THE HAWKS OF LONDON

Grant Sutherland was born in Sydney and grew up
in Western Australia. He now lives with his wife
and children in Herefordshire, England.

www.grantsutherland.net

Also by Grant Sutherland
in the Decipherer's Chronicles

THE COBRAS OF CALCUTTA

THE
HAWKS
OF LONDON

The second volume
of the Decipherer's Chronicles

GRANT SUTHERLAND

PAN BOOKS

First published 2011 by Macmillan

This edition published 2012 by Pan Books
an imprint of Pan Macmillan, a division of Macmillan Publishers Limited
Pan Macmillan, 20 New Wharf Road, London N1 9RR
Basingstoke and Oxford
Associated companies throughout the world
www.panmacmillan.com

ISBN 978-0-330-50873-5

Visit www.panmacmillan.com to read more about all our books
and to buy them. You, will also find features, author interviews and
news of any author events, and you can, sign up for e-newsletters
so that you're always first to hear about our new releases.

THE
HAWKS
OF LONDON

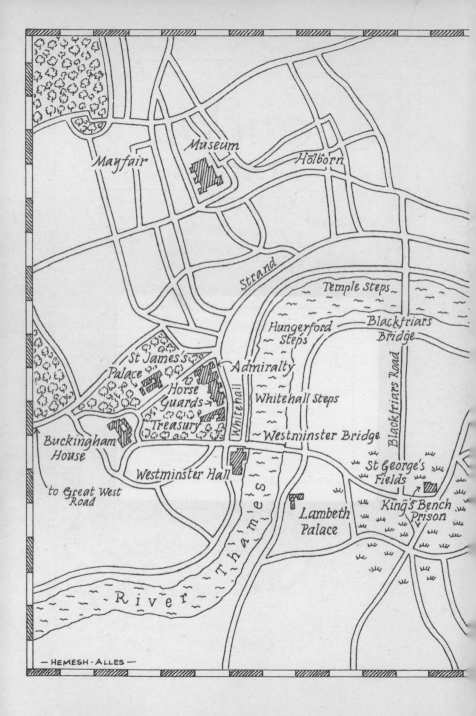

Mayfair

Museum

Holborn

Strand

Temple Steps

Hungerford
~ Steps ~

Blackfriars
Bridge

St James's
Palace

Admiralty

Blackfriars Road

Horse
Guards

Whitehall

Whitehall Steps

Treasury

Buckingham
House

~ Westminster Bridge ~

Westminster Hall

to Great West
Road

River ~ Thames ~

St George's
Fields

King's Bench
Prison

Lambeth
Palace

— HEMESH · ALLES —

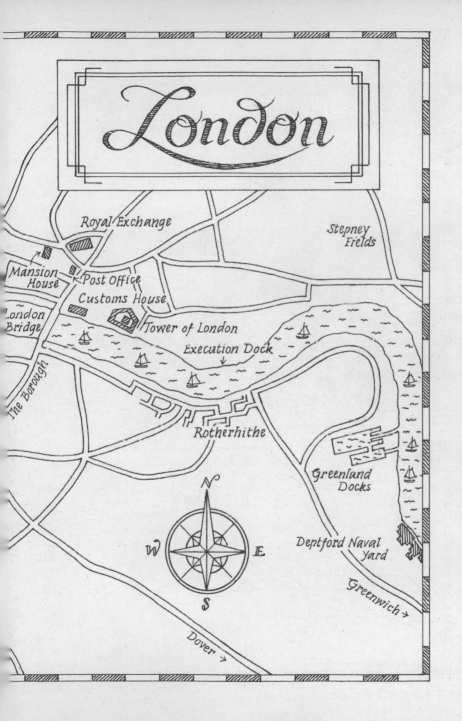

Here in the writing of these Chronicles, I am determined to make report of my actions to my own soul as to the king of kings, following truthfulness as close as any man dare. Read it who may, this is the life I have lived, such as it was and is, written for all time on the face of the world.

I, Alistair Malcolm Douglas, have roamed the earth, a spy for the Crown. God's mercy on my soul.

CHAPTER ONE

*T*he fifteenth night of November, 1767, and I upon a dock by Deptford, waiting.

'You would be warmer in the Greyhound, sir. I will fetch you when he comes.'

'How old is Langridge?'

'Eighteen.'

'Did you not think to go with him?'

'Langridge with the wherry, and me to stay and wait for you. That was Mr Carrington's order.'

'And Mr Carrington to the theatre,' said I quietly, to which Baxter made no answer, for in truth he was as little pleased as I. His hands were tucked beneath the arms of his heavy coat and his shoulders were hunched against the cold. He did not look at me but out across the river.

The lanterns on the ships standing off from us in the Limehouse Reach shone dull through the river mist, and were very still, for the tide was almost at the turn. After a time Baxter offered to fetch me a broth from the tavern and I gave him a few coppers for it. Then I went to the edge of the small dock, drew my coat tighter about me, and leaned against the great oak bollard by the water.

It was very quiet on the river. The lightermen were all abed or in the taverns, and most of the wherries gone up above London Bridge for the theatre trade, so that there were no cries upon the water now but only a faint bell from over by the far bank, which rang out three times while I listened, and then faded to nothing.

Soon Baxter returned. 'She has put it in an ale-pot for you, sir.'

'How long has Langridge been up there?'

'Not two hours. Mr Carrington ordered him to be back on the tide.'

I took the broth, grateful for the warmth of it now, and drank it very slowly.

Carrington had no business to be giving such an order. It was the two Sons of Liberty, Pearce and Flanagan, that Langridge had been sent up to the Greenland Dock for. And since my return to London in September the search for the two murdering sons of bitches had been my affair, and none of Carrington's Messengers involved excepting Baxter, and he not pushed onto me, but come to me by my own request.

Baxter mistook my unhappy gaze, which had settled upon a ship out in the Reach.

'She is another from Boston, sir. They are too many.'

'You are not asked to watch every one of them.'

'Two men, and all London to hide in. It is too much, sir. If Mr Carrington thinks he may find them – well then, let him try it awhile.'

Indeed, let him try it awhile; and there were many times these past weeks I would have passed the whole business to the chief of the King's Messengers, Nathan Carrington, and very welcome. For it was only by chance that the search for them had first fallen to my care.

I had come up from the south, my work with our Superintendent by the Mississippi completed after almost two years, and had been in Boston only to take passage back to England. I was very jaded, and my every thought upon London, so that when one of our Customs men there was murdered at the Boston docks I had kept myself clear. The killing caused a great stir in Boston, though having witnessed so

many killings in my recent time with the Choctaws and the Chero-
kees, I had thought very little on one poor fellow's unfortunate end.
It was the business of the Vice-Admiralty court, and none of mine,
and though I heard some rumours of the escape of the murderers,
Pearce and Flanagan, I had hardly thought to ever hear their names
again once I took sail for London.

But almost the first day after my arrival in England Mr Fitzherbert
had charged me with finding them. And I had not found them.

I finished the broth and tossed the pot into the river.

'Is it a Boston ship Langridge has gone up to?'

'It is a whaler, sir. She is Danish, but there will be Americans aboard
of her.'

A bell sounded again across the river, and south of us a night-
watchman called and was answered by his fellow. Eleven o'clock.
Upriver, the theatres would be emptying now, and some going along
to the Vauxhall Gardens and some going home, and the wherrymen
jostling for fares.

Henrietta must be sleeping.

The water whispered against the dock now, for the tide had turned
towards the sea, and the stench of whale oil came down.

At midnight came another bell and another cry from the watchmen,
and then the lamps went out in the Greyhound, and only the ships'
dim lanterns now lighting the water. Nothing moved on the river.

An hour more, another cry, and I said, 'The Greenland Dock is
not far.'

'Mr Carrington said I must wait here, sir.'

'I will answer for that,' said I, and then I stepped away from the
bollard toward the Greyhound.

'Sir?' he said, and I turned with a sharp word, but Baxter was
peering upriver.

It was a wherry coming down, with no oars in the water, but drifting.
It came on slowly, its bow bumping into the Stairs just above us; but
then its stern swung out, it caught the tide and moved again.

'There's no one aboard of her,' said Baxter.

She came on slow, touching the bank and turning once more, and we went down the steps to the water. I held Baxter's arm and he leaned out and took hold of the gunwale as she came by. Then he drew her in to the steps, and there was a tarpaulin lying in her and he lifted it. His head came up.

'Holy Christ.'

'Hold her steady.' I knelt and took hold of the tarpaulin and drew it back. But there was nothing more to see.

'He wasn't much more than a lad, sir.'

I let the tarpaulin fall and told Baxter to release the wherry.

'Sir?'

Rising, I put my boot on the gunwale and shoved hard, and it slipped from Baxter's grasp and went away from us, drifting slowly, turning like flotsam on the tide.

'It must be very late.'

'Aye.'

'Shall I go?'

I made no answer but only put more coals on the fire. When I sat to take off my boots I noticed the new sketchbook on my dresser. It was tied in a white ribbon, as a present for me. I took off my shirt then, and breeches, and climbed into the bed with her and she stayed almost till daybreak, when she rose and moved about quietly that she make no disturbance to my sleep. After a time she went down the stairs, and then I rolled onto my back and thought on what Baxter had told me, that Langridge had left a young widow, and a child.

The front door closed, and I heard Henrietta's light tread on the paving stones below my window, going quickly now, and away from me, back to her own house and her husband.

CHAPTER TWO

Wiilliam Fitzherbert M.P. was a member of the Council of Trade
and Plantations, and the man directly over me, though himself no
proper part of the Decipherers. It was he to whom most of my more
general reports from abroad had been customarily directed, and from
whom I had taken my infrequent instructions. And it was with him
that I walked down Whitehall to the Admiralty later that morning,
and very downcast I was then, for the murder of Langridge lay heavy
upon me.

'You may speak freely with Jenkinson,' said he, as we turned in
through the Admiralty gates. 'He is familiar with the whole affair.'

It was Charles Jenkinson he spoke of, one of the Lords of the Admiralty, who had called us here. I did not know the fellow except by
reputation, which was already considerable in Whitehall and Westminster. But I was not pleased to find myself so summoned when I
might have been down at the Greenland Dock now, and searching.
I remarked that the Admiralty had been tardy enough in their help
of us till now.

'I would not remind Mr Jenkinson of it,' said he, and nodded to the guard, who opened the door to us.

It was early yet, and inside the Admiralty lobby was nothing of the bustle of officers and clerks usually to be met with. At the rear of the lobby was one of the necessary women still at her work, sweeping the floor and chatting with a young footman who sat there upon the step. He jumped up when he saw us, but Fitzherbert waved the fellow off and we went up the great staircase unaccompanied.

It was as quiet above as below, and we started across the wide landing, but then out from Jenkinson's door came Nathan Carrington. I glanced at Fitzherbert.

'You must hold your tongue, Alistair,' said he, for he well knew my feelings at that moment towards Carrington. 'Jenkinson will not be swayed, that he has not heard from you first.'

This fellow Carrington was the chief of the King's Messengers, which is to say he commanded those two score men who must do the bidding of the King's ministers. It was these Messengers who must take the warrants from the ministers and the courts, and make arrests, and take the private communications of the Crown judges to the other courts in the kingdom. In the houses of the senior Messengers like Baxter were even lock-ups, where men might be held in temporary custody before being taken to the courts and to prison. And it was they also who must gather information for the ministers by a network of spies and informers, both within London and without.

How Carrington had risen to the topmost place among these Messengers was no mystery to any who knew him; for he was as unscrupulous as a eunuch in an Eastern court, and no secret came into his hands but was a weapon to him. And almost since the first day of my return to London in the autumn, and the assignment of two of his men to my assistance, Carrington had shown a hostility toward me as being outside his power but an encroacher upon his fief.

Now Carrington turned from the door and saw us. He showed no surprise, but rested a hand upon the hilt of his sword and came toward the staircase. He was a small man, which I think was the reason of the black tricorn he always wore; and he was a vain man too, which was why he was invariably turned out as one newly come from his tailor. He held himself very erect now as he approached us. The silver braiding of his red jacket set off his silver scabbard very fetchingly.

'Gentlemen,' said he, as he went by, and with such a look of unconcern at what had happened that I could not help myself, but in spite of Fitzherbert's warning turned and said, 'You had no business sending Langridge up there.'

Carrington checked in his step.

'Come,' said Fitzherbert, with a tug at my sleeve.

'Mr Douglas, it is you who have lost one of my men. I had thought to do you the courtesy not to remind you of it.'

'I?'

'Here is not the place for this,' said Fitzherbert, and he walked from me, and then Carrington dipped his head to me, and turned his back and went down the stairs.

Inside Jenkinson's room was a coal fire burning in the hearth, and Jenkinson seated at his table and a number of papers before him. Behind him on the wall was a number of scrolled maps and charts, resting on brackets. Otherwise the room was plain, with only a single rug on the wood floor, and no pictures but only the plasterwork cornicing for decoration. He was well informed of the events of the night, both from Carrington and from the Naval Yard where Langridge's body had been retrieved. Many of the papers before him concerned not only Pearce and Flanagan, but also the general situation in the colonies. Some of the reports that lay upon his desk, I had written.

'You seem to me not entirely certain in your views upon these Sons of Liberty, Mr Douglas,' said he, putting aside the paper in his hand.

'I have no view to speak of, sir.'

'On one page they are a violent rabble. On the next, you speak of them almost with respect.'

'There are gentlemen even in the colonies,' said I, and received for my trouble a quick glance of warning from Mr Fitzherbert.

'I think we may take it that having murdered a Customs agent, Flanagan and Pearce are not of that number,' said Jenkinson, and when I agreed that they were not, he asked me if I had any notion how they might be found. I explained that we had now received good descriptions of both men from the Vice-Admiralty court in Boston.

'If the Admiralty were to command the captains on the river to look to their newer recruits—'

'That will be done. Have you no further plan?'

'They will show themselves again. We must wait.'

'That is no plan.'

'I cannot beat a drum and call them from hiding, sir.'

Fitzherbert broke in to save me from my forward tongue, suggesting that our impatience had cost the young Messenger Langridge his life. Jenkinson disagreed, saying that it was a slim chance that Mr Carrington properly seized.

'It is but an indulgence to now wring our hands in empty regret.'

'They must show themselves before they act,' said I. 'Our patience will deliver them to us.'

'Mr Fitzherbert has recommended you to me as a bold fellow, Mr Douglas. I own myself a little surprised to discover this timidity.'

'It is care, I would say.'

'You may say what you will. I offer it to you as my observation that the two are very often one and the same. Though I am sure you will disprove the observation.'

His expression was not malicious, nor yet kindly. And I had by now a sense that he spoke the words as a goad to me, as if he must make trial to discover any weakness. I felt no friendlier towards him for the understanding.

While he talked with Fitzherbert now, I studied Jenkinson's face for some mark of the ambition that many had told me of; but in the face was nothing exceptional, unless it be an extraordinary equability (for it is very few men can keep their innermost thoughts concealed so completely). His features were in perfect balance, and also his frame, but there was too little of the stamp of any definite character to make him handsome. He was then forty years of age and unmarried.

He talked of the King's safety now, and of the need to capture and then hang Pearce and Flanagan, as if he might talk of procuring fresh supplies for the Navy. It was another piece of business he must see to, and he would see to it efficiently and well. He pressed two fingers lightly against his temple by his wig, both while he listened and while he spoke.

At last he said, 'The Customs agent murdered in Boston was inquiring into the smuggling activities of one of the merchants there, John Hancock. I understand this fellow is an agitator against the Customs?'

'He opposes the Stamp Acts, sir. It is a common opposition among all the merchants there.'

'It is not so common, I believe, to become paymaster to the Sons of Liberty.'

I said that though Hancock might have opened his purse to them on occasion, he was by no means their paymaster. Fitzherbert then offered that the Council of Trade and Plantations was well aware of the fellow. He said that Hancock's name was upon almost every petition received by the Council from the American colonies.

'Yes,' said Jenkinson, 'and you may imagine it caused me no small wonder to discover that this Hancock has had considerable commercial dealings with the brother-in-law of one Mr Wilkes.'

'John Wilkes?' said Fitzherbert, straightening in surprise.

'The outlaw John Wilkes, who I understand is a friend to you, Mr Fitzherbert. And living in Paris, beyond the reach of British justice. And also, from what I have heard, beyond his means.'

'He is not a man to be involved with the likes of Pearce and Flanagan.'

Jenkinson met this with silence, and Fitzherbert moved uncomfortably in his chair.

The name Wilkes, I should say, had even then a power to make division. Though I had not been in London at the time of Wilkes's expulsion from Parliament some years earlier, or witnessed his trial before the Lords, or his flight into exile, yet the name was as well known to me as to every man in London. The question whether the charge of seditious libel against him had been a malicious persecution was one I had heard debated in several drawing rooms since my return. There were good men stood firm on both sides of the question. Having myself been abroad during most of the time of the contention, I had been spared the firing heat that might have set me either for or against the fellow.

But Mr Fitzherbert's friendship with Wilkes was well known. And Mr Jenkinson's antagonism to Wilkes was only to be expected from one so closely connected to the Court. It was an unfortunate turn that had now introduced the outlaw into our current troubles.

Jenkinson asked Fitzherbert if he might have had any recent news of Wilkes. Fitzherbert said that he had not.

'Only there is a tale in Paris that his creditors there have some fear of his extending himself beyond his purse,' said Jenkinson. 'There is a suspicion that he might rather flee than pay.'

'Tradesmen make their sport of such nonsense.'

'His past actions have given them some reason for their concern, Mr Fitzherbert. But they must look to their own affairs. I mention it only by way of introduction to a request I must make for the services of Mr Douglas. I would have him go to Paris.'

'Pearce and Flanagan are not there,' said Fitzherbert.

'If there is any thread leading from Wilkes and through his brother-in-law to these two Boston men, we must discover it. By your own report, there is none more fitted for that duty than Mr Douglas.'

'Wilkes is not the devil he is painted. It would be to chase a chimera.'

'Our first loyalty is to the King. I am sure you do not set your friendship with Mr Wilkes above that.' This mention of the King was a shot fired by Jenkinson to some good effect, for Fitzherbert made no answer to it. And very plain it was to me that he felt himself overborne by Jenkinson's intimate connection with the Court.

I asked to whom I should be answerable whilst in Paris.

'To me,' said Jenkinson, and his look now full upon me. 'Mr Fitzherbert has at present some more urgent calls upon his time.'

I turned to Fitzherbert for some explanation of this remark (for I did not know then of his financial difficulties), but he said to me only, 'You might travel on some small business of the Council. There is a question of the French piracy off Jamaica. I might give you letters for the ambassador.'

'I leave the details to your care, Mr Fitzherbert,' put in Jenkinson. 'As to my particular instructions, Mr Douglas, I have sent a letter on ahead of you to the ambassador. You may appeal to him in an extremity, but otherwise confine yourself to the aid of his secretary. I will look to a weekly report from you. More, if you think it necessary.'

'While Pearce and Flanagan are at large, sir, it would be a negligent idleness for me to remain long in Paris.'

'The negligence, at such a time, would be to leave Wilkes a free hand to direct sedition, and worse, against the King.'

'That is too strong, sir,' Fitzherbert broke out.

'You shall remain in Paris until I recall you, Mr Douglas. As to your setting out, there is the promise of a good crossing tomorrow. I am sure that you will not wish to waste the opportunity.'

The entrance to the main Post Office in the City was by way of Lombard Street, but the door to the Secret Office of the Deciphering Branch was on the east side of the building, halfway along Abchurch Lane. The door was never locked in the daytime, and now when I went up the steps from the lane and into the first chamber, Francis's black boy Gus looked sharply around. He was standing on a chair, fixing a broken sconce on the wall. When he saw that it was me, he gave me good morning and then returned his attention to the repair while the guard opened the door for me into the steaming room. In here was only Bode at work, and as I passed by he kept his head down over the letter whose seal he was carefully lifting with a small blade.

'You will not slip, Mr Bode.'

'Never fear. I shall only blame you if I do, sir.'

There were always many candles burning in this room, for there was but one high window, and little light, and when I had begun my induction into the Decipherers it was the place that I least liked to be taught in. Set into the inglenook at the west wall was a stove, and a kettle quietly simmering, and a number of blades kept warm on an iron dish. Beside the inglenook, a door led into the quarters of the steamers and translators behind.

Passing the high workbenches, I went through a low arch and then up the stone spiral staircase. At the top was an oak door. Rapping upon it brought no answering call from inside, and so I turned my key in the door and went in. The small room was empty, which was not unusual in the mid-morning, for now it was that Francis met with the Secretary of the Post Office to give notice of any amendment to that List on which were the names and addresses of those whose letters must be set aside by the sorters for our further attention in the Lane. Relocking the door after me, I passed by the two bureaus and went directly to the shelves at the rear of the room where was kept a small archive of papers; many secret, some seditious, and all of them useful and necessary to our work.

It was two papers I sought, both pertaining to the outlaw John Wilkes. For upon our leaving Admiralty House, Fitzherbert had been very quick to try and correct the impression of Wilkes's character that Jenkinson had been at pains to convey to me. And yet it was very noticeable that Fitzherbert's answers to my own questions upon Wilkes were evasive, and never more so than when I asked him to oblige me with the loan of his copies of the two pieces of writing for which Wilkes had been tried in absentia by the Parliament and found guilty. (That is to say, *The North Briton*, no. 45, and the *Essay on Woman*.) And so I had forborne to press Fitzherbert on the matter, allowed him his evasion, and instead come directly to the archive at the Lane. Within ten minutes I had both pieces in my hand. I made only the briefest perusal of the pieces before folding them into my pocket and scribbling a quick note to Francis.

Have removed Wilkes 34 and 35 from archive. Am sent to Paris under orders of Charles Jenkinson (approved by Fitzherbert). Will write upon arrival.

After fixing the note to Francis's locked bureau, I left the room, relocked the door, and went downstairs to where Bode was now intent upon the careful and painstaking labour of fixing the wax seal upon a newly intercepted and transcribed letter, making it ready for final delivery. Bode did not look up when I paused at his shoulder. And when I complimented his handiwork he said nothing but only bobbed his head, and after a minute I left him there to continue his work undistracted while I went to prepare for my departure.

The weather when I reached Dover was far from fair, there being some question if there should be any crossing at all that day. Having been disgorged with the other coach passengers into the inn behind the dock, I now sat alone at a table by the window, and with some curiosity turned through the pages of *The North Briton*, the issue numbered 45, whilst the squalls buffeted the town from the sea. This paper, which Wilkes had undoubtedly written – though he had never acknowledged it – contained his seditious libel against Lord Bute and the Duke of Bedford and other ones of the Court; the second paper, the *Essay on Woman*, contained a blasphemous libel against a bishop.

It was my first opportunity to read with any care the two reasons of Wilkes's outlawry, and the papers lay open at my elbow while I ate my mutton. There was liveliness enough in the writing, and fluency in the pen, but the subject of Lord Bute's influence over the King, and the scurrilous insinuation of Bute's relationship with the King's mother, were things too familiar now to have the piquancy of novelty. Likewise the vilification of the Duke of Bedford's negotiations over the peace. And the brazen and public naming of high names was an innovation in the public press, but had little effect upon me, having been inured to the like by any amount of private reporting within the Deciphering Branch. As to Wilkes's posturing antagonism toward the Scots, it seemed to me almost a matter of form, as if an actor should repeat some foolish mummery at the command of the pit. This was no Voltaire or Dean Swift taking aim at universal human folly. It was a public man embroiled in the issues of the day, and fighting his corner with the weapons nearest to hand.

His *Essay on Woman* was different, but no better, and I took this with my ale. A bawdy travesty of Pope's original on Man, it possessed a low-mindedness quite exceptional. A few lines must give the flavour of it.

> Who sees with equal eye, as God of all,
> The man just mounting, and the virgin's fall,
> Pricks, cunt, and ballocks in convulsions hurled,
> And now a hymen burst, and now a world.

I own that I had heard worse, and in good company, for there is a certain type of gentleman that glories to speak vulgarities that a Plymouth tar might blush to hear. But to have spent such time and care in fixing so crude a canvas upon the frame of Pope's creation spoke an uncommon zeal to bespatter learning with the mud of the gutter. According to Fitzherbert, Wilkes claimed the piece was stolen from his papers and was never meant for publication but only for a private circulation among his friends. That seemed to me a quibble, and not touching on the deeper question of who the man must be who would choose to turn his higher faculties to such a dismal end.

The innkeeper's mother came to get the empty plate and jar that I had pushed aside after my reading. She asked if she might bring me something more.

'The mutton is worse every time I am here, Mrs Porter.'

'It is the butcher, sir. It is scrags for all but his family.'

'There is a fellow sits with his back to the fire. He did not come with us in the coach – please do not turn. He was here when we entered.'

'Yes.'

'Is he a local man?'

'Never seen him before, sir.'

'Might he have come from France?'

'There's been no ship come in today. He's likely waiting for a crossing, sir.'

I said that she might bring me a glass of port, and when she returned with it I paid her, and gave her also an extra shilling which she slipped into her apron.

'I would be obliged to know if you see any more of that fellow here. Also the direction and times of his coming and going.'

'I don't see as well as I did, Mr Douglas.'

'You see well enough, Mrs Porter. I cannot expect perfection for a shilling.'

She smiled, and then a call from her son sent her to another table, and she bobbed her head to me and went.

An hour later, with the worst of the squalls now past, the ship's boy came to call us for our embarkation. That fellow who had watched me secretly at the inn did not embark with us; but as our ship left the harbour I fancied that I saw him through the misty rain, standing alone upon the mole and observing our departure.

CHAPTER THREE

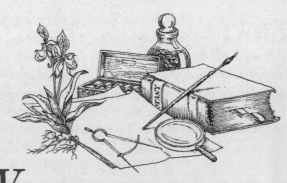

'Wilkes keeps an apartment up there,' said Barrow, to whom I had been directed by Jenkinson's instructions. This old fellow, retired from the sea, had kept watch over Wilkes for Jenkinson, and was to be an aid to me now in the same purpose. 'He has a young whore to keep him company.'

'I understand he is in some straits.'

'Straits? He has not two pennies to rub together. We can go into the park here. There's a bench gives a view of the front door and window.'

'I would not have him see me.'

'He keeps to his house in the Bois de Boulogne all the daytime. He comes here only after dark.'

We went into the park and crossed to the bench the old fellow had talked of. He had supported himself with a cane as we walked the short way from the workshop where I had found him sitting alone at his table, sewing canvas into bags with an air of penurious industry. Now he seemed relieved at the chance to ease his legs.

'Will the woman be here now?'

'She is always about. Sometimes her mother calls on her.'

I asked if he had been long watching Wilkes.

'Two months. Mr Jenkinson wrote I might speak freely with you, sir.'

'Yes, of course.'

'I do not like to spy on Mr Wilkes. I am sure he has many faults, but to my understanding, they were worse men who drove him out from England.'

'He appears to suffer little hardship,' said I, surveying Wilkes's apartment and the square where we sat. Both the district and the building were of a quality very superior for any gentleman, let alone one who had not two pennies to rub together. A marquis might keep such an apartment and not disgrace himself. Fitzherbert had told me of Lord Temple's past patronage of Wilkes, and I wondered now if an expectation of future munificence from that quarter had kept Wilkes living so far above his means. Certainly, without some such expectation it was near madness for a man to suspend himself above such a quicksand of debt as must swallow him whole at his first slip. We waited a quarter-hour there, with Barrow all the while bent forward to ease his legs and back, and then someone came out through the building's front door. Barrow looked up.

'Is it she?'

'Claire Pitou,' said he. 'It is she.'

She came into the park and passed near to us so that I saw her face very clearly. It was a pretty face, unmarked by either age or care, and on her lips was a half smile, as if she thought upon that which pleased her innocence. Her skin was white as milk, but the few loose locks escaping from her bonnet were deepest black, and she had about her the look of the Highlands. She took no notice of the park, or the people in it, but went on quickly.

'Where does she go?'

Barrow opened a hand. He neither knew nor cared.

I turned to watch her from the square. 'She is but a girl. She is not seventeen.'

'She is of an age, sir.' He asked if he should expect me later that evening at his workshop. I said that I should need him no further that day but would call upon him in the morning; and while he leaned upon his cane and twisted up from the bench, I rose and went after the girl.

There was no hurry nor yet furtiveness in her progress through the streets, but she went on steadily, as one familiar with her destination. I kept at some distance, my purpose being to make a first study of the girl in the hope that she might disclose some private path to the affairs of her keeper Wilkes. I knew already that Barrow should be little help to me in this, for he had told me what use the Admiralty had made of him in Paris, which was only to listen at the inns, and pass messages. As to any more serpentine business, I must shift for myself.

When she came to the Seine I kept back, and she went over a bridge onto the Île de la Cité. Once she had reached the far side she cast a long glance over her shoulder, and would surely have seen me had I been any nearer. But the bridge behind her was empty, and she turned again and went on into the narrow lanes. I decided at once that I should follow her no further that evening. For there had been in her backward glance something more than a casual inspection, and the place at which she had made it was just such as I might have chosen. It is possible the glance was mere accident, but it seemed to me a deliberate and considered part of her journey from Wilkes's apartments; though why she should need to practise such a precaution I could not well understand.

After half an hour she had made no return, and when the bells of Notre-Dame begun their pealing I finally came away to those rooms I had taken near to the British ambassador's hotel. And from the matron of the house, and much to my surprise, I received upon my entry the card of the Undersecretary to our Southern Department, Laughlin Macleane.

'Will you be long here in Paris, Mr Douglas?'

'That is for others to determine. I have no particular departure settled.'

Macleane bent forward from the carriage seat and looked out at the free-standing houses we were passing. 'I too am in no anxiety to return to London at the gallop. I was in Antwerp till last week, but Paris agrees with me very well. You know that Wilkes is well thought of here?'

'I am told there are some think well of him in London.'

'You are sceptical of his qualities.'

'I am indifferent to them, whatever they may be.'

'Ah, but you have not felt the charm of the ugly fellow. Wait till you have spent an evening in his company. It is his boast to talk away the disfigurement of his face in half an hour. There is some truth in it – though I think the ladies are less forgiving of his misfortune than he fondly imagines. But we are arrived,' said he as the carriage drew into the driveway of the largest house on the boulevard. 'You will remember. Wilkes has many friends here.' He was too familiar. I had met him but once before, and that only fleetingly; and though he might be Lord Shelburne's secretary, and Lord Shelburne in the ministry, yet to hear Macleane speak like this to me was disconcerting. For how should he know my business in Paris unless it be by Jenkinson or Fitzherbert? Macleane sensed my unhappiness, and added, 'I do not mean to interrogate you, Mr Douglas.'

I returned that I, for my part, intended to cause him no embarrassment after his kind invitation to accompany him, and so we got down from the carriage.

Madame Couchard, whose house we had come to, presided over one of the celebrated salons of Paris. Indeed, I had first heard of her salon while travelling in the hinterland of Louisiana, my French travelling companion remarking that we were then as far from the centre of civilization – which was Madame Couchard's salon – as he ever hoped to be. The unfortunate gentleman was killed by the Choctaws shortly after; and strange now to think that it was I and not he who mounted the steps to the place where the best literary and philosophic minds of Paris made their customary gathering each Friday evening.

Our hats once taken, we were ushered into the drawing room, where our entry passed almost unnoticed. The gathered worthies were spread in many groups about the room; men for the most part, but with several fine-dressed ladies moving among them, and some with wigs very high, for that absurd fashion was then coming in, and conversation flowing pleasantly on every side.

Macleane led me to the group by the sofa, where I must be introduced to Madame Couchard as a secretary to the British Council of Trade and Plantations.

'You are very welcome here as a friend to Monsieur Macleane,' said Madame Couchard, and we exchanged some pleasantries, and then she complimented my French and put me under the care of a young gallant standing nearby. The fellow put a glass into my hand and steered me across the room, where to my consternation he presented me to Necker, the great financier, as Monsieur Douglas, the envoy of the Council of Trade.

'I am barely a clerk, sir,' I put in quickly, and Necker graciously dipped his head to me and asked to be remembered to Fitzherbert. He enquired what arrangements had been made to replace 'Champagne' Townshend, who had died in the autumn. I pled the ignorance of my junior position, and after he had made a few half-hearted sallies to discover if Townshend's death might bring any change in the taxation of our American colonies, he seemed to accept that there was no worthwhile information to be had from me. He allowed the other gentlemen there to return him to some question of the French finances, and I soon extracted myself from that coterie and made my way to the rear wall, which was hung with so many pictures it had the appearance of an exhibition.

I regretted now that I had come. I should have ignored Macleane's insistent invitation. But amidst the usual dreary scenes pastoral and mythological hung upon the wall was a series of watercolours that soon drew my eye. They were pictures of animals and birds, but done with great skill, and I found myself leaning forward to decipher the signature.

'It is a bird of the West Indies,' said an older gentleman coming up by my side.

'Yes,' said I. 'I have eaten one.'

'Then you have the advantage of me, monsieur. I had only the preserved specimen upon my table.'

'But the work is not yours, sir?'

'It is.' He gestured over the series. 'They are.'

I expressed my admiration for his draughtsmanship, and for the verisimilitude he had achieved.

'But you do not think them lifeless?' said he, regarding the pictures now with a self-critical eye.

'They are very far from lifeless, as I am sure you must know very well, sir.'

'Buffon,' said he, and bowing very gentlemanly, gave me his hand. Buffon. Which was the name of the most celebrated naturalist in France. Feeling now an utter fool I told him my own name and he laughingly brushed aside my inept and embarrassed apology that I had not recognized him. We moved together to the next picture along the wall, which was another bird, and studied it.

'I was not happy with its colour in my studio. Here it looks not quite so pale as I had feared.'

'It is perfect,' said I, and meant it sincerely; for the shining green feathers almost brought the bird's call to me. I could very near smell the burnt cane in the hills behind Havana. And when I enquired what technique had achieved the fine shadowing, he told me at once; for he was a man far above the pettiness of professional secrets and jealousies.

Though he was thirty years my senior, there was an openness of spirit about him that made him seem almost youthful, and I liked him from the first. He was not long in discovering my own inclination for sketching, and was at once eager to urge upon me the value of flora and fauna as the best subjects for any skilled draughtsman. When I told him that I favoured architectural subjects he made a groan of theatrical despair, and I chaffingly said, 'I was in the East awhile, sir. Would you rather I had sketched an elephant than the Nawab's palace in Bengal?'

'Monsieur Douglas. I had rather you had sketched a field mouse, which is a construction more marvellous than any palace in the world.'

I had the singular pleasure of his company for several minutes more before he was wanted by some gentlemen to settle a question of natural history between them. I was then drawn among several other fellows who would hear of me the British Parliament's attitude to the present situation in Corsica. With them I made sure to listen more than I spoke, and when I must speak it was only in such generalities as were least likely to embroil me. And when Macleane joined our little group I happily deferred to him as the more proper representative of our kingdom's policy. Though Macleane's French was often flawed, his charm carried him over every difficulty. They were pleased to hear him say that the Corsican, Paoli, was not universally admired in London.

As we left these gentlemen, Macleane quietly congratulated me on what I had spoken. I averred that I had said little, and nothing of sense.

'Just so. But you have made the acquaintance of Buffon? Do not be taken in by his show of affability. It was something other that has won him the prime place at the Royal Garden. I noticed that Monsieur Necker was not so much to your liking.'

'Am I brought here to be watched?'

'You will not take offence, Mr Douglas. I must be my Lord Shelburne's eyes. It is not personal to you. For myself, a financier like Necker must necessarily be of greater interest than the keeper of a garden, however royal. Neither one of them, by the way, is any close friend to Wilkes. That fellow there, however—'

My ears closed to him. My eyes wandered. At that moment a young woman entered the room holding the uplifted hand of a toddling infant. The infant wore white lace, and the young woman was as finely dressed as any other lady present, but wearing no wig. Buffon, who was near to the door, crouched down to the child, and there was general laughter when the infant pushed an open hand into Buffon's face. The young woman withdrew the child's hand and then looked up, smiling. And in that moment I felt that I had received the death-blow.

I could not move. Neither could I speak. When her eyes met mine, the smile froze on her. All the colour went from her face.

'Mr Douglas?' said Macleane.

She was eight years older, and changed. Changed – and yet the same. But the child—

'They will not stay long, Mr Douglas. If you would meet them—'

'What?' said I, turning to Macleane, not understanding a word that he had said. I was stricken.

'I say that Wilkes's friends will not remain here long,' said he, studying me with puzzlement, and as though he expected some answer. It was several moments before I had collected myself to turn away from him. She delivered the infant quickly into Madame Couchard's care. Then I watched, dazed, as she walked swiftly back through the guests and directly out from the room.

'You must excuse me,' said I brusquely, at once detaching myself from Macleane and from that company of gentlemen about us. I hurried from the drawing room and into the empty hall, where the front door was closed, the doorman sitting quiet with his legs outstretched before the door and his hands in his pockets. He looked up at me curiously. Hearing voices in a room down the hall behind me, I turned and ran along there. But upon looking into the room, I found two servants preparing card tables.

'Have you seen a young lady pass this way?'

They had not.

I withdrew into the hall, and following more voices soon went through the green baize and descended the stone steps into the kitchen. There I stopped on a lower step and looked over the great central table. The cook and her kitchen maids were by the stove. Two footmen were eating the remains of the canapés recently returned from the drawing room.

'Was there a lady came down here?'

They looked at one another in bemusement, and I did not stay for an answer. Up in the hall again, and I made several more fruitless enquiries of other servants before at last returning to the front door. That same doorman who had lounged there was just now coming back inside. As he closed the door, I said, 'A young lady—'

'I have seen her to her carriage, sir.'

Shoving open the door, I rushed out by him.

The carriage was gone. The footman came out and stood above me on the steps. When I asked the young lady's destination, he told me that it was her own carriage she had taken, and that he had not spoken with the driver.

Leafless poplars framed the driveway and the empty boulevard. Carriages passed in the light rain. I returned inside and slumped onto the footman's bench in the hall. Setting my hands upon my knees, I stared at the floor between my feet and attempted to recover myself. Valerie was alive. Eight years after the loss of the transport with all hands. Eight years after I had seen her name in the list of the drowned.

And now when she had seen me, she had fled. And the child—

'Was the lady alone?' said I, lifting my head.

'Yes, sir.'

Rising, I returned at once to the drawing room.

'You have missed your opportunity with Wilkes's friends,' said Macleane when I rejoined him, and he indicated some fellows, with their ladies, now taking their leave of Madame Couchard. My eyes passed straight over them and stopped on the infant.

'Who is the child?'

'She is the pet of the salon.'

'And the father?' said I, and Macleane nodded toward a lone man at the fireplace. It was Necker.

'The child is a bastard then?'

'For God's sake, collect yourself,' whispered Macleane, taken aback. 'She is the child of Necker and his wife there, Madame Couchard. You will take no more wine.'

He had been till then quite solicitous of me. But now he was something more than annoyed, and I begged his pardon, saying that I had got some small fever in the crossing and was not quite myself. In truth, his stern look did not touch me, for by his words he had already drawn out the spear.

We were another half-hour in the salon, and for all the good I had of the erudite conversation I might have been at the far side of the city. Such was my distraction as I went among the remaining guests, gathering what small and broken understanding of her situation that I might, that I missed Buffon's invitation to me that I must call upon him at his studio. It was only Macleane's intervention that prompted the older man to repeat it.

'That is too kind, sir. Of course I shall come.'

Later, as our carriage drew from the house, Macleane said to me, 'This fever that you have is one you would do well to be rid of,' and I inclined my head as if I was in any state to have regard for advice.

CHAPTER FOUR

'Who is she?' said Barrow, inspecting the name and address upon the letter that I had given him. 'A friend to Wilkes?'

'You must allow me some privacy in my enquiries, Mr Barrow. You know the address?' He nodded. 'Good. Then when you are done, you shall wait for me at the south end of the Rue Lazare.'

'You have not asked after Wilkes.'

'Very well then. What of Mr Wilkes?'

He told me that Wilkes had come to the Pitou girl at eleven in the night, and was away at nine in the morning. 'If you would see him today, sir, you will find him at his house in the Bois de Boulogne with his daughter Polly. You cannot mistake the girl. Her face is her father's, but everyone gives her a good character.'

'She must be of an age with the mistress.'

'Wilkes keeps them apart. The girl must know of the other, but he makes no mingling of them. One here, one there. And Wilkes here and there between them.'

I reminded Barrow that I should expect him in the Rue Lazare, and as I left him he slipped my letter into his heavy coat.

Though I might have Valerie Beauchamp's address after my enquiries at the salon, my knowledge as to how or when she had come there, and where she had been all these past years since I had seen her in Quebec, was very meagre, and at once unclear and contradictory. The only certainty I had discovered was that several days out of Quebec she had been transferred with her father to another French vessel, and sailed on to the West Indies while the transport she had left (carrying many of the paroled French officers) had foundered in a storm and gone down.

The list of the drowned that was then posted in Quebec had of course included Valerie and her father. And since I had watched them set sail in that doomed vessel, I had no reason to doubt of their drowning with the others. But while I had grieved, she had sailed southward. And to confound me further, it seemed that upon their arrival in the West Indies the father had inherited a title, and with it an alteration in his name. He was now the Vicomte de Sarlat, but what he had done during his time in the West Indies remained obscure to me. Few in Paris made very particular enquiries of their colonies except as it touched their own pecuniary interest, and certainly I had not found the reason of his extended absence. It was known, however, that father and daughter had returned together to France in the late summer. There was a presumption that he had brought her home to make a match.

The utter disorder of my thoughts and feelings continued all the while that I wandered from Barrow's workshop and across the bridge onto the Île de la Cité. It continued still while I found a place to sit inconspicuous by the river. And even as I waited there, and watched for the girl Pitou upon the bridge, I thought only on Valerie Beauchamp.

I had been twenty, and she sixteen. And I was now near twenty-eight, and she – she had run from me. And not a letter, not a word from her in the years between, but only the silence of the fathomless deep. My thoughts turned upon themselves, directionless and with a disquieting disorder, till two o'clock, when Wilkes's mistress came over the bridge.

She made that same glancing inspection behind her that I had noticed the previous day, and then she came along the lane by the river to a place not twenty paces from me. There she turned in to an alley. Rising now, I went a short way along the embankment and stopped by a lone fisherman there. He complained to me of the cold- ness of the season and the scarcity of fish while I looked down the alleyway. Claire Pitou was there, but arm-in-arm now with a young fellow. And no gentleman, by his dress, but perhaps a journeyman carpenter. She pressed her cheek to his shoulder and they turned away from me. Soon they were gone from the far end of the alley, and I wished the fisherman an improvement of his fortune and then trailed at some distance after them.

It was but a short while before I had what I required.

I found Barrow in the Rue Lazare at four o'clock.

'Which would you see first, sir? Wilkes's tailor?'

'Have you delivered the letter?'

'I sent a boy.'

'What boy? It was you I charged with its delivery.'

'He will take it faster than I might,' said he, and when I uttered a quiet oath, Barrow seemed surprised at it. 'He will bring any answer to my workshop, sir. I have used him before. He is reliable.'

What my tongue was almost ready to say, I swallowed back. For Barrow was old, and his body bent and twisted from the life he had endured. Once he had been a sailmaker, one of Admiral Anson's idlers, who had gone around the world. But he had got no fortune by it. And now he was not in his right place, which might be a village near the sea in Devon. His best was useless to me, but he meant me no harm.

I waved a hand towards the many shops and told him we might start where he would. He produced a small notebook from his pocket and read aloud the name of a tailor, and the amount Wilkes owed, which in sterling was upwards of seven pounds.

'He will not break Wilkes for that, Mr Barrow.'

'That is but the smallest, sir. There are then the other tailors Wilkes must pay.' He turned the pages of his notebook, reading aloud the names and numbers. There were five more tailors. Wilkes's total debt to them exceeded seventy pounds.

While Barrow waited further along the street, I entered the first tailor shop. While the two apprentices cut cloth upon the table to the rear, the tailor himself came out from behind the counter. A single glance at my jacket and breeches, and he must have marked me for an Englishman. When I mused upon the possibility of a new jacket, several bolts of his most expensive cloth came down from the racks, the tailor unrolling a yard of each of them for my view. And as I inspected the cloth, he made the usual shopkeeper's enquiry of the recommendation that had brought me there.

'Monsieur Wilkes has had a good coat from you,' said I, and the change in him was instant. Though his hands continued to move over the cloth, he no longer met my eye. 'He is very pleased with all the pieces he has had of you.'

'Good. Very good.'

'He was unsure that you would have the time for a sizeable order.'

'Perhaps. Perhaps not. For a sizeable order, we must ask an advance payment, Monsieur, you understand.'

'I have a bill drawn on Monsieur Wilkes. It should cover the order.'

His hands ceased to move over the cloth, and he looked at me with one brow raised. There was nothing amused in his expression. 'I have already a collection of Monsieur Wilkes's paper. I am sure he is an honourable English gentleman, but my family cannot dine upon his hopes.'

'If the order were smaller—'

'It would make no difference, sir. Monsieur Wilkes has no credit here. I would not give you one pin for his note. If I may say, Monsieur, I think you have not been very long in Paris?' I answered that I had just come this past week. 'If you have accepted paper from Monsieur Wilkes, you have my sympathy. But you will find it no easy matter to be rid of it.'

He rolled up his bolts of cloth. I nodded contritely and withdrew into the street.

'It will be no better with the others,' said Barrow as we went further along. And at my enquiry of how Wilkes could live in such straits, he answered that he thought Wilkes's daughter Polly paid the expenses of the house. 'They say she will be a wealthy woman when her grandmother dies, sir.'

This was true, as Fitzherbert had told me. But he had also told me that Polly's maternal grandmother had bound the inheritance with a thousand legal snares to make it secure against any depredation by Wilkes. And it had surprised me to hear the tailor speak now so openly and immediately against Wilkes. On this evidence, it seemed that Wilkes's situation was fully as dire as Jenkinson supposed.

I asked Baxter if he had seen any sign that Wilkes would flee.

'No.'

'You say it with some meaning.'

'My meaning is that no sign is sometimes the truest sign, sir. If he means to run, he cannot let his creditors get wind of it, or it is the debtor's prison for him. He might run tonight, and no one know it till the morning.'

Barrow next took me to a wine merchant, and then to a jeweller. In both places Wilkes's name brought down on me a harder frost than I had had at the tailor's. After three more shops I was come firmly to the same view as Barrow and Jenkinson, that Wilkes was fast approaching the end of his financial tether here in Paris. Though some literary salons might remain open to him, the artisans and tradesmen had every one of them put up their shutters in his face.

I bought some small presents from the best milliner I could find there, and when we returned to Barrow's workshop there was a lad crouched by the fire and warming his hands. Barrow spoke to him gruffly, asking after the letter. The lad told him that it was delivered.

'Was there no reply given you?' said I.

'The footman told me I must leave, sir.'

Barrow reached to cuff the lad, but I checked his arm.

'If there is a reply, it may have gone to my rooms.'

But there was no reply waiting for me at the Hotel de Lyon, and so I sat down at my desk to write a second letter to Mademoiselle

Beauchamp. Thrice I took up my pen and thrice I put it aside. For though the note I had sent by Barrow's boy was brief – an expression of my stupefaction upon seeing her at Madam Couchard's, my address here in Paris, and a deep hope that she had fled from me only from her own confusion – what more could I yet say?

A fourth time I made the attempt.

My Dearest Valerie,

I have sent a letter to you this morning by a boy, but having received no reply, I must believe that the message has miscarried.

Since your flight from Madame Couchard's salon I have made some general enquiries, the better to understand what my eyes have seen, and what I can yet scarce dare to believe, that you and your father are numbered yet among the living. I will not attempt to trace in words my astonishment at this discovery, nor my feelings upon it. You may understand the tempest and confusion that is in me.

We must speak. Without we are together, I fear some ill chance or further misunderstanding shall make a second wreck of my hopes.

Your father must not be allowed

I hesitated, struck out these last words, and wrote instead:

None must be allowed to keep us from that happiness

I stopped again, and struck this out also. Then I read again what I had written. And once I had read it I struck two sharp lines through the page, screwed it into a ball and flung it into the fire. I watched it flare and then burn to ashes, then I rose from my chair, crossed the room, and slumped onto the bed. I was twenty again, and no wiser, but only the very same fool.

The first history between us was all come back to me now, and may here be quickly told. After General Wolfe's bold assault on the Heights in Quebec, and the collapse of the French resistance, the Vicomte (then a mere Monsieur) had surrendered himself to me and brought

33

with him his daughter and an elderly French maid. The reason of this surrender was that he well knew what fate might likely befall any woman at such a time, let alone one such as his daughter. And knowing also something of me from the role I had played as an envoy from the British side before the battle, he quickly took advantage of my adventitious presence among the French. He surrendered his sword to me, explained his fears, and together we took the women to a place of better safety.

Once the first danger was passed they remained quartered in the house we had found, and I with them; but he was soon paroled, thereafter spending much of each day from the house, visiting the French prisoners and calling on the British officers to persuade them to leniency.

I will vow to my grave that I did not then do as he believed, which was to use his absence to dishonourably make a prey of his daughter. But I was then twenty, and she sixteen, and who shall wonder at the consequence? The maid who should be a chaperone to Valerie barely acknowledged me as British, or an enemy, for to her the great business of the world was ever between men and women, and not nations. She proved almost a pander to us. Valerie's father saw his danger all too late.

I was transferred to a new billet, but that was the only concession our officers would make to his sudden agitation against me. Nor could Valerie be kept a prisoner, but I met with her daily, that maid remaining ever helpful to us.

All this was overturned by her father's announcement that they should all three of them depart with a batch of newly paroled officers. The ship's departure being but two days hence, Valerie must obey, and my only assurance her promise that she would await my release from service in Quebec. Then the *Neptune* went down, and my heart with the ship; and to my firm belief, for ever.

While I lay upon my bed in Paris now, contemplating the strangeness of finding Valerie so unexpectedly alive, and considering what should come of it, a cry from the lady of the hotel told me that I had a visitor.

Leaping up from the bed, I straightened my shirt and cuffs. I composed myself a moment, and then opened the door. My hope, like my letter, turned to ash.

'Mr Fitzherbert.'

'Am I such a disappointment to you, Alistair?' said he, coming in. 'I would have warned you, only that I would have outpaced my own letter.' Then noticing the open door to my bedroom, and the disordered bedding, he enquired, with a sudden misgiving, if he found me alone.

I said that I was, and then with no word more of explanation, he thrust into my hand a sheet of the *Public Advertiser*, a London newspaper of the day. He tapped a finger upon the first article, and then took an impatient turn about the room while I read. The paper was dated the same day that I had left London. The article gave notice that the outlaw John Wilkes was contemplating a return to England, where he might stand as a candidate in the next parliamentary elections. 'Who has written this?' I asked, smiling; for I confess at first I took it for no more than satiric nonsense.

'It is no jest, Alistair. I have a fear it is Wilkes himself has written it. It is a great mischief being made here.' Fitzherbert retrieved the paper from my hand. 'I have come to discover what Wilkes means by it.'

'But an outlaw cannot be elected.'

'As to that, the lawyers are divided. And there is a rumour at the Inns that Wilkes has taken advice on the question. Howsoever that may be, Mr Jenkinson believes the question is better left untried. And I agree.'

'If Wilkes should return to England he could not escape the court. And if he is brought before the King's Bench, how can he then keep from prison?'

'You do not know the man,' said he, and shook his head in agitation. He asked then where we might find Wilkes at this hour, and when I told him, turned for the door. 'I have a carriage waiting. You will ride with me down to the Bois de Boulogne. We must call on Mr Wilkes and no delay.'

CHAPTER FIVE

*T*he Bois de Boulogne being the pastoral retreat nearest the city, there was ever a demand for the villas there; for each villa had invariably an extensive garden or orchard where the Parisians might take their leisure, and forget for a time the malodorous stench of the tight alleys in the town. We easily found Wilkes's villa by Barrow's directions, but it was the early evening when we came into the driveway and along the arcade of pollarded willows. The villa Wilkes had taken was neither larger nor smaller than its distant neighbours, but well proportioned, and with green shutters pinned back against its white walls.

Upon our alighting from the carriage, there came hurrying up from the garden behind the villa Wilkes's servant asking our business there.

'Your master will not wish to stand on ceremony. That is he there, is it not?' said Fitzherbert, indicating the two figures in the garden, who must be Wilkes and his daughter Polly. Their arms were linked and they were coming slowly towards us, past the unpruned branches of the apple trees. We went forward across the frozen ground to meet them.

We were very near before Wilkes cried out, 'Fitzherbert, by God. And so it is, my dear.' He parted from his daughter and came forward. 'You are almost the last man I expected, and very welcome.' He pumped Fitzherbert's hand, and so I had a few moments to recover myself. For though I had heard many remarks on Wilkes's face, and had frequently seen Hogarth's cruel caricature of him on many ballad sheets and handbills, yet this first sight in the flesh was yet a small shock to me.

His squint was more pronounced than any I ever saw, and handicap enough; but in addition he had a jaw so extended (which I believe is called by the doctors a prognathous jaw) that it jutted out beneath his beaked nose, giving him altogether the appearance of a hobgoblin. Even his smile was marred by a missing lower tooth. To be blunt, his face was an unfortunate slip of the Maker's hand, and a thing thoroughly misshapen.

But his smile was warm, and he welcomed me very civilly. Fitzherbert introduced me as his secretary, and then Wilkes called his daughter forward, and I saw that she had the same jaw as her father, but not quite so extended. She had been spared the Wilkes squint, and her smile was as warm as her father's. As she walked beside me to the villa she talked very sensibly and confidently, so that I was struck that a girl of seventeen should have such a rare good sense as not to let her appearance cripple her into silence.

Within the drawing room a fire was already lit. The servant busied himself with putting on more coals, and then Polly called him away and the two of them left us. Fitzherbert apologized for our imposition on Wilkes's hospitality. 'And you must know that I have not come from London to dine with you,' said he by way of warning.

'I do,' said Wilkes cheerfully. 'I know it, but you will dine with me anyway. Both you and Mr Douglas. Had you given me some notice, we might have met in town. I might have entertained you properly there. But we must make shift as we can. Polly will take a stick to the cook. We shall have nothing to complain of.'

'She is considerably grown.'

'She is, she is. And in her mind, where her best hope of happiness must reside. But come here by the fire and I will open a jug. Put off your coat, Mr Douglas. I will not allow you to excuse yourself.'

'We must talk,' said Fitzherbert firmly, 'whether Mr Douglas be here in the room with us or no.'

Wilkes gave a gap-toothed grin, seemingly untroubled, and perhaps even a little pleased, to have this envoy from the ministry in his house. He poured wine into our glasses now, asking Fitzherbert for news of the Beefsteak, and of their mutual acquaintance in London. Fitzherbert, though he might pretend otherwise, was not by nature a hardened man of business, and would rather make a treaty than a war. And so it was not long before he was talking very freely with Wilkes, and Wilkes reminding him of times past, and genially recalling to Fitzherbert the various follies of some notable persons in the Parliament and Whitehall. Nor were all of Wilkes's stories old, but he heard much of the latest drawing-room scandals in London, and also a goodly measure of salacious gossip which he recounted very merrily.

'We do not appal you, Mr Douglas?' said Wilkes, turning to me after some minutes of this. I said that I was appalled only to think that the vices of our public men could be known so easily here in Paris. 'Tsh,' said he. 'The French give as little care to our peccadilloes as we to theirs. It is near, or it is nothing. The Chinese empress might be a harlot, and why should we in Europe care to hear of it?'

'I shall make enquiry of the point when next I am in Canton,' said I, and his squinting eye moved shrewdly over me. He seemed more amused than offended by my impudence, and was soon turned to Fitzherbert again and scandal-mongering with an undimmed enthusiasm. Watching him, it was not difficult for me now to imagine him bent over his papers by candlelight and penning his *Essay on Woman*. Penning it, and laughing at every low ribaldry. But the author of the *North Briton* 45 was hid a little deeper, and it was only when Polly returned, and we moved to the table, that this other John Wilkes raised his head.

For once at table his talk turned to British politics, and it was soon evident that he kept himself better informed on Westminster and Whitehall matters than did many people in London. Certainly he knew more than I. But his understanding was not perfect, and several times Fitzherbert must correct his understanding of some current factions and personal conflicts within the House. Wilkes took these in good spirit, but I saw how it irked him that he who had once created the rough weather in Westminster should now be obliged to take advice upon the direction of the fickle parliamentary breezes. He was at the periphery who would be at the centre, and this reminder of it truly pained him. I doubt he ever thought one moment on his outlawry; but his exile was a daily punishment to him.

'You seem to care very little for politics, Mr Douglas?' said Polly.

'I have been travelling for some years. I cannot say that I ever pined to hear of Westminster.' I asked her in my turn if she would stay long in France.

'While my father is writing his book he will need someone to watch over his house here.'

'Every author might wish for such a devoted companion.'

'A book,' broke in Fitzherbert, who had overheard from across the table. He turned to Wilkes. 'What manner of book?'

'Such a book as none will take exception to. You may calm yourself. It is a sprat.' Fitzherbert awaited some better answer, and finally Wilkes admitted that he was writing a history of England. 'I have taken this villa to give me peace from the town, and to keep me at my work. It is an honest labour. You may tell them so at the Beefsteak. John Wilkes indulges himself in honest labour.' Wilkes raised his wine and quaffed it, as if to drown his self-disgust. It was the word 'labour' had done it. He had been partaking very freely since coming in from the garden, and now he was perspiring a little at the temples below his wig.

Fitzherbert expressed a solicitous surprise that the literary work was not to Wilkes's taste.

'I was not made for drudgery.'

'It may be that your situation is more fortunate than you suppose. A steady application of your undoubted talents at such a time may produce a work fit to carry your name down the years.'

'Huh.'

'You might write a work you may be proud of.'

'I am proud of the *North Briton*,' ejected Wilkes with sudden vehemence and slapped his hand upon the table. 'I am proud of the forty-five.'

'Father—'

'You may leave us now, Polly.'

The girl looked at her father with concern. But when he kept his squinting gaze upon the table, she made no vain attempt to bring him back to his earlier light-heartedness. I had a notion she had seen the gaze before. She rose and quietly left the room. I was in some perplexity whether I should likewise excuse myself, but a quick look from Fitzherbert kept me to my place. There were several moments of silence, broken only by the crackling from the hearth. Wilkes must hear it now, what they both knew that Fitzherbert had come here to say. At last Fitzherbert drew out the *Public Advertiser* and unfolded it upon the table. Wilkes studied it awhile, and then remarked, 'Too much ink. The printer does not know his business.'

'It is not the printer's ineptitude has brought me here. Did you write it?'

'No.'

'But you have had a hand in it.'

'I had not expected to be interrogated in my own house, and by a friend.'

'You must know the concern this has caused. You have hit the mark you have aimed at. Bute will be in apoplexy, and the King can be scarcely more sanguine. What Justice Mansfield must make of your threatened return whilst yet an outlaw I cannot begin to conceive.'

'If it has ruffled feathers, I am glad of it.'

'I may tell you that your friends are not. It is a foolish mischief-making, and I fear it must return upon your own head. Though you have no such improper intention to put yourself forward as a candidate, for the ministry to see it writ so bold, and with the suspicion of your hand behind it – it is a vain struggle for me to understand why you have done it.'

'Who has sent you?'

Fitzherbert baulked at the direct but quietly spoken question. 'Is it not enough that I have come in friendship?'

'Was it Chatham?'

'He is unwell.'

'Lord Shelburne, then. Grafton? Someone has sent you.' Wilkes raised a finger and named some others of the ministry. There was now a chaffing tone in his voice. 'Come now. Is the ministry so weak that it may be shaken by a badly printed paper?'

'You will not win your pardon by provoking them.'

'I am done with waiting for a pardon. Did you hear me speak of any pardon? I will shit on the head of any man who presumes to offer me a pardon.'

'You are too rash.'

'They have attempted my life. Do you doubt it?' said he, as though offended at Fitzherbert's sigh. 'I have had the proof of it. I was baited into my duelling with Martin. He had been at his targets all the summer. He was paid well for his trouble, and might have dined off gold plate had he killed me. See here, Mr Douglas.' To my consternation he opened his shirt to show me the scar of the lead he had taken from this fellow Martin. It was a bad one. I should say he had been lucky to live.

'This is an old story,' said Fitzherbert. 'And I am come here on a new.'

'You will not speak of rashness, Fitzherbert, when you have rotted away three good years of your life in exile. Three years of waste.'

'Three years whoring through France and Italy, you mean to say,' said Fitzherbert mildly, 'for which you may have my congratulations but not my sympathy.'

Wilkes seemed at first astonished by this riposte; but he was too much a man to take hypocritical offence, and when his astonishment was past he buttoned his shirt and patted Fitzherbert's arm. 'I will confess it, Seneca had a worse time of it than ever did John Wilkes. And if I have made my grand tour as an outlaw – well then – I have made my grand tour. I climbed Vesuvius, did you know?'

'You have not disowned this,' said Fitzherbert, putting a finger upon the paper.

'I have said that I did not write it.' Wilkes took up his glass.

'You have not disowned the sentiment. You have not said that you have no such intention to stand for election to the next Parliament.'

'You are very quiet there, Mr Douglas,' said Wilkes, turning to me. But I gave him no aid, I remained very quiet – and he must finish his wine and put down his glass and at last face Fitzherbert again. 'I have not disavowed the sentiment, my dear Fitzherbert, because it is not in my nature to tell a barefaced lie to a friend.' This was the very worst that Fitzherbert had feared. He stared at Wilkes. 'It does not mean that it is certain I shall stand. The question is open before me. I am undecided.'

'I pray you make up your mind now against this ill-advised escapade.'

'I note the advice.'

'It is for Mr Douglas to note advice. It is for you, my friend, to find the good sense to take it to your bosom.'

Wilkes braced both hands upon the table. His face was red, and there was no pretence now in his anger, but it came from his very bowels. 'Not one Jack of them has lifted a finger to my aid. I have waited. I have bided my exile. All with the expectation that my professed friends would make some shift to strike out the false charge against me. And have they? Have they, sir?'

'The ministry is unsettled by Chatham's ill-health.'

'The ministry is always unsettled. And I am not so mad as to stake my future upon the good health of Chatham. I have given you my answer. I am undecided whether I shall stand. If that now cause some indigestion in the ministry, very well. I am only sorry they have not choked on it.' Wilkes turned savagely toward the door. 'Polly! Polly! More wine for our guests.'

Fitzherbert was silent as we drew out past the willows. And as we turned onto the road I looked back and saw the lone figure of Polly, lit by her lantern, going up the steps and inside the villa to attend her drunken father.

'Is he watched here?' said Fitzherbert.

'The orchard-keeper reports to Barrow.'

'Better that the keeper now report to you. And there is something else I must tell you,' said he, turning to me. 'You will no longer be under my charge, either here or in London. But Mr Jenkinson shall now be over you.'

'May I ask the reason of it, sir?'

'The reason is personal to myself. I find my attention divided, when it should not be.'

I nodded, and waited for more; but Fitzherbert seemed disinclined to speak.

'Shall I write to Mr Jenkinson of Wilkes's intentions, sir?'

'I leave for London in the morning. I will see Mr Jenkinson the hour of my arrival.'

'Wilkes means to stand,' said I.

Fitzherbert made neither agreement nor disagreement but looked out of the window. He seemed drained by the meeting with Wilkes. All was cold winter stillness outside, and only a crescent moon to light the bare trees and soft shadows beyond the carriage.

'There are those would see him dead before they would see him elected. And he must flee his creditors first. When he does, Alistair, you must stay at his heels.'

CHAPTER SIX

*T*here was no remedy for me now but that I must act quickly. I must put any thought of propriety aside, and present myself at the house of the Vicomte unannounced and uninvited. It was a smaller house than Necker's, though in the same quarter, and when I mounted the steps and knocked at the door I make no exaggeration when I say that I have entered battlefields with less trepidation.

The liveried footman took my card, and I waited in the porch while I rehearsed in my mind what my first words might be. A vain effort, for when the door reopened to me my every prepared thought scattered on the wind. Following the footman, I passed through the hall and into the drawing room, where I found myself facing not Valerie but her father.

'Monsieur Douglas,' said he, and with no move towards me he inclined his head in curt greeting. He had certainly heard of my presence in Paris, else he had shown some greater surprise to see me. But whether from his daughter or some other I had no way of telling. 'I regret that I was not told of your coming.'

'Forgive me, sir. I have taken the liberty to be my own messenger.'

'As you say. You have taken the liberty.'

'I am astonished to look upon you again, sir. Till two days past I had believed you lost with the others in the *Neptune*.'

'We escaped by the merest accident.'

'I have heard.'

'Have you, indeed? You are here at leisure in Paris, or on some business?'

'I am directed here by our Council of Trade.'

'I confess, Monsieur Douglas, that I am equally astonished to see you.'

'You believed me dead, sir?' said I, for this was the hope that I had settled upon, that Valerie had mistaken my fate just as I had mistaken hers.

'I believed that your forwardness would bring you to no good end, Monsieur. And very quickly. You have outlived my expectation of you.' He half-turned from me and took a poker to the coals of the fire. He was unchanged. A slender man, and with the bearing of a soldier, and his frock-coat not elaborate, but in impeccably fine taste. For all his courage (which I had been a witness of) and for all his devotion to his daughter, I yet disliked and mistrusted him as much as he disliked and distrusted me. 'I can only imagine that it is a good wife has preserved you, Monsieur?'

'I am not married,' said I, which must be the answer he had most feared. He attempted to cover his dismay with a quip that the English women had more sense than he had supposed, and we were back there already, on that same fighting ground where we had been when we last laid eyes upon one other.

Swallowing my pride, I attempted a conciliatory enquiry, asking if he would settle now in Paris, or if he might contemplate a return to the West Indies.

'I shall go where I am sent. I am at the disposal of the gentlemen in Versailles.'

'Papa?' came her voice from the hall, and I turned as the door opened and she came into the room. She stopped when she saw me, her hand upon the door.

'Valerie,' said I without thinking, and with no concern of her father; for in her name was all my thought.

'We have an unexpected visitor from across the water,' said the Vicomte, which gave his daughter a moment to compose herself. When she had done so, she came in and gave me her hand. 'You will remember Monsieur Douglas,' said he, as if I might be forgotten.

'Monsieur,' said she.

I bowed and kissed her hand. She withdrew it more quickly than I might have hoped.

'You come at an unfortunate moment, Monsieur,' said the Vicomte. 'We are invited to the Court. Our carriage waits, and we must be away.'

'We can spare a moment for Monsieur Douglas, Father.'

'I did not mean to disrupt your day, sir.'

'It is no disruption,' said Valerie and went to the sofa and sat down while the Vicomte remained on his feet. The years had made a subtle change between them, which I only felt at the first, but did not yet understand. 'And you have so much to tell us, Monsieur Douglas,' said she smiling, and at the same time, and to my startlement, she turned her grey eyes upon me with the cold look of a wild Cherokee. I was taken aback. All my words died in me. 'Where to begin? Quebec? You were much occupied after we sailed, I think, Monsieur.'

'I was.'

'I said so to my father. It is the press of some urgent affair, I said, keeps Monsieur Douglas from replying to my letters.'

'Valerie—'

'Monsieur Douglas has found a place in the British Board of Trade,' put in her father to silence me.

'Mademoiselle, I received no such letters. As I have explained to your father, I had supposed you lost with the *Neptune*.'

'We are not ghosts.'

'I thank God for it,' said I, and she peered at me then as if to penetrate the sincerity of my declaration. And I confess that I found her instinctive doubt of me no less alarming than her opening hostility. She remarked that I must surely have made some proper enquiry of their fate. 'The ship was reported lost with all hands. I departed Quebec myself the same week that the report of it was posted.'

'My letters must have reached you in London,' said she.

'I was not in London.'

'They would have followed you.'

'I cannot explain why they failed to reach me. I have been mostly in our American colonies. But I could not know you had survived.'

The Vicomte did not seem to like this turn of conversation, and broke in upon us, saying that he could not agree that there was time to spare, and that they must be away at once to the Court. 'I will not keep them waiting, my dear, even for the sake of Monsieur Douglas.' He proffered his hand to her so that she might not refuse him. Taking his hand, she rose.

'Sir, this has been very brief. May I call upon you again?'

'It is unlikely you shall find us in, Monsieur. I cannot recall any free hour we shall have for some weeks.'

'I must take my chance then,' said I, which I saw displeased him. But his displeasure was less than nothing to me. For when I looked upon his hard and narrow face now I was near certain of the fate of her letters. And certain too of the subtle poison he had poured into her ear throughout the missing years. There was no doubt but that he had made every effort to secure his first, best treasure against my return.

Bowing, I took my leave of them very civilly, but in my heart were feelings murderous and bloody.

'You are out of temper, Mr Douglas.'

'If I am, I do not require the reminder of it.' I stood next his fire to warm my hands, for Barrow's workshop was bitter cold, and even with the fire I could see the steam of my breath. 'Is the Pitou girl at Wilkes's apartment?'

He nodded, squinting closely at the canvas that he worked with his needle. His day's work was on the table before him, six canvas bags and a pile of cut string. And beside the string that copy of the *Public Advertiser* that I had given him. I asked had he read it. He said that he had.

'You saw there is a suggestion Wilkes will stand as a candidate in the next election?'

'I saw it.'

'You view the prospect very calmly, Barrow.'

'I have no seat in the Parliament to be put out of, sir. If Wilkes get a place there, he is welcome to it.'

'I cannot think your opinion will be widely shared.'

'It is shared wide enough to fetch you here,' he muttered, pushing the needle.

It was a just observation, and a wise one, and I might have paid it more heed. As it was, my mind was occupied with the more immediate concern of how I might keep myself apprised of Wilkes's travels between the Bois de Boulogne and the town; for it seemed certain to me that he must use one such journey as a cover for his flight from Paris, which I now expected very soon. Though the person most near to him was his daughter Polly, I doubted that she would be forewarned of it. Next to Polly in nearness to Wilkes was his manservant, and after that, the girl Pitou. And it was the girl, I had decided, was his weakness.

'You may spare yourself this evening's vigil at his apartment, Barrow.'

'Mr Jenkinson wants a daily record from me, sir.'

'I will answer for this evening. Keep yourself by the fire.'

'Shall I expect you tomorrow?'

'You may expect me when you will. I cannot answer for it.' Adjusting my dirk beneath my jacket, I left the feeble warmth of the workshop and went into the cold of the night.

The small bridge to the Île de la Cité was deserted at that hour, and the alleys unlit, and I crossed over and waited by the river. The mist was thick upon the water. After half an hour it turned to a drizzling rain, so that I was forced beneath the cover of a doorway for shelter. I kept the bridge in my view, but while I watched for one young woman, I thought upon another.

Had the fury of her eyes revealed her heart? I could not believe it, for that was only to misbelieve the best part of myself, wherein was no subterfuge but only that openness that we had once shared in Quebec. We each of us had changed – of course we had changed – but there must ever be that thread of gold in our past, immutable. Nor was her beauty altered, but only fulfilled, for the girl of Quebec was now become a woman, though even yet joined to her father. And between him and me was no golden link, but only the bare civility of men implacably opposed. It was a certainty that he had returned to Paris to see her married. And just as certain that I had no part in his plan. But to think on that was to pour hot coals on my head; for if she once gave her word to another, she would not break such a vow. Her eyes had given me no reason to hope, and yet hope was a quiet fever in me.

At last Mademoiselle Pitou came over the bridge.

'Mademoiselle,' said I, stepping from the doorway as she came near. She started, and her glance went to my face, and as quickly away. Then she hurried to get by me, but I moved now to block her path. I did not touch her. 'Mademoiselle Pitou, you need have no fear of me. I would talk with you a short while. That is all.'

'I do not know you, sir,' said she, attempting to sidestep me.

'You are the mistress of Monsieur Wilkes and you go now to your lover. It is what Monsieur Wilkes should not like to hear of, I think. Not while he pays you.'

'Let me pass.'

'Your lover's name is Renan. He is a carpenter,' said I, and when I spoke his address, she hesitated. 'Only allow me a few minutes and then you may go to him, whose name I will most surely have forgotten after.'

She asked, in some cold anger, what it was that I wanted.

'What I have said. Only to talk with you.'

'And that is all?'

I gave her my word upon it. But in her eyes was a great and very natural suspicion of me. She made no hurry to agree to talk, but neither did she move. She looked me over in a manner very calculating. 'I have seen you before,' she said.

'I do not believe so.'

'You were in the park. With the old lecher.'

'The rain is easing, Mademoiselle. We might walk a short way by the river.'

The door by which I had taken shelter now opened, and two men came out. Mademoiselle Pitou turned her face from them, and when they were past us, said to me, 'You will forget Renan once we have spoken.'

'I will forget him.'

'I will not walk with you beyond the next bridge,' she said, and turned down to the river path.

'You must know already that Monsieur Wilkes is in some difficulties,' said I, walking beside her.

'I have nothing to complain of,' said she, quite shameless.

'In five weeks the lease on your apartment expires. There is no one in Paris will advance Wilkes the sum necessary for its renewal. Nor in London, I may tell you.'

'How should you know?'

'I expect you know it as well as I.'

'You are English?' said she, looking closely at me now.

'He has drawn from a well of credit that is now run dry. There is fast approaching a reckoning for Monsieur Wilkes that may prove his ruin. In such difficulties a man is liable to act without taking due thought. Indeed, he might not fully understand what those consequences might be.'

She asked again what I wanted of her.

'If Monsieur Wilkes should choose to flee his difficulties, it might not go well for him. Nor for me.'

'He owes you money.'

'Has a creditor approached you?' She turned her head in reply, and I said, 'I would pay for such a warning.'

'You are employed by his creditors.'

'I will give you ten écus now. And the same again if you bring me a warning before he takes flight.'

'He must owe you very little.'

'Do not attempt to bargain with me, Mademoiselle. There is no more to be had.'

'I must think on it.'

'You have two minutes, and then I am from here.'

'I could meet you tomorrow.'

'I shall not be here tomorrow. And if you think to get a countering offer from Monsieur Wilkes, I would not advise taking his paper.' I took out my purse and let her see it. 'If you would like to walk on a little way by yourself, Mademoiselle, to reflect upon it, I shall wait for you.'

But she did not need to walk any further. She considered all that I had said, and she considered the purse, and then she raised her eyes. 'You will forget Renan,' she said again. When I nodded, she hesitated but a moment more, and then greed seemed to overcome her suspicion of me, and she asked where she should find me. When I told her, she took the purse.

And then, I confess it, I even felt some small pity for her.

CHAPTER SEVEN

*H*aving made my bargain with Mademoiselle Pitou I was free to return to my rooms, where I might attempt yet again to compose such a letter to Valerie as would put before her in their true light the confused depths of my feelings. But every attempt was no better than my first useless scribblings, and after an hour I gave up in high vexation with myself. I wrote instead a note to Jenkinson, which to my disgust came from my pen with an easy fluency, and in the morning took this to the ambassador's hotel, that it might be sent with the embassy's private post.

I had delivered the letter and was on my way out through the hall, when I met with Macleane showing Buffon out from the ambassador's rooms. Macleane enquired my business there, and when I mentioned the letter I had just delivered, he made a frown as if he mistrusted my discretion. But the ambassador then calling him from within, he took his leave of us with a request to me that I might see Buffon to his carriage.

'I have been boasting to your people of some specimens I have received from Captain Bougainville,' Buffon told me as we went out.

'But that is the great expedition, sir.'

'Ah, you have it, Monsieur. Though I fear your ambassador and Monsieur Macleane do not see it so. But I will not apologize for the intrepidity of my countryman,' said he, turning sideways a little now, and going carefully down the steps into the street. 'I regret only that such a voyage should happen, and I be wasting here.'

'I am sure they do not think it waste who must commit the specimens to your care.'

'Perhaps. I count myself fortunate to see such things. If the Almighty will grant me but a few years more – but it is ever the age of wonder, is it not, Monsieur, for a man with opened eyes.' We walked slowly toward his carriage, and he said, 'You are a friend of Mademoiselle Beauchamp.' At my sharp turn towards him, he added, 'Forgive me. I meant no offence.'

'It is no offence, sir. I am only surprised that you should know of the acquaintance.'

'Monsieur,' said he, lifting a brow in amusement. 'And though her father was not at Madame Couchard's, you may be certain he has heard of it. But I should not have mentioned it. You must forgive me.'

'I had not seen her in several years. It was a shock to me to see her, sir.'

'Do not look so troubled, Monsieur Douglas. I compliment your good taste. I am very fond of Valerie. She has been a frequent visitor to me, in my home and at the Garden, since she has returned from Saint-Domingue. She is a woman very like her mother. And her mother was someone I was proud to call a friend.'

'You have known her some considerable while, then.'

'Since she was—' He put out his hand to indicate the height of an infant. I remarked, though with some misgiving, that I must suppose that her father was also friend to him. 'You might suppose it,' said he, and cocked a brow and looked at me smilingly from the corner of his eye. I returned his smile, and with some relief to find the Vicomte not universally admired. We were at Buffon's carriage now, and as he put out his hand to grasp the open door a thought seemed to strike him. 'You have an invitation to my studio, Monsieur. Are you free to come now?'

'Now, sir?'

'I shall be all the morning over my first sketches. Yes. I am decided. You will come with me. You will see the new trophies Bougainville has sent me,' said he, and now he would not abide my hesitation but took my elbow and steered me into his carriage.

Now, when the world is mapped in both hemispheres, and the southern oceans are no longer the exclusive preserve of the fearless Portuguese, it is strange to think just how recently it was quite otherwise. But it was so, and in those days the arrival of botanical specimens from distant quarters of the globe had still the charm of novelty and wonder. And kneeling that day by Buffon before an open crate in his studio, I felt almost a child as he reached his hands into the dried packing moss and brought out one by one, and carefully, a number of specimens to put on a tray beside him. It seemed almost that the clean, salt winds blew over us from the far corner of the world.

Buffon had several curious plants already positioned upon his workbench, where he now took the tray. He had tied an apron about him, and his servant had put out the drawing materials for us on the bench. Buffon picked up a fantastically shaped pressed flower, the breadth of a hand, from the tray, and put it on the reading-slope beneath the window between us. He slipped a white paper behind the flower, and then he drew up his stool to the bench and sat down. Though I began to sketch at once, Buffon did nothing at first, but only rested his chin upon his hand and studied the specimen for several minutes more. It was clear he wanted no disturbance and so I remained silent at first. But when at last he took up his pencil and commenced to draw, his intensity abated somewhat and then we conversed, though his eyes never turned to me but moved continually between the specimen and his paper.

I would hear more of Valerie, but he offered me nothing concerning her now, and was instead curious to hear of my travels. He quizzed me on the strange flora and fauna that I had encountered on my way, and sighed often, and regretted to me the passing of his own youth. As I had been subjected to something of the same inquisition from Banks on my first return to London, I was able to dredge from memory some particular plants and animals that must most interest Buffon. But he was less forgiving of me than Banks, and made no hesitation to scold me that I had made no regular catalogue of these things I had seen, nor studied to complete any proper series of drawings.

'You have some facility,' he said, glancing at my sketch. 'It is a crime, Monsieur, to have travelled so far and recorded so little. A crime against natural history.'

'I am not employed by the Board of Natural History, sir.'

'A man's mind is his own, and you have no excuse.' He bade me hold up my drawing that he might see it the better. After he had studied it awhile, he said, 'I expect your facility is frequently admired.'

'On occasion.'

'And on occasion by yourself?'

'I am too aware of my blemishes.'

'No, Monsieur. You are not sufficiently aware of them, or – if you are an honest man – you would have corrected them.' This unexpected criticism, from such a source, had a most surprising sting. I think he saw its effect, for he reached across and put his hand upon my arm. 'As a boy, I had the same lesson from my own drawing master. It cannot come too early, Monsieur. It is often in my mind even now.' He smiled then, which was at least some small balm to me. Then he put down my sketch and called to a servant passing through the garden, bidding the young fellow to fetch us coffee.

He then led me on a tour of his studio, which was shaped like a broad gallery, with most of its southern side windowed and over-looking his cloistered garden. He showed me several studies that he had made for the next volume of his great work, and also the work of the artists who assisted him. There was a bureau in one corner piled high with a quantity of his notebooks. He opened one of these for me, and I read there his first quick thoughts on the specimens arriving at his studio. There were delightful sketches in the margins too, of all manner of shells and sinuous plants and insects. He would not hear my praise, but soon left me there and went to find the footman and the coffee.

When I put the notebook aside my eye happened to fall upon a small map pinned to the half-hidden side panel of the bureau. What it was that caught my attention, I cannot say, and it may have been but idle curiosity. But whatever the reason, I bent forward to examine the map more closely. And when I had the closer view, I recognized it instantly. It was a map of the known world, with additional red marks at various landfalls, and these marks labelled in French, which were clearly the places where Bougainville meant to go ashore. These labels were the only parts of the map in French, and every other word in English, as well they might be; for the map was a fair copy of one from the hand of our best mapmaker, the original of it kept under lock and key at the Admiralty. I scanned it quickly for any clue as to the hand that had made the copy, but finding none, I stepped away from the bureau as Buffon returned.

'Monsieur Douglas,' said he, coming near. 'You will not mind if I shall have another to help me with unpacking the specimens.' I said that I did not mind in the least. 'Good. I have warned her that you are here, and she too makes no difficulty.' I followed his glance to the door and in the next moment she was there, and coming towards me. 'Monsieur Douglas is pleased to have your assistance, Valerie,' said Buffon, and then turning to me added, 'I had forgotten Mademoiselle Beauchamp was to help me this morning. But I think you will forgive me.'

She was herself quite composed, so that it seemed to me he had made sure of her understanding before bringing her into the studio. She greeted me amicably, and there was nothing about her of that fierce reproach I had received from her in her father's house.

'Monsieur Douglas has been busy at his study,' said Buffon, and showed her my sketch. She looked from my sketch to the pressed flower on the slope; and then she noticed Buffon's drawing.

'Say nothing,' said I.

'Yours is very good also, Monsieur. I remember you always had a sketchbook about you.' Then she asked Buffon if she might see

Bougainville's crate, which he had promised her. He showed her the crate and put into her hand another of the dried plant specimens, wrapped in moss. She took it to the workbench beneath the window, holding it cradled to the light, and her delight in the thing was such that she could not keep from smiling. She questioned Buffon about the plant, and it was a surprise to me how knowledgeable she was. Her conversation with him was very free and their fondness for each other very evident. The winter sunlight fell upon her while they talked, and never was a woman's face more lovely to me, and in truth, when I think on it now, I believe that she hardly noticed me at all.

'Monsieur Buffon treats you almost as a colleague.'

'He is a kind man, and tolerates my ignorance,' she returned. It was an hour since her arrival, and Buffon now at his sketchbook again, and so we had come out to the cloistered garden to fetch a herb for him, which he wanted to lay alongside one of the New World specimens.

'It sounded at least a very learned ignorance,' said I.

'Oh, I am a very parrot with my Latin.'

'Valerie.'

'Monsieur,' said she.

'That is too hard.'

'You may believe so.'

'May I mention Quebec?'

'Tell me of London. What is it that you do there?'

'I am sure we do very little that is not done here, Mademoiselle. A little work. A little leisure.'

'And you?'

'I am a functionary with our Council of Trade and Plantations. And now you must think me become very dull.'

'But you have travelled.'

'I have been several years with the Council. It has occasioned much travel. And if you should compel me to speak any more of the Council of Trade, I shall dash out my brains on a stone.'

She smiled and asked me where I had travelled, and I named some of our colonies in America. As we talked of these places, I noticed, and with some discomfort, just how much there was that I might not say to her. It seemed a shadow between us, which I had not thought on. When I asked after her own life, our talk went easier, and there was no pretence in her that she had spent the years in regret of me. By her correspondence with Buffon, and with the collectors that he employed in the French colonies, she had been always connected with the greater world, and Paris. I remarked that in spite of this she must surely have felt the want of society.

'My father has had need of me. And we received more people in our house in Saint-Domingue than I can remember.'

'You have been content there.'

'I was,' said she, and twined a sprig of rosemary about her finger thoughtfully. 'And now it is you who must think me very dull.'

'I shall never think that.'

Buffon threw open his window and called out to us that he would like the plant before night if it were possible. She answered him, laughing, and we continued on our way down the path, but with no hurry.

'I was not always content,' said she. 'I think you must know the brutality of the plantations. Thank God, we did need to go often among the planters. I spent perhaps more time than I should in our library.'

'A library is no warm companion.'

'That is what my father says. So we are come to Paris, and very likely to remain here. I must make myself accustomed to good society again. Meanwhile, I can take refuge here with Monsieur Buffon. And you will now think me not only dull, but perverse.'

'I think that you know your own mind.'

'Not as I would. The suppers and the salons are not quite as disagreeable to me as I had pretended to myself. And to be in Paris, and a young woman among gentlemen, is not disagreeable to me either.' She tossed aside the rosemary and crouched down to pluck the herb she sought from by the path.

'How shall I see you again?'

'We were different people then, Monsieur. It is foolish to grasp at what is gone.'

CHAPTER TEN

'While Parliament sits, Wilkes would be a fool to parade himself. If he makes his mother's house a headquarters for himself, you may watch over him the easier.' Jenkinson had not risen at my entry into the library of his house, and kept a volume open on his thigh, with a slender hand resting upon the pages. 'It is little more you may do now, Mr Douglas, but only to watch and to wait.'

'But it is months yet before Parliament shall rise.'

'Yes?'

'It is a very long wait, sir.'

'I will have a daily report from you on Wilkes's visitors. It were better you come here to my house in the early evenings, else your days shall be wasted in pursuit of me between Whitehall and Westminster.'

'I have some business in Paris.'

'Your business is with Wilkes.'

'In Paris—'

'In Paris they may do as they will. Wilkes is here, and those two Sons of Beelzebub, Flanagan and Pearce, are here also.' He closed the book and set it upon the table, his fingers interlaced upon the leather binding. 'Mr Carrington can hardly place a man aboard the ships nor get any proper information from the docks. The coal heavers and the sailors are at each other's throats. You may believe me when I say that Wilkes could not have chosen a worse time for his inauspicious return to us.'

I remarked that it was his creditors, not Wilkes, chose the time of it.

'That is by the bye. I will know with whom he speaks and corresponds, and the names of the persons who call upon him.'

'Will the ministry order his arrest?'

'There is some hesitation over it. For now he must be managed, not exploded. Certainly his election must be prevented. If he is truly to stand in the City he must have the support of a guild. It may be a higher hurdle than he expects.'

I ventured that Wilkes might yet surmount it.

'The good citizens shall learn how he has spent his wastrel life in exile. An absconding debtor and libertine may not have an appeal equal to a pretended hero of liberty. I will discuss with Mr Carrington how we may best use the Deciphering Branch.'

'Mr Carrington is not of the Decipherers.'

He rose. 'I have troubles enough before me, Mr Douglas, than to adjudicate a petty jealousy of place. Now, will you take a glass with me?' When I said that I had some further business of my own that I must attend to, he seemed somewhat surprised by the refusal. 'Of course. I had not meant to detain you from your own affairs,' said he, almost as though I had made some slight of him.

I bowed my head. When I raised my eyes I found him weighing me from beneath his hooded lids. I kept my eyes firm upon him and at last he turned away and led me out into the hall. There was a woman's portrait there, quite striking, and at my admiring the handsomeness of the figure he was quietly pleased, and owned it to be a likeness of his mother. But almost at once he must tell me the artist's name, which was Reynolds, so that even his filial affection seemed overwhelmed by that worst part of him, which was pride.

As I came from his house, I reflected that it was a place very much like himself, with every furnishing from the best makers, and the whole done with a fine taste and discrimination, but lacking in that human warmth which was an ornament he could not purchase. In short, it felt the want of a woman, as did he.

Not two hundred yards from Jenkinson's house was another in Mayfair to which I then repaired; and this second house, though to outward appearance much like Jenkinson's, with four floors and a mews behind, was a place altogether more congenial to me. For it was the house of the Watts family, and the doorman greeted me warmly as he took my hat and coat, saying that he trusted that I was well, for he had marked my absence. He made no ceremony of my arrival, but with my coat still upon his arm, opened the drawing-room door, and called through, 'It is Mr Douglas, Madam.'

The youngest, Sophia, was upon her feet as soon as I entered, and demanding to know what presents I had brought.

'Sophia,' Mrs Watts scolded her.

'Alistair does not mind.' Sophia, who must have been about ten years of age then, took my hand and brought me to her mother.

'And if he did mind,' remarked the older daughter, Amelia, peering at her needlepoint, 'you would give him no opportunity to say so.'

Mrs Watts took both her hands in mine. 'I see that your time in Paris has been no refreshment to you.'

'Mama, you are worse than Sophia. Forgive them, Alistair. Sit here and tell me how improved is my needlework.' I dropped into the chair, and peered rather sceptically at Amelia's handiwork. 'Well, you may at least say that it is not the worst you have seen,' said she, and gave me a frowning look, very pretty.

From my pocket I produced those three pieces of Parisian lace I had bought, each wrapped in fine cotton and tied with a red ribbon. They avowed themselves pleased with the small gifts, and while I tied the lace about young Sophia's wrist I amused Mrs Watts and Amelia with a relation of my attendance at Madame Couchard's salon. I made mention also of my visit to Buffon's studio, and told them of the admirable work that he did there.

Amelia was content to draw out from me my enthusiasm for Buffon's work, but Mrs Watts said little, and was watchful of me, and I knew that she read the change in me, for she knew me too well.

Mrs Watts had played no formal part among the Decipherers since the death of her husband. Nor did she pry into my duties, but she had remained ever a support to me, and a discreet ear whenever I might need one. Mr Watts, having got a fortune of one hundred thousand pounds and more for the part he had played, with his wife's most knowledgeable aid, in the revolution in Bengal, had then returned to England to make the establishment of his family. And following his untimely death, Mrs Watts was now a wealthy woman, her son George the inheritor of the Hanslope Park estate in Buckinghamshire, and both daughters in expectation of sizeable dowries. (It was from that same fount of Bengali treasure, I must add, that I had purchased my own small house in Holborn.)

Though Mr Watts's death had been the most profound and heart-breaking blow to his family, Mrs Watts well knew that the blow had been at least partially cushioned by the high position in society that his great endeavours had made for them. And his early death had drawn the sharp tooth of envy that was even then showing itself against other Nabob families in London. (As to the effect upon myself of Mr Watts's passing, I will not claim a grief the equal of his family's, but I was for some time as bereft as any man may be who finds a guiding light so purposelessly extinguished.)

Amelia soon put aside her needlework to go upstairs and make ready for our departure to Almack's, where I was now to escort her with her mother. Sophia went with her, and so I was left momentarily alone with Mrs Watts.

'You will know that I have returned from Paris after Mr Wilkes.'

'I know it now,' said she.

'It appears he means to run the ministry a dance.'

'The likes of Mr Wilkes are never content unless they are making a big noise and putting up dust, Alistair. I am sure you are equal to him.' She looked at me shrewdly. 'And I am just as sure it is not Mr Wilkes that has made you so pale.'

'It was a hard journey.'

'Then you are not unwell?'

I hesitated, and then said, 'I believe that I told you once of a young lady that I met with in Montreal.'

'The girl who was lost at sea.'

'I had thought her lost. She is alive, and in Paris.'

'My God. Alistair.'

'Yes. You may be sure, it was a very great shock to me.'

'Have you met with her?'

'I have. It was a great shock to both of us. And before you ask any more I must tell you that I hardly know what it shall mean.'

'Is she married?' When I said that she was not, Mrs Watts looked at me with a discernment that was hers alone. 'I will say no more on it then,' she said, and when I bowed my head, she went on almost without pause, 'I have read that your Mr Wilkes means to stand as a candidate in the general election. It must be an interesting time you have ahead of you.'

Though I had been in Almack's on a number of occasions, I was no regular patron, for it was a place not nearly so congenial to me as the house we had just come from. Here was gathered the froth and gaiety of London society, everyone come out to seek some light pleasure and amusement. It was what I had thought on while I slept on the open ground in the Appalachians, and what had palled so quickly upon my arrival in London. The gaming tables were in the upstairs rooms, and in the main room below them was a large wooden floor, highly polished, with some tables nearer the walls which were mostly taken by the time of our arrival.

Having deposited my hat and the ladies' cloaks, I guided Mrs Watts and Amelia to one of these tables, more than one young gentleman turning an admiring eye upon Amelia. She rewarded each one with a pleasant smile, and left in her wake a trail of gentle conquests. Though not quite so perspicacious as Mrs Watts, Amelia had at least the rare wisdom to lean upon her mother's judgement, so that in spite of her great beauty she had been out in society a year and more, yet there was set against her name neither taint nor any dark whisper. Thrice married, and thrice widowed, Mrs Watts knew well the value of a woman's reputation, and she watched as carefully over Amelia's as her own.

Amelia touched my arm. 'Aren't they your friends over there, the Daweses?' They were standing in a group of several others. Dawes moved his glass left and right as he spoke, and gestured with his other hand very freely. His bored interlocutor gave him but half an ear, and to the other side of this fellow stood Dawes's wife, Henrietta. 'Will you ask them to join us?' said Amelia.

'They appear to be with others,' I answered. 'And our table is rather small.'

'We might stand.'

'I am sure Alistair is right,' broke in Mrs Watts, and Amelia then being hailed by friends at a neighbouring table, any thought she had of the Daweses joining us was forgotten. A minute later I glanced again toward Henrietta, but when I turned back I found Mrs Watts studying me very coolly. Until that moment I had never been sure that she had fathomed the nature of my acquaintance with Henrietta: after that moment I could have no doubt of it.

'Perhaps you will have a man bring us some refreshment, Alistair.'

I took a turn about the room and was stopped twice in my wandering by different gentlemen desiring me to pass on their good wishes to Mr Fitzherbert. But there was also in their good wishes some enquiries upon the details of Fitzherbert's West Indian losses, and so I quickly got myself free of them and was just returning to Mrs Watts and Amelia when I found my way obstructed by Laughlin Macleane. There was an older fellow with him, Isaac Barre, whom I had first met in Quebec when his eye was shot out by the French. He was now a Member of Parliament, and a close follower of Lord Shelburne. They made no circumlocution, but asked directly after Wilkes.

'You must know,' said Barre, 'that he is even now in his mother's house. But will he stand in the City?'

'Mr Barre, I am sure your information on the matter is superior to my own.'

'And I am sure, Mr Douglas, that it is not,' said Macleane.

'Perhaps he will be invited to dine at Lansdowne House, where you may question him upon it,' said I, with some hope to silence them by this mention of their master's house; for the Shelburne faction, unlike the Bedfordites, was known to be well disposed toward Wilkes. And I did not think they would like to be reminded of it just now.

'It is a nice question,' said Macleane, 'whether a man who has morals fit only for the Vauxhall Gardens should have an honourable place among gentlemen on the grounds of his laudable attachment to Liberty. What think you?'

'I think it is a nice question,' said I, and excused myself from them.

'I feared we had lost you,' remarked Mrs Watts when I retook my seat by her. 'I did not know that you were acquainted with Macleane.'

I told her of our meeting in Paris.

'He is up to his eyes in the Company,' said she. 'He has called upon me in the hope of borrowing Company stock. A charming fellow. I would not trust him with a farthing. It is a wonder to me that Lord Shelburne should let such a man into his affairs.'

'Barre is sober enough.'

'It is not Mr Barre bulling Company stock in Antwerp. And I offer it to you as a caution, Alistair. Keep clear of Macleane. He will ruin someone, and I should not like it to be you.'

At ten o'clock the Italian quartet commenced to play. And Amelia by this time having three young gentlemen about her, and Mrs Watts being joined by an old friend with two very plain daughters in want of husbands, I took the opportunity of making my way upstairs to the gaming tables. Here was not the same ferocious wagering upon the cards that happened in the gentlemen's clubs elsewhere in St James's, but there was an atmosphere quite decorous, with the music now coming up from the quartet below. It made an accompaniment to the restrained conversations at the tables and the clicking of gaming chips upon the baizes.

One table only was an exception, which was in the poorly lit rear corner, where Lord Sandwich and his coterie made as much noise as all the rest of the room put together. I was invited to make a temporary partner at another of the tables nearby, and whilst I played, I observed Sandwich quaffing his wine and making a butt of his neighbour, and inveigling the others at his table to join in his humour, and to wager more than they ought. He was a thin man, though not tall, and with a great flowering of silver braid upon his red jacket. He had made one of the Monks of Medmenham, along with Wilkes and several others, a fellowship dedicated to wine and fornication, and any godless pleasure that might satisfy their too-jaded palates. By his peers he was called the insatiable earl, but the common folk had another name for him, which was Jemmy Twitcher (who was the great betrayer in Gay's opera). For after sharing in all Wilkes's vices, Sandwich it was had led the charges against Wilkes from the House of Lords.

He was of that same circle about the Duke of Bedford as contained our present joint Post Master, Lord Hillsborough, who was also at the table there, and Barrington, who was Secretary at War, and some others that I did not recognize. They must all know of Wilkes's return to London, but it seemed to make no disturbance to their entertainment.

After half an hour I had lost a few guineas, and the first player then returning I relinquished my place and came away. And it was as I crossed the room that I saw Henrietta sitting alone near the fire.

I hesitated in my step, and in the same moment she looked up. There was such a wretchedness there to begin, and then such a look of hope when her eyes fell upon me, that a chill came over my heart. But hardly had I screwed up my courage and taken the first step in her direction, than Dawes appeared at her side, and he so thoroughly intoxicated that he must put a hand upon her shoulder for support. He did not see me. Indeed, it was as much as he could do to focus upon Henrietta. Opening a hand with inebriated care towards the stairs, he directed their departure. His other hand remained on her shoulder till they reached the stairs, where he turned to bid farewell to some fellows he fondly supposed his friends. Henrietta guided his hand to the banister, and then separated herself from him before descending (for had he fallen, he had most certainly taken her after). And in her stiff uprightness was all her humiliation and her pride, and my face burned for her, but she never looked at me or any other but fixed her eyes upon the door.

They were gone by the time I came down to the main room. But at a table by the foot of the stairs I now found Jenkinson seated with two dowagers. I paused a moment, for civility's sake; and what they were to him, or he to them, I never learned, but only thought to myself that it was a joyless party they made, and after a minute of stilted politeness I took my leave of them and rejoined Mrs Watts and Amelia.

It was past midnight when I opened my front door and sensed Henrietta's presence in the house. Upstairs, I found her in the bedroom, still dressed, and kneeling by the grate and stirring the faded embers as I came in. There was a candle lit upon the dressing table, and beside the candle the spare key that I had given her. I looked from the key to the crown of her uncovered head. At last she turned and looked up at me.

'I had intended to send word to you tomorrow,' said I.

'You have been a much shorter while in Paris than you had expected.'

'Henrietta. I have met someone there.'

She made a small movement of her head. It was not surprise, but something deeper. She had known this would happen. She had told me so almost that first time she had come to me two years past. And now it was come, as certain to her as the setting of the sun.

'I should have told you tonight.'

'Yes. Yes, I saw that you intended something.'

'It was not the time.'

'I suppose it cannot be that she is in Paris, and I am yours in London.'

'I will make her my wife, if I can.'

She was very still. And then she put aside the poker and stood and came very near to me. Her left shoulder almost touched my right.

'I can give you no advice, Alistair,' she said. 'I have not found the secret.'

And then I felt her hand grope for mine and I took her hand and she clenched it very hard.

'Henrietta.'

'There is no more to say. You did not pretend to love me. I make no complaint. You will remember me, sometimes.'

I said that I would, and she hesitated a moment, but then she asked nothing more of me. She released my hand; and with a grace and a courage I have often thought on since, she went quietly out from my house and my life.

CHAPTER ELEVEN

'You will not forget how I may be reached, Mrs Langridge.'

'The Abchurch Lane, sir.'

With her babe in her arms, she showed me out from her door.

'I am truly sorry for your loss,' said I again. 'Though I know that can be but little comfort to you.'

She offered that it was some comfort at least, and then, not knowing what else I might say, I dipped my head to her, and she made me a curtsy, and I came away from the muddy lane with some savagery in my heart against those who had done for her husband. For the young widow was barely more than a girl herself, and with every sign on her drawn face, and in the dark pouches beneath her eyes, that she had truly loved Langridge, and now suffered a keen grief at the loss of him. She had said not a word against Carrington, that her husband had been put in such danger; but someone had evidently told her of Pearce and Flanagan, for she referred more than once to the murdering Boston men.

At the south end of the lane Baxter was waiting for me, and as we went on together towards the river, I mentioned this knowledge she had of the Americans. He said that she had known it from the first, for Langridge had told her of them.

'If he was so loose-tongued,' said I, 'there is little surprise he should have ended as he did.'

He nodded, but with a look that made me wonder if his own wife might not be equally well-informed. I gave him no lecture upon it, but trusted to his better sense for the next time.

At the steps by the Execution Dock we parted, he taking one wherry upriver, and I taking another just a short way down to Shadwell, where I was to meet Carrington's second, Meadows. He had come down from his usual place in the Messengers' room by the Post Office stables at my particular request. We were to meet with a fellow called Green, one of his chief informers on the docks, and this meeting had been arranged in the most circuitous manner possible. For it was only after Meadows had directed my request to Carrington, and Carrington had refused me, that I made a complaint of it to Francis. Francis then passed word of my dificulty to the Bishop, and the Bishop to Jenkinson, and then Carrington at last received the request from a direction that he could not ignore.

There was a collier docked to the west of the Shadwell Steps, and the coal heavers at work on her as we came down. My wherryman made sure to keep wide of her to avoid the cloud of coal dust, and we came up to the Steps from below. Just beyond the head of the Steps I came upon two gangs of these coal heavers, seven fellows apiece, and the first gang coming from their labour, and covered in coal dust, and with hands and faces black; and the other gang sitting outside the tavern there, with trousers and smocks just as black from earlier days of work, but with hands and faces white. These were clearly waiting for a gang-master to call them out to a collier. There were several of them Irish to judge by their voices, and they regarded me with a wary suspicion as I went up by them; for it was just as Meadows had said, and no welcoming place for a gentleman. But the next gang of coal heavers that I met with I gave good day to, and asked after the Gravel-end Lane; which when they had told me, I heard them speaking together in the Gaelic as they went away from me down toward the steps.

I soon found the Roundabout Tavern, and in the small lane to the rear of it there was the small wooden gate that Meadows had told me of. The gate was unlocked, and I passed through into the cobbled yard, where the door to the rear of the tavern opened to me before I had knocked. It was Meadows who had opened it, and he said only, 'You are late.'

Inside was Green, the keeper of the Roundabout Tavern, and he neither rose nor offered his hand. He was a surly fellow, and by the look he gave me as he folded his arms, I feared that Meadows had primed him against me. There was the stink of stale beer in there, and a number of barrels stacked behind him.

'You'll not find them,' said this Green, as I drew up a chair at the far end of the table to him. 'They won't stay by the river.'

I glanced at Meadows.

'I have explained to Mr Green all the circumstances of your search,' said he.

'You do not know all the circumstances of my search, Mr Meadows. And you, Mr Green, will oblige me by putting aside what you have been told on the matter.'

'If they were in Shadwell, I would know. And I would have told Mr Meadows.'

'I have not come here as a Justice,' said I, and he muttered something, and I asked him sharply what it was that he had said.

'I said, "It is as well," ' said he, and looked at me very directly.

I had been there less than a minute, and I saw already that I should get nothing by an open questioning. So instead I asked after the coal heavers. He expressed an easy contempt of them. 'There seem a good many of the heavers in want of work,' said I.

'There is work aplenty if they will take a fair wage.'

I said that I was informed he was an agent for the coal merchants. He nodded, but said nothing more in reply. And Meadows made no effort to come to my aid, so I must then ask Green exactly what it was that he did for the merchants.

'The heavers live all about here. When they are not drinking here in the Roundabout, they are at the colliers and the carts. Here is the place the merchants may find them without knocking at every door.'

'The merchants come here?'

He made a smirk at my ignorance. He said that he went up into the City every few days to report on the unloadings of the various colliers, and the carting and barging of the coal from the docks. And also to get new contracts from the merchants, and to fetch the coal heavers' wages.

'It is you who pay the heavers?'

'I pass them their wages from the merchants. But the heavers get a good thirst in their labour. They soon pass their wages back to me for their drink.' He looked again to Meadows, and with such an unpleasant amusement at this business of milking the heavers that I could have no doubt then but that he was the very lowest kind of man. And at my remark that the heavers seemed many of them Irish, he replied, 'Kerry born and Kerry bred, thick in the arm and thick in the head', which I am sure he had never dared to repeat outside. 'But there are enough English heavers to keep the others honest,' said he. 'And will you ask me now if there are any Boston heavers about? There are none.'

'And you are sure of it?'

'The heaving gangs are jealous of the work. They will let no one into the gangs unknown to them. I said as much to Mr Meadows before you came. I never heard those names till now.'

Meadows spoke up then, saying something of the recent discontents upon the river, and suggesting that the ships must be a more certain hiding place for the Boston men. All of which was said only to distract my notice from what Green had just revealed to me, which was that till Meadows had come to him that morning, Green had had no knowledge of any search for Pearce and Flanagan. The Messengers' chief informer along this part of the river, and he had not been told to watch for them along the docks or in his tavern.

I thought on all the many times that I had met with Carrington in the autumn, and the many times that he had told me there was no information on the Boston men coming back to him from his spies. He had not told me that certain of his spies, like this fellow Green, had been given no instruction on the matter.

I knew then that there was no more on the Sons of Liberty that I might learn from this Green, but I stayed twenty minutes longer and asked such questions as might give me a better notion of the cause of the troubles they had there by the coal docks, and the reason of Carrington's deception of me. But as to the dockside discontents, Green would countenance no other cause than the obstinacy of the heavers in seeking higher wages for their work. And the way he spoke of them, it was a wonder to me that he could disguise his contempt of them sufficiently to take their money each day in the tavern.

At last I tired of him, and of Meadows sitting silent but watching that I discover nothing useful to me. I took my leave of them, assuring Green of a reward if he should hear of the two Boston men and pass word of it to Meadows.

From the tavern I went down to the river, where that unloading was still under way a hundred yards to the west of the Steps, and so I turned and walked along to the collier.

The heavers aboard saw me standing there on the dock by the ship, but they said nothing at first and continued with the unloading. It was a curious work they were about; for the business of the three heavers upon deck was to get great buckets of coal up from the ship's hold, which they did by running jointly up a ramp especially built for the purpose, and with the derrick rope in their hands. Then together they must leap from the top of the ramp and down to the deck, all the while hauling upon the derrick rope. The huge bucket of coal, suspended at the other end of the rope, then shot up from the ship's hold. Then the derrick was swung about, the coal emptied into a giant chute going over the side, and the coal came rattling down into the waiting cart upon the dock.

'Sir,' called down one of the heavers at last. 'There is the master aboard if you would see him.'

I knew by this that they did not like me to be there, or at least that they would know the reason of my presence. So when the master came out from the collier's cabin (for one of the heavers had fetched him) I went up the gangway. This master was a genial fellow, and happy to accept idle curiosity as the reason of my observation of the unloading. Indeed, he seemed glad to have some company other than the heavers, and pointed out to me all the particulars of the unloading, even taking me to the edge of the hold so that we might look down there and see the two heavers working below, the perspiration plastering their shirts to them, and they black with the coal dust. They loaded the coal into the great buckets that came down to them, working swiftly with their hands, and also with long-handled scuttles. It was a back-breaking labour, done amidst thick coal dust and darkness, and fit to drain any man's spirit. And no surprise to me now that they should go directly from this work to the taverns. In truth, the men were used here much like coolies.

The master told me that the heavers must make the most of the tide, explaining that when it fell the unloading would continue into a coal barge on the riverward side, which he showed me also. I remarked on the many heavers that I had seen idle ashore.

'It is the owners keeping all their vessels from the Thames. We are to Newcastle after this, but we shall not return here this winter. The seamen have forced a strike of sails here too often. These here must pay the price of it,' said he, with a lift of the chin toward the heavers.

I declined his offer to take a meal with him, but thanked him for his courtesy to me, and then I descended the gangway to the dock. And as I went down I kept in the corner of my eye that fellow whom I had first noticed following me as I came down from the Roundabout to the Steps. He was by a building near the warehouse into which the coal carts were being taken. He had been in that same place watching me all the time that I was aboard the ship.

Now I made no hesitation but set out for the warehouse, walking alongside the coal cart as if in continuance of my inspection of the unloading, and talking with the driver whilst keeping that man who shadowed me at the edge of my sight.

The warehouse doors were fixed back against the walls, and the cart went straight in, and I with it, though the driver warned me with some concern that I was not dressed for such a place. Inside was a vast space without walls, its roof trusses supported by many pillars of oak. Great hills of coal were piled in different parts of it, and at the foot of each coal hill the coal porters worked in pairs to bag the fuel and load the heavy baskets, which they then put by or loaded onto carts standing horseless in the centre. Some of the coalmen worked with kerchiefs tied around their faces, but most without, and every one of them black from head to toe with coal dust.

Two of these fellows leaped up to begin the unloading of the cart I had arrived with, and looked down with some surprise to find me standing at the other side. I asked how I might get from the warehouse some other way, and they directed me to a door hidden by the next hill of coal. I went along there, feeling already the gritty coal dust settling upon my hands and face, and very glad I was to find the door and pass out from that black and morbid dungeon.

I moved quickly along the wall to get nearer to where I must hope my shadowing observer still remained. Upon reaching the corner I stopped, pressed close against the wall, and then dared a glance across.

He was there yet. I withdrew my head quickly. And I was in no doubt now, but that it was the very same fellow who had watched me in Dover when I had first set out after Wilkes. Though who he should be, and why watching me, I could not begin to fathom.

I gave thought to what I might do, which consideration came to nothing; for when I made a second glance around the corner the fellow had left his place and was returning in some hurry toward the Shadwell Steps. He was but fifty yards from me when I came out from by the warehouse and started after him, but hardly had I started than the cart driver that I had arrived with called out to me from the open end of the warehouse, offering me a pitcher of water. My shadow looked around, saw me and ran.

I set off in pell-mell pursuit. Seeing Meadows near the Steps, I pointed and cried out for him to stop the fellow. But even as I shouted the fellow veered up into an alley. Then Meadows, clutching his scabbard to his thigh, turned and ran after him. But by the time I came up there it was only Meadows in the alley, and the fellow gone.

'Which way?' I called, running up by Meadows, who had given up the chase. He pointed to the next lane upon the right, and I continued up there. But after twenty yards this lane met another, and I stopped there in the small crossroads. I looked in every direction, but every one of the small lanes was empty.

'Was it a thief?' said Meadows, coming up by me now.

'The fellow had me under his observation. You did not recognize him?'

He shook his head. The fellow had worn a brown jacket, he said, but the face he had not seen. 'And you?'

'I saw him very well,' said I. 'I shall know him again.'

We returned down the lanes, and when we came to the Steps he left me there to go back up to the tavern. What reason he should have for his return there, I did not ask him. For I had a greater question in my mind as I climbed into the wherry, which was why Meadows had asked me no description of the fellow we had chased.

CHAPTER TWELVE

*T*he lad Tyler came to the Lane with a message from Baxter. Wilkes had fled his mother's house, and London; Baxter had gone after him.

'Towards Dover?'

'North, sir. On the Harwich coach.'

I wasted no time in pondering the possible destinations, for wherever Wilkes was bound, it was not Paris. The lad had also a list from Baxter, which was the names of all those who had called at Wilkes's mother's house during that day. I set out at once with the list to find Jenkinson.

At Admiralty House they told me he was at Westminster; at Westminster, they said he had gone to call upon Lord Bute. No sooner had I set out for Lord Bute's house than a footman came after me to say that Jenkinson was already returned from Lord Bute, and was now in private conference with Chief Justice Mansfield in a chamber off Westminster Hall. But when I arrived in that place, Mansfield was presiding in one of the courts in the Hall, and Jenkinson nowhere to be seen. By chance some members of the House had come as spectators to the court, and one of these directed me back to Admiralty House whence I had begun, and there I at last found Jenkinson, in his own room, and completely unruffled by the recent peregrination on which I had trailed him about his business all through Whitehall and Westminster.

He listened to my report now while perusing the list of Wilkes's visitors. At last he tapped the list with one finger. 'There is weight enough here to carry a candidate. We must conclude that he means to stand.' He said that if my surmise was correct, and Wilkes had gone up to Harwich to take a boat to the Netherlands, that would prove but a temporary bolt-hole. There he might keep beyond the reach of his French creditors, and the British ministry, till Parliament be dissolved and a general election called. 'And that will be in March,' said Jenkinson, though how he should know it I cannot say.

I owned myself glad to be rid of Wilkes awhile.

'You are not free of him yet, Mr Douglas.' He rose and went to a cabinet by the rolled charts that were lodged in brass brackets upon the wall. He unlocked a drawer. 'His City friends will now set to stirring the pot for him. There will be a great flurry of correspondence in the papers and gazettes. If he means to be elected he shall work at it, and with a will. We cannot stay idle.'

'The ministry might make an arrest of him if he returns.'

'The ministry is divided, and not as strong as it might be. Lord Chatham stays from London, and I do not know that Grafton is much minded to think on the business of government.' Though it was spoken evenly, I detected a certain disapproval of both of these two great men, and especially the Duke of Grafton, who was well known to prefer Newmarket to Westminster. Jenkinson now took a bundle of papers, tied in red ribbon, from the cabinet drawer, and then relocked it. 'And if Wilkes makes himself a candidate, to arrest him would be folly. He is a friend to the mob, and the mob to him.'

'If he goes openly against the ministry in the election, sir, I cannot see how I may prevent it.'

'He is a menace to the good order of the kingdom. I will not make a quarrel of this, Mr Douglas. Mr Fitzherbert has commended your many talents to me, but they must go for nothing if there is to be a contention raised over my every direction to you.' He brought the bundle of papers to me and put them into my hand. 'You will take these and read them. Perhaps then you will feel a little more sceptical of Mr Wilkes's good intentions.'

Back at the Lane, I unbundled the papers with Francis and together we read them and made our notes. They were a most curious collection of pieces. Some were private letters, some were items torn from the newspapers and magazines, and a few were printer's proofs, the ink badly smudged, as though the proofs had been torn in haste from the presses. At the top of each paper was Jenkinson's signature, and a date. The dates went back three years.

'Jenkinson has been at this for a time,' said I, handing Francis the last letter. 'It looks that he has been storing them against Wilkes's return.'

'They are not all by Wilkes,' he said, which was the same judgement I had come to. 'And it can only be Carrington that has put these into Jenkinson's hand.'

I agreed. Francis asked what further instruction Jenkinson had given me.

'The pieces are to be turned against Wilkes in the election. It is a foul business.'

'He who wrote these,' said Francis, gesturing to the papers, 'is a foul man.'

And in truth, there were many of the pieces had made a darker impression upon me than either the schoolboy vulgarity of Wilkes's *Essay on Woman*, or the mocking effrontery of his *North Briton* 45. For here was a pen dipped in venom, and driven by a malice whose cause was impossible to discern. There were government ministers held up to ridicule, and sometimes also their wives, and a pervading scorn for any person of rank, as if the author meant to flay them by the sheer power of invective and abuse.

Francis looked across the stable yard to where Carrington was just now giving some instruction to Meadows. And it was no fond look

Francis gave them, but there was a rare coldness in his eye. He saw in these pieces the same thing that I had seen when Jenkinson gave them to me, that an incursion was being made by Carrington into the Decipherers' proper affairs. He rebundled the pieces and then retied the ribbon, saying, 'I will take these to my father. You will not tell Jenkinson.'

Baxter followed Wilkes to Leyden, and to several other places in the Netherlands. And in London I received Baxter's weekly report, and with it a constant plea to be recalled, for he had an aversion for the Dutch, and was in some despair to find himself so unexpectedly among them. His reports were slight, and not so enlightening as Wilkes's own letters, of which we intercepted some two or three a week, to his daughter Polly, who had stayed with her maternal grand-mother in London. Now he was in Leyden, and now in Rotterdam, and always in gay company, as if he travelled only for his own amuse-ment and not from the necessity of avoiding arrest. The winter being as fierce that year in the Low Countries as in England, Wilkes several times joined skating parties on the Maese, and amused Polly with accounts of the happy sights he had seen, the garlanded sleighs being pulled across the ice, the festive stalls set up by the river, and the chil-dren skating. It was a picture very different from what I witnessed daily when I went down to the Thames.

Here too was ice, but it came and went, and was no delight to the people living near the river, but an inconvenience, and sometimes a danger, for there was frequently some fool, or a child, or a drunkard, put more faith in the ice than he ought.

And I in some frustration now that I should be stopped there in the bitter cold of London.

My Dear Mademoiselle Beauchamp,

It has been now some weeks since I was so urgently called away from Paris. Receiving no word from you, I have begun to fear that my own letters have miscarried. If so, a thousand pardons. I will make no prolonged excuses for my sudden departure, only to say that nothing but a matter of the first importance could have summoned me away. I am detained now in London upon the same business that took me from Paris, though with a fair expectation of release in the New Year. My duties here once despatched, I will be on the next packet to Calais.

I will not set down words that a woman must hear spoken, and from a man's heart, before she can properly judge of them. Enough to say that they are very few, but as deep as any words may be.

I therefore send this as a herald, in trust that it will be received kindly, as coming from your devoted servant,

Alistair Douglas

The world's greatest fool, I did not go to her but sent the letter in my stead.

CHAPTER THIRTEEN

By the close of December the continuing dispute of the seamen with the shipowners had clogged the river and the docks below the Bridge, with many ships anchored there, and the lighters and barges lying idle. In the lanes and streets behind the docks was endless trouble, for any who got their living by some means connected to the water trade now found themselves stalked by privation, so that the magistrates must send the constables out in pairs now for fear of their safety. In the second week of the New Year a note came up to me from this centre of the troubles, and from the hand of the young widow, Kitty Langridge. I went at once, for it seemed that she had made her own enquiries after the men who had killed her husband, and had made some discovery that she would now tell me of.

Picking my way over broken paving stones and frozen mud, I turned at last into that narrow lane and was about to knock upon her door when she hailed me from further along. She stood upon the threshold of a place almost derelict. I joined her there, and she retreated into the house and showed me into the parlour, where were some few pieces of furniture, and a bed, with her tight-swaddled child asleep, wedged between two pillows. There was no fire in the grate, and the room near as cold as the lane outside.

'We were put out of the other,' said she, seeing my eyes take in the dismal scene. Rank poverty was writ in every part of it. The floor was bare stone, the plaster broken upon the walls, and no curtain in the window but only a thin woollen blanket that she had draped there. But the room was clean, and though she was thinner in face than when we had last met, her child looked well cared for, and bonny.

I remarked the baby's good appearance, at which she brightened and told me that he was no trouble to her but only when he cried, and then only because the landlady of the house pricked her ears to hear him. I said that I hoped the landlady was not unkind to her.

'She is a witch, sir. But she takes in all the washing hereabouts, and while I help her, we may stay here.' She sat by the bed, and put a hand upon the blanket by her child's feet. The hand was red, and mottled from the washing.

I made mention then of what I had come for, which was her note. And I confess I had but little hope of her having done what both Carrington and I had failed in.

'I did not see them, but only heard of them. They took up with two girls from close by. They are not bad women, sir.'

'I am not come down to judge the women.'

'They knew the men's voices for Boston. The men would not have it. They said they were from the Newfoundland fisheries. The girls teased them for the lie. I think they had all been drinking. One girl was struck.'

I asked where I might find the women now.

'I dare not say, sir. They are married.' She saw my surprise, and quickly added, 'They are married to coal heavers. There is no work. They will not let their children starve.'

'Their husbands know then what they do?'

'Know, and know not. But if you go open to the women – that you must not, sir. Their husbands are no gentlemen.'

'I can look to myself, Mrs Langridge.'

She looked down at her boy, saying quietly, 'It was the women I thought of, sir.'

I questioned her then on these two pretended Newfoundland fishermen, but she knew little more, only that the men had taken a boat over towards Rotherhithe, and that there was some expectation of their return, but at a time undetermined.

'And these women would entertain them again?'

'They would entertain the devil, sir, if only it feed their children.'

The door flung suddenly open, and there was a crone stepped in without leave or invitation. Unabashed to find me not a pauper but a gentleman, she demanded to know what I did there. Kitty tried to introduce me, but the crone threw up her hand almost into the poor girl's face.

I rose and stepped between them. 'Mrs Langridge is the widow of a young man who was in my service. You will please to leave us while I conclude my private business with her.'

The old hag was sufficiently cowed (and I later learned, hopeful of extracting a toll from Kitty for my presence) that she withdrew, muttering some vile oath beneath her breath. I shut the door, and turned to find the child awoken and already taken into his mother's arms. I apologized that I had brought this new trouble upon her.

'It is nothing,' said she.

'It is something, Mrs Langridge, that you have told me of these men. It will not be forgotten.'

'Are they my husband's murderers?'

'It is possible.'

'They must hang, sir.'

I gave her some coins and came away, and that same day I set Baxter's nephew Tyler as a watch over Kitty Langridge. By week's end he had discovered the names of the two whores, and also the warehouse by the Execution Dock where they did service for the men.

'Mr Douglas cannot take such a responsibility upon himself, lest he break the proper discipline of my Messengers,' said Carrington, and with some exasperation now, for he had been putting this case to

Jenkinson almost since our leaving of the Admiralty and setting out across the park toward the Palace, where Jenkinson had been summoned. Now, at last, Jenkinson glanced to me upon his other side, as if to invite my submission upon the case.

'Sir, grant me but three Messengers of my choosing, and I believe I may now take Pearce and Flanagan.'

Jenkinson stopped and lifted his eyes toward the King's Palace ahead of us. Carrington would have spoken again but that Jenkinson bade him to silence. 'I am sure the discipline of the Messengers is a very proper concern, Mr Carrington. I am satisfied at the great consideration you give to it. But you have not taken these murderers, despite your first confidence.'

'Had I been given the chance at their first arrival—'

'Therefore I must allow Mr Douglas the help of three of your men. You will make no obstacle to him, but pass the three of his choosing under his authority. – Mr Carrington?'

'Sir?'

'I say that you shall make no obstacle to Mr Douglas.'

Carrington, with some reluctance, asked me to submit the names to him the next morning. I gave him the three names at once.

'We shall have to see if they are available,' said he.

'They are from this moment under Mr Douglas's authority,' said Jenkinson. 'And you shall go now to tell them so.'

Carrington could barely contain his fury at me. But Jenkinson had left him no opening, and so Carrington now bowed his head stiffly to Jenkinson, and turned back toward Westminster, where he must find the three Messengers to be passed to my care.

'I trust that you know what you are about, Mr Douglas,' said Jenkinson as we walked on towards the Palace. 'For myself, I should be happier to think that you and Mr Carringon might seek to cooperate.'

I inclined my head, but stayed silent.

A carriage then proceeding up the Mall, and Lord Shelburne's crest upon the door, we stopped to let it pass. But the carriage halted and Macleane put his head out. Jenkinson bade me wait a moment, and went across and spoke briefly with Macleane and Lord Shelburne.

'It is the election of the Company's directors,' Jenkinson said when the carriage had moved on and I rejoined him. 'Clive and Sullivan are at each other's throats. They are near as much trouble as Wilkes. But I am sure that is to tell you nothing,' said he, and looked at me from the corner of his eye as we crossed the Mall. Then this of the Company seemed to bring another thought into his mind. 'I could not help but notice, Mr Douglas, that you were with Mr Watts's widow at Almack's some while ago. You are a friend to the family, I understand.'

I nodded, but unsure of his intent.

'And Mrs Watts is aware of your work?'

'She knows I am under the auspices of Trade and Plantations. She makes no enquiry of my business.'

'But you are a friend to her.'

'Yes,' said I directly. It was a quite different enquiry to anything I had had from him before this. It seemed not guile, but an odd circumspection.

'They seem the very best type of people,' said he. 'I am told there is a son, Edward?'

I said that he had then been told by someone who did not know them. For although there was a son christened Edward, he had been known always as George.

'And Mrs Watts has two girls?'

'Yes.' He seemed to expect more, so I added, 'But only the youngest is still a girl. The other, Amelia, I think you must have seen with Mrs Watts in Almack's.'

As we turned up toward the Palace gates, Jenkinson remarked the misfortune of Watts's early death, enquired what type of fellow George might be, and some other matters of little consequence, and then asked after any attachment that Amelia might have had.

'As to that,' said I, finally understanding the tenor of all these enquiries, 'it is for George and Mrs Watts to know. I am a friend to Amelia, not a brother.'

'But of course,' said he, as if he had never spoke the startling question. And then seeming to consider the matter further as we stopped outside the Palace gates, he said, 'Your friend Banks has approached me, I believe at your suggestion. I have had it in my mind that you might come to my house also when I dine with him. And I think now it must be a more sociable occasion for the presence of Mrs Watts and her eldest daughter. And the brother, if he is in town.'

I replied that I should be glad to dine with him, but that I could not answer for my certain presence, as I might be called to my work unexpectedly.

'I have obliged you with three of Carrington's men, Mr Douglas. And I know of no such reason will excuse you.' He bade me good day and walked by the sentry and across the yard into the King's Palace.

CHAPTER FOURTEEN

*T*he plan I conceived by which to take Pearce and Flanagan was
as simple as any plan may be.

The three Messengers were to keep watch at the whores' place of
work in the warehouse, each one in his turn, both day and night. I
had decided it were best not to take the women into confidence, for
they were new to their trade, and had husbands, so that neither threat
nor promises were methods very certain, however well practised.
My order was for one Messenger to keep watch at the warehouse
by Execution Dock till the Boston men return there, and then send
word to me at once. This done, he must then signal over the river
to the other two Messengers waiting in Rotherhithe (one sleeping,
one watching for the signal). If Pearce and Flanagan went up into the
City, and I not yet arrived, he must follow them. And if they took a
boat across the river, the two watchers at Rotherhithe should trail
them. Beyond these preparations was only one necessity more, which
was patience.

We waited days.

The days became weeks.

No sign of the bastard Sons of Liberty. Nor any letter to me, nor any message, from Valerie.

I called daily upon the watchers to keep up their flagging spirits, but almost despaired myself now of any success. Then came a day I went down there and at my second rap upon the leaden pipe, the Messenger Armstrong put his head out from above and pushed down the ladder so that I might climb up to join him. Having no sword to encumber me but only a dirk beneath my coat, I was soon with him in the warehouse loft. He hauled the ladder up after me.

'It is the quiet time, sir. Nothing about now but only the rats.'

There was such a darkness in the loft, that the place was very much like some giant hold in a ship. At the far end was a window overlooking the river, and through the window were a number of masts visible against the leaden sky.

'Only remember your boots now,' said he, pointing at them in warning. I sat upon the floor while he pulled off my boots, and then I put them by Armstrong's shoes near the hatchway.

In stockinged feet now, we walked silently the twenty yards across the oak boards to the window. It seemed a ghost fleet anchored there upon the river, for no sailors moved about the decks or the rigging, and the only sign of life two seamen going down the Steps to their boat with great difficulty, both being much taken with the grog. There was no ice in the river, but a freezing malodorous vapour came up from the still ships.

'It is worse in Rotherhithe, sir. They are boiling the whale fat at the Greenland Dock. Without a good wind, the stench sits over the whole south side.'

I asked after the whores. He said he expected no return of them now till after nightfall.

'Is it possible they go also to some other place?'

He beckoned me, and we went back to the spying hole in the floor. I stretched out upon the boards and fixed my eye to the crack.

'You see they have brought a blanket now, sir. They have made a bed of the sacks. They are cosy here.'

It were by the miserablest measure indeed that the dismal little room below might be called cosy. For beside the sacks and the single wretched blanket was nothing but some small flagons, and one of these with a candle wedged into its mouth. Here were the barest necessities for fornication upon a freezing stone floor, and as bleak and dismal a place as the hardest whore might crawl to for a desperate hour before sunrise.

'Is it still the sailors they bring here?'

'Only sailors. But not one American yet.'

'You are sure.'

'I would know it, sir. We all would. There is not a one of them keeps silence down there.' Getting up from by the spyhole, I brushed the dirt from my jacket and breeches, and then Armstrong added, 'I said as much to Mr Carrington.'

'But you have not left your place here?' said I in some surprise, and, I own, annoyance.

'He came, sir.'

'When?'

'Just this morning.'

'Did he say why?'

'I believe he is stretched, sir. Baxter is away. And us three here. He would like us to waste no more time, but go back to our proper work. He is gone over to see the others now in Rotherhithe.'

I went back to the hatch without a word, sat down and pulled on my boots. Armstrong expressed a belated concern that he had spoken too freely, to which I replied that I was much obliged he had spoken at all.

Over in Rotherhithe I found both Messengers awake, and Carrington already gone. I had won some mastery of myself in crossing the river, and so I spoke at once as though Carrington's call upon them was a thing well known to me, and unsurprising, so that they had no particular guardedness in their replies but told me openly of their disappointment that Langridge's murderers had failed to enter the trap that we had set.

'But Mr Carrington is right, sir. By week's end, there will have to be other means tried.'

I attempted to draw them on any other plan that Carrington might have put to them, and it was evident from the speculative ruminations they then embarked upon that Carrington had made no definite statement concerning his intentions. But that they were to be removed from my authority at week's end, this they spoke of as a thing firmly decided.

'You have been very patient,' said I. 'And if we have only a few days more left to us, I trust that you will remain as vigilant as you have been till now.'

They gave me their word upon it. But I saw that Carrington's visit to them, and the setting of the date of their removal, had undermined my authority over them, and given them an impatience to be away from the river.

I confess, this room overlooking the water was bitter cold, as having no fire, and it was certainly no pleasant place to be. Yet I had been confined in worse places, and had imposed upon me more thankless tasks (and with no conjugal visitations), so I was little inclined to coddle the Messengers. But they felt that, I think, and held it somewhat against me. The one of them I then re-crossed the river with hardly spoke a word to me while the boatmen rowed us by the ships, but he kept himself close-muffled and hardly raised his eyes till we reached the steps. I urged him again to vigilance as he got from the wherry. He nodded, and with his eyes lowered and his hands in his pockets, went to replace Armstrong at his station over the whores.

I then directed the wherryman up to the Whitehall Steps.

'If the scum are not discovered by now, they never shall be. Not by your method, at least, Mr Douglas.'

'That is only your belief.'

'It is,' said Carrington, and continued with the polishing of his sword. I had found him in his room at the King's Palace. It was near to the stable yard, just like Meadows's room at the Post Office. But the inside of Carrington's room was nothing like the spartan interior of his second's; for here were portraits of the King and Queen upon the wall, and a fine mahogany bureau, and a dresser. Here it was that he received the letters sent up to the King by Meadows; and from here that he dispatched his Messengers with the King's correspondence. He was very secure in this place, and comfortable beneath the King's shadow. 'But it is your fruitless efforts have provided the evidence for my belief. The weeks go by, and I am without three of my best men, and you are no further on. Is it to be expected that this shall continue till midsummer?'

'That is absurd.'

'Till Easter, then? Come now,' said he, inspecting his blade and then sliding it into the scabbard by the table. 'When must an end be made?'

'You had no business to come down there.'

'It was never forbidden me.'

'Mr Jenkinson passed those men into my sole charge.'

'They were to render you some temporary assistance. And they have done so. Or have you some complaint against them?' I neither moved nor spoke, but I think he glimpsed for the first time the possibility of bloody violence in me. 'There is none of us his own master,' said he.

'You will not go down there again.'

'And you are surely not mine, Mr Douglas.'

We looked the one upon the other, and then a Messenger came in saying that the Chief Justice was upon the King's Bench inside the hour, and that Carrington was wanted there as a witness. Carrington turned on the man, asking what the fellow thought to be reminding him of his own business, and the Messenger hastily withdrew. Carrington put on his sword.

'London is not the colonies, Mr Douglas. And if you do not understand your place yet, I hope that you shall quickly discover it.'

'Do not go down there,' said I; and left him.

CHAPTER FIFTEEN

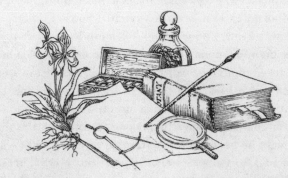

I was often a guest at the Bankses' house in Chelsea through that winter, and also at Joseph's place in New Barrington Street, where he kept his collection. I had been at Harrow with Joseph, he a few years my junior, and though there had since then been a vast diversion in our fortunes, we took an easy pleasure in each other's company. And it was more than long acquaintance joined us, for he was then already fully alive to the world beyond England. He had been on an expedition to Labrador and Newfoundland the previous year, and though his collection of floral specimens was not yet the great prodigy it became, there was more than sufficient to keep him busy in New Barrington Street, classifying and cataloguing throughout every morning. It was during these hours that I would often endeavour to call upon him, for then I might sketch, and he attend to his meticulous labour, and all uninterrupted by those many social obligations that a young gentleman of his estate must necessarily meet with.

I had told him of my visit to Buffon's studio, and Joseph, who had some small correspondence with the Frenchman, was much vexed to hear of specimens from Bougainville's expedition which he had not seen, or indeed even heard of.

'Let me get myself launched on my circumnavigation after de Bougainville,' he had said unhappily, 'and you will see then how quickly Monsieur Buffon shall write to me.'

It was the first week in February when Banks reminded me of this earlier conversation. I had come to New Barrington Street carrying with me all of my cares over those wretched Sons of Liberty, and had already spent a solitary hour in the Collection Room with my sketch-book. The hour had done little to dispel the shadows that hung over me. I had received not one word from Valerie, and that in spite of the further letters that I had sent to her. It was known by this time that Parliament would be prorogued that month, and election for the City seats held in March, and so I had begun to count off the short time before I might be freed from the tiresome business with Wilkes and get myself back to Paris. So when Banks said now, 'There is your friend from Paris, we shall see tonight at Jenkinson's table,' I lifted my head with a start.

'What friend?' said I.

'Monsieur Buffon arrived in town yesterday. Jenkinson tells my mother that Buffon will join us this evening.' When he came over to admire the small study I had done of a strangely coloured lichen, he asked me what friend I had thought of. He made no question of it when I said that it was only Buffon I had in mind.

Banks was called down to Chelsea shortly after, so I was alone in the room when the apothecary Collins came in to deliver a packet to Banks. He told me what it was, which was West African flora, and I said that he might leave it there on the bench, for Banks was already gone. Then I put my sketchbook aside.

'I have not seen you for some while, Mr Collins.'

'There is a packet for you too, sir. But Mr Banks was very partic-ular he should get this as soon as it come into my hands.'

I assured him that I meant no reproach to him; for it was I had introduced him to Banks, after Fitzherbert had introduced Collins to me, and it was plain that Collins now feared I should upbraid him that he had seen to Banks's business before the King's. Now we went downstairs and into that room which Banks had put aside for him, where Collins kept all the potions and herbs of his trade. It smelt of a thousand mingled spices, and the aniseed very strong, which was the scent that ever hung about Collins. Around the walls were many boxes of herbs, each labelled in Collins's spidery hand, and each with a well-worn brass handle. Collins went to his bureau, and after some working of his keys produced a packet, somewhat smaller than the first.

'Things being as they are here at the docks, the captain put in at Portsmouth. This came up this morning, with the other for Mr Banks.'

'I am obliged, Mr Collins.'

'That shall be the last of them, sir. My fellow is dead of something tropic. Mr Banks shall have to find another man if he wishes more specimens from the Guinea coast. There is a Dutchman possible.'

'An unknown Dutchman will not do for me. You will let me know if you hear of any Briton might take up the dead man's business.' I asked then if he had any word of Bougainville's expedition, for Collins kept up a correspondence (and a seemingly endless posting of packets) with a string of his fellow apothecaries in Europe. He told me what he had heard from them, which was that Bougainville had been expected to go through Magellan's Strait in December, but they had received no confirmation of it happening.

'You shall let me know when it is confirmed.'

'And Mr Banks?'

'What of Mr Banks?'

'He has made the same enquiry of me.'

'You need keep nothing pertaining to the botanical aspect of the expedition secret from him.'

'Of course, sir. I expect he has told you that Monsieur Buffon is in London.'

'He has. And if you have nothing else for me, I will bid you good day, Mr Collins.'

Mrs Watts was in the drawing room, waiting for me, and Amelia nowhere to be seen. 'If she appears within the half-hour, Alistair, we must be grateful. And George has cried off and stayed down at Hanslope, and Sophia demands to know why she may not come, and if you now make any difficulty for me I shall not answer for what I might do.'

I remarked that Jenkinson would be disappointed by George's absence.

'He will have to bear it. Did I tell you that Mr Jenkinson has called upon us? We had his card yesterday morning, and he followed it in the afternoon and took tea with us.'

'And?'

'As you said. More fine manners than good humour. But I am bound to say, better company than I had expected.'

'He is too dry for Amelia.'

'Sometimes I almost forget that you are a man, Alistair. But then you will say that which makes your place in that bewildered herd only too apparent. You look very fine, by the bye.'

Sophia then bursting in upon us, my belated compliments on Mrs Watts's green silk dress and necklace of pearls went for nothing

'She will be five minutes more. Hello Alistair. Mama, where is the blue ribbon from Jessel's? We cannot find it anywhere.' Mrs Watts ventured two or three possible locations, said that the maid must know, was told that the maid was hopeless, and finally surrendered and went with Sophia upstairs.

To while away the time till they came down, I took a book from the case, made myself comfortable by the fire, and drew the table-lamp nearer. But when the footman came in a few minutes later to enquire if I might want anything, he found me with the book open in my hand, and my abstracted gaze fixed not on the book but upon the fire. When he left me, I put the book aside.

A part of the bewildered herd. And so I was. For when I thought on Valerie now it was as through a mighty fog of bewilderment. My every letter had gone unanswered, as though sent not to Paris but to some Pacific island where the chance of arrival was a mere lottery, and that of a reply too slight to be thought on. I had considered the possibility of enlisting Barrow as a messenger for me, but dismissed the notion when I found how very uneasy it made me to think of allowing him into my most intimate affairs. For he was beholden to the Admiralty, and to Jenkinson; and I was very loath to place myself under any personal obligation to Jenkinson, or, in very truth, to make myself vulnerable to him. His mode of action against Wilkes bespoke a man quite able to make a cut with some weapon more dangerous than a sword.

It had seemed that I must wait a few weeks more, till the election be passed, before I might go to her and my bewilderment be lifted. But with Monsieur Buffon come to dine with us tonight, I had taken the opportunity of writing yet another letter which I now took from my pocket and turned over in my hands. I wondered if it were not as rash to trust Buffon as Barrow with such an intimate concern. Of a certainty, my head warned me against it. I looked from the letter to the fire and knew what I should do, but hesitated to do it. And in that moment Mrs Watts entered with her daughters. I quickly slipped the letter into my pocket.

Sophia led her sister by the hand. 'What will you tell her, Alistair? You must say that she is beautiful.'

'You have never looked more lovely, Amelia,' said I, which was no more than the plain truth. For she was then in the prime of her beauty, and her diamond necklace, the shimmering silk of the pale blue dress and the jewelled clasp of the black cape about her shoulders, all these fine ornaments had found their proper setting. Nor did she blush to be admired, but only smiled at me very womanly, and I had a sudden memory of the girl she had been when I had first met her in Bengal.

Outside, I helped her into the carriage, and Mrs Watts also, and we went the few hundred yards to Jenkinson's house, where torches burned at either side of his door.

Jenkinson came out into his hall to welcome us. He was probably ashamed at the flush that came to his face when his eyes fell upon Amelia, but I confess that I liked him the better for this momentary betrayal of his innermost feelings. After greeting Mrs Watts, he quickly turned to me, saying that Banks was in the drawing room, and that we wanted only Monsieur Buffon now to make us complete.

'Buffon has expressed to me a fond desire to meet you again, Mr Douglas. But I hope you will not slight the ladies with talk of business this evening.'

It was a warning that I should not raise the subject of Bougainville's expedition. How little did he know Joseph Banks.

'Though it is the summer there, yet surely a cold wind must come up from the south, Monsieur.'

'Ah, that was always the complaint from our people on the Malouines,' returned Buffon to Banks, the two of them seated side by side at the table, and talking, as they had been throughout the dinner, of the collecting expeditions gone out from France and England. 'Either cold or raining, or raining and cold.'

'Mr Banks,' said Jenkinson tersely from the table's head, with a failed effort to keep the exasperation from his voice. 'We have quizzed Monsieur Buffon sufficiently, I think.'

'Ah, but you must not obstruct me, Mr Jenkinson,' cried Buffon good-humouredly. 'It is too little I have the opportunity of such talk. In Paris I am like a hermit, *n'est-ce pas*, Mr Douglas?'

'Monsieur, if a hermit be in regular attendance at the best salons, then I grant it, you are a hermit.'

He raised his glass to me, and smiled merrily at Mrs Watts, who sat between him and Jenkinson. Then Banks asked some question concerning an earlier French expedition, and a certain plant then brought back from Patagonia, and Buffon was instantly engaged upon the subject of the rare specimen. Banks was but twenty-five years of age, and Buffon sixty, but they spoke as equals, and very openly.

'I must rely upon it that you are making Joseph aware of the many perils he will be in if he get his wished-for expedition, Mr Douglas,' said Banks's mother, who sat by me.

'He knows them well enough,' said I.

'Perhaps you believe so. But it is a wild venture to go gallivanting across the globe. What must he find at the other side of the world that he cannot get in Chelsea?'

'It will be a great adventure.'

'You have hit it, Mr Douglas. An adventure. He prattles of new species and botanizing and what not, and beneath it he is that same foolish boy who would always be wandering from the garden just to see what lay beyond the gate.'

'I am sure you would not have him idle his time away at Almack's.'

'There are other entertainments for a young gentleman in London. I will not have this notion that all the young gentlemen in town are fops and macaronis. It is what Joseph puts before me to justify himself. He would be away on his escapade, and so he must have it that to stay would be but to enlist among the idle and worthless.'

Banks, overhearing us, broke off from his conversation with Buffon to say a few laughing words in his own defence. In truth, there was a real affection between mother and son, and even if it were a thing within her power, she would not have prevented his planned expedition. Though the dangers of such a voyage were all too real – and to one who had already lost her beloved husband, the death of a son must have seemed darkness scarce imaginable – she was a better woman than that.

Amelia had been quiet throughout much of the dinner, while Mrs Watts and Jenkinson rang the changes of their mutual acquaintance; but now Jenkinson was pronouncing on some question concerning that grandiose treaty by which Portugal and Spain had once divided the world between them. And Amelia was giving every indication that she listened with a genuine interest. I exchanged an amused glance with Mrs Watts.

'You would no doubt have your own opinion on the treaty, Mr Douglas,' said she, which was but to game me.

'I must defer to the superior knowledge of Mr Jenkinson.'

'So must we all. And if Lord Chatham is indisposed, we should be grateful there is another near that the ministry may rely upon for guidance in all its actions abroad.'

Jenkinson inclined his head graciously to Mrs Watts. Amelia, however, had detected the amusement in her mother's tone, and now directed a sharp look across the table.

'The Portuguese at least have the good sense not to pretend to a power they can no longer maintain,' Jenkinson continued. 'As to the Spanish, I could wish they were as wise.'

'And the French, Mr Jenkinson?' Buffon suddenly enquired from along the table.

'The French, Monsieur Buffon, are another case entirely. They are not to be compared with the Portuguese and Spaniards.'

'Because we have a Navy the equal of your own?'

'As you are our guest, I must not be so discourteous as to dispute that question with you.'

'Mr Douglas,' said Buffon, facing me, 'you have been in America and in the West Indies. You have seen the French and the British colonies.'

'I have. But I am more familiar with the British, sir.'

'To know one is to know the other,' said he. 'For are we not at an equality there? Perhaps it should be that our two countries now make a treaty like the old treaty of Portugal and Spain. You may pass here, but no further.'

'I had no idea, Monsieur, that a natural historian might take so close an interest in colonial affairs,' said Jenkinson.

'My interest is in peace. If there is peace between Britain and France, then young men like Mr Banks may wander freely, collect and study freely, and I will not then in my old age have to endure the general idiocy of another war.'

'You may assure your friends in Paris,' said Jenkinson, 'that there is no such matter thought on here in London.'

'It is not thought on,' said Buffon sadly, 'but it will happen as it has happened a thousand times before. Perhaps I am a fool to hope for better.'

'If you are,' broke in Mrs Watts, 'then I must thank you for it. For I am as little pleased to think of a spirited rivalry between our two countries descending again by degrees to hostilities.'

'But come now, this is to stand in firm opposition to a phantom,' protested Jenkinson. 'I say again, there is no such matter thought on here in London, Monsieur. Now, Mr Banks, may I recommend to you the apple pudding.'

Mrs Banks obliged us with some inconsequential chatter about the pudding, and so the deeper matter was pushed aside, which was a relief to most of us at the table. For though we might have a great regard for Buffon and his own sincere concern for peace, there were many powerful gentlemen in Paris and Versailles only too willing to be at Britain's throat should we show any signs of weakness in defence of our colonies. Nor was it true that an equality then prevailed between ourselves and the French in America and the West Indies; for it was certain that we held the preponderance of power there, and that the French were very jealous of that power.

I had seen first-hand how the French worked to make mischief for us among our colonials and the native Indian tribes. And I confess, I had done my utmost to work a similar mischief among their people and allies. It must be as clear to Buffon as to any of us at the table that some such eruption of open hostilities between us in America was nigh on inevitable. As to Jenkinson's true thoughts, he veiled them very expertly and gave a busy direction to his servants, whereupon two more puddings were set upon the table, and all our glasses refreshed with sweet wine.

'You must think how very poorly I manage even this small entertainment,' Jenkinson remarked to Amelia now that Buffon was distracted again by Banks, and the threat of any unpleasantness gone by.

'You do it very well, Mr Jenkinson.'

'That is too generous.'

'Indeed, I cannot think that any man would do it better.'

'Some part of my life must suffer from my too many commitments and obligations. Alas, it is my own household.'

Again she demurred; again he signalled his lack of a feminine helpmeet; and always with allusion to his high public office, to the wealth he had accrued and to his association with the powerful in Westminster and Whitehall and St James's. A strutting peacock could not have put on a more flagrant display of bright feathers. And Mrs Watts spoke throughout with Banks's mother and me, and all the while listened in to this other conversation in which lay her real interest.

A quarter-hour more and the ladies retired to the drawing room, and we gentlemen to the piss-pots and the port. Jenkinson was now very firm in his direction of our conversation away from anything touching upon the British rivalry with the French, and he went so far as to have part of his collection of coins brought to the table for our general inspection. Knowing more of numismatics than the rest of us together, he was able to direct the talk into channels of his own choosing. But he had not that passionate wonder for his subject that made Banks and Buffon such agreeable tutors in botany, and so it was a very tedious half-hour we spent admiring his coins beneath the candlelight. He signalled at last for his servant to return the coins to their keeping place, and then we went to rejoin the ladies.

At the prompting of Mrs Watts, and at Jenkinson's urging, Amelia was then induced to the harpsichord for us. She played with a real charm and grace, so that even Buffon and Banks broke off from their conversation to listen awhile. Jenkinson beat the time with a finger upon his knee very poorly, and he seemed to take his eyes from Amelia only reluctantly when Banks's mother spoke with him. No one of us could hear what she said to him. But all knew that she meant to have an expeditionary ship for her son, and the King's sponsorship for it, and that Jenkinson was the man could make it happen. It was very cordially they spoke, and by some looks she directed toward Buffon it came to me that she had perhaps had some hand in bringing him here, for the reminder he was of the French expeditions, and as a prime lever for the opening of the King's purse.

After a time Amelia came to the close of the piece, and Banks at once rose from his place by Buffon and went to stand by Amelia and look through the music sheets piled on the harpsichord. Buffon was for the first time that evening alone, and just by me; and knowing that he intended to leave in the morning for Bowood House, which was Lord Shelburne's seat in the country, and fearing that he might leave Jenkinson's house without another such opportunity presenting itself to me, I leaned across to him.

'Monsieur Buffon, I have no right to ask it of you, but I wonder if

I might prevail so far upon your good nature as to ask a small service of you.'

'This is a request from Mr Jenkinson?' he asked warily.

'The service is of a personal nature, Monsieur. Personal to myself.'

He relaxed at this. He put a hand on my knee. 'But, *bien sûr*.'

I drew the letter from my pocket. 'I have written several times to Mademoiselle Beauchamp. I fear that the letters have miscarried, but there has been no opportunity till now of bypassing the general post.'

He lifted his eyes from the letter to me. And as Amelia commenced another piece, which was sprightly and cheerful, he said, 'You did not think to write to the Vicomte?'

'Monsieur, I think you know my circumstances with regard to Mademoiselle Beauchamp's father.'

He studied me a moment, and then his eyes fell to the letter in my hand. But he did not take it.

I was confused now, and, I own, somewhat annoyed at his hesitation. 'I did not intend to involve you in any intrigue, Monsieur. I had only hoped that I might be certain of Mademoiselle Beauchamp receiving my letter. If I have presumed upon you, you will forgive me.' I pocketed the letter again, in a small heat with him. He fixed me with a look that I did not understand. 'I should not have asked it of you,' said I.

'Mr Douglas, when did you last see Mademoiselle Beauchamp?'

I told him that it was that day at his studio. His look was no longer questioning, but a sudden cloud came over his eyes. It froze me.

'Monsieur?' said I.

'I am sorry that it is I who must tell you, Mr Douglas. But she has engaged herself to a French officer, Capitaine Cordet.'

CHAPTER SIXTEEN

*I*s there any pain so deep as that of one's own making? From the first moment of discovery, I had no doubt but that I had been the agent of the disaster. Letters. I had departed Paris without a word of explanation to her, and then sent letters in my stead just as though there had been no lesson to me in those lost letters she had once sent to me. What use now to rail against myself? And yet I railed with all the vehemence of the true penitent, shut up in my house that first night, pacing the rooms, dropping into a chair only to rise again minutes later, unable to quiet myself or find peace. And that the man she had chosen to be her husband should be Cordet was a touch of fate scarce endurable. For after questioning Buffon I had no doubt but that this Capitaine Cordet was the very same Frenchman who had fought us in Bengal, and whose life I had spared. All through that first night I tormented myself, and into the first light of morning, when exhaustion overcame me at last and I slept.

Waking near midday, there was a moment of surprise to find myself upon the bed, and sunlight streaming in; but in the next moment the remembrance of Capitaine Cordet returned to me and I lay there like a man stricken. When I could endure myself no longer, I dragged myself from the bed and went downstairs, where I surprised the daily woman who kept the house for me. I asked her to heat some water, and then I retreated upstairs to sit by my window and stared out over the square. Drays and coaches came and went along the road, and workmen, and sedans, and a bellman collecting letters, and to me it was purposeless movement all, and no distraction to me.

I could not conceive that it was possible Valerie had received none of my letters. And was it conceivable she would sacrifice her whole life to the will of her father? Or was it not more likely that I had presumed a place in her affections far beyond that which she had ever granted me? Whatever I might believe, there was one fact indisputable, which was that Cordet had won her, and this the fact that I circled. Endlessly I circled, like a stumbling ass at the mill, and then at last in self-loathing I washed and dressed, and took myself from the house in the hope of finding some more purposeful distraction down at the Lane.

'Your Mr Wilkes is to join with the Joiners,' announced Francis without turning from his desk. 'The Guild of Joiners and Ceilers,' he added, and tapped an opened letter that rested at his elbow. 'Posted by the Guild secretary this morning. If you would read it, make no delay. It must be resealed and back in the post to Holland within the hour.'

I took the letter across to my desk. There was no encipherment, and the Guild secretary had written the letter as a simple matter of business.

My Dear Wilkes,

You will know that membership of the Guild is not lightly bestowed, and that though the requirements of membership are not now so strict as they were in former times, yet there is a common expectation that there shall be a real concordance between all our members' interests and the interests of the Guild.

Though there has been some question raised of your ability to

*further the interests of the Guild (as having no experience or busi-
ness in the pursuit of Joining or Ceiling) yet it has been determined
by the Committee that your assurance of those good offices you may
as a sitting Member of Parliament do on the Guild's behalf are a
sufficient surety and qualification, and that the Committee shall
support any application you make to the Guild for admittance to
membership. (Your nomination being subject to the usual acceptance by a General Council, and the prompt payment of £22.)*

*The election for the City's parliamentary seats being now
scheduled to commence late March, it would be needful to have you
admitted to the Guild at the soonest. By our Rules and Procedures,
your induction to the Guild may not be done in absentia, but in
propria persona only, which I trust shall be no insurmountable
inconvenience to you.*

*You may apply to me directly upon any procedural matter. As
to any general concerns, your brother-in-law Mr Hayley is well
acquainted with several of the Committee, and has till now acted
with promptitude and discretion on your behalf.*

In hope of your near return to London,

And then was a scrawl, the secretary's signature.

I set down the letter.

'The Joiners are no power,' remarked Francis. 'I expect the better
guilds would not take him. To them, he must be only an annoyance.'

'Hayley visited Wilkes at the mother's house. And Jenkinson
mentioned the fellow at the very first. I had thought it was nothing.'

'Well, you must now correct the thought, Alistair. Hayley is in this
with both feet. I have put him on the List, so we shall soon have his
letters, coming and going. Do we know anything of the fellow?'

'I believe he is a merchant. I shall make some inquiries.'

'How went the great dinner?'

I returned the guild letter to Francis's desk, and told him that the
dinner had gone very well.

'Very well?'

'Yes.'

'That is not very particular.'

'What would you have me say? That Jenkinson is not the most convivial host in London?' Francis looked up in surprise at this curtness. I inclined my head in apology. 'I drank a little more of his wine than I ought. A full morning in bed, and even that has not cleared my spleen. As you see.'

Francis was unconvinced by this evasion and I caught him several times through the morning watching me with a look of concern.

At the Customs House down at the Keys there was little inclination shown by the officers in the Long Room to rise from their chairs by the fire and render me some assistance. For such a quiet as then prevailed on the river was unheard of, and they seemed determined to take full advantage of their unaccustomed leisure. But eventually a junior of their number, one of the Searchers of the ships, was directed to help me, and with reluctance he left the warm hearth and took me upstairs to the Records Room, where were copies of the bills of lading for all the ships that came up the Thames. The room was cold but dry, and rank after rank of shelves stretched down the room, each shelf boxed into small compartments from which binders and sheaves of paper protruded.

'Hayley,' said I. 'Hayley of Wapping.'

'Syndicate or personal?'

I said that I presumed Hayley was involved in several syndicates, but that it was such questions I hoped the Customs records might answer.

'If he trades personal, he is here,' said the lad, slapping a shelf. 'Syndicates over there.' He pointed to the far end of the aisle. Then I asked after the sorting method, and he told me that it was done by the date of the shipment, and by the type of goods being freighted.

'What is his goods?'

I confessed my ignorance, and the lad screwed up his face.

'Can it be done?' said I.

He pulled a bill of lading from the box just by him and showed me the various columns and rows and signatures. 'The merchant's name is always put here. If Hayley is trading, he will be listed. But how you shall find him without you know either his goods, or the time of his shipments—'

'It is worth half-a-crown to me.'

'It is more work than you know,' said he, very sly.

'I see that the senior gentlemen downstairs have taught you the value of your trusted position,' I remarked, and he answered me now with a smirk of open cupidity. And never was a lad more surprised than when I caught him by his coat collar and pulled him onto tiptoe, and slammed him back against the shelves, with my other hand at his throat. 'Do you mistake me now for a chiselling merchant?'

He attempted to move his head from side to side, his eyes fixed upon me in fear.

'Then you will please not be so foolish as to haggle the price with me. I say it is worth half-a-crown. You will make copies of any bill where Mr Hayley is named. When I return here next week you will have them ready.'

He made a small nod, as much as my hand upon his throat would allow. Then I released him, and he turned aside from me, cowering. It was in my mind to strike him, which was a base thought, and one for which I well knew the reason. And that reason was not the lad's cupidity, or even the difficulty of discovering Hayley's bills. Shamed by my own misdirected anger, I turned from the lad and went quickly down the stairs.

There was a darkness upon me that I could not shift, nor could I be still, and I moved continually along the docks and up into the City about my business, and back, all through that day.

At the Guildhall I made enquiry of the arrangements being made for the coming elections, and where the hustings might be, telling the guildsmen of my desire to hear the candidates' speeches. Both the hustings and the poll itself, they told me, would be held in the very hall where we stood, and they warned that I should come early to get a place there, for there was never room enough for all who thronged in at such times. As to the candidates, they knew that Beckford was standing, with the support of Chatham, and then were two candidates supported by the ministry, and two others supported by Lord Bute, and one who had Lord Rockingham at the back of him. They assured me that others would be nominated, for there were four City seats to be won. They mentioned that the Duke of Bedford had no man forward yet, and I got no hint from them of Wilkes's prospective nomination (though they had read it in the papers, and heard the rumours in the coffee houses, as well as I). I mistrusted their silence on Wilkes. Nor could I mistake their coldness toward Lord Bute's name, or their indifference to my idle speculation upon prospective candidates who might have the support of the Court.

And yet it was not at the Guildhall but down by the river that I found a mood more suited to my own. For at the docks were no gentlemen engaged in debate about the coming election, but there was despair and privation on many faces now, very naked. In the night the whole of the riverside was become a threatening place, and to wander there aimlessly was a thing that no sensible man would venture. But now, on that day, I found that I might walk there unaccosted, as if the wretched riverside dwellers should recognize a like wretchedness in me.

I must accept in the end that I could not blame the father; for howsoever he might have guided her, the decision at the last must be hers. She had chosen; and not me, but another.

Near sunset, I leaned against the wall by the Tower Steps and looked over the grey river, and there was an emptiness in me beyond sounding. There was not a sail raised on any ship, but the masts were like a forest of leafless trees in the midwinter. There was ice on the river, and nothing moving but only an empty cart on the Bridge, and then it passed over and now was silence, and nothing moved at all.

CHAPTER SEVENTEEN

*T*he click of the first pebble against my window woke me, and the second brought me from stupor and got me from my bed. Opening the casement, I discerned a blonde-headed figure in the shadows below.

'Tyler?'

'Yes, sir.'

'Wait there. I shall be down directly.'

I joined him in the street a few minutes later.

'Is Wilkes returned?' said I, for we had been expecting it for some days now.

'It is the Bostonians, sir. Mr Armstrong sent me to tell you they are with the whores.'

He had a hackney waiting, and we went swiftly through the empty streets, and then through the dimly lit narrows of the City where was no one about but only some lampmen with yokes upon their shoulders, and buckets of oil. Beyond the Pennington Street fields, I gave order for the jarvey to set us down at a place well back from the river. I told him to wait for us, paid half the fare to be sure of him, and then proceeded with the lad Tyler down to the warehouse by the dock.

The taverns were all shut at this hour, nor was there any drunken carousing in the lanes and streets nearer the dock, for the bitter cold had sealed everyone indoors save only the destitute, who were invisible but for an occasional stirring of rags in doorways that we passed. We came at last to the warehouse. I was about to knock upon the draining pipe as a signal when I saw in the darkness that the ladder was already lowered. Tyler saw it too, and whispered, 'Sir,' but I clamped a hand upon his shoulder and turned him to face me. I raised a finger to my lips.

With gestures then, I directed him to hide himself in the nearby shadows and wait for me. I was surprised, but by no means displeased, to see him draw a blade from his belt as he went. I drew my own dirk from beneath my jacket and crossed to the ladder, set my foot upon the first rung and started to climb.

The smallest sound at such a time is like a musketshot, and twice in my ascent the wooden rungs creaked beneath my boots, and I stopped and looked upward. But each time there was nothing, and so I went carefully on. Arrived to the top, I raised my head through the opening in full readiness to either strike with my dirk or leap from the ladder and risk my neck below. But there was nothing there to meet me, only the phantoms of my imagining in the darkness, and I quickly pressed these aside as I stepped up from the ladder onto the oak boards.

The dark here was thicker than below, though a pale yellow glow came in at the far window, which must be from the ships' lanterns on the river. I stood still for a few moments, and peered into the shadows and listened. There was a low sound very strange, which caused me some consternation till I understood that it came from outside the warehouse. It was the broken ice, scraping the river's edge as it moved on the tide, and so I put it from my mind and stepped away from the ladder toward the place where I remembered the peephole to be. But at my first step, my foot scuffed against something lying upon the floor. I crouched and put out my hand like a blind man. Then I felt the thing, and knew it at once for an empty boot. Recalling now how careful Armstrong had been to shed his boots by the top of the ladder, I reached all around me and felt for the other of the pair but could not find it.

Then I dared a whisper. 'Armstrong.'

Receiving no answer – nor starting any villain from the darkness – I went slowly towards the window, with some hope by that means to discover the hole in the floor. The whores' room below being unlit, I needs must crawl upon the boards, searching with my hands, till after a time I discovered the peephole. A vain discovery, for pressing my face close to the boards I found the room below an inky blackness, and no part of it visible. Rising to my knees now, the dirk still in my hand, I looked about me.

'Armstrong,' I whispered again, but again the name fell into the silence.

I rose and went slowly into the dark shadows by the wall, feeling ahead of me with my boots, and very pained by the noise that they made upon the floor. But the floor there was empty, and all the way to the wall, which when I came up against I turned and moved along, with my left hand touching upon it to guide me. Haltingly, I made my way back towards the ladder. I had gone almost the length of the place, and was about to turn from the wall to the hatchway, when my boot struck hard.

Startled, I thrust forward my dirk; and I confess, had Armstrong stood before me it was such a thrust as might have killed him. But no one stood before me, and when I was certain of it I composed myself, and then shuffled forward till my boot touched the thing again. I prodded it cautiously with the toe of my boot, and finally crouched and put down my left hand.

It was a man; I knew that instantly. But that it was a dead man I discovered only when my hand went to the face and met a tight coldness where should have been a warmth of life. I sheathed my dirk and grabbed the body below the arms and dragged it over to the feeble light near the hatchway.

'Mr Douglas?'

'Quiet,' I returned sharply; for it was the lad Tyler calling from below. 'Keep your eyes open.'

I let the weight of the body down on the boards and knelt to see the face by the dappled light from the hatch. It was Armstrong. I ran my hand over his throat. It was cold and dry. But when I touched his chest there was a wetness of blood. Then my hand went to his feet. There was a boot upon his right foot, but upon his left, only a stocking. I lifted both his hands upon his chest where he was stabbed. Then I put my hand upon his forehead, saying quietly, 'Lord have mercy. Christ have mercy. Lord have mercy.'

Seeing nothing more about me, I got myself quickly to the ladder and climbed down. Tyler asked no questions but came with me around the warehouse, and then I went alone down the steps to the river. He waited up by the river wall while I pushed my bloodied hand through the broken ice and into the water. Then I drew a kerchief from my pocket and dried my hands. I looked up and saw the lad watching me.

'You may go home now.'

'Mr Armstrong—'

'He does not need you.' The lad's eyes stayed fixed upon me. 'Mr Armstrong has been murdered,' said I. 'There is nothing more that either of us may do for him.'

'He sent me to fetch you.'

'You are not blameable, Tyler.' I came up the steps, wiping the last of the blood and the water from my hands. I felt the coldness of the river like death, deep in my bones, and I told the lad again to return to his home.

Though Jenkinson was by now confirmed as one of the Lords of the Treasury, yet he remained also a Lord of the Admiralty, and so it was at his Admiralty room that I met with him and Carrington shortly after daybreak. Though Carrington wore the face of a man stricken, it was but a mask, and he made sure with every word to remind Jenkinson of my prime responsibility for the plan which had brought

Armstrong's end. 'It was my mistake,' said he finally, 'that I did not oppose Mr Douglas's folly more forcefully.'

'You made your opposition sufficiently clear, Mr Carrington,' Jenkinson assured him. 'And I am sure Mr Douglas regrets it as much as any that your advice was not heeded. But it is done and cannot be undone. Is there a widow?' There was none, thank God. Jenkinson then asked me what I had heard of Wilkes's expected return.

'Sir, there has nothing come from Baxter these past two days.'

'I beg pardon, sir,' broke in Carrington. 'Wilkes is landed yesterday evening in Harwich.'

Jenkinson seemed as startled at this news as I. 'You had not heard of it, Mr Douglas?'

'No, sir.'

'Mr Douglas has doubtless been too busy with his close attention to the docks.' Carrington faced me, the impertinent fellow. 'You know that you may lean upon me. There is little sense in taking so much upon your own shoulders that the weight must crush you.'

'I am not crushed, sir.'

'To all appearance, Mr Douglas, you are not travelling so very sprightly.'

Jenkinson then asked when Wilkes would be in London, but of this Carrington had no certain information, and so Jenkinson said to me, 'He will no doubt send some notice to his daughter. And you will inform me of it when he does.'

'Is that all, sir?'

'You may notify the two Messengers left under your charge that they are now returned to the service of Mr Carrington.'

'But I will have need of them.'

'Pearce and Flanagan are no more your concern, Mr Douglas. I would have you turn your mind to Mr Wilkes. Once he has arrived in town as a candidate, we shall have trouble of him. He cannot be arrested now till he lose the election. But he is late to the field, and I am confident the papers with which I have furnished you shall be an insuperable obstacle to him.'

'If I may be so bold, sir, that is to mistake the City. Wilkes may be a rake, and a fugitive from justice, or the very devil. But so long as he is in opposition to the ministry, he will have the support of the City gentlemen.'

'They have not seen the full squalor of his mind.'

'I have made sure his bawdy *Essay* has found a good circulation in all the coffee houses. The laughter I have witnessed, sir, seems to offer no great threat to Mr Wilkes.'

'That is not all you were given,' said Carrington (which was a confirmation to me that he had procured those pieces for Jenkinson).

Ignoring him, I said to Jenkinson, 'An appeal to morals in the City must fail, sir. Each gentleman there keeps his conscience in his purse, and if Wilkes only takes care to make no infringement there, he will not be judged for any want of morals.'

'As Mr Carrington says, it was not bawdy alone with which you were furnished.'

'There is a question, sir, whether the seditious pieces were entirely from Wilkes's hand.'

'Question?' said he.

'The Decipherers have some doubt of their authorship.'

'The pieces were given you to be used, not questioned.'

'If Wilkes were to prove a false attribution had been made—'

'I have no inclination to debate the matter, Mr Douglas. I am surprised that you have taken it upon yourself to put up this impediment. I have pointed you to the highway and you have turned aside into the thicket.'

'I am to receive the Bishop's opinion of those papers within the week, sir.'

Jenkinson started at this. It was an unexpected turn, and clearly one he did not like; but neither could he reprimand me that I had passed them to the Bishop. And after taking some thought, he said that he would expect my report on the Bishop's judgement. 'Now if you would leave us, I have some further business with Mr Carrington.'

'I will need to retain the services of the Messenger Baxter.'

'Has the fellow a wife?'

'He has,' said Carrington, and I could not help but feel the weight of it.

'You will be careful of him, Mr Douglas,' Jenkinson instructed me. 'But you may keep Baxter by you till the ministry decide when the arrest be made of Mr Wilkes.'

There are narrows and glens in every life, and no man may pretend to know each turn in the road ahead of him, nor the troubles he will meet with, nor yet his final destination. But there are times he is in the uplands, and all the world open to him; and then it is that the skylarks sing, and the clean wind is upon his face. And just as certain there are other times when he is deep in the glen, and the cold rain falling, and no shelter for him but the sodden bracken, and the crags and rocks formidable all about him; and then every look turns inward, and every part of Creation throws only another shadow upon his soul.

From the Admiralty I took my way homeward with a step full as heavy as any I had taken. Both Langridge and Armstrong's deaths weighed on me now, and the loss of Valerie haunted my every thought. Sick at heart. Aye. And myself the only maker of my stony path into the shadowed glen.

CHAPTER EIGHTEEN

'Enjoy myself?' said Baxter, taken aback by my enquiry. 'Your Dutchman is a sour bastard, sir, and I am glad to be done with them. It was only Wilkes's credit put a smile on every face he met with. They did not smile upon me, sir. Ice is ice. Only a Dutchman could think it entertainment.' Baxter had found me in the Lane but a half-hour since, and had brought me directly to a row of merchants' houses by the Goodman Field above Wapping. This, he told me, was where Wilkes had gone to ground upon his arrival from Harwich. Now we stopped at the corner and Baxter lifted his chin. 'It is the brick house opposite where Tyler is standing.'

'Whose is the carriage?'

Baxter beckoned Tyler over from his watching place. The lad told us that he had seen a big-wigged gentleman pass from the carriage into the house. He had not recognized the face.

'Do we know who owns the place?' said I.

Baxter shook his head, but Tyler said, 'It is some fellow Hayley.'

My eye lingered on the black door and then went to the four upstairs windows. It was a handsome property, newly built, like the others in the row. Wilkes's brother-in-law. A man on the rise. And it might be a convenient place from which to fight a campaign for a seat in the City.

It was the second week in February. It was little time Wilkes now had to forge a campaign. Weeks, and not months; and the other candidates with such a start already that there must be some question whether he could make any headway, the electorate being already half-promised or bought. Jenkinson had most certainly taken care to fill the coffers of the ministry's candidates. Chatham's fellow would be similarly well supplied. Against this redoubtable opposition, the outlaw Wilkes must stand armed with nothing but an empty purse and a ready pen; and though I will not say that I admired him, in such brazen defiance a man declares himself at least no coward.

And then while we stood there, a small band of men, fewer than a dozen, came up the street and stopped outside Hayley's house. Some were coal heavers, easily identifiable by the black on their clothes, and others journeymen of the poorer sort, and now they lifted their faces to the upper windows, and some cried out, 'Mr Wilkes!' and one of them bellowed, 'Wilkes and Liberty,' like a fool. Along the street people came out from their houses to discover the cause of the cries.

'Go along there, Mr Tyler,' said I. 'Find what they are about.'

It was several minutes the men milled about, Tyler among them now, and with occasional cries of 'Wilkes!' going up to the windows. Then the front door opened, and the men pressed forward to the steps. From that distance I could not make out the fellow who came down to meet with them, but by his upright bearing I knew it was not Wilkes. The fellow had some conversation with the gathered men, and said that which seemed to quiet them. When he returned inside the house, they moved away peaceably, and the curious onlookers in the street likewise made a general dispersal.

'It was Hayley,' Tyler reported coming back to us. 'He asked them to keep away from here. He said that Mr Wilkes would show himself in the town, but in his own good time.'

'What did the men want?'

'Nothing, sir. Some sight of Wilkes? They had heard he was here, and came.'

Baxter remarked that such men were sheep, and not worth thinking on. But I own, the small scene disturbed me in spite of its seeming inconsequence. For Wilkes had been in London for but a matter of hours, and had made no speeches, nor so much as lifted a finger to bring people here. And yet here was some wealthy gentleman's carriage at his door, and the coal heavers and journeymen moving towards him like ants to the sugar.

I left Tyler to keep watch there, and gave Baxter leave to go to his wife, for he had not seen her since his return. Then I took myself down to the Customs House.

There was no waiting this time, but that same young Searcher was upon his feet the instant of my arrival, and he led me from the Long Room and upstairs to the Records. 'I have put the pieces by, sir,' said he, and went behind a counter to draw out a box filled with papers and set the box before me on the counter. 'Your Mr Hayley is both "Syndicates" and "Personal".'

I remarked that there was more there than I had supposed.

'He is not the biggest, nor yet the smallest type of merchant, sir.' As I lifted the papers from the box and drew up a stool by the counter, he asked if he might get me aught else. Then he went down the stairs to fetch me coffee, and I commenced my inspection of the papers he had found. There is always in such records a story, if only they be read with due attention. And the tale of Hayley's fortunes was told very clear in the growing duties and taxes he had paid. In the late Fifties, he had traded solely on personal ventures, and it seemed mainly through the agency of two captains who had set sail in private vessels along with the East India Company fleet. Thereafter, his attention had turned to the Atlantic trade, and here he had been part of several syndicates bringing tobacco from the American colonies and sending slaves there from the West African coast; and there was a variety of lesser ventures besides. Year by year, the value of his trade had increased steadily, with a rise very noticeable in '65. The last paperwork was from the spring of '66. When the Searcher returned, I asked the reason for the omission of any more recent papers.

'They are Current,' said he. 'Sometimes the merchants will put the taxes to test in the courts. It is a slow business. There are papers three years old and yet Currrent. I would need the Chief Officer's permission to fetch them.'

He was gone fully an hour, but at last returned and placed before me a handful of loose pages, which were the Current documents. I thanked him for his trouble, but he did not move away, and so I looked at him very pointedly. 'The Chief Officer says the papers should not leave my sight,' said he, a little wary of my temper. 'They are Current, sir.'

'Does he suppose that I shall steal them?'

'It is an order,' he said helplessly.

There was nothing to be done, and no privacy to be had, and so I bent my head over the papers. There were several large shipments for Hayley had come into the Thames since the spring of '66, the last of them in late November. After that he appeared to have suffered the consequences of the trouble on the river equally with all the other London merchants; for since then there was nothing recorded for him. But after several minutes I came across the papers for the shipment that had arrived in the early autumn. The vessel that brought the goods was the *Valiant*.

I sat up.

'Are you done, then, sir?'

'I am done. You will make me a fair copy of this piece, and lively.'

'You are sure this *Valiant* might have brought Pearce and Flanagan?' said Francis after reading the copy I had brought up from the Customs House.

'It was one of the five Boston ships that I went aboard in the autumn.'

'Who shall you tell?'

'I have told you.'

He pursed his lips, for it was no proper answer I had given him.

For who, indeed, should I tell? Jenkinson had been adamant that I should not continue in pursuit of the murdering Sons of Liberty. And Carrington would fashion any report from me into a weapon at my throat. In truth, I was myself in no wise certain of the meaning of my discovery, for there had been those other ships from Boston in the Thames at the same time as the *Valiant*, and till now she had been under a suspicion no greater than the rest. And nor had my search in the autumn been as thorough as it might, for what with all the crewmen signing off and signing on the vessels, and the officers changing, and the captains continually busy with the unloading and repair of their ships, it was not long before I had given up my enquiries shipboard to concentrate my efforts in the docks and along the river-side. It had not occurred to me then to make any question of the ownership of the goods being freighted. And the *Valiant* had sailed for the Guinea coast shortly after, and in a fashion quite regular, to get slaves for the return across the Atlantic.

'It could be that there is nothing in it,' said Francis at last.

'There is something in it,' said I. 'Only what it is, I cannot tell.'

'Jenkinson would have you look to Wilkes.'

'I have looked to Wilkes and I have found Pearce and Flanagan.'

'You have found nothing. It is very likely that you have made no discovery, but only unravelled a thread of coincidence.'

'If Hayley had some part in getting those two murderers here—'

'You are charged with the careful surveillance of Mr Wilkes. Pass beyond that, and you trespass now upon Carrington – much to your detriment, I fear.'

'Would you have me ignore this?' said I.

'I would,' said he. 'But now that you have made your token consultation with reason, I expect that you shall feel at liberty to do as you please.'

I took the copy to the window and looked across the stable yard where some fellow in the green livery of one of the Accompting Houses nearby had come to speak with Carrington's man, Meadows. Meadows rocked back on his chair, balanced against the wall, and listened to the fellow's information. It was a very deep and powerful web of informers and information that Carrington had established over London. But if I now offered up Hayley's name to the senior Messengers that they might discover for me all they could of the fellow, word of my enquiry must go directly to Carrington, and from Carrington to Jenkinson; and I must thereafter find myself dismissed to the outer dark.

Carrington was right in this at least, that London was not the colonies, and neither was the Thames the Mississippi. There were such shackles on me here as had never hobbled me while I wandered abroad.

CHAPTER NINETEEN

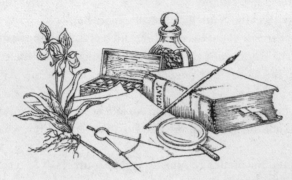

I had not spoken of Valerie's engagement to Cordet with anyone, but I had taken such a knock from it that no perfect concealment of my feelings from my intimate friends was possible. Banks had no doubt heard something of the particulars from Buffon, but he kept it to himself, and was content to leave me to my sketching in his Collection Room as before. He asked me no questions, and made no outward show of sympathy, and his silent companionship was in those days a great succour to me.

But I confess that I avoided the Watts household for some while after that dinner with Jenkinson. And that, I am ashamed to say, from a cowardly fear to be trapped in company with those whose every word of feminine sympathy must be another cut to me. (And Mrs Watts knowing Cordet from our time in Bengal, the cuts must bite the deeper.) But having excused myself from several invitations to supper, and a request to accompany them on a visit to the Museum, I found myself at last called to order by a note delivered not by any bellman but by one of Mrs Watts's own servants.

She had taken tickets for Mr Murphy's *Zenobia* at a theatre in Drury Lane. She regretted that she must impose upon me, but that George had not come up to London as expected, and so she must rely upon me that evening, else the tickets be forfeit. She would call upon me at seven that same evening.

The moment must be faced; and it being Mrs Watts alone, without her daughters, decided me.

'You may tell Mrs Watts that I shall expect her.'

At seven her carriage arrived, and I settled myself on the seat opposite while she made some idle pleasantries, and then as the carriage moved off, she said, 'And now, Alistair, you will tell me about Mr Wilkes.'

'Shall I, indeed?' said I, though in some relief that it was this public matter, and not the personal, she had broached first. 'Pray, what have you heard?'

'The whole town talks of him. And the Court. Half Mayfair have already dined with him.'

'They have not. And I am not a little surprised that they should own to it if they had.'

'He is the fashion. I think it is a happy diversion from the usual talk of the ghastly Baltimore.' Lord Baltimore this was, whose trial for the rape of a milliner girl was then proceeding. 'I have noticed Mr Jenkinson shows no fondness to hear of Wilkes's exploits.'

'You should follow Jenkinson's wise example.'

'I will not be put off, Alistair. Everyone has heard something. It is gossip, not a secret, and you will tell me.'

'Very well. Wilkes has been in London some days now. First at the house of his brother-in-law, but he is now in some idle fellow's house by Dean's Yard. There is good reason to believe he will seek election into the next Parliament. And now you know as much as I.'

'That is what I have heard. Also that he calls himself Mr Osborne, as though that should disguise his face.' The carriage passing from light to dark as we moved beneath the street lamps, her expression was harder to read than the mirth in her voice. 'I wonder that Mr Carrington has failed to arrest him.'

'Perhaps I should direct them to you, as a person remarkably well acquainted with Mr Wilkes's whereabouts and *nom de guerre*. I must assume you have had this from Fitzherbert?' She nodded and I said, 'Amelia will find herself embarrassed if she speaks a word of it to Jenkinson.'

She nodded again, and though silent, seemed altogether pleased with the confirmation of Wilkes's exploits she had won from me.

It was but a short way to Drury Lane, and we talked of Banks's planned voyage then, and the news she had just heard of the King's consent to the expedition. I had got some earlier hints of this from both Banks and Jenkinson, and so it was no surprise to me, but still cheering, and a subject sufficient to hold off any enquiry concerning Mademoiselle Beauchamp. But from the remarks Mrs Watts made, it was evident that she had spoken with Banks several times since that dinner at Jenkinson's house, and I could not doubt but that she knew what Buffon had told me. And glad I was when we drew up outside the theatre and I could get down from the unwanted privacy of the carriage. I helped her down, and we made our way across the brightly lit pavement and joined the gay throng of people passing into the theatre between the great torches by the door.

Once past the milling crowd near the ticket stall, we went straight up the stairs and found our box, which was a good one, and almost overhanging the stage. As she took her seat, Mrs Watts informed me that we were to be joined by Lady Shelburne, and a small party.

'I hope that you will not mind the company.'

I said that no man came to the theatre for solitude. And in truth I was happy enough to share the box, as the presence of others must provide a shield to me against any close enquiry of the heart. So I sat and leaned forward to rest my forearms against the balcony rail, and surveyed the scene below with the blankest indifference.

No woman was in the seats there but had made some considerable effort with her hair or wig, her jewellery and dress; and I am sure there was as much feminine beauty gathered there as in Ranelagh Gardens or Almack's, or in any other place of civilized leisure in the town. And yet, to me, all was a great nullity of chattering wigs and hairpins and face-paint. For though the cause was in me – which I knew – I could not will myself to regard them.

'The Daweses are gone to Rome.'

I turned to Mrs Watts in surprise. I had not thought of Henrietta almost since she had left my house that night.

'I see you had not heard of it,' said she.

I admitted that I had not.

'And will you not ask me now when they shall return? It is to be a long tour. A year or more. A man like Dawes is unlikely to have taken so decided an action unguided by his wife.'

With a flush now rising to my cheeks, I said, 'That is behind me.'

She inclined her head, accepting this, and I think glad of it; and then looking across at the boxes opposite, and the people coming in, she began to instruct me light-heartedly in the follies and adventures of various ones of her acquaintance. This young man had a destructive fondness for the gaming table. That young woman had almost lost her good character to a notorious baronet. And that old reprobate had made his fortune by some dubious venture in the West Indies and now spoke of nothing but God, religion and the decline in morals he saw all about him. Mrs Watts pronounced no hard judgement on any one of them, but with a shrewd remark and a lifted brow, gave the touch of life to people that had otherwise passed unnoticed beneath my gaze.

But in the midst of one recounting she fell silent, and I looked around to see Lady Shelburne and her party coming into our box. We rose, and Mrs Watts introduced me both to Lady Shelburne and to Mrs Barre. Isaac Barre, the Member of Parliament and ex-soldier from Wolfe's Quebec command, gave me a curt nod of acknowledgement. Then I shook the hand of the fourth of their party, who was Laughlin Macleane.

Macleane sat behind Mrs Watts, and was instantly launched with her on some gossip he had heard that day at India House, while Lady Shelburne turned in her seat to speak with me. She was no older than I, and almost French in the delicacy of her manners. Though she had not a half of Mrs Watts's penetration, she was both pretty and engaging, and I well saw how ably she must fulfil those public duties expected of her position. Her charm was very natural to her, and without malice, and no surprise to me that she should be a friend to Mrs Watts.

The stage-lamp shutters being then opened, a strong light flooded the boards, and we looked down to see the first actor declaim the prologue. The fellow was no Garrick, and Macleane leaned across and offered me his hip flask, which upon my declining it, he raised and took a liberal dose of the medicine.

The play was set in Roman times, but it was like a child's puzzle to determine what relation the people in it bore to each other, or indeed to understand the reason of their great contention. After fifteen minutes I almost regretted that I had not taken Macleane's flask, and I turned, only to find him dozing comfortably.

I leaned forward and touched Mrs Watts's shoulder. 'I shall return presently.'

Nor was I the first to beat a retreat from Zenobia's troubles, for beyond the door there were a number of gentlemen seated at tables, drinking and smoking, and conversing cheerfully, like men reprieved. I took a small table, and picked up a copy of the *Public Advertiser* lying near. A few minutes later and Macleane came out and sat down beside me.

'I have decided to follow your excellent example,' said he. 'Drink?'

'No thank you.'

'Is that Wilkes's piece? You might spare yourself that too.' I did not like to have Wilkes's name bandied so publicly about me, and I set the newspaper down. He mentioned then that Barre had told him I had some connection with Mrs Watts's late husband.

I explained that Watts had been my superior when I was in Bengal.

'Trade and Plantations?'

'Company.'

'Clive is in town next month.'

'The affairs of the Company have been no concern of mine, Mr Macleane, since I left Bengal. And that is several years past. And if you are wondering if I might have power over any Company stock, or that I might for some consideration oblige you by passing the stock into your hands to be split for the next vote, then I fear that I must disappoint you.'

'Barre thought you must be promised already to Jenkinson.'

'I am promised to nobody.'

He leaned toward me. 'There have been fortunes made this past year. And they will be nothing to what shall follow. You seem a man of spirit, Mr Douglas.'

'I had rather be a man of sense.'

'There is no sense in stepping over gold that lies strewn beneath your feet. But I will not insist upon it.' He sat back, and this with an air of my having wasted his time. How this brazen solicitation might affect others I cannot say, but, for myself, I felt it almost comical in its impertinence. Now I watched with curiosity as his gaze ran over the other gentlemen about us. I have seen generals look out over a battlefield thus; and pickpockets over a crowd.

'Will Wilkes stand?' said he, as though the question had just come into his mind.

'I am not Wilkes's keeper.'

He smiled as though he saw through me, and then he excused himself and went to where Hastings, whom I had not seen for some months, stood laughing with his friends. I had heard recently that Hastings was very close to securing his heart's desire, which was a return to Madras or Bengal in some good position in the Company. But the internal politics of the Company were at this time extremely fluid, with the new Court of Directors due to be elected in April, so that nothing in the way of appointments was certain.

As he turned to greet Macleane, Hastings saw me, and he raised a hand and hailed me in a manner friendly and familiar. Macleane's quick glance went from Hastings to me, and by his look I knew that he thought I had deceived him about my closeness to the Company's affairs (which I had not). He commenced speaking with Hastings, and I saw that they talked of me, which I found disagreeable just then, and I did not linger but returned to the box and the interminable tribulations of Zenobia.

After, as the carriage drew away from the theatre, I attempted some banter about the play, and the actors, but Mrs Watts said, 'I thought it not so very bad. Perhaps the subject was too heavy for your mood. Loyalty and love gone awry—' She shot a glance at me, and then said, 'I am sorry. That was a stupid thing for me to say.'

I said, 'It cannot matter now. Was it Buffon told you?'

'He told Banks. And Banks spoke to me only out of concern for you.'

'The concern is unwarranted.'

'Alistair—'

'You know it is Cordet.'

'Yes. And if you are wondering, I have mentioned it to no one. Nor shall I.'

'I am not the first man in the world to take such a blow. Most have survived it. I fancy I am not so weak as to go under.'

'It is no weakness to feel a grief. You told me so when William died.'

'It is not the same.'

'Except only that one of us must offer consolation and the other accept it. Else how should we pretend to any friendship between us?' The carriage rattled over the paving stones and we said no more for a time; but when we reached my house, I opened the carriage door and she said, 'I hope you are not angry that I spoke.'

'I am not angry,' said I.

'Did Macleane want money of you?'

'That, and some better knowledge of Wilkes.'

'You must be careful of him.'

I bade her good night and got down from the carriage.

CHAPTER TWENTY

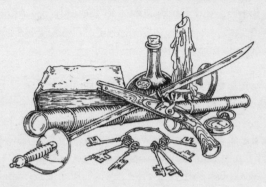

'As Wilkes has now moved from Hayley's place,' said Francis as we crossed the Lambeth Palace quadrangle, 'you might do well to move your attention also.'

'Hayley is in Wilkes's business with both feet. You said so yourself.'

He raised his hat and nudged me, and I bowed my head to the elderly prelate that we passed. It was the first time I had been within the palace walls, though to Francis it was a place altogether familiar. 'If you continue in that line,' said he, 'Carrington will hear of it. You are providing shot for his cannon. And he will not hesitate to use it against you.'

'Let him do his worst, and welcome.'

'My God, but sometimes you are an ass.' We passed beneath the portico, and he pointed to the great door upon our left. 'The library. It is my father's sitting room while he is in London. His proper rooms are above.' We ascended the broad staircase and emerged in a long and well-lit gallery. Along one side were glazed windows overlooking the quadrangle, and the other was hung with portraits of churchmen known, unknown and long forgotten. A young novice rose from a table halfway along. He went and rapped at the first door and opened it. 'Mr Willes and Mr Douglas, My Lord,' said he, though how he should know my name I could not say.

The room was darker than the gallery, and darker still when the novice closed the door at our backs. But there was more than enough light coming in at the arched window to reveal the kneeling Bishop by the sofa. He did not rise upon our entry. The folds of his surplice were spread in some disorder about his legs and on the floor. His hands rested upon the sofa.

'I have brought Mr Douglas, Father.'

'I trust you are well, Mr Douglas.'

'I am, My Lord.'

He remained kneeling, and dropping lower now, peered beneath the sofa. I glanced at Francis, who seemed not in the least perturbed by this singular reception.

'I hope we do not disturb you, Father.'

'I am well accustomed to disturbance, Francis. It is by disturbance that we live, is it not? Change is life.' He put his hands now upon the floor and almost lay down. I was reminded, for a strange moment, of the Moors at their prayers. 'I am told that Wilkes runs you a merry dance, Mr Douglas.'

'He has not been idle, My Lord.'

'Will you help me here, Francis? It is the cat. She hides herself away here the better to claw at my ankles.'

Francis took his sword from its scabbard and went and joined his father on the floor. He poked and prodded beneath the sofa until the cat hissed and came scurrying out, sleek and black, and leaped first onto the sofa and then up on the window ledge where it settled. I stepped forward and helped the Bishop to his feet.

He was then about seventy-five years of age, and a lifetime of moving between his books, his church and his table had taken its sedentary toll. He was a little breathless now, and red of face, and I held his elbow a moment to steady him. There was a likeness between them which I had not noticed before. Perhaps it was that Francis's face had

143

filled out in the years since we had first met; or perhaps it was the slightly stooped shoulders, very noticeable now as they stood side by side.

'Thank you, Mr Douglas. Now if you will bring me that key there?' I brought him the key from the table. He took it to the bureau, unlocked the top drawer and brought out some papers that looked to be those that Jenkinson had first passed to me. He set them in two small piles upon the table then returned to the sofa. There he reclined, stretching out his legs so that his red slippers peeped out from under his surplice. 'Where to begin? You have both read through them all?'

We confirmed that we had.

'You have no doubt reached your own conclusions.'

'We have made this list,' said Francis, passing a sheet of paper to his father. 'We believe half the pieces to be the work of Wilkes. About the rest, we are in doubt.'

The Bishop perused our list awhile and then put it aside. 'And you were not instructed to pass them to me.'

'I was instructed to use them against Wilkes's election, My Lord.'

'And have you?'

'I have had copies of his *Essay on Woman* printed. The paper boys have made some circulation of them about the City.'

He passed no comment on this; but I felt that it displeased him to have the Deciphering Branch so used, just as it had displeased me to have received that instruction from Jenkinson. 'And what is my part in this now? To give you my approval for it? Mr Jenkinson is your superior.'

'My Lord, I had feared lest Mr Jenkinson's personal disapproval of Wilkes should happen to cause harm to the Decipherers.'

'I agree,' put in Francis.

'Then I shall set your mind at rest over those pieces you have both attributed to Wilkes. They are most certainly from his hand. Though how they should do him harm in the election I am at a loss to understand.'

'I have said as much to Mr Jenkinson.'

'To which he replied?'

'He insisted that it must be done. He seems little accustomed to any questioning of his commands.'

'Yes. I did not think you would find him quite so accommodating to your wishes as Mr Fitzherbert was wont to be,' said he, and looked at me very directly; for it was the Bishop himself who had written to me while I worked with the Superintendents in America, warning me of the dangers of the great liberty I had there. Certainly, when he had recalled me to London, I had half suspected an intention to properly break me to the bridle. 'And did Mr Jenkinson say how all of these pieces came to him?'

'It must be Carrington,' said Francis.

'That may be,' the Bishop agreed; but then he seemed to put this by, and asked me now of Wilkes.

I told him of everything I had done, and each enquiry undertaken; and told him too of that discovery I had made concerning Hayley, and my increasing suspicion of some connection between Hayley and those two fugitive Sons of Liberty, Pearce and Flanagan. He made no remark upon any of these speculations. His mind had moved on again, and he then turned to Francis, enquiring if Lord Hillsborough had yet paid any call upon the Secret Office with the name of the new joint Post Master, Lord Sandwich.

Francis professed himself unsurprised. And indeed it was but a confirmation of what was generally expected, that one of the Duke of Bedford's supporters should replace another.

'There is to be a new department for colonies, and Lord Hillsborough will get charge of it,' said the Bishop, and seemed gratified to find that we had not heard of it. 'While Chatham insists on staying from London, his friends must be weakened. Grafton has not the same sway with either Parliament or the King. And Bedford's men are making the most of their opportunity.'

I asked what a new department of colonies must mean for the Council of Trade and Plantations, under whose aegis I had usually worked whilst abroad.

'That we must wait to see. But it will most surely not strengthen them. You need have no concern of it now that you are under Jenkinson.'

While the Bishop and Francis now discussed the many political implications of this new department, I found myself unable to keep fully abreast of their talk. For I had spent too long out of England these past years to have any feeling for all the Whig factions, and the Court; and, I confess, too little interest in political manoeuvring to apprise myself of all the subtle connections, obligations and enmities that one must first be schooled in before engaging in any meaningful debate. But both the Bishop and Francis were steeped so deep in the business that they spoke almost in code to each other, with one word or name standing for a web of connections indecipherable to me.

But there was one thing clear from their discussion: the Bedfordite faction, from their stronghold in Woburn Abbey, the Duke of Bedford's country seat, had with this one bold stroke seized a power over the colonies that till then had been shared by all the other factions through the Southern Department and the Council of Trade. Lord Weymouth being already head of the Northern Department, the Bedfordites now constituted a ministerial power truly formidable.

And from this even I understood the fiercer enforcement this must bring of those taxes we levied upon our American colonies; for on this matter the Duke of Bedford had made his views publicly known (and Hillsborough, after Fitzherbert had carelessly put one of my colonial reports into his hand, had in the autumn summoned me up to his room at the Post Office and lectured me on the same matter).

'But we bore you, Mr Douglas,' said the Bishop.

'It is not boredom, My Lord, but unease.'

He put a cushion beneath his head, and shook the curtain, and the cat leapt down from the window ledge. 'Draw up the side table here, if you will, Mr Douglas. Francis, bring those papers.'

And thus we returned from political abstractions to the very real business of those letters and papers that I had from Jenkinson.

When we had brought up our own chairs to the side table by him, the Bishop instructed us to read again those pieces that we had agreed were from several pens, but not by Wilkes. We did so, and as we reread the pieces he rested his head upon the sofa cushion and closed his eyes as if to doze. But he did not doze. While we read the letters aloud to him, and in turn, he made a commentary upon each one, focusing our attention upon subtleties so inconsequential in the pieces that it seemed he gave us lessons in style and grammar and philology. There were subtleties apparent to the Bishop that continued to elude me even after he gave us the explanation of them. But I had no doubt of him. As who could doubt a man who had, whilst still in his twenties, made a brilliant deciphering of a Jacobite plot by the Bishop of Rochester against the King, and followed this with fifty years of deciphering to keep safe the Crown? Through his guidance now, Francis and I both saw much in the pieces that we had previously missed.

And after we were done, which was an hour and more, Francis said, 'But they are all from the one hand,' which was the same realization that I had just come to.

'One hand, and not Wilkes,' agreed the Bishop. (They were, it transpired years later, early effusions from the poisonous pen of 'Junius', whose identity Francis at last uncovered only by chance. But neither these letters, nor 'Junius', had any connection with Wilkes – as Carrington surely knew.) 'And I am much obliged to you, Mr Douglas, that you did not put them into public circulation.'

Francis said then what I had only thought. That Carrington must surely have known better than to put such pieces as these into the public light.

'No doubt,' said the Bishop. 'And I shall make some enquiry of it. Tie up the papers now, Francis. I shall need them in good order when Mr Jenkinson calls upon me tomorrow.'

As we retraced our steps across the quadrangle toward Lambeth Palace gates, Francis said to me, 'It was a black hour for Jenkinson and Carrington when they thought to use the Decipherers as their instrument.'

I remarked that the Bishop seemed to have taken it with a surprising calm.

'I promise you, he is furious. I would give much to be there tomorrow.'

'Will he rebuke Jenkinson?'

'Rebuke him? Do you suppose Jenkinson has risen so quickly, and with no secrets, nor enemies? Alistair – my father will put the fellow's feet to the fire.'

CHAPTER TWENTY-ONE

The following day, and for several days after, I was turned away from Jenkinson's door in Mayfair when I came to make my regular report to him. It may be that he was consumed by the press of greater matters (and as a lord of both the Treasury and Admiralty he certainly had many calls upon his time), but Francis was convinced it was the private meeting with the Bishop had caused this temporary self-seclusion.

But whatever the cause, I took the opportunity of this unexpected freedom to acquaint myself with the business of Hayley. And not at a distance, rifling in the Customs House paperwork, but by a close surveillance of the fellow. Baxter I left to keep a watch over Wilkes, with Tyler for an aid; for I was confident by this time that Wilkes meant to keep himself wisely sequestered till the Parliament be prorogued in early March.

Nor was it any trouble for me to rise early and leave my house in darkness, as I slept very poorly all through this time, and was glad to be about some business at every minute rather than have overmuch time for repose and personal reflection.

There were three full days that I devoted to trailing after Hayley, and each one of them he followed the same round. In the uppermost windows of his house, where his servants were quartered, the lamps were lit at five o'clock; but the drapes in the main windows remained drawn till after eight. Then a short while after ten o'clock, Hayley, wearing a tricorn, a short wig and a sword (and the satisfied look of a man who has breakfasted well and intends to dine better), emerged to greet the day. There was on each occasion a sedan chair waiting near his door, and from his house by Goodman Fields he was taken to the Jamaica House coffee house, close to the Post Office. It was a simple matter for me to find a table in a corner, to buy a paper from one of the lads who hawked them all about Change Alley and get a small pot of coffee. Then amidst the noisy throng I might sit quietly and keep Hayley and his friends under observation.

In each of the shops near the Alley were similar gatherings of frock-coated gentlemen, but in each place a variation according to the trading interest. In some it was the Company investors held court, in other places the Baltic and Muscovy men, and here in the Jamaica House were assembled the West Indies merchants and captains. Upon the wall by the fire was an enormous slate, and on this was chalked the previous day's sugar prices from the Royal Exchange and the latest arrivals in the port at Bristol. There was a fug of tobacco smoke filled the room, with trays of long clay pipes on every table.

Hayley seemed almost a peripheral figure among those dozen men near the fire, but he sat very contentedly there, laughing when one of the boisterous fellows made some jest, and adjusting his scabbard, and chatting amiably with the others nearby. He was a portly fellow, florid in complexion, and invariably with too much powder on his wig, so that the dust of it lay upon the shoulders of his coat.

I never stayed in the shop much after eleven, but Hayley lingered among his acquaintance till after midday, and then with a few of those same fellows came out and strode along the pavement very purposefully to the Eagle, where they lunched themselves for an hour and more. Then, some time after two o'clock, Hayley emerged from the Eagle and with the purposeful stride of an important fellow about important business, made his way across to the Royal Exchange. Francis kept private rooms on the Exchange's second floor, above the shops and overlooking the central courtyard. This was a place where he might take refuge from the Lane on those nights when he could not get back to his home in Hampstead. And to these rooms, I kept a key.

Though there were no walls dividing the Exchange's courtyard, the merchants conducted their business in different parts of it, so that the informal divisions of the coffee shops here took on more formal and necessary separation. Shipowners stood in one place, sugar traders in another, and so on through the great commodities, and also the Jews had their own place, and the Spaniards. As in the coffee shops, here also was conversation among the merchants, but directed now, and with pocketbooks and pencils in hand. Beneath the colonnade a number of ledgers stood open, and the clerks there made records of the transactions being made.

Hayley went the same route each day. First to the sugar traders, then to the shipowners, and last of all to the tobacco merchants, where he seemed well known, and where his own pocketbook came out at last. And there, for twenty minutes among the tobacco men, he gave every appearance of transacting some business.

On the first two days that I followed him, he left the Exchange before four o'clock, climbed into a sedan, and went directly home. On the third day, however, there was among the tobacco men some deep conversation that Hayley was part of, and when it concluded he and two others came back across the courtyard, so that I must descend in haste to keep them in my sight as they passed out into the street. They went no great distance, but only as far as the Eagle, where another gentleman seemed to await them. And recognizing this other, I checked my step, turned away and walked, and after reaching the next corner looked back and found them gone into the public house together.

'If you were so anxious to know what Mr Fitzherbert did there you might have asked him,' offered Francis.

'He was the last man I thought to see meeting with Hayley.'

'You speak as though it had been a den of thieves. Mr Fitzherbert has a hand in many a commercial venture. The whole town knows of his recent troubles. What surprise that he should be in the City, or in such company? How else shall he right himself but by a close application to his affairs?'

'The presence of the tobacco men bespeaks an American interest.'

'Their presence bespeaks nothing but their fondness to be entertained. If we should seek to know the reason of every such meeting in every such public house in the City, we should end in the madhouse. You are overreaching. I am almost glad now that Jenkinson has recovered himself.'

'You have seen him?'

'He stood where you are standing, and not two hours past.' Francis took a printed paper from his desk and gave it me. It was the latest *St. James's Chronicle*. 'He brought this for you. And I may tell you, he did not seem overjoyed that you had made no report to him.'

I read the marked piece in the paper. Most of it was a transcription of a petition which it was claimed that Wilkes had made to the King. It outlined Wilkes's grievances against the ministry, rejected the charge of outlawry, and made great play of the public service Wilkes had performed by his opposition to those General Warrants used in the seizure of his private papers, of his own person, and of many more innocent men besides.

It claimed further that the King had sent the petition back, unopened and unread. The piece was signed by 'A Friend to Liberty', a nom de plume, but which surely must be Wilkes.

I looked up from the paper, appalled.

Francis said, 'Jenkinson is unhappy that Wilkes should drag the King into this so publicly, and worse, that you should give Jenkinson no warning of it. Though he did not say so, by his temper I would think that Jenkinson came here directly from the Palace.'

'But I have heard nothing of this. '

'It is little wonder. It was only this morning Wilkes sent his servant with the petition to the Palace gates.' My bewilderment now was complete. And Francis at last took pity upon me and gave me his judgement. By avoiding a proper presentation of the petition at a levee, Wilkes could be sure of it being sent back to him. And the piece in the *Chronicle* must have been set by the printers some days since. 'It is Wilkes raising himself by tweaking the King's nose. Wilkes the upright and wronged citizen. The King an unheeding tyrant.'

'Christ in Heaven,' I muttered.

'Indeed. But I would waste no time in prayers. Your fellow Baxter may have more to tell you. And were I you, I should be careful to inform myself of all the circumstances before I met with Jenkinson.'

Within the hour I had met with Baxter in his watching place by Dean's Yard and learned from him all that he knew of Wilkes's petition, which was nothing. He confirmed that a servant had gone out from the house very early, and returned at mid-morning, but he had no notion of any importance attaching to it. I was rather shorter with Baxter than he deserved or I intended. He bridled at my rebuke of him, saying, 'Unless Wilkes's man be in our pay, sir, I do not see how I might know the purpose of every errand he is sent on,' to which I confess I had no good answer.

At last I could delay no longer, but took a hackney to Jenkinson's house in Mayfair.

Jenkinson received me in his library. He was at his table in the middle of the room, with several books lying open before him. He glanced up at my entry, waved his doorman away, and then returned his attention to the coin that he was examining through his magnifying glass. He let the silence speak his cold fury at my negligence. It was very clear to me that whatever wound the Bishop had inflicted upon him should be no protection to me now.

'If Wilkes is to be contained, sir, he must now be arrested.'

Jenkinson continued his inspection of the coin. He made no response to me.

'Sir, I regret that you learned of his petition in a paper rather than by me, but how any should know of it—'

'Your report, if you please, Mr Douglas.'

'Sir?'

'You are offering me advice. It is not what I require of you.'

'While Wilkes remains at liberty, and in a private house receiving callers with no impediment, my report of that fact can serve little purpose. How should any such report have prevented his petition to the King?'

'That is none of your affair.'

'Then I could give orders that all who leave the house be searched. Or Mr Carrington's men might do it.'

'Do not provoke me, Mr Douglas,' he said mildly, and put down the coin and the magnifying glass. He had a far greater control of himself than I had expected. 'You are put out,' said he, 'and I am glad of it.' Rising then, he closed the books upon his table. 'I have no doubt but that what you say is true. But the decision not to arrest Mr Wilkes has been taken. I may tell you, the judgement was no easy one whether he is a greater threat to the public safety as a man at large, or in prison. But that is by the bye now. We must suffer him to run his low campaign and so let him fail in the election.'

'And then, sir?'

'We will have the freedom of the next Parliament to move against him.' He glanced across as if daring me to contradict him. When I refrained, he took the coin across to the display cabinet and locked it inside. 'And I expect that you must know I have had some discussion with the Bishop,' said he.

I inclined my head and kept silence. His manner now was strained but not uncivil.

'It seems that there has been some misunderstanding over those pieces ascribed to Wilkes that I gave you. The Bishop has determined that I was misled in being told they were all of them from Wilkes's pen. It seems Wilkes is responsible for only a part of them.' He took out his kerchief, wiped it over the glass door of the cabinet, and looking over his shoulder gestured to a small side table across the room. And there I saw that bundle of papers which I had last seen in the Bishop's room in Lambeth Palace. 'Take them. I understand there is a safe archive where they may be kept at the Lane.'

I went and put them in my jacket pocket. He seemed almost relieved to have the papers removed from his sight.

'Is that all, sir?'

'How should that be all, Mr Douglas, when you have made no mention of Mr Hayley?' He came back to the table, sat down and put the magnifying glass away in its case.

'Hayley, sir?'

'Do not take me for a fool. You have made enquiries of him at the Customs House.' He paused for some reply, but I gave him none. 'Will you not justify yourself?'

I turned my head.

'Because you cannot,' said he.

'Because I have had no success in my enquiries.'

His eyelids came down a little. He examined me, as if weighing whether he should tolerate my impertinence or have my head.

'I should tell you, sir, that I have done more than that. For I have for three days now followed Mr Hayley about the City.'

'Under whose direction?'

'My own.'

'Do you wish me to remove you from the Decipherers?'

'It is the very last thing that I would wish for.'

His steady gaze stayed on me several moments more. Then he said, 'Sit down, Mr Douglas.'

'If you would have an apology of me—'

His fists slammed suddenly down on the table. 'For God's sake, man, sit down and hold your tongue. I will not be braved in my own house.'

I sat down.

The flush had not entirely left his face when he began to speak. 'You have made your concern only too plain. And I must believe this was not your usual manner toward Mr Fitzherbert, else he had not recommended you to me as he did. Very well. As you have paid me the unlooked-for compliment of an honest directness, I shall in this instance return it to you. My wish to see Pearce and Flanagan taken is equal to your own. And after my recent meeting with the Bishop,

I have begun to have a doubt of my own decision to pass the charge of it back to Mr Carrington.'

'I am sure that he is very pressed with other matters.'

'Yes. I am sure. But let us not enter into any debate of Mr Carrington. It has been brought home to me of late that my knowledge of these affairs is not as full as I might wish it.' Which pressing, I well knew, had been done by the Bishop. But to my surprise the effect of their private meeting upon Jenkinson was something more than either Francis or I had expected. For Jenkinson seemed not a man brought to heel, but rather one brought to reason. 'I have reflected further on the death of the Messenger Armstrong. It is apparent to me now that you were at least casting a shadow over them that caused them some fright. You were very near to them.'

'That moment is passed.'

'You could make another.' He waited to have my agreement, but when I kept silence, he said, 'If you thought it necessary, I might first speak with Mr Carrington.'

'If Mr Carrington should feel himself slighted, it would make it the harder for me, sir.'

'You would need some of his men to watch over Wilkes till the election.'

'I need nothing but to know that I am unobstructed. Even then, I can give no assurance of any success. The Boston men know that they are sought for.'

'You will not be obstructed. Well. Have you nothing more to say?'

This offer of freedom was something I had not for one moment thought to have when I first came into his library. Nor, indeed, the more general freedom with which he spoke to me. We talked of Hayley a short while, and of the reason of my enquiries. But like Francis, Jenkinson was little concerned when I mentioned Fitzherbert's meeting with the fellow. I took the opportunity of Jenkinson's unexpected reasonableness to mention what I most feared now in the coming election, which was how Wilkes's name was in the mouths of all the City's poor. 'It would take nothing now, sir, for him to call them up as a mob.'

'The mob is no freeholder and cannot vote, Mr Douglas,' said he, very sanguine (as even wise men may be who have never been caught in a riot). 'They will be the concern of the justices and the constables. Now, if we are done—'

I rose, and bowed my head to him, and he looked at me as if to make me understand the great trust he now placed in me. And I own, I saw that in him which I had not seen before, which was simple good sense, and understood a little better how the King should lean upon him in the Parliament.

At the library door I turned back to him. 'Sir, I said that I should need no one else. But there is one person I would have to help me.'

He replied that I might have whomsoever I wanted, if only it be someone within his command. I told him who it was, and he granted my request, and I then bowed my head again and departed.

CHAPTER TWENTY-TWO

'*I* fear you must be a little uncomfortable here, Mrs Porter.'

'Oh my, sir,' she said, looking through the attic window and across to the shabby little house across the alley. 'But isn't it a great coming down though for Mr Wilkes?'

I told her of the information we had that Wilkes would move to a place in Birdcage Walk by Westminster within the next few days. 'I have taken a room for you overlooking his building. You shall be more comfortable there. Tyler will come to you in the mornings for your report.' I gave her the address and the keys to the other watching place, which she slipped into a pocket of her dress. Then she went and brought her portmanteau from by the door where Tyler had left it. She put it down by the chair near the window, and rummaged inside and brought out a thin blanket, and also her knitting. Then she settled into the chair and spread the blanket over her legs. 'Shall I follow Wilkes if he leaves, sir?'

I told her that she should, and send word of it to me as soon as possible at the Lane.

I then went with Tyler down to Rudd's coffee shop, where Francis had come up to wait for me. He was seated by a window, with several of the weekly and daily journals upon the table before him. He had his head tilted back and his eyes half-closed, as if enjoying the first feeble rays of the spring sunshine. I left Tyler in the street and went in.

'Parliament is prorogued,' said Francis, 'and here are the papers.'

'Have you looked at them?'

'I have. You need not trouble yourself. Your friend has a piece in the *Chronicle* and the *Advertiser*. It is more of the same.' As I folded them together for a later inspection, he said, 'I see you have Baxter's young fellow with you.'

'We will go down to Wapping.'

'I hope that you know what you are about.'

'I am about my work.'

'And what work is that? We have not seen you in the Lane for days. And this morning I had Meadows knocking at my door and making an enquiry after you.'

'You must give him my good regards.'

'He seems to have some suspicion that you are encroaching again upon Mr Carrington.'

'Did he say so?'

'He will say so soon enough when he has evidence of it. And not to me but to his master.' He lowered his voice. 'If Meadows knows, Alistair, and with little enquiry, that you have followed Hayley about the City, how shall that escape Carrington's attention? Or Jenkinson's?'

'I cannot concern myself with Carrington.'

'He has more people beholden to him than you know. Here is another thing that will interest you. Your Friend to Liberty is to be inducted into the Joiners and Ceilers Guild in two days. His name will then be put forward as an official candidate for the parliamentary election.'

'He will not win a seat.'

'I am told that the news has not been taken so well in a place not so very far from here.' It was the King's Palace that he meant. And now when Francis looked at me I saw that he searched my eyes for some clue as to my intentions. He must assume, of course, that my meeting with Jenkinson, following Wilkes's provocative petition, had gone very badly for me. And he must therefore believe that I was now proceeding on a rash and wilful course, and directly contrary to Jenkinson's instruction. It says much that it occurred to neither one of us that Francis might report my actions to Jenkinson, who was nominally his superior. Francis answered only to his father, and I had his father's approval, and the powers of Westminster and Whitehall were to one side of that, and secondary. 'You will take care what you do, Alistair.'

I said that I would.

'You will not,' said he. 'But perhaps you will take a warning. If you stumble, Carrington will make sure that it is no easy matter to right yourself. You may then find that you do not have the defence against him that you suppose.'

I embarked with Tyler from the Hungerford Steps, and our wherryman rowed us out to the mid-river where the retreating tide caught us and carried us east, down past Somerset House and the Inner Temple, and on below Blackfriars towards the great dome of St Paul's. The ice was now all gone from the river, but many boats had been damaged through the hard winter, and many lay half-submerged, but still tied to bollards on the shore. Others had been drawn up beside the few slipways on the south bank, with the boatwrights and carpenters very busy at the repair of them, the hammer blows ringing out to us across the grey water.

Seated comfortably on the wherry's cushioned bench, I propped myself against the gaily painted backboard and made a casual inspection of the papers that Francis had given me. I had by this time read more than sufficient of the thoughts, complainings and self-justifications of Mr Wilkes, "Friend to Liberty". And as Francis had told me, there was in these recent papers nothing extraordinary or new. Wilkes's whole purpose now seemed to be to keep his name and his supposed plight before the public, and always with a low stab at certain members of the ministry. In some places he ventured to make an equivalence between his own particular situation and the recent sufferings endured in the poorest quarters of the City, which sufferings I had glimpsed in the person of Kitty Langridge and some others, and so found Wilkes's protestations almost contemptible.

But I confess that having witnessed the frequent scurrying of Wilkes's servant from that wretched hiding hole in Dean's Yard to the various printers' offices about Charing Cross, and also the steady stream of visitors that Wilkes received, it was a wonder to me that a man in straits such as his could put up such a continual dust from his wheels.

Apart from Wilkes's pieces, there were several articles in the papers that touched on the battle then proceeding within the Company, with some for the redoubtable Mr Sullivan and some against, and much talk of honour and obligation, and none of money or power, which was the real concern of every one of them. These gave me some amusement, several of the actors being known to me, but by the time we were by St Paul's I was drifting from my reading, and then the conversation between Tyler and the boatman came into my ear. They were talking of the many ships lying at anchor all about us, and tied two and three deep at the docks both sides of the river.

I caught Tyler's eye, and with a tip of my head back toward the boatmen, encouraged a continuance of their conversation. Tyler thought a moment, and then said, 'You have no sympathy with the coal heavers.'

'As much as they have for me or any other on the river. They are scum. When you go ashore down here, you watch yourself, lad. Keep your purse close about you.'

'I was told it is the sailors are the trouble.'

'They are rough boys, but no trouble if only the heavers leave them be. The sailors have struck sails to get fair pay. They need no bloody heavers to tell them how to go about it.'

Craning around to look up at him, I asked if the wherrymen might have a general opinion on Mr Wilkes.

'Our opinion is that the coal heavers are for him, and so we are against him. We are for the seamen, sir.'

'And they are also against Mr Wilkes?'

'They do not give a tuppenny damn for any man ashore. If they would only have their asking, they would be from here, and the devil take Wilkes and any other they left behind them.'

'You would be left behind them.'

'The river joins the sea, sir. I have two lads gone before the mast in the Navy. God knows where they be now.' He fell silent then, and steered us through the many ships lying at anchor, sails struck, below London Bridge. Once past the Tower, he brought us closer in to the ships along the docks, and then he came down into the middle of the boat and rowed us the rest of the way in to the Execution Dock where Baxter was waiting.

Baxter reached out from the steps and took hold of the wherry's gunwale. But rather than climb in, as I expected of him, and tell us where we should next go along the river, he said, 'I am sorry, sir, but you will have to come up.' I left Tyler with the wherry, and went up the steps with Baxter to the strand. 'The women will not speak to me, sir. Kitty warned me that I should not press them. She believes they will be more free in their answers if it is you who questions them.'

'You have got nothing from them?'

'No, sir,' said he, abashed that he must admit to the failure. 'If I had pressed them, we should have lost them. It is all I could do to keep them with Kitty till you should come down.'

That lane where Kitty Langridge lived had not quite the dismal aspect of the deep winter; but nor was it a place where any would wish to tarry. There was washing put out on rods from many of the upper windows, and slicks of mud on the lane beneath. In one of the cottages a woman was screeching like a fishwife at her children, her lad shouting back at her, and not a person in any doorway or window, but everyone closed up inside.

When she came to the door, I saw that Kitty Langridge was very uncertain to discover Baxter with me, and so I sent him back. 'Thank you, sir,' said she as I stepped by her into the passage. 'The girls must be away soon or they will be missed.'

'I shall not keep them long.' Then I noticed the old woman,

Kitty's landlady, peering down from the landing. 'Good day, Madam,' I called, that Kitty be warned.

'It is you again,' the old bitch said.

'It is. And I trust I shall not be disturbed for the brief time I am here.' Without awaiting the landlady's reply, I followed Kitty into her own private room and secured the door behind me.

Turning, I found the two whores that I had sent Baxter to question standing silent. I say whores, but two young women with less the look of whoredom about them would be difficult to find in all of London. They had jumped to their feet at my entry, and as Kitty gave me their names now, they each dipped a quick curtsy to me. They wore white bonnets, as if it might be a social call that they made upon their friend. And their dresses were more than modest, being the usual heavy cloth of the workers' wives, and buttoned at wrists and throat. Each made a careful study of the floor between us, as being mortified with shame to so stand before me, and in some fear, I believe, of what I should ask them. I understood at once the great pains Kitty must have been at to get them to this point, and also the reason of Baxter's failure to question them.

'You need not stand,' said I, and they sat down in immediate obedience. Kitty went and sat on the edge of her bed, and made some small play with the bedding covering her infant, whose hands were upraised to either side of his head upon the pillow as he slept. I took my seat at the only chair left by the table, and glanced at Kitty, for I hardly knew how best to begin. But finding no help there I said to the two women, 'I think Mrs Langridge has told you that I am not come here to involve you in any magistrate's inquiry into the murder.'

Kitty said, 'I promised them that you would not, sir.'

'Nor shall I.' For the first time since my arrival one of the women lifted her eyes. She had skin very pale and eyes near as dark as her hair, and I was reminded of Valerie for one moment. The fear was visible in her, but there was boldness too, for now that she had dared to look up at me she neither blinked nor turned away. 'But you must know I cannot prevent all that others may do. I trust you will believe me when I say that your best hope lies in giving me the information that I need.' Receiving no reply from either the woman who watched me, or the one who did not, I said, 'I am sure, Mrs Langridge, that your friends are aware of the dangerous predicament in which they find themselves.'

'They need no reminder of it, sir.'

'Then I will not dwell on it. But I must tell you that it is not in my power to obstruct the actions of a magistrate's court. And you must know that if I have found you, any agent of the court may do the same. I promise you that such men as they are will show no delicacy towards you, but seize you directly from your homes.' At this, even the bold woman shrunk a little. It was very clear that they were neither one of them born strumpets but that they had made the dangerous venture into whoredom, as Kitty had told me, from necessity. That it was Pearce and Flanagan they had caught in such an early cast of their unpractised net was a piece of misfortune very rare, and thoroughly pitiable. But if I was to be any aid to them (and to myself) I must not show them pity now but fix the darkest shadow over them, and so I said, 'There is but one way in which I may help you. And that is if I can find those men who did the murder. It is they, and not you, should take the journey to Tyburn.'

There came a groan from the timid one; and the other turned in her wretchedness to Kitty, who said to me, 'Sir, they know this. They are ready to answer you.'

I said, 'How many men were there that night?'

'Two,' said the bold girl. 'Two men,' she added, as if surprised to hear herself speak.

I asked after the men's names, and she told me they had called themselves Samuel and Caleb. Their family names she did not know.

'Can you describe them to me?' said I, and the bold one began, the timid one intervening occasionally to support her. The two men they described were unremarkable. In truth, they sounded much like a hundred young fellows to be met with any day about the docks. Not yet thirty years of age. One dark-haired, one blond. Each of average height and build. There was a disagreement between the women on what colour eyes the men had, which confusion might have come from the couplings happening in the dark of night, or the unremarkableness of the men, or possibly from the women shutting their eyes as they lay back upon the stone floor of the warehouse. They agreed, however, that both men were from the American colonies, and with an insistence upon it that only grew with my questioning. And I had little reason to doubt of their judgement, for there was a constant traffic of different peoples about the docks, and those like these women who lived near the river knew well the accents and voices from many parts.

I asked how often they had kept company with the men. They said it was only their second time of meeting when the murder happened.

'How did you first meet with them?'

'On the strand above the steps.'

Kitty said quietly, 'It is where the men come to find a woman, sir.'

'You met them by chance, then?'

The bold girl nodded.

'And how did you meet with them on the night the murder was done?'

'In the same place above the steps. They sought us out from the others and we went to the warehouse.' She was uncomfortable now, and looked down, so that neither one of them would now meet my eye.

'My concern is with these men, not with you. But I must know how the murder happened.'

'I didn't know what he was about, sir,' broke out the timid one, looking up. 'How should I know? He said I should wait, and be silent. When he came back, he was no different.'

The bold one said, 'I was with the dark one in that private room. She and the fair one were done, they were outside.'

I turned from her to the other. 'And while you were waiting outside the room, he left you?'

'I did not like to be alone. I went to find him. There was another man there,' she said. 'I hid myself.'

'A man you knew?'

'No. He came across to the warehouse. There was a ladder. He went up.'

165

'You kept yourself hid?'

'Yes.'

'For how long?'

'Not long. It was two or three minutes, no more. Then – then he came down.'

'The same man?'

'No sir. The fair one, Caleb. I could not know, sir, what had happened. I hurried back to where he had left me, outside that room. When he came, he was no different than before. I swear it, sir.'

She might swear it all she wished, but in keeping herself hid from this blond fellow, and retreating in some hurry to the same place where he had left her, she had shown her alarm all too clearly. And I had no doubt but that it was Armstrong she had seen go up the ladder that night. And whether she had heard something from the loft after Armstrong went up, or whether it was another thing had warned her, she had perceived at once that she must keep her unwanted knowledge secret. Before a magistrate, she would be in great danger of putting a rope about her own neck.

'When he first left you outside the room, did it seem to you a thing he had planned? Do you suppose that he knew he should find someone in the loft?'

'Likely enough. How else should he be so very much the same after what he done?'

'Though she did not know it then, sir, that he'd done murder,' put in the bold one quickly. 'Neither of us knew it, sir. They took a boat from the steps as before, and we have not seen them since.'

'Have you an idea whence they came, or where they went?'

'They never said.'

'That is not what I asked.' From the way they glanced at each other, I had a notion that there was that which they kept from me. I rose, and said to Kitty, 'Perhaps I should not have come.'

'Wait, sir,' said she, and stood up from the bed and turned on the women. 'If you would have any help it is here,' she told them with a quiet and forceful anger. 'Do you suppose Mr Douglas cares what those men will say of you? It is your good fortune that he seeks for them. If you give him no help in it, I am ashamed that I have asked him here. I am ashamed.'

'We do not know their staying place,' said the bold girl at last. 'That is the truth, sir. But we have a suspicion of it.' There was yet some reticence in her manner, and I let her be for a moment, but I could plainly see the fiery blush upon her cheeks. But finally she found the courage to say, 'They wore new clothes, but there was a smell about their bodies. It was on both of them.'

'We both smelt it on their skin, sir. It was the whale oil.'

'What attention did Mr Carrington give to the Greenland Dock after Langridge's murder?' I asked Baxter as we turned from the lane and towards the Execution Dock.

'I took no part in it, sir. After you went off to Paris, I was given work to do at the Common Pleas.'

The Common Pleas was the very lowest work for the Messengers, and done almost invariably by the junior men. I glanced across at Baxter, but he kept his eyes ahead.

'You never mentioned this.'

'It is nothing to boast of.'

'Was it to punish you?'

'Mr Carrington had said some harsh words to me after Langridge was killed. They were no harder than I had said to myself. A month in the Pleas is very little against what his widow must live with. And in such a place—'

I asked him how many Messengers had been sent to search the Greenland Dock. He did not know.

As we approached the steps we saw Tyler slouched like a ruffian against the wall and holding some cheerful banter with two women across the way. I called him from there, and he pushed off the wall and came to meet us by the small Execution Pier. No hapless sailor hung then from the gallows over the water, but it was an ill-omened place, and no one about, and so I might speak privately there. I told them frankly and at once what I had feared for some time now, that Pearce and Flanagan had since their arrival in London been informed of every step taken against them. Not only of my own search for them in the autumn, but also of Langridge's approach to them, and likewise Armstrong's. 'It can only be someone from among the Messengers has passed them such information. And whoever has done it has murdered Langridge and Armstrong just as surely as if he had wielded the knife.' Neither of them showed any astonishment at this, but rather looked at each other as if I had but confirmed a thing they had already speculated upon. 'To proceed now in any safety,' said I, 'there must be secrecy. I would not ask it of you but from a concern for your own lives.'

'If Mr Carrington should ask of me—'

'It must be a secrecy with no exceptions, Mr Baxter. If that is impossible for you, you must tell me now.'

There was but a short time he considered it, then he said, 'Langridge would have done as much for me.' He asked then if Mrs Porter should have no aid from them in the watching of Wilkes.

'We will give Wilkes our attention till the election is done. Once he has lost, he may then be arrested. I shall call on your services as I need them.'

CHAPTER TWENTY-THREE

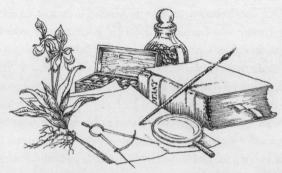

*I*t was but a short while after, on the first day of the election, which was the sixteenth day of March, that Tyler arrived at the Lane with a note to me from Mrs Porter. She informed me that Hayley had come in a carriage to Birdcage Walk, and was gone in to breakfast with Mr Wilkes. She suggested that I might proceed at once to the Guildhall, where she was sure I should find Wilkes arriving but a short time behind me. She was wrong in this, for when Francis, Tyler and I came near to the great crowd spilling onto the neighbouring streets from the Guildhall, Wilkes's carriage had just halted a short way ahead of us. Wilkes and Hayley alighted into the crowd and were greeted with a terrific cheering and waving of hats by all the people. Wilkes smiled very merrily, and acknowledged the cheers with a princely wave of his own tricorn, as if his new white shirt and blue jacket had made him something other than a penurious outlaw kept out from the debtors' prison only by the charity of friends.

'What do you think, Mr Tyler?' said I, for I saw that he was much surprised to see this reception of Wilkes. 'Shall he be elected?'

'They are fools, sir.'

'Wilkes will have no concern of that, if only they be freeholder fools.'

'If they had seen him skulking like a dog in Dean's Yard,' said he, 'they would not cheer.'

But the time of Wilkes's skulking was well and truly over; for since the proroguing of Parliament, and his move to new quarters by Bird-cage Walk, Wilkes had tested the ministry by proceeding about the town with all the freedom of any English gentleman. And finding himself unarrested, he had then established a motley court in the King's Arms tavern in Cornhill (where we had watched him, but at Jenkinson's instruction done nothing more), and from there had dispatched yet more letters to the papers reminding the good electors of the inestimable good service he had done by his defeat of the General Warrants. Against this torrent of publicity (for which, it must be said, he had a particular genius) our own distribution of those pieces given me by Jenkinson had been but damp squibs, disappearing at once and unnoticed.

I gave Tyler an instruction now to remain outside, and Francis and I then followed after Wilkes and Hayley through the crowd and into the Guildhall.

The confusion and clamour was almost as great within as without, for at one end of the hall a high wooden platform had been put up as the hustings, and on the hustings were the gentlemen candidates, not seated but moving about and talking with each other, and lean-ing upon the hustings rail to speak with their supporters below. The whole floor of the hall was filled with City folk, both journeymen and merchants, many with their wives, and all come dressed as to a fair on a high day, and more yet in the galleries above.

As Wilkes moved through the crowd and nearer hustings, the general commotion near to him drew every eye in the hall. And at his climbing of the hustings steps there were several cries of 'Wilkes!' and 'Wilkes and Liberty!', but he put out his hand and stroked the air as if to calm the mad fervour that his campaigning had done so much to encourage. He seemed though very content, and even pleased with his reception. Wilkes being the last of the seven candidates to arrive, the chamberlain in his ceremonial cloak and chain now went up to confer with them.

Francis and I got a place on the step at one side of the hall, and he leaned towards me saying, 'There shall be some difficulty in any arrest of him here. But my God, his face is the very image of the print. I could almost pity him.'

'He will win few votes from pity.'

'The bear come out from his winter cave, and the keepers unsure of his strength.' He nodded towards the other side of the hall, and there I saw Carrington standing with Meadows, and both men watching Wilkes impassively.

There came a sudden commotion in the gallery, and we soon saw that the cause of it was Wilkes's daughter, Polly, who had just arrived. There had been a place saved for her in the front row, and as she sat down there she received a great cheer, with people pointing her out to their neighbours now, and others calling up 'Polly Wilkes!' and 'Daughter of Liberty!' which I confess shocked me the first time that I heard it.

The chamberlain stamped his foot several times upon the hustings boards, calling for silence. He did not get silence, but once the talk and hubbub had subsided, he announced that the candidates would now give their speeches. He prayed that consideration be given to each one of them, and said that he would tolerate no unruly disruption. This last was greeted by laughing jeers from some few places, at which the chamberlain looked very stern. He then invited the first candidate forward, who was the Lord Mayor.

The fellow was no great speaker, but nor did he have to be, for he held such influence in the City that his election into the next Parliament was all but certain. His speech was a mere show, but the crowd paid him the respect due his office and did not talk overmuch while he spoke. He kept his speech brief, a courtesy for which they thanked him with a solid applause as he returned to his seat.

'There is one of the four places filled,' Francis remarked to me quietly. 'What odds against Mr Wilkes now?'

'Our friend seems untroubled,' said I, for Wilkes was now

congratulating the Lord Mayor, and then leaning over the rear railing of the hustings to share a few convivial words with his own supporters, Hayley among them. There was a general air about Wilkes of gaiety and good cheer, and he joked and laughed with his fellows very freely while the other candidates stepped forward one by one to solicit the votes of the freeholders.

The only disturbance came when there was an objection raised to the noise and laughter coming from that part of the gallery where Polly Wilkes sat; for there it was that many of Wilkes's drunken supporters had taken their seats to see the show. When the chamberlain called them to order the fellows baited him merrily, which he wisely ignored, and so the speeches went on till at last was Wilkes called up from his seat.

Francis nudged me, and I followed his gaze. Carrington was whispering to Meadows, with a hand raised to cover his mouth. There was some intent in it, but no way of knowing what it was, which disturbed me.

'Friends!' Wilkes cried, stepping forward, and then again, 'Friends!' with both hands opened to them. 'So I hope I may call you, the good men of the City. For I think we know, you and I, how few friends I have at the other end of town.' A great cheer at this, and laughter, for it was his enemies in the ministry he meant, and there was little regard for them here in the City after the fall in trade through the winter. 'I stand here before you supported by no faction, but as an independent man among independent men. I trust in no wallet or pocketbook, but only in the native good sense that is the birthright of every freeborn Englishman.'

'Hear, hear!' broke from all sides now, and Wilkes bobbed his head and smiled like the very devil. It was a leer that put me in mind of that story concerning Lord Sandwich and the 'Monks of Medmenham', when Wilkes was said to have set loose a baboon in the midst of their carnal revelries. The sight of Wilkes now, so very delighted by the sway he had over the people, made me believe him capable of almost any devilry.

Francis nudged me again, and now I saw Carrington and Meadows moving quickly through the crowd and then exiting through a side door.

'I will go,' said he, and then left the hall through the door behind us.

Wilkes's speech continued, but I was distracted now and had only half an ear for the hot winds of liberty, freedom from General Warrants, and the rights of every Englishman. In truth, Wilkes's power in speaking was all in the first sally, the fine phrase boldly proclaimed, but ever after repeated with little variation and decreasing effect. Far from being a second Chatham, he was not even Barré's equal in oratory; and though the crowd continued to give him that near attention they had withheld from the other candidates, it was only for his person they gave it, and not his words.

After some minutes, Carrington returned to his place across from me in the hall. Meadows did not. And very soon Francis reappeared at my side.

'Meadows is gone off in a hackney with another of the Messengers,' said he. 'Carrington seemed to urge them to make haste about their errand.'

I watched Carrington now, as his gaze wandered over the crowd and up to the gallery. His arms were folded, and he paid no mind to Wilkes's speech. I could not believe that he was here to make an arrest of Wilkes if it transpire that Wilkes fail to be elected. Carrington's gaze moved down from Polly Wilkes in the gallery, and back over the crowd, and then he saw me. He made no pretence that he had not, but rather fixed his eyes upon me a good while. I at last dipped my head to him. He returned a curt nod and then faced the hustings and Wilkes again, for Wilkes was just now concluding his speech.

'Therefore, good men of the City, do I offer myself to be your humble servant in the Parliament. And not only the humble servant of my fellow Joiners and Ceilers, but all of you.' At this, there were cheers and laughter from several quarters. 'If you grant me the favour to represent you, you shall have in the Parliament a man who cannot be bent to the influence of any powers that hail from without the City walls. I think I am proven an independent man, who will not be driven hither and thither like an ox till I end a noble but lifeless carcass in Smithfield market. I am done now, friends. I must place my trust in your good sense as true-born Englishmen.'

There was general applause, and mad cries of 'Wilkes and Liberty!' and when he waved up to his Polly she was forced to her feet by those about her, and she was cheered also, to her own evident embarrassment. It was some few minutes that the chamberlain took to quiet the hall. He at last called the two sheriffs onto the hustings, and it was understood then that the vote was near, and so the conversation and shouting died away.

'The seven worthy candidates have now fulfilled their duty in appearing before you,' proclaimed the chamberlain. 'It is now for you to do yours by electing four of their number to represent the freeholders of the City in the next Parliament. I will now call for a show of hands, your raised hand to signify your vote for the candidate I have named. You will please keep your hands upraised till the sheriffs have completed the counting. As is the custom, we will begin with the last speaker and proceed up to the first. Pray silence for the voting.'

There fell now, and for the first time since our arrival, a real silence. On their seats behind the chamberlain the candidates had no uniform appearance, but some seemed relaxed and others, in spite of their smiles, apprehensive. Wilkes had his fists clasped upon his knees, and leaned forward with a look of eager interest, almost as if he was there only to witness a scene he might later report on in the papers. Of apprehension there was little sign. He smiled and nodded to some of those he recognized in the crowd to the front of him.

'Those freeholders who would declare for Mr John Wilkes, the candidate properly endorsed by the Company of Joiners and Ceilers, please now raise your hands.'

The hands went up. And almost at once a general gasp rose from the crowd, for it was half the people, perhaps more, had cast their vote for Wilkes.

'Well now,' said Francis to me quietly.

I could not reply. For I own I was struck dumb with astonishment at the forest of hands all about me. And through that forest I then saw

Wilkes slap his fists upon his knees, and turn a devilish smile upon the candidates to either side of him.

The sheriffs looked to the chamberlain for guidance how to proceed, but the chamberlain himself seemed at a loss how to count so many, and now the crowd put off their silence and there was a buzzing as of bees, and then a loud voice from the midst of the hall called out, 'Wilkes to Parliament!'

The Lord Mayor hurriedly rose from beside Wilkes and came forward to whisper with the chamberlain, who appeared pleased to be given some direction. The chamberlain now stamped his foot for silence.

'There are votes being cast by non-freeholders, who have no right to vote. Therefore have the candidates requested a poll taken. You may lower your hands, gentlemen. The polling books will be opened here by the hustings for a week, till the twenty-third day of March. You will be required to identify yourselves as a freeholder before you cast. The books shall be opened within the hour. If you are not a freeholder, you will please to leave the hall peacefully.'

Now came an eruption of noise, not angry or wild, but almost exuberant, as if the raising of all those hands together had for the first time shown Wilkes's supporters their own true strength. Certainly the joy was not universal, for some of the merchants and gentlemen pressing past us with their wives to the door wore looks severe and spoke together unhappily. But these were far outnumbered by the many other men and women who pushed forward to the hustings, crying for Wilkes. Some drummed on the husting boards with the flat of their hands, and cheered Wilkes, who was soon alone up there, and laughing, for the other candidates had quickly absented themselves. And now that this separation of the crowd had happened, it was plain to see by the dress of those who went and those who stayed that it was the poorer journeymen who were the main body of Wilkes's support, for there was hardly a frock-coat to be seen anywhere near the hustings.

These poor journeymen were no freeholders, and I recalled then what Jenkinson had said, that there were no votes in the mob.

'My father bade me write to him how this went,' said Francis, with his eyes upon Wilkes. The fellow beamed down at his cheering supporters with an unalloyed delight. 'I hardly know what I shall tell him.'

Polly had by this time descended from the gallery, and Wilkes now came down from the hustings to embrace her. The crowd opened, and I saw that Hayley was there also. But so intent was I on this merry party that I did not notice Carrington till he was almost upon me. He stopped at my shoulder, saying, 'I see we now have the reward of your neglect, Mr Douglas.'

When I turned a blank eye upon the miserable fellow, he spoke across me, reminding Francis of certain letters that he had earlier requested from the Private Office, and then they both left me and joined the general throng towards the door.

'Is he elected, sir?' asked Tyler when I found him outside. 'Some say as he is, and some say no.'

'Neither elected, nor yet passed over,' said I. The crowd in the square was even greater than that which had been inside the hall, for here had gathered all the poorer people of the City, and every one of them pressing forward now for a glimpse of Wilkes, who was lost somewhere in the midst of the tumult near the Guildhall door. Here was no pretence of decorum, but the shouting and celebration were on all sides, and hats flying upward, and the bells of St Lawrence Jewry pealing across the square, which set the crowd to cheering the fiercer, with ever more cries of 'Wilkes and Liberty' and 'Remember the Forty-five' and 'Wilkes to Parliament!'

'They are mad, sir,' shouted Tyler.

But they seemed to me not mad, but drunk with the joy of Wilkes's empty victory. And Hayley was visible now, standing upon a block by the Guildhall door and waving his blue tricorn over the heads of the crowd, signalling to the coach and pair that now came through the crowd to fetch Wilkes. The crowd parted very sprightly at the sound of the hoofs clacking upon the flagstones and the warning cries from the jarvey, and soon it was stopped near the door. Then Wilkes was suddenly thrust up by the people into the open coach, and Hayley seemed to make some objection to this manhandling and ordered several men there to stand aside. But far from obeying him, these fellows only pressed in closer to the coach, two of them barring its way, and two more taking hold of the reins. The jarvey protested and was at once hauled down from his seat.

'It is the coal heavers,' said Tyler, who had climbed up to a ledge of the church. 'They are uncoupling the horses.'

For a few moments there was a confusion as to what the coal heavers meant by their actions, and Wilkes, standing in the coach, suddenly gripped its sides as if alarmed and in fear that he might be thrown down. But then one of the heavers got onto the footplate and spoke to Wilkes, which seemed to reassure him, and Wilkes took his seat, though holding on tight, for the coach now rocked like a small boat at sea.

'What are they about?'

'I cannot see, sir. Wait, now – the heavers are taking up the shafts.'

The crowd opened again, and amidst a frenzy of cheering and huzzahs the coal heavers hauled the coach whilst others turned the coach wheels to help them. The coach then coming towards us, I pressed back against the church to avoid being trampled. Wilkes laughed now, and waved back to Polly and Hayley and his other friends left behind at the Guildhall. An excited coal heaver just near to me shouted up at Wilkes, 'You are a man, Mr Wilkes, and you will be drawn by men!' and many other voices called, 'To the King's Arms!' and yet others cried 'To the Parliament!' so that as they went out into the street there was no knowing their destination. Trailing after them came the pair of unhitched horses, and these led by two coal heavers. A crush of people now surged past the church, and I saw staggering and dazed in their midst the jarvey, who had been struck such a blow he was now bleeding from his mouth and with the blood now streaming all over the front of his white shirt.

'Come down,' I called sharply to Tyler, and he came down and we followed after the crowd, whose wild high spirits threatened to turn them at any moment into a mob.

We had followed but a short way after Wilkes when his coach and its surrounding people turned up toward the King's Arms tavern in Cornhill. But as this part of the crowd peeled away, a greater part broke off in a different direction, and seemed to follow after that pair of unhitched horses and the heavers who led them. These we followed, for there seemed about them some certain purpose, and no good one. After a short distance they turned into a side street of shops and free-standing houses, and from the way the heavers now looked about them, I had a notion that this was no random turning.

At the corner I stopped, and put out my hand to stop Tyler.

'Wait,' said I. The heavers now mustered the crowd before the second house in the street. There were ropes brought out from some place, and the heavers began to tether these ropes fast to an upright of the front porch. 'Go back to the Guildhall. Find the justices or the chamberlain. Tell them men will be needed here at once to keep the peace.'

Tyler went without question and I hurried towards the mob. I was almost among them when I saw in an upper window of that house the face of an old woman. She was there and then gone, and I pushed forward now, calling sharply, 'There are people inside. Hold off there! Hold off!'

At the edge of the mob as much surprise as hostility greeted my arrival among them, and as I went through they gave me leeway as a gentleman. But nearer to the horses was a hard core of the coal heavers; and with them several other big fellows, who by their dress must be chair-men. Coming among these, I was jostled, and many of them murmured darkly against me, till I came at last to the pair of horses. A true giant of a man was now tying those same ropes to the harnesses, and the horses wild-eyed and tossing their heads, so that the lads who held them were almost lifted from the ground.

'There is a woman inside,' said I, which the giant ignored, and continued tying the ropes. 'Will you kill her?'

'She has legs.'

'You may stop this foolery now,' I told him, for he seemed as much a leader of the mob as any man might be.

His answer was to finish tying the ropes, and then he stepped back and called, 'Haul hard!' and brought down his platter-sized hand on the flank of the nearest horse. The ropes jerked taut, the horses scrabbled to get footing on the stones, and the upright timber of the porch creaked, and groaned; and then, with a mighty crack, gave way. Half the porch came down, the tiles and bricks spilling onto the street amidst the whooping and cheering. Already the giant had hold of the ropes, and he called up his orders of how they should now be tied to the newly exposed lintel above the door.

'If any die here today,' I said, raising my voice to be heard by the fellow, 'you will not be innocent of their blood.'

He looked at me very threateningly and said, 'You are a friend to the coal merchant who lives here?' I confessed that I was not. 'Then stand clear.'

The front door was kicked down, and a hole was now being broken through the wall so that the rope could be looped around the lintel. There was a wildness in many eyes now, and a fierce frenzy in their actions. To reason now was waste of breath, and so I said no more but stepped over the broken tiles and bricks of the porch and entered the house. Some fellows had slipped in before me and these were busy stripping the silver and candlesticks from the dresser, and snatching up anything movable. I hurried past and on up the stairs.

'Madam? You must come out now. It is dangerous to stay.'

This last word was scarcely from my mouth when the door above me shattered from a pistol shot, the splinters spraying like deadly grapeshot over my head. I dropped very sharp upon the stairs.

'Hold your fire! Do not fire! I will come up and fetch you down safely. Do you hear me, Madam? Hold your fire!'

With a little more circumspection now, I went up the last stairs. Hugging the wall, I reached around and pushed open the shattered door.

'I have another pistol loaded,' the old lady shouted fearfully.

'For God's sake put it aside. I am no part of the mob. Are there others in the house?'

'My son is at the Guildhall. What do they want from us?'

I put my head tentatively around the door. It was the old woman I had seen at the window. She had no second pistol, but only the one she had fired, and which she had now dropped by her feet. 'You must come away. They will pull the floor out from beneath you.'

At last she came towards me, but uncertainly. She was in confusion, and began to say that she had never fired a pistol till now. I took her by the elbow and began to lead her down the stairs, and at this moment the giant appeared below us, brandishing a pistol of his own. He levelled it at me, and demanded to know who had fired upon him.

'You were not fired upon,' I told him angrily. 'It was I who was almost hit, and here is the lady marksman who has put you in such a fright. There is no other person in the house.' Those who had been plundering now came to his side, and very vicious they looked now, for the shot had badly startled them. I went on down the stairs, holding tight to the old lady's arm. We stopped on the last step, for the giant still barred our way. 'Let us pass,' said I, and turned aside his pistol with my hand.

He appeared abashed to have been put to fright without cause, and he said now, 'Get her from here. The place will be down about your ears,' and then he turned and he and his fellows went out into the street, and we after them.

The horses were harnessed to the ropes again, and the giant at their side by the time we came out. He looked over his shoulder, saw us stepping over the rubble of the porch, and slapped the nearest horse, crying, 'Pull!'

The horses pulled. I threw my arm about the old woman and hauled her into the mob and safety just as the main lintel came free. The face of the house collapsed into the street, and the cheering of the mob was now like the baying of a pack.

The woman slumped against me, and shrieked at the sight of the wreckage. But there was no saving the place now, and so I supported her through the mob. When we were clear of them, and but a short way along the street, a fellow, in great alarm, looked out from his own front door and cried, 'Mrs Green? What the devil have they done to you?'

I took her across to him. 'Keep her with you, sir,' I said, and when a woman came out and fetched the old lady inside I said to the man, 'You called her Green?'

'Yes.'

'Her son is never the tavern keeper in Shadwell?'

'That is a wastrel of their family. The son is a coal merchant, and a gentleman.'

'Send word to him that his mother is unharmed. Tell him that he must not come here. It will not be safe for him. You are not a coal merchant, I hope, sir.' He shook his head and looked with fear along the street, and I said, 'Do not let her go back to her own house. Keep her inside with you till they are gone from here. And keep yourself inside also.'

He retreated from the street and hastily shut his door.

Back at the Green house the horses were scarce manageable now, and bucked and reared as the men struggled to get the ropes tied to the harness. But there was no sign of any stopping. A thick dust hung in the air from the broken bricks and mortar, and in the men a fierce lust of violence. This time when the horses pulled it was something central in the house collapsed, and there was a great tearing of timbers inside.

What power these men had was in their hands and sinews. They used it now with a will, and unnerving it was to see the depth of the ferocious hatred that burned in them. No justices came to stop the destruction, nor any sheriff or constable. Brick by brick, and wall by wall, the men pulled the place to the ground. And I stood at the corner and watched them.

CHAPTER TWENTY-FOUR

'You are in no doubt of this, Mrs Porter?'

'No doubt at all, sir. There were two of them.' She pointed through the window and down to Birdcage Walk. 'The hackney stopped there by the oak. One fellow stood there, waiting. Looking here and there, keeping his eyes open. The other fellow was up and inside Wilkes's apartment all the while.'

'It may have been Wilkes's servant.' I looked over at the two large windows across the way. 'A face is not always clear at this distance.'

'His servant went out straight after Wilkes left for the Guildhall. It was not the servant, sir. It was the fellow from the hackney.' She told me the exact time of the hackney's arrival. I asked her how long they had stayed. 'Twenty minutes. Time enough for a good old look about. Back and forth he went.' She pointed again to Wilkes's windows, moving a finger to indicate this fellow's searching of the rooms. 'I would recognize the one below if I saw him again.'

'It is a long way from here down to the Walk. Too far to recognize a face.'

'Exactly my thought, sir. Which is why I took myself down there.

He is scarred from the pox.' She raised a hand to her right cheek. 'All on this side, and on his forehead.'

'Did the fellow searching the apartment bring anything away with him?'

'If he did, I never saw it. Straight into the hackney he went. Wilkes's man came back an hour after the hackney left. No one else.' She asked after my news of Wilkes then, and whether he had been elected.

With my gaze upon Wilkes's apartment, I told her of the day's events in the Guildhall and the City. I said that Wilkes must find himself uncommonly occupied this coming week in the business of gathering votes and running his campaign from the snug of the King's Arms tavern in Cornhill, and that she might expect to see a little less of him here in Birdcage Walk. 'But he must sometimes return here to sleep, Mrs Porter. And no doubt there are those will find it more convenient to call upon him here than in a City tavern.'

'If you could spare five pounds, Mr Douglas, I believe I might make some good use of it.' At my look of surprise, she said, 'I am sorry, sir. I did not mean to embarrass you.'

'No, of course, you must have it,' said I, fetching out my purse.

'It is only that Mr Wilkes's man has run short. And I thought I might put myself in the way of helping him.' There was nothing in her eyes, or in any part of her expression, to suggest what it was that she was, in fact, suggesting. In truth, she was the wiliest of women, and very glad was I to have called her up from Dover to my service.

I gave her the five pounds, and would have given her more but that she would never have taken it.

'You are very quiet, Mr Tyler.'

'Nothing to say, sir.'

'You recognized her description of the man.'

He pushed the lock of blond hair from his eyes and glanced at me. 'It is Meadows from the Post Office stables.'

'You will remember what I asked of you and Mr Baxter.'

'I can hold my tongue, sir.' As we walked on a little further towards Horseguards Parade, I saw that there was that which weighed on the lad. I presumed it must be this newly acquired knowledge concerning Meadows, till he said, 'How does she know such a thing about Wilkes's man?'

'Want of money is not unusual.'

' "Wilkes's man has run short," she said – like she knew.'

'She does not sit by that window all the day. While you and I were not yet born, Mrs Porter was going about the shops and streets with her eyes and ears wide open. If she says the fellow has run short, you may trust in it. How she came by the information is more than I care to enquire of her. And it is quite possible she would not tell me if I did.'

'What business had Meadows there?'

'And that is more than you should ask me.'

I sent him then to discover if Baxter was returned yet from Deptford, and if so to fetch him to my house in Holborn. Then I went myself to find Jenkinson.

The Parliament having been prorogued, there was not now that same scurry of important gentlemen near St Stephen's Hall that I had grown accustomed to during the autumn and winter. Nor would I have thought to find Jenkinson there in Westminster, but that I had met a secretary of the Southern Department who stopped me outside the Treasury to ask me of Wilkes's fate in the election. I told him, though omitting any mention of the mob; and upon my saying that I must now take the same news to Jenkinson, the fellow directed me to Westminster Hall, whence he had just come. The courts were in session, and he was sure that he had seen Jenkinson there in the company of Lord Chief Justice Mansfield.

The Common Pleas and the Chancery were both sitting when I came into the Hall, but when I put my head around the screen of the King's Bench court I found no case being heard, but only a few idle lawyers and spectators amusing themselves with a game of cards and the casual perusal of the latest papers. I told a clerk of the court my business there, and he took me into an anteroom off Mansfield's private chambers and left me there while he went in to fetch Jenkinson. He re-emerged almost at once to tell me that I should go in directly.

'But I had not intended to disturb the Chief Justice.'

'I should not keep them waiting, sir.'

After a hasty straightening of my jacket, and a tug upon my cuffs, I nodded to the clerk and he opened the door for me. They were both of them seated, Mansfield behind a broad desk and Jenkinson on an armchair nearer the fire. Neither man made to rise at my entry. I bowed my head towards Mansfield as Jenkinson introduced me.

'Mr Douglas has worked for some years now as an agent of the Deciphering Branch.'

'I am surprised we have not met till now, Mr Douglas.'

'I have been but little of that time in England, My Lord.'

His gaze was very steady upon me, neither hostile nor friendly. A Scotsman himself, but he was not the kind of fellow to let that dispose him towards me. He wore his full court regalia, both the red cloak and the wig, whose rows of curls reached almost to the arms of his chair. Behind him was a wall of leather-bound books.

'You have come from the Guildhall?' Jenkinson prompted.

'There is nothing settled, sir. The chamberlain has opened the polls for a week.' They had the news already, but now Jenkinson mentioned the rumour that had first come to Westminster of Wilkes being elected by a general acclamation. I explained what had happened concerning the show of hands for Wilkes. 'Not all were freeholders, sir, yet it gave his supporters much heart.'

'And much good may it do them,' said Jenkinson. 'They are rabble.'

'They are a well organized rabble at least, sir. A party of them has destroyed a merchant's house near the Guildhall.'

'How destroyed?' said Mansfield, suddenly furrowing his heavy brow and tilting back his head to study me. It was such a look as he must have used to intimidate a good many of the accused persons who came before his bench. I told him what I had seen of the mob's actions. I gave it as my opinion that the whole proceedings were done for reasons pertaining to the coal heavers' dispute, and were in no direct way caused by Wilkes. 'And the justices?' said he.

'They kept away, My Lord. As did the constables.'

'Kept away, and the house pulled to the ground? And near to the Guildhall?'

'Yes, My Lord.'

Mansfield looked to Jenkinson with some meaning, as though my report had some bearing upon words previously spoken between them.

Jenkinson said, 'Is it possible they were called to their duty elsewhere?'

'The other part of the mob retired to the King's Arms with Wilkes, sir. The justices and constables only kept from the coal heavers out of fear.'

'The heavers have taken their permission for riot from the example of Wilkes. He has flouted the law with an absolute impunity,' said Mansfield to Jenkinson. 'Even if it be not by his direct order, he calls them up by his very presence.'

'We must endure it only a short while more,' said Jenkinson. 'The poll closes in a week, Mr Douglas?'

'Yes, sir. But if he is elected—'

'He shall not be elected, Mr Douglas. The numbers have been against him from the first. Most of the City votes were promised before he entered the fray.' Jenkinson spoke this as a certainty, and as though he had never ordered me to distribute those scurrilous pieces about Wilkes around the City coffee shops.

'Had Grafton but taken the advice given him upon an arrest,' said Mansfield, 'this had not happened.'

Jenkinson, I saw, thought this an injudicious remark for the Chief Justice to make in my presence. For though the Duke of Grafton was known by all to be fonder of the gaming table and the horses than ever he was of the business of government, yet he was a nobleman, and Jenkinson not a man who could set that by. And so he broke in upon Mansfield to thank me for my report, and then he invited me to return to the Lane.

'Sir, there are some other matters—'

'Then you may wait for me. But outside, if you please.'

'My Lord,' said I, dipping my head to Mansfield as I withdrew.

That Jenkinson should want privacy for their talk now was unsurprising; for what should they talk of but only the various attitudes toward Wilkes within the ministry. And the attitude of Lord Shelburne or Lord Weymouth toward Wilkes, or Grafton's evident neglect in dealing with the problem, or Lord Chatham's unaccountable indifference, these were not matters to be aired before any they might doubt of. And yet I found Jenkinson's graceless dismissal of me irksome, as being an unwelcome expression of this doubt.

After several minutes in the anteroom I grew impatient of the wait, and went out to the terrace by the river. There I strolled up and down, near to the Speaker's house, till at last stopping to rest my forearms upon the river wall. The Archbishop's pennant flew above the Lambeth Palace across the river. It put me in mind of the Bishop, before whom I would much rather have set all my troubles rather than turning, as I now must do, to Jenkinson. But the Bishop had long since returned to his see in Wells, and my only communication with him now was through Francis. The river below me was grey and sluggish. A boatman at the Westminster Steps helped two gentlemen into his wherry and then pushed off, striking out eastwards towards the City. How often I had made that same journey in the autumn; and how often I had returned to Mr Fitzherbert in Whitehall to report my failure to discover Pearce and Flanagan. Indeed, they had disappeared so completely that by November I had almost begun to doubt of their continued presence in London.

Then Langridge's murder had happened. Jenkinson had replaced Fitzherbert over me. Carrington had taken up the search for Pearce and Flanagan. And I had been sent to watch over Wilkes in Paris. But now all the winter was gone by, and what had I to show for that bitter season? Armstrong murdered while under my command, and I deceived at every turn, but scarce knowing by whom, and the reason.

And behind all of this, and deeper, a continuing numbness of the heart.

While I was pondering in this melancholy fashion, I became aware of some gentlemen approaching along the terrace. They were arm in arm, and as they neared I recognized them for the new joint master of the Post Office, Lord Sandwich, and the previous incumbent in the post, Lord Hillsborough.

'Have you not some business to be attending to at the Post Office, Mr Douglas?' said Sandwich, smiling upon me with a supreme condescension. 'I expect there shall be any number of letters going out from Wilkes's people now.'

'That is not my affair, My Lord.'

'No? And what part of your affair is it to be here?'

I told him that I waited for Jenkinson to conclude his private conference with the Chief Justice.

Upon hearing this, the thin smile vanished from his lips. They were just by me now and they unlinked their arms. Sandwich's hand rested languid now on the hilt of his sword. 'Mr Carrington tells us that you have advised against Wilkes's arrest.'

'I have given no advice to anyone.'

'I hope you do not say that Mr Carrington has lied.'

'Perhaps he has misunderstood.'

Hillsborough snorted at this evasion. I did not like to be trapped in such a conversation, for I trusted neither man, nor the report of it they should undoubtedly take to Carrington. It crossed my mind even that they might be happy to provoke a duel between Carrington and me, though I could not think what reason they might have for it but only a malicious and idle self-amusement.

'And I do not believe, Mr Douglas, that you have brought me yet all the papers that I requested from the Secret Office.'

'As to that, My Lord, you must apply to the Bishop.'

'Apply?' said he, and smiled unpleasantly.

'Douglas!' came a sharp call from behind me. It was Jenkinson, come out to the terrace with Mansfield, and Mansfield still wearing his wig and gown. Jenkinson beckoned me to him, and I took my leave of the Bedfordite pair with some relief. But as I came away, Mansfield joined them, and all three now turned at once along the terrace. Sandwich took Mansfield's arm, and they bent their heads together in earnest discussion.

Jenkinson, who had none of Sandwich's poisonous charm, stood stiffly beside me and watched them go in silence. And I believe that the sight of Mansfield joined so familiarly with the Bedfordites was still in Jenkinson's mind as we proceeded in his carriage up by St James's towards Mayfair. Certainly he listened only distractedly to all the details of what I had witnessed in the City, both in the Guildhall and in the street. Which when I had given him, I added, 'Mr Carrington was there also in the Guildhall.'

'Mr Carrington's whereabouts are hardly my concern.'

'There was his second, Meadows, with him. Meadows left just as soon as Wilkes began to speak from the hustings.'

'If I care little for Carrington's whereabouts, you may believe I care even less to know the business of his second. As to your man, has he discovered anything down by Deptford?'

I told him that Baxter had heard of a Danish whaling ship that had been for some months in the Greenland Dock. The vessel was now gone downriver for refitting. 'Several of the crew that moved her were Americans.'

'That is very little.'

I could not deny it. But I told him that I would soon meet with Baxter down in Deptford to have his report, and now I offered to bring Baxter up to him. Jenkinson declined, saying that he did not doubt me and was very sure that I knew my own business.

'I believe that I do, sir,' said I. And Jenkinson was too well acquainted with the dealings of committees, and the hidden meanings of gentlemanly conversations, for my tone to escape him. He knitted his brow and peered at me, awaiting the explanation of it. 'When Meadows left the Guildhall, he went to Birdcage Walk,' I said. 'He had another Messenger with him. He sent the fellow up to search Wilkes's rooms.'

'A search at whose order?'

'I had wondered, sir, if you knew of it.'

'I know of it now,' said he tightly.

He continued to peer at me, and I to watch him, for I had been ready to see any small sign might betray him; but there was nothing in his eyes of deception, not so much as a flicker. He reached up in silence and struck two sharp blows upon the top of the carriage. The carriage slowed, and then stopped. He looked at me now in such a way that I could have no doubt of his fury at me, that I should raise this doubt of him. Nor could I doubt of his meaning in stopping the carriage. I opened the door and got down. Without a word to me, he thumped the top of the carriage again, the carriage drew away, and I was left standing alone by the side of Park Lane, knowing well that I had given the gravest offence to the one man in London whose aid I most stood in need of.

It was seven o'clock and dark when Tyler came to my house. He told me that Baxter's wife had complained to him that she had not seen her husband for some days now, and that she had talked of going to Carrington, and so Tyler had been forced to tell her that Baxter was well, but delayed about his work south of the river.

'And did that quiet her?'

'She is not a quiet woman, sir. But she will not go to Mr Carrington.'

I gave him an instruction to go among Wilkes's supporters at the King's Arms tavern the next day, as one of them; and again each day after, till the polling was done. He must make himself familiar with any plan they made there for riot in the City. And if he heard of any such plan, he must find me at the Lane, or pass the information to Francis Willes.

'Come by here in the evenings to give me your report. If I am out, put a blank paper beneath the door to signify that all is well with you.'

When he had left me, I returned to my sitting room and took up the sketching pad that I had put aside when he had knocked at my door. There was a candle yet burning on the table by me, and next to the candle a shell of such curious twisting form that Banks had sent it to me that I might make a detailed study of the thing. For two weeks it had awaited my attention. I know not why the events of that particular day should have made me take up the task at last, unless from need for some inner voice of my mind to be stilled. I sat down again now and set the pad upon my knee. The shell was the size of a man's fist, with a double spiral running half its length, and a serrated opening where some creature of the deep might once have found refuge. I studied it now, just as I had seen Buffon study that specimen in his studio, with a rapt and singular attention. Then I took up my pencil and traced out very carefully the twisting lines of this shard of Nature. There was no regularity in any part of it, and no symmetry. I turned my whole concentration upon it, and finally, line by gentle line, its form and shadow began to emerge in slow but accurate relief from the blankness of the page, and so I lost myself till sleep.

CHAPTER TWENTY-FIVE

*T*he Temple Stairs wherrymen worked mostly that stretch of river between the Westminster and London bridges, so that I was several minutes debating the tide and the price (and no use appealing to the fixed rate set by their guild) before one of them agreed to take me as far down as Deptford. And that agreement I got only once I had settled with him that he might ferry some people from the City over to Rotherhithe on our way downriver.

The tide was low, and so the boatman rowed, and I sat upon the stern seat and gave him warning of those many other boats ahead, forced like us into the narrow central channel. Near Blackfriars, on the south side, there were women and children had come down to dig in the mudbank for whelks. This was no recreation to them, but necessity. The women hardly spoke to one another, or to their children, but they laboured joylessly, their feet and calves sunk in the mud with the heavy hems of their dresses. The children were no better, but equally silent, and with faces careworn and pale.

Below London Bridge the ships were as thick and unmoving upon the river as they had ever been whilst trapped in the winter ice. The several vessels that had got themselves out past the Medway had been replaced by others whose owners must now regret the chance they had taken in coming up. The ranks of ships we now rowed under seemed not so much anchored as becalmed, and in a doldrum beyond anything to be met with at sea. There were few sailors visible aboard any vessel, and not a man in any ship's rigging. I asked my boatman if he had heard what the seamen intended; for it was evident to all that it could not continue in this way, with the seamen enforcing strike-of-sail upon the ships, and the owners refusing the seamen's demands for higher pay. But my boatman would not be drawn, and began to complain instead of the price of meat at Smithfield, and the foul smell now coming from the bilges of all the ships.

Three fellows got into my wherry just below the Tower, and they were merchants going now to inspect a ship they were equipping over in Rotherhithe. They were making her ready for a voyage to the West African coast, and it was some amusement to me how they talked, for they were fellows like Hayley who spent all their days in the coffee shops and the Exchange, and now they spoke very lightly of the prospective voyage to Sierra Leone, thence to Boston and home again, as men will only speak who have never undertaken such a journey. Small wonder it was to me that there should be so little understanding between the seamen and fellows such as these. But I heard from their conversation that the refitting they were engaged with was causing them a much greater expense than they had expected, so that it seemed even they were not spared from the general discontent upon the river.

Once they had disembarked, we continued down past the stench of the Greenland Dock, and so came at last to the Steps before the Royal Naval Yard, which stretched almost half a mile along the southern shore, with a high brick wall enclosing the many buildings and the several wet docks cut into the bank there. A number of naval vessels in ordinary stood off from the docks and as we drew near to the shore we saw the ribs of two ships under construction within the Yard, the timbers jutting up like whalebones. There were boats moving between the Yard and the anchored ships in ordinary, and men moving about near the Yard buildings. And yet it was noticeable to me that both the Yard and the river here were very much quieter than when I had last come down. Jenkinson had already given me the reason of it, which was the Admiralty's concern to have its own seamen clear of the Thames, lest the trouble crippling the merchant fleet should spread. For this reason a good number of the Navy ships had now sailed to other harbours along the coast. But though I knew the cause of it, the unusual quietness of the place unsettled me as following after the other things I had seen in coming down.

Once ashore, I took the path beside the Yard wall and around to the village of Deptford, two minutes' walk inland behind the docks.

I passed by the inn of the village, which was the White Bear, and saw in the first window some old fellows of the kind who are always to be found at such places, and in the second window, Baxter, with an ale pot before him on the table. He saw me, and I made no signal but continued directly on to the church of St Paul's. It was ten minutes later that Baxter came into the church and found me seated at the base of one of the Corinthian columns inside. He cast a wary eye towards the vestry.

'I have made a search of the place, Mr Baxter. You may speak.'

'I had expected Tyler, sir.'

'He is busy with our friend at the King's Arms.'

'You were right, sir. The Boston men have been moving all the while. All through the autumn and winter. From here down to Greenwich, and up again to the Greenland Dock. They must have been keeping themselves ahead of you.'

I stood and almost embraced him. 'If you have found them, Mr Baxter, then you have done in days what I could not do in months.'

'It was the two whores pointed us back to the Greenland Dock. And the men are not found, sir. But I know now where they have been. They have been most of their time upon a whaler in the Greenland Dock. But sometimes they have moved down here, or on to Greenwich.'

'You have not seen them then.'

'A few days more, sir, and I think I may find them.'

I asked if he had gone aboard the whaler. He shook his head.

'It would be like a beacon to them if they heard of me there. But I have felt myself very close to them.'

'You will remember that Langridge and Armstrong were both close to them, Mr Baxter. And I would not have another widow upon my conscience.' He smilingly told me that if I lost him, his wife would make trouble to parts of me other than my conscience. I laughed, which pleased him. We were both of us greatly cheered by his success, for it was too long we had taken in getting close to Pearce and Flanagan. Then I stepped into the nave and turned about, facing anew those same questions that had vexed me through the winter. How had the damned fellows lived? Had they worked? We must surely have had some report of it. I said, 'It is months they have been here.'

'I am sure they may steal as well as any, sir,' Baxter replied, for he knew well the questions in my mind, and how poorly we had answered them till now.

'They must then sell what they steal. And if they do it by the river, Meadows would surely hear of it.'

'They might have done some light duties aboard the whaler, sir. I might speak with the captain.'

'Leave the captain be. Your first thought was the better one. We must light no beacons now to warn them.'

'And Wilkes is still campaigning?'

I told Baxter in brief what had passed at the Guildhall.

'Down here, sir, they are saying he has raised a mob.'

'Whether he has raised a mob or merely rides it, we shall see. But I will need you up there when the result is declared. You may continue down here a few days more if you think it worthwhile.'

'I shall be the closer to them at the end of it.'

He needed money for his lodging at the White Bear, but nothing more, and so I gave him some coins from my purse, telling him that he should make no approach to Pearce and Flanagan if he should find them, but send for me directly. 'I will call on the Chief Shipwright in the King's Yard when I leave you now. If you find yourself in any extremity, and I too distant, you must go to him.' He nodded, and I knew that I might trust him upon it. 'Is there nothing more?'

There was not. But as I turned to go from the church, he said after me, 'Is it to arrest Wilkes that I must come up to the Guildhall, sir?'

'If he fails in the election, those who now curb themselves will no longer be in any fear of him. He will be arrested.'

On the evening before the declaration in the Guildhall, I walked up Red Lion Street and met Tyler coming down from my house in the square. He turned when we met, and fell into step beside me.

'I thought I had missed you, sir.'

'All quiet at the King's Arms, Mr Tyler?'

'They have been on the ale. But there is no trouble.'

'And nothing planned for tomorrow?'

'Not as I know of, sir. There is a belief common among them now that Wilkes will not be elected.'

'Let us hope that the ale shall get them past their disappointment.'

He told me then of what he had learned of the giant, that same fellow who had used the horses against the coal merchant's house. For this man, Tyler had reported to me, was now a frequent visitor to the King's Arms.

'They call him the Infant, sir,' he concluded. 'He has control of the chair-men in some parts of the City.'

'And was he there again today?'

'A short time, sir.'

'Did he meet with Wilkes?'

'Not as I saw.'

'And what of Mr Hayley?'

Hayley, Tyler said, had come at midday as before. And as before, had stayed an hour, done no particular business, and then departed. 'He spoke with Wilkes very little, sir. It is some other fellows who are Wilkes's men of business. They are writing all the day, and sending lads off with their letters to the printers.'

'I am obliged to you for your close attention, Mr Tyler. You have done very well.'

We reached the door of my house on the north side of the square, and I put my key in the lock.

'Has Baxter found the Boston men, sir?'

'I have asked Mr Baxter to come up to the Lane tomorrow. Whatever shall be the result of the election, I may have need of you both.'

'He has not found them, then.'

'I shall see you at the Lane at midday. Good night, Mr Tyler.'

'Good night, sir,' said he, and turned and went off across the square.

I went in, and noticed at once that he had forgotten to slip a blank paper beneath my door. It was a carelessness that I should have rebuked him for, only that when I turned he was already crossing the square, and as I watched he leaped up and touched a cherry branch, and I knew then that he was full of my congratulation of him.

I could not rebuke him then. He was young, and it was almost the first error that he had made, and so I said nothing but only watched his second touching of the cherry branch, and then closed my front door.

Upon coming up from the Lane to the Guildhall on the next afternoon (which was the twenty-third day of March), I found the scene there not near so raucous as I had feared. For though there were many people come to hear the result of the polling, everyone from the chamberlain down to the printers' lads had an understanding by then that Wilkes had lost. As Jenkinson had foreseen, too many votes were already promised to the other candidates before Wilkes ever entered into the lists.

Outside the Guildhall, Wilkes's journeymen supporters had gathered, but they seemed to be there only to await the announcement of their hero's defeat with a sullen acceptance. There was no sign of the coal heavers, or of the Infant and his chair-men, and without this violent centre there was no focus for the general discontent and unhappiness of the milling people. And while the official declaration of the result was yet to be made, there was likewise no trigger to fire them.

'You will wait here, Mr Tyler. If Wilkes attempt any flight this way, you will follow him.'

'Mr Carrington's Messengers are at the Guildhall door there, sir.'

'And I have put Mr Baxter at the other. And you will take no part in Wilkes's arrest, but the Messengers shall take him. Only if he elude them, then you shall follow. And what I have said to Mr Baxter I now say to you. There shall be nothing excuse us if we should lose him from here. Have you any question of me?'

He had none, and I left him by St Lawrence Jewry and went with Francis across the paved courtyard and into the Guildhall.

As we passed through the people and into the hall I saw some gentlemen jostled by the poorer journeymen there, and heard some harsh words spoken, and I was not then so sanguine that the day should end peacefully. There was an anger and frustration very palpable within the hall, and I was only spared a jostling of my own by the accident of donning a blue jacket that morning. Blue being the colour favoured by Wilkes in his dress, it was the colour all the Wilkites had adopted in their campaigning for him, and here in the hall were blue cockades in many hats, and blue ribbons tied in the hair of the poorer women.

The feeling was very different now from that first day of polling the week before. Up in the gallery, the ladies of St James's and Mayfair had been replaced with the ladies of Shadwell.

Francis and I found that same step we had shared earlier. Then he leaned toward me and whispered, 'Carrington would be a madman to bring the Messengers in here.'

On the hustings the Lord Mayor held court among his fellow candidates, with only Wilkes standing off from him and leaning over the side rail and holding his own conference with Hayley and his other supporters. Wilkes, somewhat to my surprise, seemed quite unruffled, and even laughed as he talked with these fellows.

To one side of the hustings, the chamberlain was with the sheriffs and overseeing the final counting of the votes recorded in the polling books. In truth, had Wilkes run at that moment, and Carrington's men taken him, I would not have been displeased. For when Baxter had come up to the Lane from Deptford just an hour since, it was to tell me that he had at last laid eyes upon Pearce and Flanagan. They were at the Greenland Dock still, though no longer hiding in the whaler. He was very eager now to get back there, and I just as eager to go with him.

The chamberlain mounted the hustings with a paper in his hand, and he called the hall to silence. There was no preamble made to the declaration of the result, but once he had silence the chamberlain read out the name of each candidate along with the number of ballots cast for him. The Lord Mayor and three others were declared the elected parliamentary members for the City. And Wilkes was not one of the three.

There came at once an uproar from many places in the crowd.

'Pray silence,' cried the chamberlain. 'The candidates must make their acknowledgements.'

First the Lord Mayor spoke, and then the other candidates in the order of polling. Nobody listened, for the shouting and cries from the floor had become general now, and the cries of 'Wilkes and Liberty!' no longer joyful but ugly and threatening. At last Wilkes came to the front of the hustings to make an acknowledgement of his supporters.

'Friends,' said he, and the cheers broke out from left and right. He raised his hands and said again, 'Friends! For so you are, good Friends to Liberty every one of you. And what is it to us, you and I, the Friends of Liberty, if there be practised against us the many low tricks and chicanery of men who think more of power than of their honour? Shall we be disheartened?'

A thousand voices answered him, 'No!' and 'Never!'

'No my friends, we are not disheartened, for we came into this election not as innocent babes, but as men, and knowing full well that we should have our honour traduced and our good name blackened. While we have fought in the open, as befits free men, they have stabbed at us from the dark.'

'Shame!' came the cry now. 'Shame on Bute! Grafton, for shame! Shame on the ministry!'

'Hold, my friends, name me no names. Keep yourselves from the vile gutter where they would drag you. Though they have spread such scurrilous nonsense about me, yet they have not touched me in the one place that would wound me, which is your honest affections.'

There was a loud cheering at this, and Francis glanced at me and I at him.

'But let me not blame such inconsequential sprats as these for my defeat. For I know what has defeated me. It was my own tardiness.' Wilkes slapped his hand upon the husting rail as though to pass judgement upon himself. 'Had I but offered myself in good time, and before half your votes were promised, then – I am sure you will acknowledge it with me – we had seen a very different end to the polling.' The crowd acknowledged it with a great cheer. 'Friends, I say, we are not disheartened. And I thank you in all sincerity for the lesson you have taught me. I shall not make the same mistake again. And that is why I ask your aid now, that you keep faith with Liberty, that this day be remembered not as a defeat, but as a first bold step in our campaign to win for Liberty one of the parliamentary seats for Middlesex.'

Wilkes, with both hands, now gripped the hustings rail, and looked across the hall with a defiant cross-eyed gaze.

'What the devil is this?' whispered Francis, but I was in some shock and could not reply.

'Friends – fellow Joiners and Ceilers – while you stand by me, I cannot leave off from our common struggle. And that is why I have today entered myself as a candidate in the Middlesex election. No sirs, we are not disheartened.'

Understanding of his meaning broke at last over the people. Cheering broke out, and mad laughter.

'Wilkes!' they shouted, and 'Wilkes and Liberty!' and all the wild cheering and shouting caused those outside the hall to come pressing in through the main door. The crush of bodies was suddenly very great, and amidst the wild shouting were cries of anger, and fists flying. Francis and I now got down from the step. We pushed and shoved our way to the side door to get to safety, and met Baxter there. He asked if Wilkes was arrested, for he had heard nothing from outside, but only the wild noise.

As we were swept out in the crush I looked back to the hustings.

The mob had lifted Wilkes from the platform, and now carried him above them, shoulder-high. He grinned over their heads like a knave, and waved his hat, glorying in their adulation like a king.

'He will not be arrested today, Mr Baxter.'

CHAPTER TWENTY-SIX

'Who will rid us of this wretched man?'

'I have seen the list of the Middlesex candidates. He is properly registered.'

'You were to watch the man, both day and night.'

'His presence was not required to enter himself as a candidate. Beyond his most intimate friends, I doubt that any man knew of it.'

'It is certain, at least, that you did not know of it, Mr Douglas.' Jenkinson, in his anger, shoved back in his chair and rose. He had moved now altogether from the Admiralty building, and several boxes of his papers had followed him across the Horseguards Parade and into his room at the Treasury. These boxes were now piled up around his desk awaiting the attentions of a clerk. He picked his way around them now and went to the window. He held one arm behind his back as he looked out at the drilling ground, and in his agitation his hand made a continual clutch and release. 'I cannot recall who else is standing for Middlesex.'

I told him the names of the two candidates. One a lawyer, and one a junior paymaster to the Army and supported by the ministry;

and neither one a fellow of any great distinction. 'And now Wilkes, sir.'

'That is all?' he said, turning in startlement. 'Three?'

I nodded.

'Dear God, but there are two Middlesex seats.'

Until this moment I do not think that Jenkinson had paid serious heed to the possibility of Wilkes's being elected to the Parliament. With the battle confined to the City, he had always believed that it was beyond Wilkes's capacity to enter so late and yet win. Those scurrilous papers we had put about had been but an insurance. But in Middlesex was a situation very different. The other candidates were little known, and neither one had campaigned, as believing themselves certain to be elected unopposed. And now Wilkes's campaign would be transferred there, so that he would enter that election at a gallop while his opponents were not even mounted.

'These were being sold in Lombard Street when we came out,' said I, producing from my jacket a copy of the *Advertiser* in which Wilkes's intention to stand in Middlesex was announced. Jenkinson read the sheet.

'This was more than the labour of an hour,' he remarked, getting a better control of himself now, and facing the matter square.

I gave him my opinion on it, which was that the printer must have set the piece privately, at Wilkes's instruction; for if the printer's assistants had known of it, Carrington must surely have heard. Jenkinson warned me quite curtly against any speculation upon Carrington's business, and then he asked me the date of the Middlesex election.

I told him the date. It was inside the week.

His jaw clenched tight. He was too astute a judge of such things to deceive himself. He knew at once how little chance there must now be to hold off Wilkes.

'Sir, I believe that we have found Pearce and Flanagan.'

'Believe, Mr Douglas?'

I told him of Baxter's report. 'I would be at the Greenland Dock now, but for chasing to discover Wilkes's business in Middlesex. And if I may now be excused, I will go down to the dock directly.'

'And what of Wilkes?'

'Sir?'

'Have you not thought how he might be dealt with?'

'It is in the ministry's hands if they would arrest him.'

'You know very well that he has made that impossible now.'

'I have no reach beyond your order, sir. Or that of the Bishop.'

He told me that I must think on it, and come to him at eight the next morning in Mayfair. I answered that I could not promise myself free at that time, as having no way of knowing how this business at the Greenland Dock should end.

'At eight,' said he firmly, and still in some vexation at me for what had happened with Wilkes. 'And if you are not there, I must then look to the assistance of Mr Carrington.'

On the south side of the London Bridge my hackney was about to turn in to Tooley Street, toward Rotherhithe, when I directed him on to the Long Lane and thence to the Blue Anchor Road, where he set me down by the Halfway House in the fields. There were a number of men digging in the market-gardens near the house, and I walked on by them, and down the road toward the landward side of the Greenland Dock. It was quiet and no one else on the road till Baxter came out from the Halfway House and caught up with me.

'I hope there is some good reason you have put me in the mud, Mr Baxter.'

'From where they hide, sir, they can see the Stairs and the river. Coming up from this side we are hid from them.'

'And you are certain they are still there.'

'They are there,' said he. 'I made very sure of Tyler's safety before I came away. I have warned him against putting his head up.'

'I am obliged.'

The smell of the whale oil rose up to meet us as we went on. The Greenland Dock was bigger even than the main wet dock in the Deptford Yard, and about its perimeter was a double line of tall poplars that acted as a windbreak for the ships berthed in the basin. These poplars stood directly ahead of us. To our left, but a good way across the fields, was the line of buildings about Jamaica Street up on the river, the buildings thinning eastward, and stopping altogether before they reached the trees. To our right, but a half-mile distant, and across more fields, were the buildings of the Deptford Yard.

Standing up from the line of the river was a thick forest of masts, and all without sail. It was evening now, and the pale sun hanging low at our backs, the light turning grey, and weakening.

Upon reaching the first of the Greenland Dock buildings, we skirted south and stayed close to the field wall by the windbreak, and went on till we were within fifty yards of the river.

'There sir, in that big shed, that is the vats. There is no window this side.'

We turned away from the field wall then, and towards the dock-side. Till now it was only a few field workers we had passed, going homeward from their labour, but here close by the water we came upon men of a different stamp entirely. Sailors for the most part, though not so many as I had expected from the score or more ships at berth there in the basin. These fellows paid us no heed, but pursued their card games and their idling, and we were soon by them, and the air very thick now with the stench of the oil. Baxter led me into a narrow alley between two buildings, and then into one of these buildings and on up the stairs. At the top we paused, and Baxter made a low whistle at the door. There was the sound of movement within, and after a few seconds came an answering low whistle. Baxter whistled once more, and then we heard the door bolt go back, and Tyler opened the door to us. His face was very grim.

'There is one of them gone upriver,' said he unhappily as we entered.

Baxter crossed straight to the window, and I with him. Their hiding shed was twenty yards from us, its lower floor open to the dockside. Three huge vats stood in a line inside.

'They have made a place for themselves in the loft above,' Baxter told me. 'The chimneys go up by them. I should think it has kept them warm through the winter.'

I asked Tyler after the one who had gone upriver, but there was little he knew; only that the fellow had gone in a wherry from the Steps. I stared across at the vat-shed. Months of searching, and they at last beneath my hand; but if I closed my hand now, I should take only one of them.

'Is there no other way out from the shed?'

'None. They must come out by the vats, sir.'

'And you are sure, Mr Tyler, that the other remains in the shed.'

'He is there, sir.'

They looked at me now in expectation of some order. And I own, it was a great temptation to set them loose upon that single fellow we had cornered.

'We will wait.'

'Sir, it will be dark in half an hour.'

'We will wait all the night if we must, Mr Baxter.' I told him that at dark he must go down and find a place to keep watch by the Stairs, which were near the entrance from the river into the basin. 'You will have warning of the other if he returns. And if this one makes to leave, you may then stop him there. If the wretch is not returned by midnight, I will come down to you. Mr Tyler, you will keep watch here. What weapons have you?' They had knives, which I thought should answer any need that night. We waited a half-hour together, and when the dark came, lanterns were lit upon several of the ships in the basin, and then Baxter went down to the Stairs.

I watched Baxter into the darkness near the Stairs, and then I left Tyler by the window and turned up my coat collar as I sat upon the floor in the corner to wait. Langridge was in my mind then, for he must have been murdered somewhere very close to this place. It must be that they had cut his throat ashore, and then put him in the boat in the basin and pushed the boat out by the Stairs, and Baxter and I waiting downriver. I did not try to sleep.

It was a few minutes before midnight, and the watchman of the Dock just gone by, when I went down to replace Baxter at the Stairs. He had gone off from there to wait in the shadow of the field wall till the watchman was past, but now when he saw me he came out, we spoke briefly, and then he retreated to the room where I had left Tyler.

For the next several hours I remained by the river, withdrawing to the shadow of the field wall at each advance of the watchman's lantern. There were but few lights upon the ships in the basin, and from the vat-shed came neither a glimmer of light, nor any sound. At the mouth of the basin, no boat came in and none went out, but all was quiet, the night moonless, and very dark, and still. I might have been on a night watch at sea, but for the smell of whale oil that hung all about me.

I did not like to be in London. This thought, which I had held off for some months now, came upon me very strongly while I kept my solitary watch. While I had been away from England, in whatever quarter of the world, Mr Fitzherbert's instructions had been but a guidance to me, and had arrived in my hand so infrequently that there was by necessity a tremendous freedom allowed me in all my actions. God knows, there were times I had wished it otherwise, for I had not entirely avoided every pit that was dug for me (and some good few, I confess, which I had dug for myself). And yet I had, through both chance and a slowly increased understanding, survived my errors. But in London there could not be that same freedom afforded me, which though I always knew, yet it had proved a heavier yoke to me than I had prepared for. In London I should never be allowed to steer my own way unobstructed. And if Mr Fitzherbert had been no Mr Watts to me, at least he had not tried to bridle me. But with Jenkinson over me now, it seemed that I could move neither left nor right but at the tug of his hand upon the reins.

I knew that I could not endure it for very much longer. And Valerie would soon be married to Cordet. By some means, I must put London and Paris far behind me.

The eastern sky greyed before the sunrise, and I left the Stairs and rejoined Baxter, who kept watch now, and Tyler who was sleeping.

By seven the sun had risen, and men moved about the Dock, and I stood with Baxter at the window.

'How long will we wait, sir?'

'Nothing is changed. Till the other return, we have but half our quarry.'

'It is a bird in the hand.'

'You may be right, Mr Baxter. But we will wait.'

Tyler woke then. He came to stand by us at the window, with his hands tucked beneath his arms for warmth, his blond hair awry, and his eyes very bleary. I gave him money and told him to get bread for us, and milk or beer if he could find it; and I warned him not to go far, but to keep by the Dock. When Tyler had left us Baxter sat on the crate by the window, and I on the floor by the wall. I remarked to Baxter that his wife had seen as little of him lately as when he had trailed Wilkes into Holland.

'I will hear about it, you may be sure.' He continued to watch at the window. 'Will Wilkes be elected for Middlesex, sir?'

'I am no fortune-teller, Mr Baxter.'

'He has put up enough noise. There are those who wish him to hell.'

'And you do not?'

'I did when he took me among the Dutchmen.' He glanced over. 'I think you must be a Middlesex freeholder, sir.'

'I am.'

He said nothing more, but folded his arms then, and leaned forward on the crate and watched out the window.

Eight o'clock was the time that Jenkinson had ordered me to report to him. But when Tyler returned with only a pitcher of boiled water and a handful of biscuit for our breakfast, I checked my pocket watch, and it was already more than a half after seven.

'Do you expect someone, sir?'

'No, Mr Tyler.' I put the watch away, and took some of the biscuit. Eight, Jenkinson had said. Eight o'clock, or he would then look to Carrington for his aid. And I knew that I would not get there. My tardiness in the face of such a direct order would be forgiven me only if I now made sure of Pearce and Flanagan. I finished the biscuit and washed my mouth with the water. 'There has been no sign of this fellow since you fetched me.'

Baxter looked to Tyler, who said, 'He is there, sir.'

'If he has not shown himself by midday, or the other has not returned – it is your bird in the hand then, Mr Baxter.'

The refitting of the berthed ships, which was the main business of the Dock, went on throughout the morning, but with no urgency; for here was that same feeling of discontent that had settled over the river in the winter. The fuel beneath the oil vats remained unlit. Rope lay uncoiled by the sheds, and many timbers discarded. In the mid-morning the whaler by the vat-shed was untied and pulled across the basin to another berth on the far side. At the Stairs, several boats came and went, but there was no sign of the missing Bostonian.

At midday I said, 'We can wait no longer.' I touched the dirk beneath my jacket, then rose and went to the door. Baxter came down with me, and I set him at the corner of the vat-shed to watch along the Dock and the Stairs. Then I signalled Tyler down and he followed me into the shed and past the great vats. The air inside was scarce breathable, for the smell of the whale oil clung like a pestilence. Tyler pointed to the ladder fixed upon the rear wall, and we went across there silently. I looked up at the closed hatch directly above. Tyler stepped by me and set his foot upon the first rung. I put a hand upon his shoulder and drew him back. Then I mounted the ladder.

It was a high wall, but the rungs were secure, and so I was quickly to the top, where I paused to glance down. Tyler's pale face looked up at me in apprehension. I signalled him to wait, and then climbed the last rung and placed my hand upon the hatch, and very slowly pushed it open.

There was no sound of any movement in the loft. I quickly put my head up, snatched a look, and back down. But what I had seen was only a chimney and a wall, but no person, and so I raised my head and looked again. The wall divided the loft from front to back. On this side, where the hatch was, the whole floor space was empty. By the chimney was a closed door.

I carefully eased the hatch fully open till it rested upright against the wall, and then I climbed into the loft. I signalled for Tyler to follow me up. He was soon at the top, and I took his arm and helped him to step silently into the loft with me, and then I pointed to the closed door. He nodded, and we crept across there, and I signed for him to keep himself close by the wall. Then I clasped the handle, and with my other hand took my dirk from the sheath beneath my shirt. Tyler drew his own blade, and when he was ready I eased open the door.

There was no sound, but only the crying of the gulls out by the ships. Then I glimpsed a figure upon the floor.

'Stay down!' I cried, rushing in. 'You are taken! Stay down, or you are a dead man.'

Tyler rushed in after me, and we stood over the fellow who lay beneath the grey blanket, but now I saw the face was half-hidden, and just as grey. I bent and drew the blanket from his face, and then threw the thing off altogether. There was no doubt but that he was dead. There was a thick rim of ants and other small creatures around the blood, and I rolled him by the shoulder and wiped my dirk across his bloody jacket till I found the three places where he had been stabbed. Then I dropped him onto his back again and knelt to search his clothes.

'You may call up Mr Baxter. This fellow's friend shall not be returning.'

'I knew he had not come out from here.'

'Do as I have asked you.'

We remained there fully an hour, searching in every corner, and Baxter and Tyler speculating very free and wide on what must have happened. Both of them seemed relieved to have found the fellow there, even though he was dead; for they had understood more than I had supposed of my growing doubts of them through the morning. Their best speculation was that a question of money had divided the two Sons of Liberty, and that the one had killed the other and taken the whole of it.

Leaving Tyler in the loft to gather together the clothes and some few personal items we had found there, I finally went down with Baxter to the dockside. We were standing by the shed, and I instructing him how to proceed, when of a sudden he squinted and peered over my shoulder toward the river. I looked around, and there was a boat drawing in to the Stairs. And the fellow rising from his seat in the stern was no Bostonian.

'Sir—'

'Yes. I see him, Mr Baxter.'

The boat touched the Stairs, and the three fellows in the bow disembarked, and then from the stern came Mr Carrington. He made no hesitation, but strode toward us in his sharp military manner, and Meadows beside him, and two more Messengers at his heels. Baxter said to me quietly, 'How are they here?'

'Where are Pearce and Flanagan?' called Carrington, looking about the Dock.

I told him that Baxter's nephew had Flanagan under his charge in the loft above the vats. 'Pearce is escaped,' said I.

'Take me to Flanagan,' said he, and with such a confidence in his command that I knew he must have Jenkinson's authority. I led him into the shed and climbed the ladder, and he came up after me and I took him into the room.

Carrington looked from the body up to me.

'We found him an hour past,' said I.

'Get out,' said Carrington to Tyler, and the lad left us.

Then Carrington went and crouched by the body. He turned out the pockets of the dead man's jacket, asking me now who had killed him.

'Pearce. We found the body as you see it.'

He glanced up. 'And nothing upon him?'

'A knife. Some few things.' I pointed to the bundled kerchief by the door. Carrington rolled the body and made an inspection of the floor beneath.

'You have seen Mr Jenkinson this morning,' I said.

'Baxter is no longer under your command.'

'I have need of him yet to watch over Wilkes.'

'Then you must make your appeal to Mr Jenkinson.' He rose from by the body and looked about the room. 'And nothing found here?' said he.

I turned my head in reply. And when he moved towards the door, I said, 'How did you know that you should find us here?'

'Mr Jenkinson informed me that you were near to the Boston men. And you are not invisible to the wherrymen, Mr Douglas,' said he, and he went out the door and down from the loft.

I had no doubt but that Jenkinson had told him of the Boston men, nor did I doubt that he kept a good many of the wherrymen in his pay. But I had come down here in a hackney. And very glad I was now to have made the first search of the body, and to have discovered that which Carrington looked for.

CHAPTER TWENTY-SEVEN

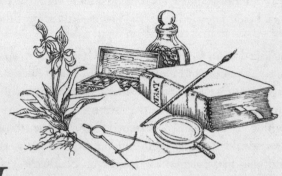

'*H*ave you shown this to Jenkinson?'

'No.'

Francis put the bill of exchange down on his desk between us. It was much creased, but every word clearly legible. Not only the sum, which was two thousand pounds, and the drawee, which was the company of Willing & Morris in Boston, but also the two signatures, which were those of Hancock and Hayley.

Francis studied the bill thoughtfully. 'You must have some notion how this came into Flanagan's hands.'

'None at all.'

'It may be that they stole it from Hancock and brought it over when they fled Boston.'

'I have seen Hancock's strongroom, and also the precautions that he takes. If they have his bill in their hands, it was not by stealing it from him.'

'From some other then?'

'Possibly.'

'You do not believe so.'

'I do not see how the likes of Pearce and Flanagan should have any expectation that the bill would be honoured. If they were to present it, suspicion must fall upon them on the instant.'

'Hayley?'

'He is the drawer.'

'It is a peculiar transaction.'

'It may be no transaction at all. The only thing certain is that Hayley must have a better knowledge of this business than any other man in London.'

Francis asked me if I would confront Hayley with it, and I folded the bill into my pocket and looked out at the Post Office stable yard. Meadows was sitting at a table outside his room, and with him that fellow Green, his informer from the tavern down in Shadwell. They were laughing together and I watched them awhile, thinking how I had never seen that fellow again, the one who had observed me at Dover, and who had escaped my pursuit in Shadwell. Then I went to my desk and fetched out my daily logbook, where in the Corby cipher I must record Flanagan's death.

'Whatever I shall do,' said I, dipping my pen, 'it is certain that Carrington and Meadows must not hear of it.'

The Jamaica House coffee shop was crowded when I came there the next morning, and when I enquired the reason was told that a fellow of the Royal Society would be along presently to give a demonstration of putting air into water as a cure for the scurvy. The merchants and shipowners being every one of them touched in their pocketbooks by that dreadful disease, they had all arrived early to see the demonstration. I could not discover Hayley or Fitzherbert to begin with; but as we were only a short way from the King's Arms in Cornhill where Wilkes had re-established himself for his Middlesex campaign, and as I had a notion that Hayley and Fitzherbert both thought more of their own purses at this moment than of any election, I was sure that if I but waited, they would come.

The natural philosopher arrived a minute after me, trailed by two servants who carried the apparatus for his demonstration. The philosopher proceeded to set up some bottles and flasks upon a table near the serving stall; but there was soon such a press of gentlemen about him he must make a fierce and general rebuke of them lest they overturn everything. It was shortly after this that I saw Hayley enter, and in company. And one of those following him inside was Fitzherbert, who when he saw me broke off from the others and came across to my table.

'Speculation pecuniary, Alistair, or speculation philosophical?'

'We have found the Boston men,' said I, and at once his genial expression changed. He sat down, easing aside his scabbard and resting a forearm upon the table. There was no one who might hear us, for all were circled around the philosopher now, the conversation loud and the din very general. 'Flanagan is dead, murdered by Pearce.'

'And Pearce?'

'Fled. Sir, you will take it as no offence, but I would know a little more of the affairs of your acquaintance, Mr Hayley.'

'Is this to satisfy Jenkinson?'

'It is to satisfy me.'

'The ministry's troubles with Wilkes should not be made to fall upon every member of Wilkes's family.'

'Wilkes is not my concern here. I enquire after Hayley as he is trading with Boston.'

Fitzherbert, guarded now, asked me the reason of my curiosity. The bill was in my pocket and I might have shown it to him, which was my first intention; but now he was here, and I did not. I glanced toward Hayley where he stood with his friends, ready for the philosopher's demonstration.

'I will not be coy with you, sir. I have a suspicion that he has known of Pearce and Flanagan's presence here in London for some while.'

'He has said nothing of it to me.' I made no reply to this, but only turned to look at him again. It was a moment before Fitzherbert understood me. 'Alistair, I do not believe he knows anything of the Boston men. But if he does, it is assuredly not by me.'

I believed him, and at once. For Fitzherbert was not a bad man, and certainly no liar. But what I had suspected of him for some time was now very plain to me, that his judgement was unequal to his position. While I had served him at a distance, and he had taken direction from the Bishop, there had been no reason for me to doubt of his capacity. But in his friendship with Wilkes, his West Indian losses, and his acquaintance with Hayley, there was ample proof that his good nature might end in his own shipwreck. And I found in that moment, and to my own considerable surprise, that I was almost glad to have been removed from his stewardship and put under Jenkinson.

Fitzherbert made to rise now, a little offended I think at my doubt of him. I put my hand upon his arm.

'I must trust to you for your silence, sir. And if I may be so bold, I must warn you against too close an acquaintance with either Hayley or Wilkes for the present.'

He looked down at my hand, and when I lifted it from his arm, he rose and went to join the merchants and shipowners gathered at the philosopher's table. And I must leave the coffee shop then, and think again on whom I might use to hang the bill over Hayley.

While I still thought on the bill, I called upon Mrs Porter at the watching room in Birdcage Walk, and she put a note into my hand, which note I think was the most curious that I ever had from her. It was a short list that she had written.

> W elected for Middlesex.
> W to Bath.
> W returns London. Surrenders himself at King's Bench, first day
>   of session.

'What is this?'

'That is Wilkes's thinking, sir. I have it from his man.'

I looked again at the list. And I confess it seemed now not so strange, or even unlikely, as upon my first perusal. For that Wilkes should be elected for Middlesex seemed almost certain now, and what should he do then till the new Parliament be sworn? But if he not appear before the court before the first sitting of Parliament to have his outlawry lifted, how should he be sworn at all?

I went to the fireplace, and crouched and put the note onto the hot coals, where it shrivelled and burned. 'It is time for you to return home to Dover, Mrs Porter.'

'I cannot speak with Wilkes's man in Dover.'

'I had thought that you would be happy to go.'

'Oh, but I am, sir.'

'Well then.'

'You will not take it wrong, Mr Douglas, but in my belief Wilkes will be elected.'

'And if he is?'

'While he is in Bath, I cannot see that you will need me. But if he comes back to London, and the King's Bench court—'

'Then I shall send for you directly.'

She was pleased at this, and would have me take a makeshift tea with her, but that I insisted upon the urgency of some other business I must attend to.

'You will not mind,' said Banks, as we put on our coats in the hall of his mother's house in Chelsea, 'if I just look in upon Collins before we go.'

I said that I did not mind, and so we turned aside into the front room which Banks's mother had temporarily surrendered to her son's expeditionary preparations. There were charts on the wall, and upon the central table a sextant and a number of brass measuring instruments. And perched like a gangling bird on a stool by the table sat Collins the apothecary, inspecting a sheaf of papers. Banks went across to him, and they put their heads together over these papers, falling at once into conference upon the details of those items listed there, which to judge by their talk were the implements and potions that Collins recommended as necessary for the botanizing that Banks intended during the expedition. Some of these Collins had already ordered, and some he had in stock; and though Banks had the experience of his Labrador expedition behind him, yet was it evident that he leaned upon Collins's advice. There was a businesslike understanding between them, and they might have talked together for some good while longer except that Banks saw my impatience to be away. After fifteen minutes, we were finally from the house and strolling though the Physic Garden and down toward Ranelagh near the river.

As we walked, Banks talked; and his talk was all of his great hopes of the expedition, and the thousand preparations he must make. At another time such talk might have been a tonic to me. The world was opening before him in an endless vista of possibilities, and never was a man more ready to embrace his opportunity than he. It filled his whole mind, which I think is why we were almost to the end of the Garden before he realized that I had not spoken a word since leaving the house.

'But I am embarked upon no expedition, but only a damnable lecture,' said he apologetically.

I answered that I would cheerfully have him re-embark, for I was very happy to know that there was some better horizon in the world than my own thoughts.

'Is it Wilkes?'

I glanced at him. I knew that he had some knowledge of my work, though he never enquired such things of me directly at this time. But howsoever the knowledge of it came to him, I never doubted of his kindly feeling toward me. 'In part,' said I.

'And in part, it is Mademoiselle Beauchamp,' said he; but upon seeing my expression change, and for the worse, he began to beg my pardon that he had spoken.

'You must not apologize, Joseph.'

'I meant no interference.'

'I cannot whimper like a child at every mention of her. I must brave the shot till I get such scars that I no longer feel it.'

We walked now in silence along the avenue of pleached hornbeams, the lamplight shining brightly from every window of the Ranelagh dome up ahead, and from the torches in the garden. There were several carriages went by us, and as we came near to where they had halted by the entrance gate I made some idle remark upon the music we might hear tonight, and what acquaintances might be here. But Banks had yet that other matter in mind.

'Alistair,' said he. 'I think you cannot have heard it, but Mademoiselle Beauchamp shall be in England next week.' I stopped. 'No. I see that you had not heard. I had thought it possible that she had written to you. I had Buffon's letter on it only this morning.'

'She comes with Buffon?'

'She will be with her father. He comes as an envoy from Versailles. They will stay as guests of Lord Shelburne while they are here.'

'It is no good time to come,' said I, and spoke of the troubles there must be over Wilkes's election, while I thought, I confess, on the cannonade that her near presence must be to me.

Banks told me that the Vicomte and his daughter would go out to Bowood House in Wiltshire, and that any trouble caused by Wilkes's mob in London would not touch them there. 'She will be quite safe, Alistair. I would never have mentioned it, but that if you must brave the shot, as you say, it is best you should know its direction.'

We paid our shillings and passed into the Ranelagh Gardens.

At the Chinese pavilion there were many lanterns hung, and many torches planted, so that yellow streamers of light rippled prettily in the pond nearby. But though there were a number of people promenading on the paths there, I could not find Mrs Watts or her party, and so after we had taken a turn about the pond we went into the rotunda. The best part of the town's society had come to hear some old music of Mr Handel, but the band was not settled yet, and so the great space was filled only with the sound of voices, the noise rising from the crowd to be lost in the lantern-lit dome far above us.

'I might have remained at home with my beetles,' Banks whispered in my ear, though in truth he was always very comfortable in such a gathering (which was not true of his beloved sister), and quite happy to move with me now into the throng. We met very soon with a party of Banks's acquaintance from the Royal Society, and after conversing there awhile, we joined another group, which was mainly Admiralty men and their wives. Here Banks buttonholed Sir Philip Stephens, a secretary at the Admiralty, and while these two talked very earnestly of the expeditionary ship that Stephens was now negotiating the purchase of on the King's behalf, I made polite conversation with Lady Stephens and ran my gaze about the rotunda till at last I espied Mrs Watts.

The bandmaster announced the first piece. When the music commenced, there was a minute attention given the players before the conversations restarted, and then people moved about as freely as before. I extracted Banks from his conversation with Stephens and guided him to where Mrs Watts stood with Lady Shelburne, and Barre and his wife, and Laughlin Macleane.

Lady Shelburne congratulated Banks on securing the King's backing for the expedition. Banks owned that it was the good offices of Mr Jenkinson had won the King to the cause.

'But I am sure all your conversation that evening with Buffon concerning de Bougainville's expedition was not wasted upon Mr Jenkinson,' said Mrs Watts, smiling; and at Banks's light-hearted protest that it had certainly been no strategy, she remarked that no strategy was perhaps the best strategy of all.

Barre with his usual gruff directness enquired what opinion I had on Wilkes, and whether it was likely he should be elected, and, if he was, whether I thought the ministry should let him take his seat in the new Parliament.

'You know more of any parliamentary business than I, sir.'

'That may be, Mr Douglas. But it is not Parliament will decide the question. And what is this I have heard of Wilkes offering to present himself at the King's Bench court next session?'

'The betting is that he will get a seat in Middlesex,' said Macleane.

'And have you wagered upon it?' asked Lady Shelburne, with an outward tone quite jesting; but in her look was something very like distrust of her husband's man of business.

'I wager only upon certainties, My Lady. And that is not Mr Wilkes.'

She made no answer to this, but turned from him to converse with Mrs Watts upon the building works at the house in Berkeley Square that her husband had purchased from Lord Bute, and all the excavations at Bowood House, and the replanting of the park there. 'I sometimes wonder,' said she, 'if I shall ever live in a house fully completed. But you shall come out to see us out at Bowood next month, Mr Banks. You must advise my husband on the planting.'

'If all goes well, I shall have then a ship in Deptford for refitting, My Lady. I regret that I must therefore remain in London.'

'Then you shall come, Mr Douglas.'

Banks said quickly, 'Mr Douglas has promised me his assistance while the refitting is under way. If I were to release him, I should pay the price of it the whole voyage. I hope you would not be so unkind to me, My Lady.'

She would not. But she had from me a promise that I should come to Bowood very soon, and from Banks an undertaking that he should spend a week of recuperation there upon his return from the great expedition. Our conversation continued now in this lighter vein, till at the next stop in the music Banks excused himself, and went to seek out Stephens again. One of those entertainers employed in the rotunda then approached us, and Lady Shelburne beckoning him forward, he stepped into our midst with a deck of cards splayed open in his fingers like a fan. His sleight of hand was very deft, almost the equal of a remarkable old Spaniard I had once seen in a canteen in Havana. The women took turns to choose the card that the fellow should make magically disappear from his left hand, only to reappear in his right. Mrs Watts, in the most natural manner possible, and which even I hardly noticed, then obliged Barre to become involved in one trick. And while he held the several cards, she asked Macleane if he and I might fetch some refreshment, for the press of people and the closed doors and windows had made the place now uncommonly warm, she said.

'I have twenty pounds riding on our friend Wilkes,' said Macleane, when we were out of earshot of the others. 'My only regret is that it might have been a hundred.'

'I have given some thought to our conversation at the theatre,' said I. 'Is it possible that we might take a private turn outside?'

'How much do you have?'

'I should not like to risk it all.'

'It is Company stock, Mr Douglas, not the gaming table.'

'The price is very high at present, is it not?'

'Very high against what it was last year. Very low against what it will be next.'

'And you are in,' said I, that he might think me wary, but still a fool.

'I am. And shall be in deeper. While the stock runs, only a coward or a lunatic would keep his money tied up in his purse.'

'And Barre?'

'I respect Barre's privacy as I shall respect yours.'

'It was not to pry.'

'Of course,' said he.

'If I could only have some assurance—'

'My word is your assurance. And if that be insufficient, we need talk no more but return directly inside,' said he, a little haughty. I put on my face now some appearance of thought. And Macleane upon his own some appearance of indifference.

'I am in,' I declared at last, and told him then of the bill I held for two thousand pounds.

'It is no fortune,' said he. 'But if we are quick – I believe there is some line of stock to that amount I may secure within the next few days. I am taking the bigger lot myself, but there may be sufficient left over. Mind, we cannot delay.'

'Days? I am not sure—'

He recited me some nonsense of the Exchange, and ended by saying that I must see the reason of haste.

'Yes, I well see the reason,' said I. 'But I have a doubt that the drawer of my bill shall pay such a sum at so little notice.'

'If the bill is good, and the fellow wish to keep his reputation, he shall pay.' We stopped then, for we had been walking all this while, and now stood near the little bridge over to the Chinese pavilion in the pond. There were some gentlemen in the pavilion, with their ladies, and now Macleane put his arm through mine and turned us back toward the rotunda. 'You are certain that the bill is good, Mr Douglas?'

'There is nothing wrong with the bill.'

'Then you may get cash for it in the City.'

'I will not sell it at a discount.'

'Then take it to the drawer, and he shall pay you. Come, this is to make a difficulty where none can be. If you have some aversion to presenting the bill – why, I shall present it myself.'

'That is very obliging of you, sir. But I think, too much to ask of you.' When he deprecated his offer with a brisk wave of the hand, I added, 'But perhaps, if you are willing, you might make my intention known to the drawer. If he is forewarned, there will be no chance that he be embarrassed by want of funds when I present the bill.'

'And if he is forewarned by me,' said Macleane, thinking he had finally discovered the bottom of my manoeuvring, 'he shall then make no difficulty with the payment.'

'I have the bill on me now, if you would see it.'

He seemed almost amused now at the stratagem, and as we stopped beneath a lamp fixed to the exterior wall of the rotunda, I showed him the bill, saying, 'Hayley is the merchant. You will find him invariably at the Jamaica House coffee shop at eleven each morning. I would not have him know my name till I present the bill.'

He studied the bill by the lamplight.

'I am sure the bill is good,' said I.

'Yes, I am sure,' said he.

'Perhaps I might wait.'

'No.' He returned the bill to me. 'No, we must not wait. We will lose our opportunity.'

'Only if you are sure.'

'I will call upon Mr Hayley tomorrow.'

It was two hours later that I rode with Mrs Watts in her chaise from the Ranelagh Gardens. I held the hand-grip by the door and stared out at the night, thinking that Mrs Watts dozed, till she said, 'Do you mean to tell me how you fared with Mr Macleane?'

'He thinks that I will be worth four votes in the Company to him.'

'Which you will not.'

'Which I will not.' The chaise rocked, and Mrs Watts now took the hand-grip upon her side. I said, 'I am obliged to you that you brought him down. And for ridding me of Barre.'

'You might ask my assistance more often, Alistair.'

'There is not often the need.'

'I know.' Now she looked from me and out at the night, and I saw that there was some melancholy or regret upon her. I do not think it had occurred to me till then that Mr Watts's death had robbed her of not only a husband but also an occupation. She said, 'I expect that Banks has told you that Mademoiselle Beauchamp will stay with Lady Shelburne. And that is why he saved you from the invitation to Bowood.'

I nodded.

'I will leave London with Lady Shelburne tomorrow, Alistair. Lord Shelburne will join us later with Mademoiselle Beauchamp and the Vicomte. If there was some message, I might pass it to her.'

'There is no message.'

'Alistair—'

'I will not be a plague upon her life. There is no message for the lady.'

CHAPTER TWENTY-EIGHT

I alighted from my hackney the next morning just by the Mansion House, and being early I then wandered along Cornhill past Wilkes's headquarters at the King's Arms. Here were so many people gathered that a number of small tables had been put out onto the pavement, and benches also, and these were crowded now with young gentlemen sporting blue cockades in their hats, and with hair tied back with blue ribbons. It seemed to me that many of these fellows were students come down from university, or pupils come over from the Inns of Court. For a certainty there were no coal heavers among them. Hand-bills were plastered up in the tavern window, and Wilkes's name visible from across the street. Men came and went with yet more handbills, and there was an air of merry madness over the place.

I went on by and came back to linger near the turning into St Michael's Alley, down which was the Jamaica House coffee shop. It was a half-hour later, and almost eleven o'clock, when Hayley came down from the direction of the King's Arms. He was alone. There had been a servant tipped out some chamber pots in the corner gutter, and Hayley now put a white kerchief up to his nose and stepped wide as he turned in to the alley and then along to the coffee house.

It was but fifteen minutes more I waited before Macleane arrived. He also came alone, and spoke to the jarvey as he got down, at which the fellow cradled his whip and settled his reins as if to wait there for his client's return. Macleane then went down the street, and into the alley, and I watched him into the coffee shop.

I stayed in this place where I might have a view down the alley and myself unobserved; but while I watched and waited, a lad passed with a sheaf of newspapers beneath his arm, and crying, 'Lord Baltimore! Lord Baltimore! Mr Wilkes! Lord Baltimore!' and so I called him to me and bought one of the papers. It was the *Public Advertiser*, which frequently published Wilkes's letters.

I kept one eye upon the alley as I turned the loose sheets. Wilkes's latest letter (and perhaps the most portentous he had written) was upon the second page, following on from the extensive report of Lord Baltimore's trial for the rape of that milliner girl the past winter. And this letter of Wilkes's was reported to be a duplicate of that which he had sent to the solicitor general. In it he made a bald promise to deliver himself to the King's Bench court towards the end of April. It was a confirmation of Mrs Porter's information to me, and of Barre's speculation at the Ranelagh Gardens the previous night. And coming as it did from the pen of an outlaw, it was a letter, and a promise, of a quite breathtaking impudence. For it was as much as to publicly declare that he and not the ministry would dictate the time of his arrest. There was more in the paper concerning Wilkes, and something of the troubles between the watermen and coal heavers in Wapping and Shadwell, but nothing to match Wilkes's remarkable letter, and so I soon put the paper by. Francis would know better than I the implications of it, and I must go to him in the Lane when I was done with Hayley.

Twenty minutes after entering the Jamaica House coffee shop, Macleane came out from there, and back up the alley, and then he stepped straight into his waiting hackney, and away. And in the next minute came Hayley from the coffee house. And he turned not towards me up the lane as I had expected, but south. There was a hurry in his step now such as I had never observed in him before, and I was in no doubt but that he was badly shaken.

I had thought it must be Wilkes at the King's Arms, or someone close to Wilkes, to whom Hayley would run to tell the tale. I was wrong in that, but I was not wrong in the greater matter. For Hayley most certainly knew it was no ordinary bill that Macleane had warned him was about to be presented. He knew exactly where that bill had come from; but how he knew it, and the nature of his connection with Pearce and Flanagan, these I must only pray now that he was frightened enough to help me discover. I hurried across the street and followed him down St Michael's.

He never looked about him but went straight on, and into Lombard Street, and where he should lead me after this, I had no notion. I began to calculate where I might find the nearest chair-men, or whether it might be quicker to get a horse from the Post Office stable. But twenty yards ahead of me, Hayley turned off the street in through a large door there, and I stopped.

I had no need to go on, for the place was one well known to me. It was but thirty yards along from the Post Office and the Lane. But though it was known to me, yet it provided no answer, but rather a sense of stumbling upon a deeper darkness. For it was the Accompting House of a certain City fellow, who was Lord Sandwich's man of business.

'Hayley might have any number of reasons to call upon Jones.'

'He was not calling upon him. He ran to Jones the moment that Macleane left the coffee shop.'

'Alistair,' said Francis, attempting to play the part of reason. 'You cannot be certain what was said between Macleane and Hayley.'

'But I have told you.'

'You have told me what you believe was said.'

In the stable yard outside the window, the last of the Post Office coaches was being hitched and made ready for the midday post. The head groom shouted down from the balcony at the stable lad fixing the harness. Just along from the groom, Gus passed into the

Messengers' room with a satchel of letters newly come from our translators, and ready for Meadows to have taken up to the King and the ministry.

'Allow that you are right,' said Francis. 'May it not be that Jones has some commercial interest in the bill? There are a thousand possibilities.'

'It is only the one possibility that concerns me. And you know it as well as I. It is our new Post Master.'

Francis reminded me that Jones had clients other than Lord Sandwich.

'There is something in it, Francis.'

'If there is, you have not revealed it. But what shall you do now?' It was a question I had not answered yet in my own mind. I said that I supposed Jenkinson should be told. 'But you do not wish to tell him?' said he.

'I cannot think who should be trusted among them. If I tell Jenkinson, do I thereby reveal myself to Sandwich? And to Carrington?'

'You will tell my father,' said Francis decidedly. 'And while I make the arrangement, you will please dig yourself no deeper into the mire.'

While I waited for Francis to make the arrangement, that I might go to the Bishop in person, I sent word to Macleane that I was indisposed for several days, but would call upon him directly I was free from the press of other business. Though what my other business might be at this time was a question very difficult to answer; for now that Jenkinson had shut his door against me, and removed any Messengers from my charge, I had no proper instruction, nor yet the means to carry out an instruction if it came. As to Wilkes, his campaign for the Middlesex election was proceeding so openly, and with such a universal acceptance that he should succeed, that the position of the ministry was now farcical. That they were in too great a fear of the mob to now arrest him was evident to every person in London; and by his public announcement that he would deliver himself up to the King's Bench court near the end of April, he had secured himself a few weeks more of absolute freedom during which he would surely continue a public spectacle and an affront to lawful authority in the kingdom. And my part in the farce was now that of a walk-on player who must wait offstage, arms folded, and watch the principals work toward their unpredictable conclusion.

Having a concern not to meet with Macleane at this time, I kept from the Watts house and all of that part of society, and ventured out only twice, which was to visit Kitty Langridge and to pay a call upon Banks. From Kitty Langridge I learned that the troubles down by the river continued, but mingled now with the discontent of the Spital-fields weavers whose prices had fallen on account of the Company's March sale. She expressed no fear to be living in a place grown such a regular scene of violence, saying that the men never gave her any trouble, and that her greater concern was the expense of bread, which was an abiding worry that often kept her from sleep. Nor would she take any money from me at first, and relented only at my firm insis-tence that she would have it for her child's sake, and accept it also as the due of her departed husband.

At Banks's house in New Burlington Street, I was pleased to spend an entire afternoon and evening in sitting at my sketchbook by his cabinets. Banks gave me then no disturbance, but came and went in pursuit of his preparations, sometimes with his friend Solander, some-times alone, and always in a great hurry. Those few times when he stopped to talk with me, it was of my sketch, or the specimen before me, or his expedition, and not a word of the Parliament or the ministry or Wilkes. He easily extracted from me a promise that I would come to see his ship when it arrived for its refitting in Deptford, that I not make a liar of him before Lady Shelburne.

It was the following morning, and the day of the Middlesex elec-tion, that I received a note from Francis to say that the Bishop expected me at his palace in Wells five days hence. And it was but an hour later, in the midst of my preparations for departure, that Mrs Porter called at my door.

'I wouldn't have troubled you, Mr Douglas, only the Museum is so near.'

'Your diligence is no trouble to me, Mrs Porter. But you are sure of the girl's name?'

'Pitou, sir. Wilkes's man was very much put out by her.'

We made haste into Bloomsbury, and I with some disquiet at the arrival of Wilkes's French mistress in London at such a time. I asked if it was the first time she had seen the girl.

'Yesterday she came to him twice. It was only last night that Wilkes's man told me she was French. When she left Wilkes this morning, I came after her. She came to the Museum here, and you being so close by . . . She is a pretty girl.'

'She is a trollop.'

'I supposed so, sir. She could not like Wilkes for his face.'

There was a loud cry from the street behind us, and we stepped aside as a line of three coaches rattled by, the coachmen's whips entwined in blue ribbon, and handbills for 'Wilkes and Liberty' fixed to the doors. A young fellow put his head jauntily from one window to enquire if I was a freeholder, and, if I was, whether I wished transport out to the hustings at Brentford. I declined, and he withdrew, and the coaches carried on westward.

As we approached the gates of the Museum (which was then but the old Montagu House without extension), we saw four carriages waiting before the main steps, and so we stopped outside the gates.

'Will you go in, sir?'

'Is that a crest there, Mrs Porter? Upon the first carriage.'

'I never saw it, sir,' she said in apology; but she peered now, and then said, 'Is it Lord Shelburne's, sir?'

But even as she spoke, there were several people came to the Museum door, and so I turned Mrs Porter from the gates. Across the street was a bookseller with a window facing the Museum. Once inside, I pretended to examine the leather-bound folios near to the front window, while Mrs Porter kept the bookseller busy with some rambling enquiry at his counter.

The party on the Museum steps was led by Lady Shelburne. Nor was it a surprise to me to see Mrs Watts and her daughter Amelia keep her company, nor Barre and his wife; I had myself sometimes joined them on such an excursion, either to the Museum or to a lecture at the Society of Antiquaries. It was a great surprise, however, to see Mademoiselle Pitou come out and join with Lady Shelburne's party. And by reason of her standing so near to Lady Shelburne, though taking no part in the conversation, my first notion was that the girl had somehow inveigled herself into that lady's service. But then another woman came out onto the steps, and Pitou went and stood with her.

'Pitou is wearing the red,' said Mrs Porter quietly, for she had now dispatched the bookseller on a search of his shelves. 'And who is her mistress there?'

The whole party now moved down the steps and separated, and Pitou now at the heels of the young woman undoubtedly her mistress, for they climbed into a carriage together. The line of carriages then made a wide turn before the Museum and came out the gates and down the street and away.

When I had recovered myself, I took Mrs Porter outside. I told her that she might now return to Dover, for we had now done all that we could in our observation of Wilkes. 'If they have not arrested him before today, it is certain they will not arrest him after. They will wait till he present himself at the King's Bench.'

'The French girl—'

'She is nothing in this.' I felt Mrs Porter's eyes upon me, but she made no open challenge to my judgement. 'I am grateful, as always, Mrs Porter, for your care. But your duty is done for the present. You may leave your keys when you take the Dover coach from the Lane.'

Returned to my own house, I slumped into an armchair with a yoke of lead upon my shoulders. Mademoiselle Pitou, Wilkes's whore, was now the maid of Valerie Beauchamp. The fact was so strange that I should not have believed it had I not been witness to it with my own eyes. Nor could I begin to discern its meaning, so great was my shock. It came to me that I must speak with Mrs Watts, or Francis, and that someone with no affectionate engagement must help me see my way clearly; but hardly had the idea arrived than I dismissed it, for to mention this newly discovered connection to anyone must be to cast an ugly suspicion over Valerie Beauchamp's name, which is what I would not do. And yet how must I act? For if to reveal the connection was wrong, it was equally counter to my sworn duty to conceal it; and so I was like the ass between two bales of straw, looking from one side to the other, but remaining fixed by an idiot confusion. After an hour, and I no further on, I took up my satchel in disgust and departed my house for the livery yard, and with some forlorn hope that I might clear my mind upon the road.

CHAPTER TWENTY-NINE

*T*he Great West Road towards Bath was also that day the route of Wilkes's supporters to the Brentford Butts for the Middlesex election, but I was surprised to be among them – and they in such great numbers – just as soon as I came to the Hyde Park Corner. They had gathered not only on the pavement, but wandered the highway as if it were a village green; and no coach could pass freely but each was stopped and the number 45 chalked on its doors, and the passengers made to pay a forfeit, which was to shout for Wilkes, before they might pass on.

By a few judicious cries of 'Liberty!', and the purchase of a blue ribbon from a flower girl who then tied it about my wrist, I was quickly through them. But though they seemed then in high spirits, I noticed among them that giant they called the Infant, and several of his chairmen, and they holding one coach to a jocular ransom. I well knew then just how quickly the high spirits might sour, and so was not surprised when I later heard how these same ruffians, at this same spot, had pulled the Austrian ambassador from his coach some hours after my passing, and held him suspended by his ankles while they painted the numbers 4 and 5 upon the soles of his boots. Along that first part of the road, to Chiswick and beyond, this number 45 was chalked on most of the house doors, as if to mark out a triumphal avenue for Wilkes.

At Brentford I turned briefly aside to the Butts, where many coaches and chairs were stopped, and where a crowd of some several hundred people were gathered peacefully in the square. Wilkes was upon the hustings set up on the road and facing the green. It being now past midday, the polling had long since commenced but was not yet closed; and as each elector went towards the voting table, Wilkes and the other two candidates spoke with them from the hustings, but mildly and in no wise hectoring.

I took a cordial in the square, for the day was warm, and then I strolled among the people to hear what was said. And from every quarter the judgement was repeated, that Wilkes had surely won, and the only point of contention now seemed to be which of the two others should take the second Middlesex seat. Then a curious thing happened, which was that a young lad touched my arm to stop me, saying, 'Sir, Mr Wilkes asks if you have voted yet, sir. And if you haven't, he asks if he may rely upon your vote.'

In some surprise, I looked toward the hustings. Wilkes, his hands upon the railing, had his face turned in my direction. And cross-eyed though he was, I was in no doubt of his genial smile being directed over the heads of the milling journeymen and at me. He raised his blue tricorn, and bowed his head to me very gentlemanly.

'You may assure Mr Wilkes,' said I to the lad, 'that whensoever I choose to vote, it shall always be for Liberty.'

He weaved his way back through the crowd to the hustings and I watched him give Wilkes my answer. Which when he had heard, Wilkes looked at me again. I nodded to him, very gentlemanly, he turned his back upon me, and then I left the Butts and went to fetch my horse.

I was at my breakfast at an inn on the road the next morning when a coach arrived there with news positive that Wilkes had been elected, and that there had been some small celebratory rioting in the west end of town and near the Mansion House in the City. The Wilkites had evidently gone about demanding illuminations to be set in the windows of all the private houses as a tribute to their man, and had promptly smashed those windows whenever the owners had refused to comply. The coachman and the innkeeper soon gave up on their attempt to involve me in their discussion of Wilkes's triumph over the ministry, and within the hour I set out again upon the West Road.

There were many miles I travelled almost without noticing, for in my eye was ever the picture of Valerie at the Museum steps, and the Pitou girl with her, playing the part of her maid, and though I searched continually for some good reason for this strange pairing, yet there was nothing that sufficed to quiet my deep disturbance of spirit.

I scarcely slept through the nights either, at the inns where I stayed, and whilst I rode in the daytime I made no effort to converse with the other riders that I met on the road, nor even with the gentlemen and ladies from the coaches when I happened to share their wayside rest.

Nearer Bath, I was surprised from my heavy thoughts by a young fellow rising from his sitting place by the road to hail me. He was a lad dressed in livery, and he looked very much out of place there, so far from any habitation. He asked if I had passed a certain red coach in the last several miles, for he was awaiting his mistress, and feared that she might not come now before nightfall. He looked very down cast when I answered him. He was little more than a boy, and I gave him some bread from my saddlebag and advised him to return to his mistress's house directly, for there was no place near about where he might take shelter for the night. I asked if the house was very far.

'Not so very,' said he. 'It is two miles to Calne, and two more again to Bowood.'

'Your mistress is the Lady Shelburne.'

'Yes, sir.'

A little more conversation, and I discovered that he was from the Bowood lodge-house, and sent out by his father. I gave him a shilling, saying that he must eat properly when he reached Calne, which though he was surprised at, he thanked me with a touch to his brow. We parted, and I with a hope that he should remember me with a friendly feeling, for I was determined now, and on the instant, that I should go to Bowood once I had seen the Bishop, and make an end of the mystery that had preyed upon me since London.

I made good time into Bath, where I had some difficulty in finding a bed owing to the great multitude of people come out from London to pursue fashionable entertainment in the interim between Parliaments. (And also, though few would confess it, the recent disorders in the City had caused some fright, and there were those only too happy to shut up their London houses awhile.) From Bath the next day I rode down to Wells, arriving at the gates to the Bishop's palace near midday.

'May I have your shoulder, Mr Douglas?' The Bishop rested a hand upon me for support, and we walked now down the north path of the palace's walled garden very slowly. He had taken a fall since I had seen him in Lambeth, and though his present infirmity would surely pass, yet I found that I was myself a little shaken to find him so weakened; for it was undeniably his years upon him, and a reminder, should I need it, of the mortality of every one of us. 'God Himself first planted a garden,' said he, admiring the green shoots pushing up through the turned earth. 'Were I a wiser man I might have taken more time in following His example.' I was silent, and he said, 'In a garden is no authority but only God's. You will see my experiment with the trained vine there. A complete failure. I shall try again next winter. One must live forever upon hope in a garden.' I thought of Valerie that day in Buffon's herb garden in Paris, and the Bishop, through his hand upon my shoulder, felt the change in me. 'But it is not to hear my homilies you have come, Mr Douglas.'

'I believe Francis has written you, My Lord.'

'He has,' said he; but then spoke nothing more to help me.

'I hardly know where I shall begin.'

'You may begin where you will, Mr Douglas. I have put by the afternoon. There is no hurry.'

And so I began with Langridge's murder at the Greenland Dock.

It was an hour and more we remained in the walled garden, and much of the time seated on a bench near the whitewashed dovecote at its centre, from which place we could see the garden door, and the two gardeners working by the wall there. The Bishop made scarce any interruption, but lifted his head back and half-closed his eyes as if to enjoy the warmth of the sun while he listened. As I related the tale of my watch over Wilkes in both Paris and London, my pursuit of Pearce and Flanagan, and Carrington's continued obstructions, Fitzherbert's carelessness and Jenkinson's lack of trust in me, and all these crowned by the final discovery of the apparent involvement of Lord Sandwich's man of business, I was ever more certain that I had done right to come here to put the great tangle of affairs before the Bishop.

'And the morning I left London, Wilkes was visited by that same French girl he had kept in Paris,' I concluded, and with a hope it must be thrown into the shade by the greater matters I had just now related.

'The girl Pitou. She who brought you word of his flight from Paris?' said he, and when I confirmed it, adding that I did not believe she had any connection with this business of Pearce and Flanagan, he said, 'Perhaps not. But when you return to the Lane, you will write her into the List. She is evidently in the pay of the Cabinet Noir.'

'That cannot be certain.'

The Bishop raised an eyebrow. He had no doubt at all, and that only from what I had told him, that the girl worked as a secret agent of the French ministry. And nor, in my heart, did I.

'I shall place her on the List, My Lord.'

'You have pursued no enquiry of Sandwich's man of business.'

'None. But Carrington has known for some time where Pearce and Flanagan might be found. If I guess right, Lord Sandwich has known it too.'

'It will need more than a guess to stand against an earl.'

'Pearce and Flanagan have been protected.'

'That is your judgement.'

'It is, My Lord,' said I very firmly.

'I little wonder,' said he, 'at the vexation you have caused Mr Jenkinson. Lend me your arm if you will, Mr Douglas.' We rose from the bench and went slowly along the path, stopping several times for the Bishop to examine the work done by his gardeners. The speed with which he had made the connection between Pitou and the Cabinet Noir alarmed me somewhat. For how long should it be now before Pitou's association with Valerie be known, and Valerie herself put down in the List?

As we made our gentle circuit of the garden, the Bishop questioned me on every loose thread of the perplexing entanglement with those Sons of Liberty that I had put before him, so that when he had done I had told him near everything I knew. And very clear it was to me by then that his mind took no part in his body's infirmity.

We broke off at last when his secretary came to fetch him to the cathedral.

All the rest of that day, and the greater part of the next, the Bishop was fully occupied with some other affairs, and with the business of his See, and so I was left in idleness. There were others staying in the palace as the Bishop's guests, for such a place is treated by travelling lords and ladies as a superior kind of inn; but these I avoided, which was an easy enough matter, for the palace was large, and with several parts quite separate. But by the end of that second day I was grown very restive, for a light but continual rain had kept me inside for some hours, and in that time I had exhausted what little diversion was to be had from a solitary wandering of the galleries. My sketchbook likewise had not its usual power to divert me, and when the Bishop's messenger came to me that evening he found me lying upon the chaise longue, my stockinged feet resting upon the arm, the sketchbook closed upon the floor by my boots, and my gaze fixed upon the ceiling.

'The Bishop's compliments, sir. The Bishop trusts that you shall be ready to accompany him tomorrow. He will leave for Bath at ten o'clock.'

I told the fellow that he might instruct the groom of my departure, and assure the Bishop of my readiness to join him at that hour.

*   *   *

The Bishop called me up into his carriage with him, and bade his footman ride behind us on my horse. The carriage had hardly moved away from the palace steps when the Bishop addressed me.

'I have that to say to you which I would not have interrupted.' It was spoken very solemnly, so that I felt a tightening of apprehension in my chest. 'I think you must know the great concern that your report has given me. You cannot know, however, the many reasons for that concern. I have taken considerable thought on it, and I have decided that you must be told that which in any other circumstance I would not have you know. But I must require of you that that which I open to you now shall remain closed hereafter. I hope that you understand me.' His gaze, which had been fixed ahead, he now directed at me where I sat at the opposite corner of the carriage. I inclined my head, and he continued.

'To begin with the least matter – the troubles you have had with Mr Carrington are no surprise to me. For I fear he must know – from Mr Fitzherbert's loose tongue I must presume – what you do not know. That is, that you were brought back from your duties in the American colonies with the hope that you might become a replacement to Mr Carrington as the chief of the King's Messengers.' I made a sound of astonishment, for how should I stay silent at such a revelation? The Bishop raised a finger to stay any question. 'At the time you were recalled, Mr Carrington appeared to have done a fatal harm to his position by his overly zealous dealings with the printers. That is no matter here. Enough to say that he has made sure of himself again since that time. I tell you this only that you may see Mr Carrington's distrust of you in a true light.'

'May I speak, My Lord?'

'No.' He looked out of the window, and I had never seen such a strain upon his face. He did not like to address me so openly. Nor could I easily suppress my desire to question him. But with my newfound knowledge, when I thought of the whole course of my dealings with Carrington, so much was made clear to me that was before hidden in shadows. He must ruin me to save his own position. He was an enemy to me before I had even arrived in London the last autumn. And that fellow who had followed me to Dover, and in Shadwell – that must surely be but a part of Carrington's need to arm himself against me. But though I understood so much more, and that at once, with understanding came no forgiveness; it rather served to lay a better foundation for my contempt of the King's chief Messenger. We came to the end of the palace's driveway and into the parkland, and the grazing deer there startled at our passing. As they disappeared into a fold in the ground and were lost from our sight, the Bishop turned back from the window. 'The greater matter is this. Since Chatham's retreat from Westminster, the government has had no firm hand over it. Grafton would rather be at his leisure, and there are no few others too happy to join him there. This weakness at the head, I fear, has made the body fractious. All this last year there has been such a shifting for places and preferment as the country has hardly witnessed since the passing of Walpole. It has been an underground river running violent through Westminster and the Court. I need not rehearse every name to you, but you know already that Bedford's people are well to the front of it. I am at my prayers every day to give thanks that I secured Mr Jenkinson early to us.'

'My Lord—'

'No. I am come now to the main point, and you shall listen.' He looked at me now with a directness that I must struggle to meet. 'The Decipherers are not like to any other part of the government. Let the Northern and Southern departments be led by whom you will, the kingdom may be hurt, but it will not be poisoned. But once give the wrong man sway over the Deciphering Branch, and there must come such a malignancy into the kingdom that I do quake to think of it.

'While I have been over Fitzherbert and the others, I have had no concern. But look at me now, Mr Douglas. Do you see a young man before you? Do you see a man who will live ten years more, and with his faculties secure?'

'I cannot say, My Lord.'

'No more can I. And that is why I have chosen Mr Jenkinson. He is a rising man, and near to the King. He may do what my sons cannot.

I have but a few years left me now to guide him. It will be no easy position to him when I am gone. And if Mr Jenkinson seems not so congenial to you as was Watts, or even Fitzherbert, then I tell you, Mr Douglas, that is nothing to me. And it must be nothing to you either, if you are to continue your work with us.' He leaned back in his seat. I waited awhile, but he only gazed out from the window now, silent.

'May I speak, My Lord?'

'You may speak.'

'I would never wish to lead the King's Messengers.'

'The place is not offered you. Carrington has secured himself again and will not be displaced.'

We continued then several minutes in a general silence while I reflected – as I am sure the Bishop intended – upon all of my dealings till now with Jenkinson. Indeed, so intent was I upon these reflections that I hardly noticed our carriage slowing till we were almost at a stop. And when I looked to the Bishop for some explanation of it, I found him already studying me. The carriage had stopped entirely. Outside was a keeper's lodge, with no garden but only the cropped parkland grass going up to its stone walls. The thatched roof was old, and there was a fern drooping from one gable-end.

'You will get down here,' said the Bishop.

'My Lord?'

He did not wait for the footman, but opened the door for me. I hesitated, and then in some perplexity got down. Then it was that the door of the keeper's lodge opened, and out from there came the fellow I might least have expected to find in such a place.

'Mr Douglas,' said he.

'Mr Jenkinson,' said I.

'You will make an accommodation now,' said the Bishop to me quietly, 'or you must leave the Decipherers.' He pulled shut the carriage door and left me there.

CHAPTER THIRTY

*J*enkinson had been in Bath when he received the Bishop's summons, and it was to Bath that I returned with Jenkinson that same evening. I will not say that we rode together in any great friendliness, for the words we had spoken each to the other in the keeper's lodge had been very frank, so that I made no doubt now of his expectation of my better obedience, and nor was he in any doubt that I could not work but with an independence that he was little accustomed to allowing either to me or any other subordinate. But above this was the immediate necessity that we act undivided, in accord with the Bishop's will. For the troubles then crowding upon us were great ones, and many. And in truth, I knew even then that Jenkinson's loyalty to the King was the fixed star of all his public exertions. If he sought his own aggrandizement (which he did) it was ever from the reflected glory of the Crown; so that when in the keeper's lodge we had discussed Lord Sandwich and Carrington, and Wilkes and those murdering Sons of Liberty, his whole concern was with the better safety of the kingdom. And this it was gave me hope, that in that common concern we might do as the Cherokee, and bury a hatchet in the ground between us to make a peace.

We came presently to the hills over Bath, and paused there to admire the town below, which in both its buildings and its situation is among the most delightful in the West Country. The late afternoon sun lit the pale stone of the abbey, and also the Pump Room and baths. The church bells were sounding, some carriages and horses moved along the London Road, and there were still many trees on the higher slope where now are only houses.

'Will you not come down to see Mr Wilkes?'

I replied that I had seen quite enough of the fellow.

'He was last night in the Pump Room,' said Jenkinson. 'The insolence of the man is beyond anything.'

'A Member of Parliament may go where he will, sir.'

'His outlawry is not lifted yet. He is not sworn into the Parliament, and may never be.'

We made our farewells then, and with no mention of the better understanding we had come to between us, as if it were a fragile thing, and one which we both knew might be broken by an ill-chosen word. He turned his horse down into Bath, and I took the other track, which must lead me to the Great West Road and London, and no need for me to tell Jenkinson that I should travel by way of Bowood.

The lad whom I had sent from the Bowood lodge-house with my note to Mrs Watts was less than an hour gone, and brought me her written reply. After breaking the seal and quickly perusing the note, I asked the boy the direction of the river, which when he had told me I gave him a shilling and set out southward across the park.

Long-horned cattle grazed the spring grass, and the ash trees shimmered in new leaf. Though the swallows had not yet come, it was just such a day as I had often thought of, and even pined for, when I had been caught in the Appalachian snows, or wallowing through the Mississippi delta. But there was an inner cloud over my soul now, knowing a certain person so near and yet beyond my reach, and it was all one to me whether I was in the midst of beauty or a wasteland, for my heart could not get out from beneath the shadow. At the river I dismounted, and leading my horse upstream I soon discovered the summerhouse in a clearing by the riverbank.

It was half an hour before Mrs Watts came. Though not a formal gown, it was yet a very fine dress that she wore, crimson silk, and with a dark cloak thrown loose about her shoulders, so that it seemed she had risen from some occasion at the house and come in haste.

'I would say that this is unexpected, Alistair, only that it is more than that,' said she, emerging from the woodland path just by me.

I asked at once if Mademoiselle Beauchamp was at Bowood.

'She is at the house. And though I offered to pass a message for you, please do not ask me. I know now that her heart is set upon Cordet. I am sorry for it, Alistair, but it is the truth. And there is nothing I can do. Nor you, I think.'

'I have not come for that,' said I, but with the feeling of a knife having raked over my heart. 'Has she a maid?'

'Certainly.'

'Is it Mademoiselle Pitou?'

'It is. But how should you know her?'

'She was Wilkes's mistress when he was in Paris.'

'She is a girl.'

'It was she that I paid to inform me of Wilkes's flight. And now, when she was in London before you came here, the girl has called upon Wilkes again.'

Mrs Watts looked at me closely, and in puzzlement. She asked me what reason the girl might have for calling upon Wilkes, whether it was payment she sought, or some re-establishment in London of their Parisian arrangement. I confessed that I did not know. She enquired then whom I had told of this. I said that Jenkinson and the Bishop both knew, but that I had informed neither one of them about the girl's connection with Mademoiselle Beauchamp.

'Alistair,' said she, with a sad turn of the head.

'Pitou can have nothing to do with Valerie. It must be the Vicomte that she truly serves.'

'You cannot know that.'

'I am not come to discuss it, but to ask you to help me. The girl must be removed from Bowood.'

'But that is too much,' she said in surprise; and then she hesitated. She had not been as swift as the Bishop, but now she had reached the same mark. 'My God, but you believe Pitou is Cabinet Noir.'

'She has no business in Mademoiselle Beauchamp's service.'

'Alistair, pray hear yourself. She may not stay in Mademoiselle's service, but you have allowed her to wander Lord Shelburne's house, and he to have no word of warning from you? Alistair—'

'That is done.'

'What is in your mind? Half the ministry and Court must call here in their coming and going from Bath.'

'I need no lesson on it. We must drive the Pitou girl from the house, and neither embarrassment nor suspicion fall upon Mademoiselle Beauchamp.'

'It is no time to concern yourself over her mere embarrassment. Pitou must be got from here, and at once. Which you know as well as I.'

I was in some fear now lest Mrs Watts go directly to Lord Shelburne. For he would not hesitate to turn Pitou openly from his house, and that must put all the obloquy of it upon Pitou's mistress. And if that were to happen then Valerie's name must certainly be entered into the List along with that of her whorish maid.

We heard voices at the far side of the wood.

'You must let it be known that I am to call at Bowood this evening,' I said, picking up the reins of my horse and remounting. 'Make sure that Pitou hears it. If she is Cabinet Noir, she has my name already, from Paris. She will not wish to see me here.'

'Alistair—'

'For pity's sake, must I beg?' She looked up, startled, for I had spoken nothing like a friend. I saw that I had cut her, and I was instantly ashamed. 'Forgive me. It is only that I have no other that I may rely upon. And I cannot do this alone.'

She looked from me and into the woods. And when she faced me again, she said, 'I have had a letter from Sophie this morning. It might have brought me news of her ill-health, and a request for my swift return to London.'

Along from the lodge-house and by the stony road was a wooded place that had a fair prospect over the undulating ground and across to Bowood House. Through all the remainder of the day I waited here, and with my spyglass made a frequent survey of the scene. As with his house in London, Lord Shelburne had entered upon a great refurbishment and rebuilding, and there seemed two large parties of workmen employed here, one by the stream working with shovels and horses, and scouring the earth as though they meant to make a lake there, and the other a party of masons up by the main house and working to join this main house to a lesser close by. All the ground to the front of the house had been recently reshaped, and no grass yet grew there, so that from a distance it appeared that a plough had been put over the best lawns. Several times during the day a small group of Lord Shelburne's guests came out from the main house and walked down to see the work proceeding at the stream. And there was a party of several riders rode out from the stables at midday, and returned then in ones and twos through the early afternoon. A pair of coaches arrived at the house, but it was evening, and I almost despairing, before a coach was brought out from the yard to the front door. I was at too great a distance to make out any faces, but it appeared that two women came from the house and climbed into the coach. It came along the first part of the driveway over the stream, and then I put away my spyglass and went up to wait in a hiding place by the road.

It was less than ten minutes later I heard the coach rattling toward me, and when it came into sight I sat very still. The coachman never saw me where I hid in the leafy bower; and nor did he see Mrs Watts's hand come out from the coach window, nor the white kerchief which was her signal to me that she had got Pitou with her, and that they were now for London.

When the carriage was gone, I went down and untethered my horse. The labouring men and the masons had finished their work for that day, and now they walked across the fields, returning to their villages before nightfall. At the main house were several ribbons of smoke coming up from the clustered chimneys; and I could well imagine the scene within, and the ladies there by the drawing-room fire, and one lady making pleasant conversation for her father's sake, but all her thoughts turned now towards her fiancé, Capitaine Cordet, in Paris.

I cannot speak the emptiness of my heart at that moment, and no consolation to me the silent service we had done. I mounted then and rode up through the wood.

CHAPTER THIRTY-ONE

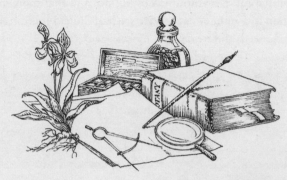

*T*he first few days after my return to London I kept from the Lane, and would have kept away longer but that Francis heard of my return and sent Gus to fetch me at my house very early. Gus said that Francis had bidden him tell me that the Post Master, Lord Sandwich, would speak with me that same morning.

'I have nothing to say to him.'

'Is that your reply, sir?'

Upon reflection, I told Gus that he might say to Francis that I would come into the Lane that day, but at a time of my own choosing. And when Gus had left me, I went down to the river and to the place where I had gone each day since my return from the West Country, which was to the Greenland Dock. I wandered about there, and onto the whalers and other ships at their refitting, and climbed into the loft above the vats and also into the room from which we had watched. There was much that I did not understand, both about how Pearce and Flanagan had kept themselves here secret, and how Flanagan had died; for it could not be that Pearce had no knowledge of the bill. And why then should he have left it upon Flanagan for discovery? It was a decipherment of things, and not words, and pen and paper no help to me, nor any aid to understanding.

From the Greenland Dock I took a wherry up and over to the north side, and went to that warehouse where Armstrong was murdered. And there I did as I had done at the place of Flanagan's murder, making a more careful inspection of the buildings and the alleys round about, and up in the loft also. And it was while I was in the warehouse loft that I heard a drummer beat a tattoo outside. I thought little of it to begin, but after a minute the drum beat again, but more insistent now, and closer. And when I heard loud voices I came down from the loft and went along an alley that took me to a place above the Execution Dock. A crowd was gathering there, and as I came near the Steps I saw the reason of it. A party of armed marines and two naval officers was coming up the Steps, and in their midst a seaman being led as their prisoner. A clergyman stayed close to the seaman and continually whispered in the fellow's ear, which the condemned man did not seem to like. The crowd, which was mainly the workless coal heavers and dockmen and their wives, pressed upon the rear of the party, and at first with no more than the usual curiosity to see a hanging.

It was then I saw Kitty Langridge behind the people. She was holding her child in her arms, and standing with her were several women, two of them those who had played whore to Pearce and Flanagan.

'Mrs Langridge,' I called. She was too distant to hear me over the crowd, and so I began to make my way through all the people towards her; for I meant that those two women should come with me to the warehouse. And I was but halfway to them when a loud and angry shouting broke out from the crowd behind me, near to the marines. What had caused it I could not see, but the mood of the people had turned in an instant. By the time I turned there were already stones being thrown, and none of them pebbles. It was no bid to save the condemned prisoner, for he was struck in the first hail. He cowered behind the marines, alongside the clergyman, and with his hands over his bleeding head to protect himself from the increasing rain of rubble coming out from the crowd.

The two officers drew their swords.

'Stand off! In the King's name, get you to your homes!'

'Damn the King!' cried one bold fellow, and another volley of stones clattered over the seamen.

'Fix bayonets!' commanded the first officer, and the marines needed no second order. But as they fixed, some within the crowd abused them and pushed angrily forward, while others shouted warnings and fell back, and all was a furious confusion.

'Mrs Langridge!' I cried, for I saw now that her friends had deserted her, and that she stood frozen in fear, shielding her child with her body against the wall.

I dropped my shoulder and pressed on through the mad herd, striking with fists and elbows at any who set themselves in my way. When I reached her at last, I put my hand upon her shoulder and she swung around and lashed at my face with the back of her hand. And then she saw who it was.

'Oh, sir.'

'Let us from here, and quickly.' I took the child into my arms for its own better safety. Kitty followed after, and asked no foolish questions, so that I soon had them both away from the mêlée. I took them up a lane away from the dockside, and when I saw that we were safe I gave her the crying child.

I asked if she had seen the cause of the incident.

'There is no cause, sir. The heavers and the seamen will fight over nothing now. It is hatred, sir. Hate is the cause.' She held the child close, soothing it with a gentle rocking, and I walked her back to that grim room she had, and stayed with her awhile, though she insisted that she had taken no harm from the fright. She put the child upon the bed, and sat by him, and with her hand upon her son's breast until he slept. After half an hour, and she assuring me that those heavers who passed in the lane were no menace to her, I left her and returned to the Execution Dock. The trouble seemed over by this time, and there were neither coal heavers nor marines now, but only a few boys throwing stones at the body hanging from the gallows. Its head was bloody, and its feet washed by the incoming tide. I chased the boys off and they abused me roundly for it, and as I went up to find Francis at the Lane the chair-men behind the docks looked at me very sullen. I knew then that it must be but a short while before the trouble should return here.

Francis was with Bode, and both of them inspecting the seal of a letter when I came into the room. They were at the table nearest the stove, Bode with his head down over the letter that lay flat upon the table, and holding his sharp blade very carefully as he worked its point gently beneath the seal. I made no interruption, but stood by them, and when Bode required a second blade I went to the stove and fetched it from the iron dish where it was warming.

'Will you try your hand, Mr Douglas?'

'It would only spoil your work, Mr Bode.'

He took the new blade and continued with the opening, Francis telling me now that the letter was for Wilkes. It had come from the Chevalier D'Eon, and very curious Francis was to see what it might contain (for this D'Eon had been the French ambassador in London till falling out with the court at Versailles, and by his notorious behaviour and continued residence in London had been a source of much useful information to us). But once Bode had lifted the seal and opened the letter, we saw at once that it was not in cipher, but plain script, and in French. It was the offer of a gift of wine to Wilkes from the Chevalier's vineyard, and a congratulation to Wilkes for his staunch defence of liberty.

Bode said, 'To be destroyed or resealed, sir?'

'You may reseal it, Mr Bode,' said Francis, handing it to back him. 'I would not deprive Mr Wilkes of his drink.' Francis came away from the table then and led me out through the antechamber and through the door into the main Post Office. 'It was not taken in any forgiving spirit, Alistair, that you ignored the Post Master's summons.'

'I am here now.'

'And Sandwich may be gone. I hope you had some joy of your visit to my father?'

'He would have me reconciled with Mr Jenkinson,' I said, and when Francis sniffed I quipped that he should write to his father that I was making the attempt.

'When I have seen the evidence of it, I shall certainly do so.' He was himself, I saw, not altogether pleased with me that I had failed to come to the Lane when he had sent Gus to fetch me. I do not think that he was in fear of Sandwich, for the Bishop's hand was over the Lane, and protecting the Decipherers from any real incursion by the joint Post Masters. But Francis's method with Hillsborough had always been to act with deference, and be willing to give any request a hearing, even those he must finally ignore. And while Sandwich was still establishing himself in Hillsborough's old place, Francis should have liked, I am sure, to have given him no cause of strife, or any reason for interference.

We came into the sorting room, where the sorters stood around the five great tables, piled deep with letters, which their hands expertly sifted and dropped into the proper bags for the next stage of their journey. Gus moved about the tables, collecting up those letters put aside as being to or from persons on our List, and also those foreign letters the sorters thought might interest us for any reason (usually a known name or address). More mailbags were now arriving from the front hall, for the coaches had just come in from the secondary post offices about the town, and we stepped around these fellows and mounted the stairs.

'Wilkes has had so many letters from his Paris friends that I am reading two or three a day. There is nothing in them. They are all of a likeness with the Chevalier's.'

'Does he reply?'

'Invariably. The fellow has ink in his veins. But there is as little in his letters as in theirs.'

I asked had there been mention of Hayley.

'None. But here is something may interest you. That other you mentioned, Jones – Sandwich's man of business – he has hardly been out from Sandwich's rooms here. I suppose it is some speculation he has running for the earl upon the Exchange.' I remarked that it might be the splitting campaign the ministry was running in the Company, and Francis agreed the possibility. 'Whatever it may be, Sandwich makes himself very busy at it. But have a care now, Alistair,' said he, lowering his voice. For we had come to the top of the stairs, and walking directly towards us was Lord Sandwich, and to one side of him that same fellow Jones, that Francis had just spoken of. And to Sandwich's other side, Carrington's man Meadows.

'I cannot see you now, Mr Douglas,' said Sandwich, and he stopped when he reached us. 'You have been chasing after Wilkes?'

'I have been on some business for Mr Jenkinson. Had I known earlier of your wish to see me—'

'You knew of it soon enough.' For Francis's sake, I bowed my head in apology. 'There is talk come to me that you are involved in some speculation, Mr Douglas.'

'My Lord?'

'A man in such a place of trust must be very careful of his actions.'

'I am sure I am very careful.'

'You make no denial of it then.'

'I hope, My Lord, that I have done nothing in my private affairs that might warrant a denial.'

He looked at me then very sharply, as any man might who had wallowed in the depravities of Medmenham, committed his wife to an asylum, and sired a number of bastard children upon an actress. But I held his look, and so he was unsure if I had aimed a deliberate stab at him. His man of business, Jones, was watching me, and so was Meadows. And I was very certain now that Sandwich must know I held Hayley's bill.

'You must pray that Wilkes makes his promised appearance at the King's Bench, Mr Douglas. For if he fail of it, I am sure there are many will blame you. And I shall be one of them.' With this parting shot Sandwich swept down the stairs, Jones and Meadows following close at his heels.

CHAPTER THIRTY-TWO

*T*he murmur of the crowd in Westminster Hall was like to the murmur of an audience in Drury Lane. Every seat around the King's Bench court was already taken when I arrived there and found Mrs Watts waiting for me; for it was not only the gentlemen of the town and their wives had come to see if Wilkes would brave the court, but the scribblers and the printers were down by the bench waiting. On the chairs at the front were several lords and their ladies, and Sandwich one of them, though without his actress, and Lord and Lady Hillsborough also. I escorted Mrs Watts up into the gallery.

'I almost think I shall be disappointed now if Wilkes does not come,' said she.

'He will come,' said I, but in truth the whole course of my dealings with Wilkes had taught me to keep always some doubt of his actions. My only surety of his coming was that I had been that morning to our watching room in the Birdcage Walk, and seen Mrs Porter there. She had promised me of Wilkes's continued presence under her eye, and the presence also of his closest supporters and legal men.

In the gallery, Jenkinson had kept two seats for us, to the front, and near enough to the bench below that we might hear any judgment.

I own that while we waited for the judges to appear I was too much distracted to get any enjoyment from Mrs Watts's light talk of the people there. She soon gave up on me and turned to Jenkinson upon her other side. Jenkinson, after his first greeting, said not a word more to me, but talked with Mrs Watts, and asked after her daughters, and gave no sign that he had any doubt of Wilkes's arrival, which I had promised him.

I assumed, I confess, that Jenkinson must know the sentence the court would pass upon Wilkes now, and that his silence to me on the subject was but a politic discretion. It did not occur to me that he might himself have been kept in total ignorance.

At last the clerk of the court announced the judges, and they came in very gravely and took the bench. Lord Chief Justice Mansfield sat central, with fellow judges one to either side, and a Recorder at the end. All four men wore the judicial wigs, hanging almost to their waists, and black gowns, and upon the table before Mansfield the clerk now laid the golden mace as a token of the court's sovereign power (Mrs Watts whispering in my ear that if the Law was to be an ass, it must at least be a golden one). Near to the judges sat the government's newly appointed attorney general, de Grey. He spoke with the clerk, who then proclaimed the new session open.

And hardly had the judges settled than there was a cheering audible, and coming from without the hall, and every eye turned now to the door. I own, it was a considerable relief to me when Wilkes made his entrance.

He had his legal men to either side of him, Glyn foremost among them, and his closest supporters behind. He whipped his tricorn from his head and passed it to one of these fellows as they all of them strode up the central aisle toward the bench. Wilkes nodded left and right, as though he saw friends all about him, his left hand grasping the lapel of his frock-coat as he advanced.

'You might have the name of his tailor from him,' whispered Mrs Watts; and indeed he was dressed in such a fashion as might put all but the lords there to shame. His frock-coat was blue, with silver braiding at the buttonholes and lapels, and his shirt snow-white. His breeches were without mark or crease, and the buckles of his shoes shining like new. His effrontery never wavered, but he stepped directly onto the dais before Chief Justice Mansfield and promptly declared that he was delivering himself to the court as he had promised, and that he had a short speech that he would make before they gave judgment against him.

'A speech, Mr Wilkes?'

'It is but a short speech, My Lord,' said Wilkes, and promptly took the paper from his coat.

Mansfield seemed almost at a loss what to do. But perhaps fearing some legal consequence of a refusal, he nodded his permission, and Wilkes at once turned a little to address himself to the hall, planting one foot forward and lifting his paper.

'My Lords, according to the voluntary promise I made to the public, I now appear before this sovereign court of justice to submit myself in every thing to the Laws of my country.

'Two verdicts have been found against me. One is for the republication of the *North Briton*, number 45, the other for the publication of a ludicrous poem.

'As to the republication of that number of the *North Briton*, I cannot yet see that there is the smallest degree of guilt. I have often read and examined with care that famous paper. I know that it is in every part founded on the strongest evidence of facts. I find it full of duty and respect to the person of the King, although it arraigns, in the severest manner, the conduct of His Majesty's then ministers, and brings very heavy charges home to them. I am persuaded they were well grounded, because every one of those ministers has since been removed. No one instance of falsehood has yet been pointed out in that pretended libel, nor was the word "false" in the information before this court. I am therefore perfectly easy under every imputation respecting a paper, in which truth has guided the pen of the writer, whoever he was, in every single line, and it is this circumstance which has drawn on me, as the supposed author, all the cruelties of ministerial vengeance.'

There was open laughter now from every part of the hall that Wilkes should maintain this threadbare fiction that he had no notion who the author might be. And Wilkes himself now looked up and smiled, as though he shared in the joke. When I glanced at Jenkinson I saw that he did not share in the laughter, but his jaw was set tight.

'As to the other charge against me for the publication of a poem, which has given just offence, I will assert that such an idea never entered my mind. I blush again at the recollection that it has been at any time and in any way brought to the public eye, and drawn from the obscurity in which it remained under my roof. Twelve copies of a small part of it had been printed in my house at my own private press; I had carefully locked them up, and I never gave one to the most intimate friend. Government, after the affair of the *North Briton*, bribed one of my servants to rob me of the copy, which was produced in the House of Peers, and afterwards before this honourable court. The nation was justly offended, but not with me, for it was evident that I had not been guilty of the least offence to the public. I pray God to forgive me, as I do the jury who have found me guilty of publishing a poem I concealed with care, and which is not even yet published, if any precise meaning can be affixed to any word in our language.'

This mention of the House of Peers was an undoubted thrust against his past friend and fellow of Medmenham, Lord Sandwich, who had led the trial of Wilkes in that House. The whole hall knew it too, and none better than Sandwich, who when I looked down at him now had his gaze fixed upon Wilkes with such ferocity that I feared for a moment that he might draw his sword. Perhaps Hillsborough had a like fear, for he leaned across and spoke to Sandwich and touched his arm. But Wilkes seemed to notice none of this. Or if he did, he had no care any longer for any offence that he might give to any man in England, and he continued straight on.

'But, My Lords, neither of the two verdicts could have been found against me, if the records had not been materially altered without my consent, and, as I am informed, contrary to law. On the evening only before the two trials, Chief Justice Mansfield caused the records to be altered – against the consent of my solicitor, and without my knowledge; for a dangerous illness, arising from an affair of honour, detained me at that time abroad. The alterations were of the utmost importance, and I was in consequence tried the very next day on two new charges, of which I could know nothing. I will venture to declare this proceeding unconstitutional. I am advised that it is illegal, and that it renders both the verdicts absolutely void.'

Mansfield, at the naming of him, had started in amazement, nor was he alone, but almost every person in the hall was shocked by this sally from Wilkes against his own judge. There was a general stir and whisper all about, and Mrs Watts said to me quietly, 'Has the fellow turned mad?' Only Lord Mansfield and his fellow judges sat still now, with their eyes upon Wilkes and their faces set like stone. It was a new and unhappy experience for the Chief Justice to be accused of perpetrating a malicious illegality, and accused in his own court to his face by an outlaw. It is a wonder to me yet how he then managed to stay silent and seated. Now Wilkes turned even more fully towards the floor of the hall. He hurried on now as if he feared to be stopped.

'I have stood forth, My Lords, in support of the laws against the arbitrary acts of ministers. This court of justice, in a solemn appeal respecting General Warrants, showed their sense of my conduct. I shall continue to reverence the wise and mild systems of English laws, and this excellent constitution. I have been much misrepresented; but under every species of persecution, I will remain firm and friendly to the monarchy, dutiful and affectionate to the illustrious prince who wears the crown, and to the whole Brunswick line.

'As to all nice, intricate points of law, I am sensible how narrow and circumscribed my ideas are; but I have experienced the deep knowledge, and great abilities of my counsel. With them I rest the legal part of my defence, submitting every point to the judgment of this honourable court, and to the laws of England.'

Wilkes then lowering his paper, Attorney General de Grey rose instantly and began to announce what everyone expected, which was that Wilkes must now be taken into custody. But he was interrupted in this, and that quite forcefully, by Chief Justice Mansfield.

'Sit down, if you will, Mr de Grey,' said he. 'I believe it is my court you are in.' The attorney general looked at Mansfield in surprise; but then he sat down as instructed, though with a colour in his cheeks now that was visible from the gallery. While Mansfield then held some whispered conference with his fellow judges, Wilkes stepped down from the dais and rejoined his own legal men, and all of them in as much perplexity as any of us at this turn. I looked to Jenkinson for some clue to the reason of it, and found him leaning forward, and his face a very picture of concern. At last Mansfield had finished his consultations. He looked not at Wilkes but past him, as if to address the hall.

'The court had information that there was to be an accused person brought here today. The court sees no such person. There is a fellow here, indeed, who I am told is an outlaw. The court does not recognize this fellow as a legal person. The court has no business with this fellow.'

'Uh,' broke from Mrs Watts, and an astonished whispering swept the hall. It was stopped only when Mansfield, with a show of irritation that he could not have felt unless he be a fool (which he was not), turned upon Attorney General de Grey. 'What do you mean to be wasting the court's time by bringing this non-person before us? The law is very clear on the question who is subject to the court, and it should be well known to you. But as you appear to need some instruction upon it, it is a warrant *capias ut legatum* that an outlaw must remain an outlaw, and unrecognized by this court or any other in the kingdom.'

'My Lord—'

'There is no more to be said, Mr de Grey. There is no prisoner before us. We can make no judgment who have no one lawfully before us. Get you to your books, sir. I must presume you have no other case prepared this morning. Then we are adjourned. You may find me in my chambers.'

Mansfield rose, and departed through the side door, and his fellow judges with him. Wilkes showed no jubilation at this startling turn, but consulted with his legal men and supporters, and they remained in consultation together as they departed the hall the same way they had come, only now with a surprise at last turned upon them, up the central aisle and through the main door, in a continuing perplexity. But almost the moment Wilkes was from our sight, a great cheering erupted outside.

'They think he is freed,' said Mrs Watts.

'He is free at least, that is certain,' said I; and I would have spoken with Jenkinson then, but that he was upon his feet now and hastening towards the gallery steps to get down to Mansfield's chamber, in which direction Sandwich and Hillsborough below were already moving.

Among the spectators in the hall was a general confusion, and everyone talking now and gathering in different groups, to get some understanding of the farce to which we had all been witness. As the people in the gallery started down, Mrs Watts and I stayed in our seats and watched the people empty from the hall. Soon we were alone in the gallery, and my arms resting on the rail, and I said, 'I have put Mademoiselle Pitou upon the List.'

'I had it from the girl that it was not Mademoiselle Beauchamp that employed her, but the father.'

I said that I had never doubted of it. 'We will know her if she comes to London again. I have not thanked you yet for what you did.'

'It was the girl's own doing that she returned to Paris, Alistair. I can only think that she received a new order when we arrived here.' While we watched the ladies filing out through a side door, she asked me if I knew that the Vicomte and his daughter should return from Bowood within the next few days, and then depart for Paris. I confessed that I had not known of it.

'If you should wish to meet with her before she returns to Paris—'

'No.'

'You must know your own heart.'

'It is not my heart I must think on, but hers. And that is now Cordet's.'

I looked over the hall now, that Mrs Watts not see into me. But she saw into me anyway, and briefly touched her hand upon my arm. After a few minutes more, and the hall emptying, we came down from the gallery, and I excused myself from her a moment, for Jenkinson had beckoned me from where he had come out by Mansfield's chamber.

'You must keep your watch over Wilkes,' said he, after first making sure we were not overheard. 'De Grey is ordered to prepare the proper warrant. Wilkes will be taken into custody before the new Parliament.'

I gestured toward the bench, remarking the farce of the proceedings.

'I would not have advised it, but it is done. And I am sure the Chief Justice shall never again allow Wilkes the freedom of a speech in his court.' He adjured me once again to keep my watch set over Wilkes, and then he went back into the chamber where Sandwich and Hillsborough must still be in conference with Mansfield.

Upon passing outside with Mrs Watts, we saw an open carriage at the far side of the square, surrounded by a cheering mob. Wilkes was in the carriage with Hayley and some of his people. Wilkes rose from his seat to address the crowd, but he could not be heard for the cheering. He quickly sat down, but waving his hat now, and the carriage and the crowd swept up towards Piccadilly. And then it was Laughlin Macleane approached us.

'*Capias ut legatum*,' said Mrs Watts. 'You are a scholar, Mr Macleane.'

'I am no lawyer, thank God.'

'I take it that someone must be blamed that Wilkes has got himself elected while an outlaw,' said she. 'And Lord Mansfield has chosen poor Mr de Grey for the scapegoat.'

Macleane agreed the likelihood of it, but had no interest to pursue the question, though it was almost the only one being discussed all about us. He turned to me instead, saying that he had not seen me for some while. And saying it, I own, with no friendly meaning. I told him that I had been away in the West Country.

'Indeed,' said he. 'I should have been at Bowood myself had there not been such a press of business here in town. I do not like to delay any business. I think it is a great fault in a man to delay in business, Mr Douglas.'

'If I have missed my opportunity, the fault is entirely mine, sir.'

'As you say, the fault is yours.'

'I hope there has not been any misunderstanding.'

'There has been no misunderstanding, Mr Douglas. It is only that I do not like to be made a sport of. It shall not happen twice.' He wished me well of my duties in relation to Wilkes, and then he bowed stiffly to Mrs Watts and departed.

'He knows that you have used him,' said she, when he was gone.

'Yes,' said I, watching him return to his friends; and I knew that I had no choice in it now. For Macleane was right in this, that it is a great fault for a man to delay in business. Now that he knew, and Sandwich seemed to have some hint of it, I could wait no longer for the answer to my difficulty but must act directly upon Hayley's bill.

CHAPTER THIRTY-THREE

I made sure to mention the bill to the footman when I handed him my card, which indiscretion was not welcome to Hayley, who turned upon me just as soon as we were alone together in his study.

'My footman is not my clerk, sir,' said he in some heat. 'Pray what is your business? You have a bill, he tells me.'

'I think you know what bill I have.' Without waiting his invitation, I crossed the study and sat down.

'I have no time for this.'

'I am sure that your brother-in-law may spare you for one evening,' said I, and took out the bill and unfolded it upon his desk. The sight of it had a quite salutary and sobering effect on the fellow. 'You will wish to sit down, Mr Hayley.'

'Do you present the bill?' said he. 'You must come to me at the Exchange.'

'This is not a Change Alley dispute, sir. Men have died. And you will sit down.'

Furious to be so bearded in his own house, he tried to meet my cold eye with a pretence of outrage, but he was not equal to it. With some haughtiness, he came and sat down.

'You know who I am.'

'I have your card, Mr Douglas.' He tossed it down upon the desk. 'And if it is money that you want, I must disappoint you.'

'The bill is yours, is it not?'

'I have not owned to it. Nor is this the manner in which it should be presented.'

'What dealings had you with Pearce and Flanagan?'

'The names are not familiar to me.'

'Then you will allow me to give you some reminder of them. In the summer of last year, Pearce and Flanagan murdered a Customs agent in Boston. The agent was at the time making an enquiry on behalf of the Vice-Admiralty court. There had been a suspicion of smuggling by a Boston merchant, John Hancock. I think that his name is familiar to you.' I put a finger on Hancock's signature on the bill. Hayley glanced down and quickly up again. 'Pearce and Flanagan fled Boston, but not before they had made some drunken and foolish boasting against the Customs agents and the King. They arrived by one of Hancock's ships, the *Valiant*, here in London in the autumn. There were twenty bales of tobacco that you took delivery of from that ship.'

'How can I be a merchant if I do not trade?'

'How can you be a merchant, sir, if you lose your reputation?' His brow came down. He gave me such a look as might have terrified his clerks. I said, 'How came your bill into Pearce and Flanagan's possession?'

'If it was in their possession—'

'It was.'

'It did not come to them by me.'

'That is not what I asked of you, sir.'

'A stolen bill is frequently presented about the City. And forgeries also.'

'This is no forgery.'

'I cannot tell how it came into their possession. You must make your enquiries in Boston. If you insist upon it, I will make a time to speak with Mr Fitzherbert. These are matters requiring a mature commercial understanding. Which I fear you are in want of.'

'You will find Mr Fitzherbert not so accommodating of you when he discovers how your bill was found.'

'My business with Fitzherbert is no concern of yours.'

'You may believe that is a very near concern to me.' Hayley answered me nothing, but only looked defiance at me. 'I must assume that Pearce and Flanagan presented the bill to you. And that you had refused them.'

'If you are not come here to present the bill to me, Mr Douglas, I do not see what business we may have together.'

'You will not protect yourself with silence,' said I, but I saw that what advantage I had had over him by the surprise of my arrival with his bill was now gone. He eyed me coldly, and from behind the fastness of his middling fortune; and were we in some place out of England I should not have hesitated to thrash him into the street. But while I considered some more civil way to shake his foundations there was a sudden commotion outside the study door. A woman (and, by her extended jaw, undoubtedly Wilkes's sister, Hayley's wife) then burst in, with the footman at her heels.

'They are smashing the windows. Illuminate. We must illuminate.' Rushing to the window, she pulled back the drapes. The footman set a candelabra in the window, and, with his lit taper, now lighted the candles.

'They know the house,' said Hayley, coming out from behind his desk. 'They will do us no harm.' He crossed to the window and looked away down the street. The sound of distant shouting was audible now, and while we listened there came a shot, and then a brief silence; and then the shouting increased along with the sound of breaking glass. 'It is some damned fool has put a shot over their heads,' said Hayley, not quite so steady now as at first. He ordered his wife and the footman to go and illuminate the upper windows. 'Shout down to them. Make sure they know it is Mr Wilkes's sister who resides here.'

Mistress and footman hurried out, and then with a hand upon the curtain, Hayley said, 'We are done, Mr Douglas. You may avoid the riot if you go at once.'

I took up the bill from his desk and folded it into my pocket. Then I came and stood by him at the window. The rioters were coming up from the direction of the river.

'You are wasting time standing about here,' said he. 'I will not answer for your safety.'

'You may ask after me at the Red Lion in Holborn if you would have the bill returned to you.'

'It is money you are after then.'

'The payment I require for it is only that you tell me what you know of Pearce and Flanagan. Tell me that, and you may have the bill freely. The Red Lion in Holborn,' said I, and then I left him.

The rioters had made no further advance up the street, but were stopped some dozen houses short of Hayley's. All those dozen houses had candles or lamps now illuminating their front windows to show their support for Wilkes (or their fear for their windows). But as I came into the street, those who had been putting stones through the unilluminated windows further down suddenly ceased in their entertainment; for there had come a shrill whistling from nearer the river. The whistling was like a regimental drum to them, and they straightaway turned south and hurried to answer its summons. And now I heard the sound of pistol shots from that same direction.

It should have been nothing to me. And I would most certainly have left them to their violent revels, only that the shots seemed to come from that quarter down by Execution Dock where Kitty Langridge had her dismal lodgings. And so I turned south and hurried after the window breakers.

Night was fallen, and the alleys toward the river very dark, and with a threat about them now that I had not felt before. It was partly the cries and shrill whistlings that came and went, and partly the knots of men I saw moving in the side streets like wolf packs between the houses, intent upon a prey I could not see. I drew my dirk and kept it in my hand as I went. But I met none of these wandering bands face to face, and was soon come safely to Kitty's lodgings. There was a lamp lit somewhere behind the ragged cloth draped in the window. I rapped at the window and spoke directly, that she be not frightened.

'Kitty? It is Mr Douglas. Will you open the door to me?'

The cloth parted, she saw that it was me, and I was soon in her room and the front door firmly locked again.

'You should not be out, sir. It is devilry.'

'Have the sailors come ashore?'

'It is the coal heavers. They will kill Mr Green at the Roundabout.' I had the story of Green's stupidity from her very quickly. The heavers had refused to make any more unloadings unless their wages be raised. And Green had replied to their demand by putting up notices in Shadwell that if the proper heavers would not work, others might do just as well. And these others were notified that they might apply directly to Green at the Roundabout Tavern.

'Green is a fool.'

'He is, sir. But no one should be murdered.' She spoke it with such feeling, and with such a look of such raw pain, that it caught at my heart.

I asked if she knew of the magistrates being called.

'They would never go there. They are afraid of the heavers. No one will go there to help him.' There were pistol shots again, and she turned sharply to the window.

'You need not fear. They are not close by.'

'I am not afraid for myself, sir.'

'No. I believe that you are not.'

I warned her not to go out, but to lock the door after me; and then I left her and returned into the night.

The alleyways I stayed clear of and went instead by the streets, for though the lamplighters had kept away and the streets were near as dark as the alleys, yet there was not there the same danger of stumbling into the armed coal heavers. Whistling and calling rose several times ahead of me, and I saw and heard others in the darkness running to answer the calls. What they were about I cannot say, but many of these fellows now carried cutlasses, and if they should meet a seaman in their way I have no doubt but that he must be cut to pieces. I kept my dirk in my hand but hidden, and walked very brazenly in the centre of the street, as if in no fear of them. Some fellows called to me as they passed, and seemed like to threaten me, but I answered them with Wilkes's name, and declared myself a supporter of the coal heavers and liberty. Though my voice surprised them they left me unmolested and ran on.

I came at last near to Green's tavern and turned aside from the main thoroughfare and into the Gravel-end Lane.

And here I stopped. For even in the darkness I saw that they were too many for me. They were a hundred and more, and not only crowded into the lane before the Roundabout, but there was a great coming and going from the alley to the side, and very evident that the heavers had surrounded the place. Stones cracked against the building, and oaths of blood-curdling ferocity went up against Green. There was shouting from above, which must be Green, begging them to leave off, that he had done only the merchants' orders, and they shouting in reply that by Jesus, they would drown him in the river if he only be a man and come down to face them.

It was more than bravery needed now to save the wretched fellow's neck. I turned upon my heel, and went back along the main street and made no stop until I came to the Tower.

The captain of the guard was very loath to send his men into the City streets. And when I told him of the heavers armed with cutlasses, and of Green's idiocy, and of the mob's intent upon Green's life, I saw that he had then an even smaller inclination to let his men out from the safety of the Tower. I cannot say that he was wrong. What skill his men had at soldiering must have availed them very little upon such a night. And Green was truly no man worth dying for.

'But you do not mean to go out there again,' said the captain when I took my leave of him. 'You must stay here till the morning.'

'Be sure that you are well armed if you go down towards Shadwell,' said I, and I went out from the Tower, and made my way back along the river, past the Execution Dock, and up into the dismal alley. The windows were still illuminated, and unbroken; but it was the merest chance had spared them. And chance would not last them till the morning.

When Kitty Langridge opened the door to me, I did not go in, but said only, 'Fetch your boy, and quickly. You are coming away from here.'

CHAPTER THIRTY-FOUR

I never liked to have servants always about me, and so the two attic rooms in my house were unused, and it was here that I put Kitty and her son. She was at a fret for the imposition upon me those first few days, and said that she must return to her lodgings, and to her washing work by the river. In the end I must forbid her to speak of it, for now that she was in the better surroundings of my house I could see the more clearly how thin she was, and wan, which to my shame I had hardly noticed while she was in that dismal place that I had brought her up from. And though I urged her to rest herself and look only to the child, she would not bend her pride so far, but the first morning she discovered an apron from beneath the stairs, and commenced to sweep the floors, with her son looking on curiously from the bed of cushions that she had made for him. It was the boy who softened the heart of my daily, an elderly woman, and childless, and very grateful I was to have such an instant peace between the old lady and Kitty. For I had troubles enough to face beyond my door, and no such simple innocence out there to help me.

That Green had saved his wretched skin by a desperate escape was news that Kitty gave me the credit of, and which was more than I deserved; for in truth I had been indifferent had they killed him as they most certainly intended.

Nor had I heard one word from Hayley by that day when Wilkes had agreed with the attorney general to present himself again at the King's Bench court to be taken into custody. In the early morning of that day I had gone down with Banks to see his ship, that was come south from Whitby and now lay in the basin of the Yard at Deptford for refitting. He would have no other answer from me but that I must go down with him to see the shipwrights' first work. I went, and saw, and in spite of Banks's great happiness, came away with an estimation that they who sailed in her were more likely to die of suffocation in the tropics, or to drown in a shipwreck, than ever they were to make a successful circumnavigation.

'She has a flatter hull than I had thought. But Lieutenant Cook says she will suit us very well.'

'Yes,' said I as our boat drew away from Deptford, and his ship fell away behind us. 'She is very fine.'

'I should have liked more space for our collections, though I must not complain.'

'I think you are the only man in London who has no thought of Wilkes.'

'But I shall sail around the world,' said he, and thumped my knee. There were a thousand preparations yet to be made, and I had heard a good many of them as we went down to Deptford; and now I heard a good many more as we returned. But as we went up past the Greenland Dock, Banks noticed my gaze fixed upon the place and asked me what I saw.

'Nothing. It is only that a man was lately murdered there.'

'A fellow known to you?'

'He was likely a murderer himself, and certainly no friend to me.'

'Well then, perhaps it was a fitting end for him there in Bedford's graveyard.' Banks relaunched upon the subject of his expedition, but I in my puzzlement interrupted to ask what he had meant by his strange reference to the Duke of Bedford. He gestured broadly with his arm. 'This all was Lord Bedford's. Then it was called the Great Howland Dock. You see the big house at the far end? It was Russells living there even when I was boy. I once stayed there with my father.' With a glance at our boatman, he made me understand that he would explain further when we had disembarked at the Whitehall Steps.

An hour later, at my prompting, he did so.

'Bedford had no care of his men when the Howland basin was dug. There were a number of men died in their labours there, and also from accidents that a better master might have stopped.' Banks mentioned Bedford's reputation for rapacity, and his own father's view that the duke's reputation was well earned. 'Though I would not have that repeated,' said he quickly, and upon my assurance of it Banks seemed relieved, for he had spoken more than he intended (and Bedford had more than sufficient power to do his planned expedition harm). Then Banks asked if I would accompany him to the Admiralty, for he was sure that Stephens must have some questions for me now that I had seen the ship. I declined the invitation, we parted outside the Admiralty, and I turned, full of thought, towards the Treasury, there to receive my instructions from Jenkinson on the matter of Wilkes.

'Wilkes shall be bound over by the Chief Justice, but not sentenced,' Jenkinson told me the moment I entered his room. Wilkes, he said, would of certainty present himself at the King's Bench that same afternoon. Jenkinson had it from Carrington, who himself had it from a spy recently bought from among Wilkes's close supporters. 'The man may then stay quietly in the King's Bench prison till after the new Parliament commences.'

'It is not Wilkes's way to sit quietly, sir.'

'It is the best we may hope for. If he is not bound over, he will present himself to be sworn in at the Parliament. The King will not have it.'

'His people may not be quiet either.'

'His mob are no less subjects to the King, and to the King's law, than any other. I have had your note upon the riots in Wapping. I need not tell you of the danger of any false step. I have advised that the soldiery be kept in their barracks. Regrettably, the King has other counsellors than myself.'

'Is it Lord Weymouth, sir?' said I (for the Northern Secretary was of the Bedfordites).

'That is more than you need know.'

'It would be almost to make a war in London.'

'It is our business to see that it does not come to that. Wilkes shall cool his heels in the prison while the new Parliament comes in, and Lord Mansfield will no doubt deal with him in earnest after the Parliament has settled. You need not instruct me on the troubles that may come from this, Mr Douglas. But I hope that you understand that it is to forestall troubles much worse. Much worse, and very much more bloody.'

A month earlier and I might have made some dispute with him. But a month earlier he would have kept from me his true concerns, and Mansfield's intentions, and his own conflict within the ministry. And this was also the first time that he had spoken openly with me of the King. It was the Bishop made an invisible third party in the room with us, and after taking some thought I said, 'I understand very well, sir. Let us have no war in London.'

'You might spare yourself the trouble of attending the court. But I would have you make sure of Wilkes's incarceration down at the prison. The head warden should know the heavy consequence he must bear if his prisoner cannot be kept secure within his walls.'

'I shall be sure he knows of it, sir.'

'The warden would not be alone in feeling the weight of the ministry's displeasure,' said he with a glance of warning. He gave me the letter of authority then, which he had already drafted, giving me a temporary command over the warden. 'You will lend the fellow your every assistance, Mr Douglas.'

Baxter was now under my charge again, and I went with him to wait on the south side of Westminster Bridge; for it was this way that the tipstaffs must bring Wilkes from Mansfield's court and down to the King's Bench prison in Southwark. Baxter had been down to the prison already that morning, and discovered there that Wilkes had sent linen and clothes on before him in expectation of Mansfield's judgment. Before coming over the bridge we had seen the mob gathered in the square outside Westminster Hall like a great carnival of menace, awaiting the court's disposition of their hero Wilkes. They were so many that their joined voices came to us as a deep rolling murmur across the bridge. After a half-hour of waiting there came a great swell in the sound, so that we knew Wilkes must be out from Westminster Hall.

'If the court has freed him again, what shall you do then, sir?'

'The court has not freed him.'

'Mr Carrington has put Messengers about the Buckingham House and by St James's,' said he, as if that were any more than the most feeble precaution against the mob should they rise. For if that happened, then neither Messengers, nor magistrates, nor constables would stop them, but perhaps only the soldiery, which I did not like to think on. Across the river the murmur now swelled into a dull roaring, and the crowd on the north side fell back towards us and onto the bridge. I stood in my stirrups.

'Is it the prison coach, sir?' asked Baxter, for he was on foot beside me and could not see. 'Is Wilkes sent down to the prison?'

'It appears so,' said I, but hardly had I spoken than I saw how the advancing prison coach now made some difficulty in its progress onto the bridge. Its difficulties worsened the further it came, for the crowd now poured about it on every side. The more the tipstaffs and coachman waved their arms and shouted, the more tightly the crowd hemmed them in, till at last the coach was forced to a stop.

Baxter climbed onto the wall. 'Will they free him?' said he in amazement at the mob's audacity in this place so near to the Court and the Parliament. 'I think they will free him, sir.'

Once the coach was stopped, people clambered onto the foot-boards, and then onto the roof, like the locusts they were, and others mounted the four horses, and the door of the coach was suddenly flung open. Wilkes, in his distinctive blue jacket, put out a hand, but whether to protect himself or to be heard I could not say. He appeared to be thrust back into the coach and the door closed upon him again.

The harness was quickly broken, and the tipstaffs and coachman pulled down, and then the coach was turned, with Wilkes aboard and at the window now, and the mob drew him back into Westminster.

I spurred my horse onto the bridge.

'Are they under Wilkes's command?' I called sharply to those dishevelled tipstaffs so recently thrown down. They were still in some shock at what had happened, so sudden and unexpected had been the mob's assault. The coachman scurried about them, hatless, urging the tipstaffs to retrieve his horses from the laughing remnant of the mob. The dazed fellows now told me that Wilkes had begged the mob to leave him be, but that the mob would not listen. Wilkes, they said, had promised to bring himself down to the prison just as soon as he was able.

It was clear to me that these fellows had no intention of going after Wilkes, so badly were they shaken by the mob's rough handling.

'You may wait for me down at the prison, Mr Baxter.'

'Will he go there, sir?'

'I have no belief in the word of Mr Wilkes.'

The mob was departing with its new-won prize by way of Great George Street, the coach seeming almost to float in the midst of the people like a rudderless boat on an onrushing tide. Riding quickly on to catch up with the rear of the mad parade, I saw hats snatched from the heads of some bemused gentlemen in Birdcage Walk. Too frightened to draw their swords, they must then suffer the exuberant cursing of the mob, and the sight of their fine hats going from unwashed head to head before finally disappearing.

The crowd soon had the coach before Buckingham House, where some fellows climbed onto the railings to taunt the Queen's guardsmen, who wisely stayed well back from the road. But it was as the mob now turned the coach eastward that I saw Wilkes. He had his face at the opened window of the coach, and looked about him now very cheerfully, and waving. He made no incitement of the people, but nor did he urge upon them any restraint. He seemed to have surrendered himself up to them, as though he would ride as their mascot wheresoever they chose to take him.

And where they took him next was to St James's Palace, and here was repeated that same taunting of the guardsmen as at Buckingham House, only with an increased ferocity, and there were boots flung over the railings to signify the general detestation of Lord Bute, Jenkinson's old master, and the erstwhile favourite of the King. 'Wilkes and Liberty' had been their cry since Westminster, but now some mad fellow began a cry of 'King John!' and others joined in with laughter. When I saw Jenkinson and Carrington hurrying across the park from Whitehall, I rode across to them.

'Is he escaped?' called Jenkinson.

'He is abducted,' I replied, drawing up.

'What – willingly?'

'They do not appear to have him in irons, sir,' said I; and then I told them what had happened down at Westminster Bridge, and what the tipstaffs had told me of Wilkes's promise to them.

'The King's guards shall retake him,' said Carrington, and ignoring my protest he hurried toward the Palace.

Jenkinson seemed in some quandary now what order to give.

'Sir, I have no doubt but that Wilkes would break his word in an instant if it might profit him. But he has sent his clothes and linen before him to the prison. He will go there. It would be an unnecessary folly to send the guards out.'

'I pray you are right, Mr Douglas,' said he, going after Carrington. 'Send me word when you have him secure.'

But now the mob was moving again, and the coach with them. From St James's and up into the Strand I followed, and some now trailing off from the mob and others joining. It was the chair-men and heavers pulled the coach, and quite evident to me now that they meant to draw Wilkes all the way to the City. People appeared at the upper windows of the houses and shops along the Strand, and the windows were flung open and many cried, 'Wilkes and Liberty', but whether from love of him or to protect their glass, I could not say.

At the far end of Fleet Street, there was a reinforcement of journeymen and weavers waiting, and the coach moved up by the Bank and into Spitalfields, where it halted at last in a slow milling crush of people near the Three Tuns tavern.

The coach door opened, and a mighty cheer then broke from the gathered mob, and Wilkes stood upon the footstep, one hand on the opened door and the other flourishing his hat. There was a wild huzzahing as he stepped down into the crowd, and the only sign of him now the waving hat which he brandished all the way to the Three Tuns and inside.

The passing carnival had drawn many out from the coffee shops, and also from the Exchange and the Accompting Houses along the way; but these onlookers stayed back from the main crowd, and cried up their questions to those dozens of us who had trailed the mob on horseback and in hackneys. And it was among these onlookers that I spied Gus and called him to me, and gave him a message for Francis, and also my horse to take back to the Post Office stables.

Wilkes did not show himself again but kept close-sequestered inside, and so after an hour the crowd had begun to make a dispersal. But throughout that hour several of Wilkes's gentlemen supporters arrived, leaping down from their hackneys, and looking, I own, more concerned than delighted by this surprising turn in their man's affairs. There was Wilkes's lawyer Glyn among them, and also Hayley, who I made sure got no sight of me as he went by.

When it began to rain, the crowd thinned quickly and I got myself into the hackney, for which I had paid a six hours' hire. After an hour I told the jarvey that he might wait in an alehouse just by us, but in the window where I might see him. No magistrate came to fetch Wilkes, nor any constable or Messenger or guard. I sat quiet in the hackney and watched the door of the Three Tuns through the rain.

It was ten o'clock, and my jarvey seated in the cab with me and dozing, and the sound of drunken revelry very full now from the Three Tuns, when I saw Wilkes's legal man Glyn step out into the lantern light. At Glyn's signal, Wilkes was then out from the tavern the next instant, clutching his hat to his head as he climbed into the waiting hackney, and Glyn climbed in after him.

Reaching over, I shoved my jarvey's knee.

Our way through the City streets was unimpeded, for there was this night a greater thirst for drink than for riot, and very soon we were on London Bridge, and the lanterns of the ships glowing faint in the soft rain all the way down to the Execution Dock, and across the river at Rotherhithe. There was a strong odour that came off the river now, for the ships had been too long there unmoving; and the rain had flushed the City gutters, putting another layer of stench across the water, so that I must lift my sleeve to my mouth and nose till we were across to the south side.

Wilkes's hackney ahead of us went directly on towards St George's Fields, and when there could be no doubt of its destination I called up to my jarvey to go easy, and so he walked his horse the last hundred yards to the King's Bench Prison. When we arrived at the gate, Wilkes and Glyn had already got down from their hackney and were passing inside.

'Stop here,' I said, but I did not get down. I watched the gate. It was lit by a heavy torch set in the prison wall to one side. The great dark of St George's Fields ahead of us was unlit and quiet. Glyn's hackney waited for him near the gate.

'Is it here then, sir?'

I instructed the fellow to wait, and it was some minutes before Baxter came out from the prison. I got down then, and met Baxter at the edge of the torchlight.

At my asking if Wilkes was securely in the head warden's custody, Baxter pointed to a lit window just along the prison wall. The yellow light from the high window spilled out now onto the edge of the field. 'He is in his rooms. He has sent the turnkey to bring wine.'

'Is he drunk?'

'He is not very sober. What will the mob do when they find he is in prison, sir?'

It was twelve days yet till the new Parliament be opened, and the newly elected members swear their oaths to the King. Twelve days we must keep Wilkes secure. For if he be not kept in the prison where Mansfield and the King's law had sent him, where then resided authority in the kingdom? He had made mock of the ministry in going freely to Bath since the Middlesex election. Now in prison, at last, he must await the law's judgment upon him, else the King's law be no law, and this perilous Wilkite anarchy rise to rule as sovereign in its stead. I looked into the darkness of St George's Fields, and then to the dark shape of the barn behind us, and across to the high building facing the prison. If the prison were a fort, and with ramparts and guns mounted upon the walls, even then it could not be defended.

'I little know what they shall do, Mr Baxter.'

CHAPTER THIRTY-FIVE

It was not Hayley came up to Holborn the following morning, but he sent one of his clerks to fetch me; and the clerk brought me not to his master's home, but to the counting house that Hayley kept in Wapping, by the river. The clerk led me through a small and poorly lit room where two of his fellows were perched on stools, and scribbling at their ledgers. Upstairs in his room overlooking the docks, Hayley expected me.

'Mr Douglas,' he said, rising; and he jerked his head towards the door for the lad to leave us. He let his hand fall to his waist then, and hitched his thumb on his breeches. Outside the window behind him were many unmoving cranes upon the docks. All the sails upon the masts were furled. 'It is not a pretty sight to any merchant,' said he, following my glance. 'There must be an end to it soon or we shall all go to the wall.'

'I have not come here to commiserate with you, sir.'

'No. No, I understand that you have other calls upon you. But you have brought the bill?'

'You will see it again when I have had the truth from you.'

'I hope you do not imply, sir, that I have lied.'

I moved at once towards the door, and when he called after me to wait, I faced him. 'Give me some reason I should wait, Mr Hayley, or I am gone from here directly.'

'Perhaps,' said he, avoiding my eye, 'there are some few other things I might have told you.' It was the first tentative self-breaching of his wall, and I knew by hard experience that I must be careful now. And so I stayed silent and watched him as his hand went to the pile of sovereigns upon the green baize cloth of his table. Without thought, he began to make the coins into small towers. 'Till last September, I had never heard of Pearce and Flanagan. They were not even names to me. And you may believe it was a considerable surprise to me when they brought themselves here with that bill. Two men I did not know, in the attire of common sailors, and expecting two thousand pounds of me.'

'You refused them.'

'Of course I refused them. How should such fellows have come by the bill except through dishonesty?'

'You did not report them to the magistrates.'

'I wrote to Hancock the same hour.'

'And he confirmed your suspicion?'

'I await yet some certain answer from him. You know what delays we have had in our shipping.' I did. And I knew also that the post across the Atlantic had escaped the worst of it, for the packet boats since December had sailed monthly out from Southampton. 'I made it known at the Accepting Houses that the bill might be presented. I instructed them that it should be refused till I had made my enquiries.'

'But you made no attempt to have Pearce and Flanagan arrested.'

'They told me a tale of Hancock's having given them the bill. And they were certainly well acquainted with some of his people. I had thought the whole matter best dealt with privately.'

'You were not sure, then, that they were thieves.'

'I hesitated to have them hanged till I had received some better confirmation of my suspicions. You will not blame me for that, Mr Douglas. It was but Christian charity. I am no Jew, to be crying on the instant for my pound of flesh.'

'And once your Christian charity was exhausted, Mr Hayley?'

His hand stopped its play upon the towers. He looked up at me and could not veil his dislike. 'They threatened me. And I am not a man to be threatened. I reported them to Mr Carrington.'

If he thought to have some surprise of me, I disappointed him. For this was by now but the final confirmation of all my own suspicions. I asked Hayley when he had reported the Boston men to Carrington. He replied that it was in the early part of November.

'And what then?'

'Then they were no more of my affair. Mr Carrington kept them from me. I made no enquiry of his method. You must apply to him if you would know more.'

He seemed pleased with his performance, and sat down and leaned back now, one hand clasping the lapels of his jacket, and his girth straining his waistcoat buttons. With his other hand he rearranged the coin towers. He was well prepared to parry the many more questions he expected that I must now put to him. That is to say, to answer me with that same admixture of truth and lies that I had received from him at every turn.

'Good day, sir.' I was at the door before he had recovered himself sufficient to ask his bill of me. 'The bill cannot be divided. And as you have given me but half the truth, Mr Hayley, I must give you nothing.'

At the King's Bench Prison was a crowd of some thousand and more people already gathered in that part of St George's Fields under Wilkes's barred window. Most were journeymen and coal heavers by their dress, and many had wives there, and children. But the scene was peaceful, and I felt no menace from them as I went up to the prison gate. Before the gate stood three fine carriages, which I wondered at till the turnkey let me inside the prison and Baxter told me the reason.

'It is Wilkes's daughter and a pack of Wilkes's friends, sir. And there have been letters for him all the morning.' I asked him if Carrington had been down and he answered that Meadows had left an hour past to take Carrington some report on the mob by the prison. 'But there has been no trouble. They are very quiet.'

We passed by the turnkey's room, through the lobby of the prison, and out by the secondary gate into the central yard. Here it was that the prisoners spent most of their days in useless idleness. I had been in the prison before (and upon my first return from Bengal, very often), and though there had been a number of brick buildings added to the place since that time, it was just the same feeling of wretchedness that now struck me as I entered the yard. The stone pavings were broken, the cobbles slick with mud, and a green fringe of slime and mould clung to the lower parts of the brick walls on every side. There were no warders to be seen, but upon a bench in the sun to the far side sat three well-dressed gentlemen. Baxter confirmed to me that these were debtors on a grand scale, and the acknowledged aristocracy of the prison till Wilkes's arrival.

He led me up the steps of the inner wall, where on the upper level was a long walkway overlooking the central yard to the left, and to the right, a line of small rooms. Baxter took me into the first of these. From below our feet came a sudden loud roar of laughter, and then a gaggle of voices joined in merriment.

'Wilkes's main room is directly under us. The wardens will keep this room empty for our use while Wilkes is here. It has a good vantage of the field. Here, you can see, sir.'

It had a good vantage not only of St George's Fields, but also of the road before the prison gate, and the two-storeyed building opposite. I enquired the use of that building, for a lad had now brought up a cart there. It was a storehouse, Baxter told me. Owned by a local innkeeper, the place was used also by the prison coachman to keep the dry feed for his horses.

At the north end of St George's Fields more people were arriving, in twos and threes and small bands, all coming down from the river.

'There is no parapet sir. This is as high as we may go.'

'We will need to have muskets brought down. But for God's sake, let the mob get no sight of them. You will need no more than a dozen, and be sure it is understood that they are under my command.' Baxter nodded, but I saw by his face how little pleased he was. 'It is a precaution only, Mr Baxter. If they should try to break into the prison to fetch him out, we must be prepared. You must put the muskets into the hands only of those warders you trust to be steady. There will be no firing upon the people while they are without the wall. But if you judge it necessary, and in an extremity, you may order a shot over their heads. If they break down the prison gate, we must have the means to defend ourselves.'

'Any shot will be an incitement to them.'

'I have requested that we have no soldiery here. If we can hold off from any shooting, no one shall be more pleased than I.'

'Meadows spoke of the soldiers being brought down.'

'I will see to Mr Meadows.'

In the yard again, we found that the door to Wilkes's room had been propped open, and a number of the prisoners had gathered there to pay their respects to him, which they offered by a general pushing and shoving among themselves, and a gawking in at the door. They were poor men, and would not think to go in to him, nor he to come out to them; for though he might proclaim himself to be for them, he was not of them, which they and he both knew. But his name was become a talisman, and he the idol the poor had fixed their best hope on.

Through Wilkes's open door I glimpsed the merry party, Wilkes presiding at the table's head, with his daughter Polly to his right. And upon the table a number of platters, and every one spilling over with breads and cheeses and fruits, and a carved leg of mutton up by Wilkes. There were many pitchers at the table's centre, and many glasses of wine. A fiddler stood up on a small table behind Wilkes and began to play a jig, at which the prisoners in the yard set up a foolish whooping. Two of them linked arms to make a dance like a pair of drunkards.

As I left the prison I espied that lad with the cart still across the way at the storehouse. I spoke to him briefly. He told me that his father owned the storehouse, so I had his name, which was Allen, before I came away and went up to the Treasury.

*　　*　　*

Jenkinson being in conference with Lord North when I arrived, he sent a message by his secretary that I might await him in his room. This room was upon the first floor, with a view eastward over the Horse Guards toward the Admiralty. And very splendid the room was, from its pillared fireplace to the fine plasterwork of the cornices, and with a pair of glassed bookcases reaching from floor to ceiling on either side of the door (a welcome elegance after my recent call upon the prison). It was by one of the tall windows that Jenkinson found me when he came in. For I was looking down, and with some disquiet now, at the soldiers who were at their drill in the Horse Guards Parade.

'It is only Barrington at his games,' said Jenkinson in answer to my enquiry, and crossing to his desk he added, 'I was grateful of your message of Wilkes's incarceration last night. I confess that I slept the easier for it.'

'Is there some particular reason that Lord Barrington has ordered the drill, sir?'

'The Secretary at War's whole business is to be playing at soldiers.' Jenkinson had brought some papers with him and now he made two neat piles of them on his desk while he asked my news of Wilkes. I made my report to him of everything I had seen, both the carnival-like parade through the streets to Spitalfields, and Wilkes's belated but peaceful going down to the prison. 'Did it seem to you,' said he, 'that there was any organization of the rabble?'

I gave him my opinion that there was not. 'Any trouble we may have now will not be stopped by a few arrests, sir. At the prison there is a crowd gathering. Not as many as yesterday, but that may happen yet.'

'It is their own infernal champion Mr Wilkes has put himself into the prison,' broke out Jenkinson, in exasperation with the headless mob. 'What shall they do, pull him out by the ears? I cannot think what they intend. He is no less subject to the law than any other one of us.'

I remarked that it was not any firm intention that now seemed to drive them, but a general feeling against injustice.

'If it is injustice concerns them, they might look to themselves. They have broke half the town's windows, to speak nothing of the houses they have destroyed. The new Parliament cannot come soon enough. We must put this behind us.'

There was a bellowing of orders down on the Parade, and Jenkinson came and stood by me. The lines of redcoats below went purposefully about their drill now; advancing, kneeling with muskets raised, and their officers inspecting the lines. The soldiers stood, moved forward, and knelt again. I had witnessed many such lines at their bloody work in places as far distant as Bengal and Louisiana, but God knows it was never then so neat and orderly as the scene now playing below us. Nor were there smart carriages stopped in the road to watch, as there were here; nor yet fine ladies standing by in bright-coloured dresses to admire the manly display.

'There should be no soldiers sent down to the prison, sir.'

'I am not their commander, Mr Douglas,' said he, turning to me from the window. But though I said nothing more on the subject, the dread of what might happen if the soldiers met the mob was written on my face and in my eyes, and after a moment he said that he would speak with Barrington and see what might be done to prevent the soldiers going down to the prison. 'I think we have all had our fill of these recent disorders. I grant you, we must be fools indeed to provoke any more of them.'

Though it was hardly disorder I feared now, but slaughter, I did not tell him so. I must be content to let him proceed in his own fashion; for every room in Westminster and in Whitehall was open to him, and he could make the argument to the likes of Barrington and Weymouth, and even to the King, whilst I should never be received in such company. I reflected that the Bishop had chosen his man more wisely than I had first understood.

When he looked to his clock I knew that I should soon be dismissed, and so I said, 'I have called upon Hayley this morning.'

'This can wait, I think, Mr Douglas,' said he, sitting down at his desk.

'Hayley has long known of Pearce and Flanagan's whereabouts in

London. In November he passed that information to Mr Carrington.'
Jenkinson looked at me in astonishment. But then as he turned it over
in his mind, his doubt of it surfaced in his eyes. It was too aston-
ishing. He could not bring himself to believe it. 'It is not Hayley's
word alone makes me believe it, sir,' said I, and then I told him all
the other circumstances that had troubled me in my pursuit of those
two murderous Sons of Liberty, the sum of which might be stated
very simply: they had evaded me too often, too easily, and too well.
'And when we found Flanagan's body, Carrington was to the Greenland Dock before I had sent word to him.'

'Mr Carrington had you under watch.'

I said that I did not believe it, and I told him the reason.

'But why should he protect them?' said Jenkinson. 'Have you spoke
with Fitzherbert?'

'Mr Fitzherbert gave no order for it.'

'Then there is no reason.'

'There are two reasons, sir. The first is that Mr Carrington had
some fear that I might displace him. My failure to find Pearce and
Flanagan made sure that I would not.'

'And the second?' said he, unconvinced.

'When Hayley understood that his part in this might be discovered, he went at once to Lord Sandwich's man of business.'

'You will be careful what you say now, Mr Douglas.'

'The Greenland Dock was once the Great Howland Dock. And
that was built by, and till recent years owned by, the Duke of Bedford.
It should be no surprise to anyone if the senior men there are still
tied to him.'

'That is not careful.'

'It is the truth.'

'You are reaching your hand dangerously high.'

'Would you have me be silent?'

He made no answer at first, but studied me now closely. Nor did
I turn away, for I would have him see me very plain. I would have
from him now that same trust and freedom that I had once had from
Mr Watts. Either that, or the harness put over the pair of us by the

Bishop would now break, and nothing for it but that I must now leave the Decipherers.

'I would not have you be silent, Mr Douglas,' he said at last. 'But I do not fully understand your imputation.'

'Nor I, sir. And that is why I have told you.'

CHAPTER THIRTY-SIX

When I came out from the Treasury, the soldiers remained at their drill on the Parade, and by now there were even more people arrived at the edge of the drilling ground to watch. But this was a small crowd, much different from that gathered outside the King's Bench Prison; for here were no journeymen or coal heavers, but the ladies were in brocaded jackets, with French lace at the collar, and pretending some attention to their frock-coated gentlemen who instructed them on the nicer military points of the drill.

'Will you cut us then, Alistair? You must pay a forfeit.' It was Amelia Watts, who had stepped out from a group of women to block my path.

'Then you must let me pay, and let me pass,' said I; but she smiled so cheerfully that I could not help but return it.

'It is a forfeit not a toll,' said she, and took my arm and led me around to her friends. Mrs Watts I saw first, shielding her eyes to the sun, and observing the drill with a sharp eye. And beside Mrs Watts stood Lady Shelburne. And beside Lady Shelburne, and to my dismay, Mademoiselle Beauchamp.

I felt my heart jolt in my chest when I saw her, and almost hated myself for it. Then I took the hand of each lady in turn, and dropped my eyes at the last.

'So, I have found our escort,' said Amelia. 'We are taking a tour, Alistair. But the gentlemen have all deserted us.'

'I cannot stay. You must forgive me.'

'Mademoiselle Beauchamp leaves with her father this afternoon,' said Mrs Watts. 'We had promised her the Abbey before she goes.'

'I hope that you shall enjoy it, Mademoiselle.'

'Come now, that will not do,' broke in Lady Shelburne, frowning playfully; and turning to Mademoiselle Beauchamp she said, 'I think you know Mr Douglas? He is too good a gentleman to disoblige us. Let us take our opportunity of the Abbey while we may.' Having so deftly put the brass ring through my nose, she then gave her maid the instruction to go with the carriage around to the Abbey and await her there; and then with Mrs Watts's arm in hers, Lady Shelburne set off around the drilling ground and towards the arch into Whitehall. Any protest from me must now be an insult to her ladyship. Amelia took my arm, and we followed after her mother and Lady Shelburne, and Mademoiselle Beauchamp walking silent at my right, till Amelia leaned forward and spoke past me, asking the Mademoiselle how she might know me.

'Monsieur Douglas was in Paris in the winter. We have a mutual acquaintance in Monsieur Buffon.'

'But it was he who dined with us at Mr Jenkinson's, Alistair.'

'Yes.'

If Amelia had not her mother's deep penetration, she had at least a quick perception, and she said to me now, 'I see you had rather I had not waylaid you.'

'It is untimely, that is all.'

'But you must go then. We shall release you. Lady Shelburne will not mind.' And so saying Amelia released my arm, and would have called ahead to her mother and Lady Shelburne, but that I prevented her, saying in my turn that it was done now and that I was content, and even happy, to be their escort. Quite why I should say such a thing, I am at some wonder to understand even now; for nothing could be changed. Mademoiselle Beauchamp must return to Paris to marry Cordet, and I must turn myself to iron and close up my heart. But I suppose if there is any explanation of my action, it must be that I was like to a drowning man who raises himself one last time to look up to the bright sky before he sinks down finally, and for ever, beneath the waves.

Mademoiselle Beauchamp barely spoke to me, or I to her, all our way along Whitehall to the Abbey. And Amelia I think grew ever more aware of my discomfort and silence, which must strike her as unaccountable, having no proper clue to its cause. But nor was Amelia immune to the great troubles at every side in the town, and she several times mentioned Wilkes, and the mad abduction by the mob, and it came to me that she thought on some incidents that she had been near when still a child in Bengal. And upon my assurance that Wilkes was now secured in prison, and that the people gathered there in support of him stayed quiet, Amelia remarked that Mademoiselle Beauchamp must think us perfect savages here in London.

'I am sure we must have our own such troubles in Paris,' came the reply (which seemed then but a polite courtesy, and nothing like a prophecy).

At the Abbey door, Amelia went to join her mother. I put a foot on the stone threshold and opened my arm to Valerie. She met my look then, and she had not that gaze of the wild Cherokee that she had turned upon me in Paris.

Would to God that she had.

I felt the waters close over me, and we passed together into the Abbey.

'How pleased shall the Vicomte be to hear that you have spent the last of your visit in my company?'

'Who shall tell him?' said she, and smiled very pleasantly at me. We walked on slowly down the side aisle, me with my hands clenched behind my back, and both of us pretending an admiration of the stained glass and speaking nothing that was in our hearts. I was melancholy now, but almost glad of my forfeit. There is a strange peace comes when a man finally sinks beneath the waves.

'Shall you be in Paris again soon, Mr Douglas?'

'I should not think so. I will be sent after our trade.'

'To America.'

'It is likely. But there are many places possible.'

'I have had enough of travel,' she said. 'I wish only to stay at home now.'

'A year past I had thought that I should like the same.'

'Shall I be disappointed then?'

'Your life in Paris must be unlike mine here in London, Mademoiselle. I hope that you shall not be disappointed.'

'I am ready for a new life. When you were in Paris last year, perhaps I was not then quite ready. My time in Saint-Domingue was still on me. And Quebec. But now – now I find that I am very settled, and happy.'

'I am glad of it,' said I, and almost choked upon the words.

We continued our slow wandering about the Abbey, and sometimes the other three ladies joined us, but they mostly kept off from us, which I think was by Mrs Watts's invisible direction. I made but a poor guide, for my gaze could not help but fall blankly upon the memorials and effigies, and the stone floor, and the brasses. And though we talked, we talked only as two friends near to parting, for that was how she had made it between us, and I knew that I must respect her wish or be no decent kind of man.

But when the leisurely tour of the Abbey was near to ending, and Mrs Watts glanced over her shoulder to us as she went with Lady Shelburne and Amelia down the nave toward the door, then it was that Valerie at last stopped and faced me. She could not quite meet my eye, and very clear that she had wrought herself up to say something to me. 'We will not have the chance to speak again, Alistair. And so I must tell you now that I regret any hurt that I have done to you.'

'It is I have done the injury. You have not hurt me.'

'That is not true,' said she quietly, but with feeling; for such is a woman, that she would rather think to have cleaved a man's heart than to have left him indifferent.

'It is not,' I confessed. 'But I will not die of what cannot be. I will think on you still. And perhaps you will sometimes remember me.' (And this the very echo of Henrietta's words to me, which I blush now to think on.)

'You shall ever be more than that to me, Alistair.'

'If you are ever in need, you must send for me.' She thanked me for the gallantry and began to turn toward the door, but that I dared now to put a hand on her arm. I looked directly into her grey eyes so that she might not mistake me. 'It was not a politeness. You must send for me. And you will promise me that.'

She was surprised, I think, by my intensity; but she bowed her head to give me the promise. I lifted my head from her arm then, and we went into the great nave and towards the door to rejoin the ladies. And outside, I must give each lady in turn my hand as they climbed into the carriage; and they must thank me, and all the civilities be said, and then I must get no last look at her, but only the talk starting up in the carriage, and a waving of hands, and Lady Shelburne thanking me from the window, and the carriage moving now, and drawing away around the square and into Great George Street, and finally gone from my sight.

I drifted down the last fathoms, and settled quiet upon the sea floor. That night there was rioting again in Wapping.

CHAPTER THIRTY-SEVEN

*E*ach day the crowd that gathered in St George's Fields was greater than the day before; and each night was more trouble up by the City. Soon not a butcher's shop in Whitechapel but was half destroyed; and though the cry was 'Wilkes and Liberty', Kitty promised me it was the price of meat was the spur. The drovers now feared to bring their cattle over the bridge, and the fishmongers to take their carts through the City lanes. Smithfield and Billingsgate stood empty. It could not go on for very much longer.

And glad though I was when Mrs Watts sent me word that she was retiring out to Hanslope Park in Buckinghamshire to spend a month with her son George (and taking both Amelia and Sophia with her), I needs must decline her invitation to join them all there. The Wattses' departure from London, and that of some other good families that I knew, was evidence to me that I was not alone in my disquiet. All through this time I went daily to Jenkinson's room in the Treasury to make report of both the troubles in the City and of the crowd in St George's Fields by the prison. And then came a day I arrived at his room and he was at the window and looking down at the soldiers on the drilling ground. He seemed not so sanguine as on that earlier day when we had watched them there. And I soon understood the reason of it when I came up by him, for he said, 'Barrington will have soldiers down at the prison tomorrow. I cannot stop him.'

'Sir, they are three or four thousand strong now in St George's Fields.'

'He knows it as well as you, Mr Douglas. If it were Barrington alone, I might dissuade him. He has others he must answer to.'

'Is it Lord Weymouth?'

'The Northern Secretary's opinion must carry a great weight. It is only the King has stayed Barrington till now.'

I asked him how many soldiers might be sent. He replied that a decision was not yet made.

'It will be a spark to the powder, sir.'

'Our business is to see that it is not,' said he, turning from the window to face me. 'Which is to say, Mr Douglas, that it is your business.' But how I might maintain peace by the prison when Weymouth and his Bedfordite gang were set upon the use of the soldiers, that he could not tell me. He returned to his desk, informing me that Wilkes's lawyers were to make a plea before Chief Justice Mansfield, and that Mansfield had expected Wilkes would be brought up from the prison to answer the court's questions. 'I have told him that to have Wilkes out from the prison at this moment may cause you some difficulties.'

'It would be a madness. It cannot be done.' There was a quick shadow crossed his face at this bluntness; but he did not overrule my refusal of the Chief Justice's expectation. I said again that there must be some way to keep the soldiers in their barracks, adding that I feared that Lord Weymouth had no proper understanding of the mob.

'It may be, Mr Douglas, that he understands the mob only too well. It may be that if he cannot face them down, then the ministry has no authority, and the mob and Mr Wilkes rule us all. But the Bishop arrives at Lambeth tonight to be ready for the new Parliament. I will surely speak to him of the soldiers.'

But the next morning, and in spite of any conversation Jenkinson might have had with the Bishop at Lambeth Palace, the first of the soldiers came down to the prison. I was without the prison wall when they came, and talking with Baxter and the lad Allen who had the cart (for though there was a well inside the prison, we must be better provisioned, and so I would have the lad go to a mill to fetch flour for us). Between the prison gate and the storehouse across the way, the turnkey had hammered in a row of wooden palings, and strung up between them a rope, and this to mark out a flimsy boundary between the crowd and Wilkes's visitors in their carriages, and also for the prison coach and the general coming and going of the warders. The sudden whistling and jeering against the soldiers started at the far side of the crowd, and I climbed up onto the cart with the boy Allen to see.

The soldiers were not many, certainly no more than fifty, and though my heart filled with dread at the sight of them it came as some relief to me to see that they had not fixed their bayonets, and that their officer kept them wide of the crowd as they came towards the prison.

When I climbed down the lad got his cart quickly away from there.

'Make no show of it, Mr Baxter, but put yourself outside Wilkes's door. If there is trouble, take him from there and secure him in the room above.'

I ducked beneath the rope and walked along by the prison wall. Wilkes's face suddenly appeared at his barred window in the wall high above me.

'What is it, Mr Douglas? Will they fetch me up to the court?'

Ignoring him, I continued on my way till I found out the captain of the guardsmen. He was a sensible fellow, and little pleased to be sent there with his men, who now appeared to watch the crowd nervously. It seemed he had got no particular order from his colonel, but only a general instruction to keep the peace near the prison; and when I told him that I was under the ministry, and with a charge to look to the safe keeping of Wilkes, he accepted that very readily, soon agreeing to keep his men from passing into the crowd.

And the crowd, though they had whistled and jeered at first, now saw that the troops did not come against them; for the captain gave his men the order that they stand easy with their muskets, which when they had done, the angry jeering turned to a railing mockery of the soldiers. The captain then went among his men, talking calmly with them, and I heard him enjoin them to restraint, and after a time he had talked them from their dangerous fear of the crowd. I heard him promise them a peaceful return to their barrack before nightfall.

Several times during that day the mob pressed up to the prison wall and cried out for Wilkes to show himself at the window, which scenes I watched with Baxter from the room above Wilkes's own. Wilkes obliged them each time, and though he made no general harangue he could not help but talk of himself, and that he would see justice done to him, and an end to his outlawry, and all for the good of the kingdom. He made also some remarks on the illegality of the General Warrants, but I saw from the blank looks of the people that it was all Dutch to them. It was never a Levelling debate that they had come for, but only to stand with the bold fellow who had poked the eye of the King and the ministry.

'Say the word, Mr Wilkes,' cried one barrel of a fellow, who must be a smith to judge by his thick arms and neck, 'and we'll come in and get you out from there.'

Wilkes's answer was to send out the fiddler who had been playing to Wilkes's feasting friends inside. And with the fiddler was sent out some part of the food that was then continually being brought to the prison for Wilkes by well-wishers of every degree.

And so a day which had opened threateningly ended with that fiddler playing in the field outside Wilkes's window, and trays of bread and fruit being taken into the crowd by the warders of the prison.

Near sunset the crowd began to make a dispersal towards the river, and that wise captain of the guardsmen let them go without shepherding. Then he marched his men back to their barracks, and neither pipe nor drum sounding, and by nightfall St George's Fields was near empty again, but for a few drunken fellows come up from the Dog and Duck to make a nuisance outside Wilkes's window. But Wilkes soon sent these troublesome fellows away, and after that it was peaceful, and any trouble gone with the dispersed crowd up into the City.

I was then an hour with the head warden, and he very happy to have my advice on the prison's defence, for it was a great novelty to him to be obliged to think on the best means by which people might be kept out of the place. But that we should need some plan he well knew; for he had heard those cries from the crowd that Wilkes must only give the word and they should have him out. When I told the warden of the order that Wilkes must not leave the prison to go up with his lawyers to the King's Bench court, he understood at once my fear that the mob might take this as a provocation.

'If it happen they break the gate, Mr Douglas, I shall look to you. I will tell my warders so.'

Upon leaving the warden, I came down the stone steps and into the prison yard. The night was moonless, and the yard but dimly lit by the several torches mounted upon the inner wall. The door to Wilkes's rooms lay open. Inside were a half dozen or more gentlemen gathered about the table, with a lively talk and laughter coming out from there, and jugs passing around. There was a fellow standing outside, along from the door, and with his back to me. He had one hand braced against the wall for support, and he was pissing into the gutter. I did not recognize him for Wilkes till he looked over his shoulder, squinting.

'Douglas?'

'Aye.'

'You are charged with my safe keeping, Fitzherbert says. They will never hurt me, you know.'

'There are others in the prison beside yourself, Mr Wilkes.'

'If they take me out, I shall only come back,' said he, turning again to the wall.

'If they take you out, you cannot know what may happen. They are a mob.'

'They will never hurt me,' he said again, which made me believe he had at least some small fear of it. He shook himself, and buttoning his breeches stepped away from the gutter. 'Will you join me at my table? I believe I have now almost the best cellar south of the river.' When I declined, he said that I should then feel myself at liberty to call upon him at any hour. 'And if I am out, it must mean that you shall find me somewhere about Westminster,' said he, and smiling as though this was all a sport to him, and not a vicious battle being fought in deadly earnest. We bade each other good night, and he returned to the merry company in his rooms, and I to Holborn and the last rest I should have for many days.

No soldiers came down to the prison on that day when Wilkes and his lawyers were due to appear again in the King's Bench court. I know not why this happened, though on my own way down through Westminster I had been surprised, and not a little alarmed, to see the many soldiers that were gathered on the green by the Abbey. (It is likely, I think now, that the disorders of those days had brought a confusion even in the ministry, and that Barrington had fully expected Wilkes to come up from the prison to the court.) Whatever the reason, the soldiers were not there to face the crowd in St George's Fields, and as the crowd grew through the morning I was very glad of the soldiers' absence; for there was not the same good feeling that there had been when Wilkes's fiddler had played. The mob had come now for a definite purpose, which was to make an escort for Wilkes up to Westminster. But as the morning drew on, and they saw no sign of the prison coach, they grew restive. A few of the worst sort began to throw stones over the prison wall, and called for Wilkes to be brought out to them.

By midday they were five thousand strong, and the head warden in a great agitation when he came up to see me and Baxter in the room above Wilkes's.

'They have struck one of my warders with a cudgel,' said he. 'You must send up for the soldiers.'

I made no answer to him, but continued to watch that party of a score and more fellows I had noticed to the front of the crowd. It was they who were making the loudest of the cries for Wilkes to be brought out, and they who had sent the first stones over the wall. They were coal heavers for the most part, and it looked to be some weavers with them.

'If you will not call out the soldiers, Mr Douglas, then I must send for them.'

I told him to quiet himself, and I beckoned him to me. He came and looked out of the glassless window. 'See you any muskets or guns?'

'By Christ, have they guns?' said he, and with such a fear as made me wonder at his worth.

'You must calm yourself, sir. They have no guns, nor any muskets. It is not troops assembled at your wall, and I will have no troops brought against them.'

'My men are ill-used.'

'Then call your men in.' He began to protest that some of his men at least must remain as marshals to stand at that makeshift cordon of rope ten yards out from the wall, but I cut him off impatiently. 'Your walls will not be pushed over, sir. You have had a man struck. Take the lesson of it. Your marshals are now targets and you must bring them in.'

This seemed to reach the poor fellow, and he hurried out, but I sent Baxter after to make sure that it was done. A minute later I saw there was a prison lad sent out from the gate to call the warders back within the walls. There was a jeering followed the warders' withdrawal, and at first there came no great press forward from the crowd after them. But then that front body of men broke free of the crowd and quickly pushed over the stakes and trampled the rope cordon into the ground. And they were near to the gate now, where I would not have them be.

'These are issued you as a precaution only,' I told the warders when they were reassembled beneath the lean-to in the yard, and Baxter distributing muskets and shot, and I the powder and wadding. 'You will keep yourselves from the rooms overlooking the field. Mr Baxter will give you your positions. It is at my order alone that any man shall fire, but I do not think it will come to that.' There was then a loud crack like a musket shot, and every man flinched; but then came a clattering above our heads, and down the slates, and a stone fell from the slates and onto the cobbles just by us. A nervous laughter ran over the men, and Baxter soon after took them to their places while I went to pay a call on Mr Wilkes.

I had ordered his door to remain unlocked, and so I knocked now and went straight in. It was a curious scene in his rooms, for he had received for several days now not only many visitors but a great quantity of gifts, and there was now a profusion of empty baskets inside his door. And there was new linen draped over the backs of his chairs, and good plate on the table; and stacked in one corner enough crates of wine to supply a decent cellar. From the central beam was suspended a small birdcage, its two canaries chirruping brightly. Wilkes was upon the sofa, propped on one armrest and with his legs stretched out over the cushions. He had a book in his hand, which he lowered as I came in.

'We must have you out from here awhile.'

'To Westminster?' said he, a little surprised; for I had told him already that he would not go up there that day. But when I explained that I would remove him to the room above, and the reason, which was the general safety of all the prisoners as well as his own, he made no difficulty of it but swung his feet to the floor.

'Before we go, Mr Wilkes, you must speak to them from your window.'

'They are in no temper for listening,' said he, as one who had attempted the thing and failed.

'I need them only to see you. You must show your face that they believe you remain here after you remove upstairs.'

We passed into the next room, which was his bedchamber. It was this room had the barred window set into the prison wall, but it was set very high, and so he must climb onto a chair, while I watched him, and from the chair onto a table, before he could put his face up to the window. The moment that his face appeared to them on the other side, there was a cheer went up, and when it had died, shouts for Wilkes to come out, and never to fear them for they should get him safely up to Westminster in spite of the King.

'If you were to request of them that they cease from throwing stones over the wall,' said I, 'then I am sure that your fellow prisoners would be grateful of the courtesy.'

He shot me a dark look and then gripped the bars and got up on his toes to address them.

'Friends,' he called down to them, 'friends, I am content to remain here. My lawyers are about their pleading. They have no need of me there.'

This was greeted by cries of 'Come out!' and 'We'll fetch you out, sir!' and Wilkes was now in some embarrassment that I should see how little they heeded him. He tried several times more to speak but they gave him no ear, only shouting up to him that he must not be frightened of them, but come out. He finished by requesting in some annoyance that they throw no more missiles over the walls, and then he got down from the table in some disgust of the people without, and came with me into the yard, where we must hurry to the steps for fear of some injury from the stones that continued over the wall and onto the cobbles.

Once we were in the room above I directed him to the sleeping platform, well away from the window; but he would not go there at first but called me back out to the verandah and questioned me on the disposition of the armed warders both in the yard and upon the far verandah. I explained to him that if the crowd broke the main gate we might be compelled to surrender the prison lobby, but that the mob should be prevented by the threat of the muskets from coming out from the lobby and into the yard. He approved the plan in a general way, but suggested some small amendments; as if I should think to take the military advice of a fellow whose whole life's concern had been only for his pen and his prick.

'I shall think on it, Mr Wilkes,' said I, and then I left him in Baxter's care while I went to settle the nerves of the warders who must be now my musketmen.

In the late afternoon Baxter came to warn me that those worst troublemakers in the crowd had brought lump hammers and crowbars to the main gate. I hurried down with the head warden, and he locked the secondary gate between the lobby and the yard, and then I barred it, which I had held off doing till now lest it worsen the apprehension of the warders, which was already very great. The lobby gate had made a loud scrape and clang as it shut, and now shouts broke from the prisoners locked in their rooms, for that noise of the gate was very familiar to them. They seemed in a fear even greater than the warders, as being more helpless.

Then the hammers began to strike hard against the outer gate.

'Mr Baxter!' I called, and he came out onto the verandah with Wilkes at his heels. 'Mr Wilkes will remain in the room out of sight. You will keep yourself at his door there.' Wilkes began to protest, and I went closer, so that I was almost under their place on the verandah, where only he and Baxter might hear me. 'You will do as you are ordered, sir, or I will put you in irons for your own safety.'

He saw that I would do it. So when Baxter stepped aside for him, Wilkes muttered an oath against me and retreated into the room.

I fetched the last musket and went and propped it against the corner post of the lean-to. And here I waited. For from this place I could see through the lobby to the main gate, and now it juddered beneath the blows of those without. At last the small door in the gate broke from its hinges and crashed onto the lobby floor, and the fierce fellows huzzahed like demons and came stumbling and shoving into the lobby.

They knocked over the lobby benches and some rushed at the secondary gate into the yard, and some went directly into the turnkey's room, and all of them shouting, but in some confusion what to do with their success.

'Come out, Mr Wilkes!' cried one, and another almost delirious with triumph, 'Wilkes to Westminster!' and some of them laughing now, and the chair came from the turnkey's room and was smashed in the lobby, and there was more crashing inside, which must be the table and cabinets being broken to pieces.

They had seen me through the iron bars of the lobby gate. And they had seen my musket, which was leaning on the corner post at my side. As they continued their wild spree within the lobby, there were some of them came and took hold on the iron bars of the second gate and shouted for Wilkes, but they could not fail to see now all the warders with muskets awaiting them in the yard, and on the upper floor. No musket was raised (which I own was a better obedience to my order than I had expected) but every musket visible, so that there could be no mistaking what must happen if the lobby gate break open and the wild party enter the yard. That was the reason, I think, that when a rash young fellow brought up a hammer to strike the bars, some others hauled him back from there. And after a minute I saw that there was no general press from the crowd without the walls, but only this worst of the mob was come in.

One burly coal heaver gripped the bars now and cursed me. He spat into the yard, but the trouble it took him to keep up his anger in the face of my indifference grew too much for him and so he soon let go of the bars and went back to his fellows. With nothing to set themselves against, and no sign of Wilkes to draw them on, the general laying waste of the lobby became their only concern, which when they had achieved to their satisfaction they began to come and go through the outer gate, taking with them as trophies some broken sticks of furniture.

I looked up at the head warden. His hand was upon the verandah rail, and his musket just by him. His face was white. About him his warders stood steady, and by them their own muskets. None had answered the taunts that were shouted up from the lobby. I could not have asked any more of them.

Another hour I waited, watchful. My only fear now was that soldiers might be sent to our aid; but whatever the reason of it, no soldiers came. And as the evening cold began to settle upon us, the exuberance within the lobby faded with the light, and in ones and twos, and then severally, the fellows went out by the broken door of the main gate. With laughter and cheering, they called loud to tell Wilkes somewhere in the prison that they should return in the morning, but that now they must go down to the Dog and Duck to drink his health, and a pint or two for liberty.

I slept that night in Wilkes's dining room in the prison, and with no little fear of the morning.

CHAPTER THIRTY-EIGHT

'The soldiers have come, sir,' said Baxter, hurrying into Wilkes's room from the prison yard.

Rising from my breakfast, I went into Wilkes's bedchamber. He had been dressing in there, and having heard Baxter's announcement of the soldiers, was now climbing onto the table beneath the window.

'Which regiment is it?' he asked Baxter. 'Did you see?'

Baxter told me that it appeared to be the same steady captain as before. Wilkes, from his vantage at the window, now reported that the soldiers were assembling before the main gate. I made no delay then, but turned on my heel and went out. I was halfway across the yard with Baxter when Wilkes came up between us, and pulling on his jacket.

'What is it that you want, sir?' said I.

'Bring the captain in to me. I would forbid him the use of his muskets.'

I stopped, and put a hand on Wilkes's chest to stop him. 'You would forbid him? You will not forbid the captain anything, sir. He is come here to keep the prison secure, which would not have been needed but for your calling up of the mob.'

'It was not my summons brought them,' said he, pushing off my hand.

'It was your actions, Mr Wilkes. And your words. With every letter in every newspaper, and each handbill that you have written, you have shoved yourself and your grievances forward. Now we must all endure the outcome. And you no less than any other.'

'Silence is no answer to injustice.'

'They without the walls have in silence abided worse injustices than ever fell to you, sir. But you have taught them speech. We shall see now what profit they may have on it. Go to your room, Mr Wilkes. You have no business with the captain.'

Outside the front gate, which had been hastily repaired in the night, I found that same captain of the two days earlier, and with him that same troop of guardsmen. Though there were people coming towards the prison across the field, it was early, and only a few hundred yet gathered near Wilkes's window. I took the captain into the lobby and showed him the inner gate, and explained to him all that had happened the previous afternoon and evening. Then passing outside again, I looked along the front line of the crowd for any faces that I had seen during the destruction of the lobby; but there was not a one I recognized among those early arrivals.

'They were at the Dog and Duck till after midnight, sir,' said Baxter. 'They will be abed a while yet.'

It was as we were standing there by the gate looking about us, and I with a hope now that the level-headed captain and his troops might do a peaceful service by their presence that day (which was the ninth day of May, and one day before the new Parliament should open), that there arrived a Post Office coach. And leaping down from the coach came Gus. He came up to me directly and handed me a scribbled note. It was but a sentence, and not in cipher but plain text only.

Come up to the Lane at once,
Francis.

There was no more to be had from Gus as to the meaning of it, and I confess I was in some annoyance that Francis should summon me up there so peremptorily, for he well knew I must be needed at the prison. But the captain assuring me that there was little I might do to aid him for the present, and Baxter saying that he would send up for me at once if there was more trouble, I climbed into the coach with Gus. We went up by London Bridge, but as we crossed over the river I saw a sight there made me bang my fist hard against the carriage roof. 'Stop! Stop at once!'

Getting down, I ran across to the wall, and set my hands there and looked east along the river, almost disbelieving my own eyes. The ships were thick upon the water, and not a man aboard, but every sail was struck. And flying on every topmast a red flag. Red flags all the way from the Tower across to Rotherhithe, and out of sight down the river. The red flag of battle, the seaman's signal of a general engagement.

'How should I know the reason of it?' said Francis testily as he came out from his room and locked the door. 'And nor is it only upon the river.'

As we descended he told me what he knew, which was that when he had come down from his rooms at the Royal Exchange that morning, there had been armed watermen at the Exchange's main door. They had made no threat to him, but answered him very civilly, saying that they had come to protect the place. 'Protect it, mark you, Alistair. But no one there to attack it. And have you seen the Post Office?'

I said that I had not, for I had come up the back way.

'Come there now,' said he.

We went out through the steaming room, and Bode calling out after Francis, asking what we knew was afoot, and if the post that day was stopped. The translators sat idle, with their feet upon the fender by the stove. Francis told Bode to wait there, and then we went through to the small entrance chamber, and from there passed into the main part of the Post Office.

There should have been a great noise at this hour, and the post arriving and going out, but instead was a deathly quiet. I looked at Francis and he at me, very grim. We soon came out into the main post room, where the deliveries must come, and the sorting be done. Here was no one standing by the sorting tables where should have been twenty hard at their work. And most curious of all, over at the far side of the receiving counter, to the front of the building, was a motley collection of watermen and sailors, and all armed with muskets. They were seated on the floor with their weapons resting beside them, or standing by the main door and talking together, and their muskets propped against the wall.

'What is this?' said I quietly, and walking on.

'Whatever it may be,' said Francis, 'my father has had no warning of it.'

Then we heard voices above us, and looking up we saw at the head of the stairs Lord Sandwich and Carrington. It appeared Carrington was getting some instruction, but the moment they saw us they fell silent. And then Sandwich nodded Carrington down. But as Carrington started down the stairs, Francis put his foot on the first step and called up boldly, 'My Lord, may we know the reason of all these armed men? Are we to defend ourselves?'

'That is as you please, Mr Willes. These are here for our general security.'

'We have guards that we may look to for our security, My Lord,' said I. 'There is no reason these men should be here.'

'I have advised it,' said Carrington, stopping on the stairs, and with his hand resting upon the hilt of his sword.

'For what reason?' said I.

Sandwich came forward to the balustrade. 'You may tell Mr Carrington how to conduct his business once you have first looked to your own. I was informed that you were at the prison.'

'I have just now come up, My Lord.'

'Then you shall easily find the way of your return, Mr Douglas. Good day to you.'

Carrington now came down and straight past me and then out the front door without a backward glance. And Sandwich pushed away from the balustrade and went back to his rooms.

Some word then passed among the watermen, and several of them went outside, and I beckoned to Francis and we followed after these fellows. Lombard Street was strangely quiet, and many of the shops there still with the night boards bolted over their windows, and very few people about, though it was a day of business. But as we followed the watermen to the corner of Cornhill and Poultry, we saw them join with many more watermen gathered there. And as we came up to them, we saw beyond, coming down Cornhill, a great parade of seamen, with a red flag carried to the front of them, which was a startling sight. The watermen cheered the seamen as the parade came on westward.

I asked the nearest watermen, whom we had followed from the Post Office, the meaning of this massing of the sailors.

'They have made a general strike of sails,' said he. 'They will take a petition to the King for better pay. But it will be done orderly, sir. We are no Wilkites. You are from the Post Office, sir?'

'I am. Who has put you under arms?'

He said that there had been a great gathering of watermen and sailors in Stepney Field very early. Volunteers had been called for, and so he had come up. He had been put at the Post Office by some fellow he was told was a King's Messenger. All of this was very disturbing to me, and when I asked the fellow his orders, he said, 'We must keep your place secure from the Wilkites, sir,' and then he moved away from me, to make his huzzahs for the sailors in the van of the parade.

'My God, but they are thousands,' said Francis as we watched the sailors come on.

And so they were; but thousands very different from that mob down by the prison. For these were all hard men, and just as the watermen had said, very orderly; a fighting force, and among them no women or children. We hurried back to the Lane, Francis at once ordering Gus to lock and bar the door that joined us with the main Post Office. He spoke to Bode and the translators then, telling them they should return to their homes and come back to the Lane only when he had sent for them.

Up in his room, Francis penned a note to his father. 'He was to spend the morning with Jenkinson,' said he as he finished. 'They will be at the Treasury.'

'If the sailors cross the river, if they go down to the prison—'

'We cannot let it happen,' said Francis, and sealing the letter he gave it me and bade me make haste up to Whitehall.

I took a horse from the Post Office stables and soon caught up with the rear of the sailors in Fleet Street. After some awkwardness in getting by them (for they filled the whole street) I finally got past their red flag in the Strand. Though there were shouts came up to me from the sailors, and some sang as they went, there was an air almost of solemnity as they proceeded, and nothing like the wild atmosphere of carnival that had surrounded Wilkes in his abduction the opposite way. And this was almost the first thing I said to Jenkinson at the Treasury while the Bishop read Francis's note.

'I think they will make no menace here, sir. But soldiers must be posted at the bridge.'

'It was at your advice, Mr Douglas, that I have pressed to have the soldiers kept in their barracks.'

'The situation is changed, sir. But neither soldiers nor seamen should go down to the prison.'

'Where are these seamen now?' said the Bishop, looking up. When I told him that they were not ten minutes behind me, he said to Jenkinson, 'You must do what you can. Douglas is right, we must get some soldiers to the bridge. You will find me across the park when you are done.'

Jenkinson made no hesitation but hurried away at once, and I was soon assisting the Bishop down the Treasury stairs and out to his carriage. He gave the order for St James's Palace, and then he bade me get in with him. As we moved off he said, 'What is this that Francis writes of Sandwich and Carrington?'

'My Lord, it is impossible that Carrington had not been forewarned of such a gathering in Stepney. And it seems the Messengers have had some part in the organization of the armed watermen about the City.'

'You knew nothing of this gathering in Stepney.'

'My Lord, I have been with Wilkes.'

'Allow that Carrington knew of it, I cannot see that he has done wrong in securing the important places of the City.'

'By appearance it is done under Lord Sandwich's instruction. And not with soldiers—'

'You wanted no soldiers.'

'I wanted no soldiers at the prison, My Lord. And yet they are now down there. And in the City, armed watermen primed against Wilkes's people.'

'What is that?' said he suddenly, and looking from his window up the Mall. It was the seamen, and at the front of them the red flag held high.

'It is a flag from off one of the ships, sir,' said I. 'There are such flags broken out upon all the ships on the river.'

The Bishop needed no instruction upon the signification. His lips were pressed tight as he watched the red flag come on. At the gate of the King's Palace he set me down, commanding me that I should not stay in St James's nor return to the Lane, but go at once to make sure of Wilkes at the prison.

The captain being from the gate when I arrived, and only his soldiers there, I went directly into the prison and up to the room above Wilkes's window, and there I found Baxter stretched out on the wooden platform with his jacket folded beneath his head. He sat up when I entered.

'When did the soldiers fix their bayonets?' said I.

'That was done just after you left, sir. But the people pay no mind to it. The captain has made no challenge to the crowd. He has stood his men quiet all the morning.'

I crossed to the window. The crowd stood thick as locusts upon the field. I told Baxter then of that mustering of sailors and watermen in Stepney, and of their presence in the City, and of the march to

St James's Palace. 'There is nothing we may do now, but only wait,' said I, turning from the window. 'And God grant that the mob have no meeting with the sailors.' When I asked after Wilkes, Baxter told me that he was just now awaiting Wilkes's return from the head warden's room. For Baxter had sent him there upon the arrival of Wilkes's daughter Polly, and the lawyer Glyn, and that fellow Hayley.

'Hayley is here?' said I, and he nodded. 'Keep a watch up towards the river, Mr Baxter. And fetch me if the sailors come.'

I went down the steps and was almost across the yard when Polly came out from the warden's room. 'Miss Wilkes. You are very far from the Bois de Boulogne.'

She smiled, but the smile was strained. It was evident that she had heard from her father of my presence at the prison. 'I would be back there in an instant, Mr Douglas, were it only possible.'

'It is a pity your father does not share your taste for quiet.'

'That is how little you know him. He would be the quietest man in England if only they would let him be.' At my asking if she had come alone, she told me that her father was now in conference with Glyn and Hayley and some other of his supporters. 'I am only in their way now. I will come again in a few days when he is not so occupied.'

I escorted her to the gate, and outside. A cheer went up from the nearest part of the crowd at the sight of her behind the line of soldiers. She made no acknowledgement of it, and we turned and walked away from the prison. Some from the crowd set out to follow us briefly, but others called them back, for there was a strange courtesy in these people, and a respect for one of Wilkes's own. Around the corner we found her carriage waiting. As I offered her my hand to help her onto the step, she said, 'You will see that no harm comes to my father.'

'I will do my utmost.'

'You seem almost as doubtful as he.'

'I think your father has no reason to complain of the protection afforded him,' said I, for I was little inclined to allow any slur upon the warders who had held so steady in spite of their fear. But she said at once that he made no complaint.

'It is only some presentiment my father has. You will laugh, Mr Douglas, but there was even a time he had a suspicion of you.' I could not conceal my surprise. And Polly seemed now to regret that she had spoken. 'He does not think it now,' she said quickly, and got into her carriage. I closed her door, and she spoke to me now through the window. 'He knows that you have looked to his safety, Mr Douglas. It was only when he was newly elected. There were many friends who warned him of the danger he had laid himself open to.'

'The man was no friend to your father who warned him against me.'

'It is past.' She adjured me again to take care of his safety. But when her carriage departed, what she had said stayed with me; for there were but two people might have given Wilkes such false warning of me, and one of them within my near and certain reach.

'I must trouble you a moment, Mr Hayley,' said I from behind the desk in the turnkey's room. Hayley and Glyn had been on their way through the lobby, but now they stopped and looked in through the open door. Glyn appeared curious; but Hayley was highly displeased to find me there.

'I am not here on my own affairs, Mr Douglas. You know where you may properly find me.'

'This goes to Mr Wilkes's safety.' Glyn at once stepped towards me, but I said, 'You will not be needed, sir. It is Mr Hayley alone that I would speak with.'

Glyn glanced from me to Hayley, and then withdrew, saying that he would have their carriage brought around to the gate. Hayley came in then, though reluctant. He sat, but very forward on the chair. He kept his hat on, and did not unbutton his coat.

I said, 'What warning have you given Mr Wilkes against me?' His eyes narrowed, and his head turned a little away as he peered at me. 'Do you hear me, sir?'

'I hear you, Mr Douglas. But you must explain yourself further if you would have me understand you.'

'It was an evil day for you when you first wrote that bill.'

'If I cannot write bills, sir, I have no business in the City,' said he in irritation. 'Now what is this of my brother-in-law's safety?'

'You will recall that Mr Macleane came to you at the Jamaica House to give you notice of that bill.' His look was instantly wary. He recalled the moment very well. 'And I think you must also recall where it was that you ran to when you learned that the bill might be presented.'

'I did not run anywhere.'

'But you did, sir. For I saw you. You ran to Jones, Lord Sandwich's man of business.'

'If I have some dealings with that house, it is no affair of yours,' said he rising.

'Mr Hayley, tomorrow the people will come again to St George's Fields, and they will be many more than we have had here till now. And the soldiers, they shall also be more. And north of the river, the seamen today have marched in their thousands to petition the King. With all that to concern me, do you suppose that I would waste one minute in any idle enquiry into your commercial affairs?'

'And yet you do.'

'I am out of patience with you. If you will insist upon secrecy, there is nothing for it but that I must tell Wilkes and Glyn of your connection with Lord Sandwich. A man you know to be the sworn enemy of Wilkes.'

'I have no such connection,' he said hotly. He was fully risen now, and he put his hands upon the desk and leaned toward me. 'None.'

'You feared that I might reveal your connection to Lord Sandwich, and so you made sure to first blacken my name with Wilkes. You have warned him against me.'

'You are wrong, sir.'

'If I am, you have not convinced me of it.' He pushed away from the desk and looked about the walls of the small room like a man cornered. 'Wilkes and Glyn are both close at hand,' said I. 'Now what shall it be, Mr Hayley? Will I at last have the truth from you?'

'Would you slander me?'

'I would do much worse than that, sir.'

He looked at me now from the corner of his eye. But whatever calculation it was that he made, he got no comfort by it. At last he saw that he had little choice now but to speak, and he directed his gaze to a place on the wall by my shoulder. 'It was by Carrington's instruction that I went to Sandwich's man. Carrington told me that the bill might be presented by another party. He instructed me that if it should happen, I must convey the news at once to Jones. I have no connection besides with any of Sandwich's people.'

'Carrington instructed you it might be presented by a party other than Pearce or Flanagan.'

'Yes.'

'And when was this?'

'I cannot recall precisely. Around the time of the Middlesex election. Around then.'

'You might have told me this before now.'

'And you, sir, might have treated me more civilly, and not like a common thief.'

He was a ridiculous man, and even now half hidden from himself. His sole concern from the first had been to evade a proper redemption of the bill. It was an evasion had drawn him into deeper waters than he knew. For what I saw now was that Hayley had first gone to Carrington in the hope that the Messengers would rid him of Pearce and Flanagan, and hence their claim upon him through the bill. But my retrieval of the bill had thwarted this miserly hope, and introduced me as a nuisance into whatever it was that Carrington had afoot with those two sons of damnation. The pretence Hayley now made that he was but a good man misunderstood might do very well for his fellows in the Jamaica House coffee shop. Its effect upon me was only to turn my stomach.

And yet he had not warned Wilkes against me.

'Do not return here tomorrow, Mr Hayley. It would only stand to put your own life in danger.'

CHAPTER THIRTY-NINE

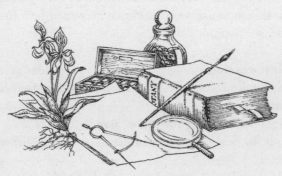

*T*he morning of the tenth of May broke clear and bright, and the people came early to the field. When they arrived they found the captain and his guardsmen already making a line at the gate and along the prison wall beneath Wilkes's window. I walked down the line of soldiers with the captain, and we stopped at the end and looked over the field at the many people coming down from the river.

'They expect that Wilkes shall be taken up to Westminster today to give his oath,' said the captain.

'Then they shall be disappointed,' said I, for it was certainly no part of the ministry's intention to allow Wilkes – still awaiting the court's judgment on the charge of sedition against him – to take his seat in the new Parliament.

'Yes,' said the captain, looking with worry over the fast-growing crowd. 'That is my fear.'

Inside the prison, I had made the same preparations as before, only that now I had a better faith in the warders and so made no delay in the distribution of muskets. The head warden had very sensibly turned out from the prison a dozen of the elderly prisoners upon their promise of a return the next week, which made it the easier to look to those who remained. At a half after seven, I gave the order for each of these remaining prisoners to fetch a pail of fresh water from the well and a loaf from the kitchen, and then to return to their rooms, where they must expect to be confined for their own safety till sunset.

The only prisoner untouched by these preparations was Wilkes, whose door stood ajar, and whom I now went to call upon.

'You are up and doing early, Mr Douglas,' said he, from his place at the head of the table. He was taking his breakfast alone, but it appeared that he had been up and doing for some good while himself, for he was dressed in a blue frock-coat trimmed with gold piping, and beneath that he wore a red silk waistcoat. He had powdered his hair, and it was tied back in a black bow, for which small duty I suppose he had paid one of the warders. Indeed, he was as well turned out as he had been that day when he had made that bold speech to Mansfield's face at the King's Bench court. 'Will you take coffee with your new Member of Parliament?' said he, raising a silver pot, and smiling as though he enjoyed the whole predicament he had created.

I went into his bedroom and climbed upon his table. Then keeping my face a little back from his window, and to one side, I looked out. The shouting for Wilkes started upon the instant, everyone calling for him to come out, and many cries of 'Wilkes to Westminster!' and a new cry that jolted me, 'Damn the soldiers! Damn the King!'

I saw, and with no small alarm to me, that those worst fellows who had destroyed the lobby were now returned. They were to the front of the crowd, and already pressing against the captain's line. I got down from the table and went back to Wilkes's dining room. He was tasting his coffee.

'What is your business with the French whore, Pitou?'

'Sir,' said he, putting down the cup as though I had made some affront to his delicacy. He instructed me to remember myself.

'What I will remember, sir, is that she was your mistress in Paris, and that she came to your apartment here in London the morning of your election. I ask you again, what is your business with her?'

'This is very low.'

'Polly may well think so, if you compel me to go to her for an answer.'

Wilkes swore.

I said, 'Pitou is in the pay of the Cabinet Noir. You will not pretend to me that you had no knowledge of it.'

'Is this what the ministry must stoop to, that I be kept from my rightful place in Parliament?'

'For God's sake, forget yourself for just one moment, sir. Did she warn you against me?'

'Yes,' said he sharply. 'And what would you know more? How often I took her?'

'What manner of warning did she give you?' He shrugged, and I stepped nearer. 'What did she say?'

'Nothing that I did not know. She said that there was some plot upon my life. Her people had a suspicion of your part in it. And you may wonder now if I knew her to be Cabinet Noir while I had her in Paris. The answer is that I did not, sir.'

'Why should they look to your safety?'

'Because they are fools and think me an enemy to my King. Which I have never been, nor ever hope to be.'

'She gave you my name?'

'She said it was the ministry behind it, which I hardly doubted of. They have tried it before, you know,' said he, and with a theatrical touch to his breast where he had been shot in his duel with that fellow Martin. Then gesturing towards me, he added, 'The ministry behind it, and the man come from America would finish me. But I do not distrust you, Douglas. I wondered even if she told me it as a tale to frighten me back to Paris.' He pushed aside his plate. 'But now you have spoiled my breakfast, sir. And for that I cannot forgive you.'

I went and found Baxter, and told him to fetch Wilkes to the upper room.

In the late morning the captain came to tell me that both he and his soldiers were to be relieved. He said that the third regiment of foot-guards had come down, which did not trouble me unduly at first; but then I went out with him, and found this third regiment already taking up their positions. And the captain leading these new men was shouting his orders like a crazed fellow, and was clearly in some fear of the crowd (which I own he had some reason to be, they being now more than ten thousand strong, and in high expectation of taking Wilkes up to Parliament). This new regiment by their mere presence seemed to have given a provocation to the people, the cause of which I only understood when I heard the soldiers speaking to each other, and from their voices knew them for Scotsmen.

The departing captain introduced me to his replacement, but this new captain was little impressed by the notion he might benefit from my advice, or indeed from the advice of his departing fellow officer.

'My men are not drilled to lean upon their muskets. They will use them if the need arise.'

'The crowd will hold off from violence if they are not provoked,' said I quietly.

'Indeed,' said he. 'And they shall find my men of much the same temper. If you look to keep the peace within the prison walls, sir, I shall make sure of it without.' He went off with his hand pressing his scabbard to his thigh, and with another barked order upon his lips. I looked at the departing captain, and he at me, and then he wished me well, and I saw how glad he was to be getting his men away from there.

Within the walls I made sure to speak with each warder as I went on my rounds. But each hour I found them a little less steady; for they heard very well the officer shouting beyond the walls, and the rising voice of the crowd as the day drew on and their champion Wilkes made no start toward Westminster to be sworn.

And then a stone came over the wall; and shortly after the first, another; and before the rain should turn general I went into that upper room where Wilkes was, and told Baxter to close the shutters now for safety. When he had done that, Wilkes went and peered out through the narrow slats. Baxter asked him what he saw.

'I see that they are not happy to find that the coach does not come for me. I see that they do not like it that the ministry will deny me my right to swear my fealty to the King.'

'Do you suppose that they are so concerned for your election?' said I.

'They care more than you know, Mr Douglas.'

'They would cut your throat for a guinea,' Baxter said. 'And if I had a guinea to spare, they might have it.'

Wilkes took no offence at this, and even smiled a little. He came from the shutters and sat upon the sleeping platform where he had left his book. Then I went myself and put my eye to the slats.

It was no longer a field of grass before the prison, but a field of angry people; and nothing but the line of soldiers, with bayonets fixed, keeping them back from the prison gate and walls. The people were more now than they had ever been, and in a greater agitation. When they abused the soldiers, the soldiers answered them with an equal scorn, and no laughter anywhere in the crowd now but was ugly and menacing.

'Have you called Tyler down, Mr Baxter?'

'No, sir.'

I stepped aside from the shutter, and beckoned Baxter over. I directed his attention to the storehouse across the way.

'Shall I call him in, sir?' said Baxter, peering through the slats at Tyler by the door there. But I said that I must go out there presently, and would speak with him.

There was a change then in the sound coming up from the crowd. Many people shouted all at once, and Baxter, with his eye still at the slats, said, 'There is a troop of horseguards, sir, come down the west side.'

I pulled one shutter open an inch. The mounted troop was a hundred strong, and riding in a file to the west of the crowd. Their sabres were sheathed, but the guardsmen rode very upright and purposeful, the gold trim of their cocked hats glinting in the sun. Their officers halted them midway along the crowd, but at such a distance that they might be clear of any missiles. Then the whole troop wheeled to face the people, and the officers rode down their line to keep them steady.

I knew at once that Jenkinson had lost his battle in Whitehall. First the Scots regiment, and now the horseguards. It could only be by the order of the ministry, which the crowd knew as well as I. Many voices now put up vicious cries against the whole ministry, and the King.

There was a bold fellow in a red jacket just below us, now harangued the crowd about him, urging the people against the Scots soldiers. And these soldiers now held their fixed bayonets levelled against the front lines of the people. A stone struck the wall by my face, and I banged the shutter closed.

'The horseguards may be my escort up to Westminster,' said Wilkes, which was a misreading so complete and contrary that I had no answer for it.

'Keep him from the window,' I told Baxter, and then I went down to the gate.

Outside the prison, that damned captain had worked his men up to such a pitch that the crowd had taken the infection from them and now made almost an opposing regiment. Those hard men to the front had now armed themselves with wooden clubs and iron spikes. And that fellow in the red jacket was the worst of them, drunk on his own fury, and the captain provoked by him and shouting in return, which was a weakness he had better kept under restraint.

I told the captain that I must go through his line.

'You will stay within,' said he, very sharp, and then he ordered six of his men to go into the crowd and fetch out that red-jacketed fellow.

The moment the soldiers moved the fellow ran. The crowd opened for him, and when he had passed, closed at his heels against the soldiers. And now was the first time I saw someone in the crowd struck, for the leading soldier swung up the butt of his musket and battered the first fellow who stood in his way, who fell crying, and with his hands covering his smashed face.

I went east from the gate, along by the prison wall, and away from the crowd. And as I came onto open ground, I saw those six soldiers break from the crowd and run across to the barn by the storehouse in pursuit of their red-jacketed quarry who had disappeared there ahead of them. But hardly had the first soldier entered the barn than the crack of a musket shot sounded, and upon the instant the crowd stopped their furious shouting.

Tyler, who had not seen me, retreated into the storehouse. But I ran now towards the barn, and as I came to the door, a soldier challenged me, but then one of his fellows told him who I was, and so they gave me entry. There were three soldiers standing over the body when I arrived, and some argument proceeding among them.

'You were ordered to take the fellow,' I said angrily, 'not to shoot him. Is he dead?'

'Aye,' said the sergeant, who seemed himself none too happy with what had been done.

And when I looked down at the body, I saw the reason. For it was not the mad fellow they had killed, it was the lad Allen. The boy was wearing his own red jacket, and staring dead-eyed at the rafters above. I looked to the sergeant. He well knew the weight of the error they had made. At the barn door, some fellows from the crowd were now appearing.

'Take your men back to the prison gate,' I told the sergeant. 'And go at once, lest they fall upon you and tear you to pieces.'

He mustered his men, and they left Allen's body lying by the straw. I followed the soldiers out from the barn as the first of the crowd entered, and while the soldiers made their hasty retreat, I went along to the storehouse to find Tyler.

Inside was a small room on the ground floor, and not finding him there, I mounted the wooden stairs, calling, 'Tyler! Come away now. We must be back to the prison.' Receiving no answer, I continued up. On the first floor were two rooms; I looked into each of them, but there was no sign of him. I looked from the window, and many people had broken off from the crowd now and were hurrying across to the barn. What might happen when they all knew of the lad Allen's death I did not like to think on. Over at the prison, the people still cried for Wilkes to show himself at the the window.

'Tyler!' I shouted again, and started up the next flight to the uppermost floor. But halfway up I stopped. For a sound had come from above, as of some heavy thing dropped or knocked over. No sound followed the first, and I took my dirk from beneath my jacket, and went on up, watchful.

At the top of the stairs were two doors, but only that upon the right side open, and I looked in warily. But the room was empty, save for some crates and ropes. Then I stepped across to the other door, and away to one side of it, and I called again, 'Tyler! Come out from there.'

'Is it you, Mr Douglas?' came the uncertain reply, and knowing the voice for Tyler's, I opened the door. Tyler was by the window, kneeling, and another fellow stretched out on the floor before him, and a musket lying near. Tyler looked up at me. 'It is Pearce, sir. I have killed him.'

I went across and bent down and rolled the dead man by his shoulder onto his back. He had a dark beard, and was dressed very simply, just as Flanagan had been – breeches, a white shirt, and a plain woollen jacket. I glanced at Tyler, and he was staring at Pearce. I saw now the bloody knife beneath his hand on the floor.

'Have you followed him here at Carrington's instruction?'

'Yes sir. It was feared he would kill Wilkes.'

I looked out. There was a fine view from this point, and over the crowd and the soldiers, and straight into Wilkes's window. Had we not moved Wilkes upstairs, he would have been often at that window during that day. And Pearce, from his vantage here, could very easily have put a fatal shot through Wilkes's head. When I looked down at Pearce now I saw that there was no blood on the front of his shirt. I rolled him again, and the blood showed all upon the back of his jacket.

'Sir, I must tell Mr Carrington.'

'Of course,' said I, and I took up the fallen musket. 'But first check Pearce's pockets. There may be some indication whence he has got his instruction.'

Tyler was still on his knees, and he bent forward over the body, searching the pockets. 'What was that shot, sir?'

'The soldiers have killed a lad.'

'Did you see the horseguards come down?'

'Yes. Where is Mr Carrington?'

'I cannot rightly say, sir.' He reached across to Pearce's far pocket, and as Tyler's blond hair fell over his eyes, I raised the musket and drove the butt down hard into the base of his skull. He dropped like a rag, face forward onto Pearce, and I went back into the other room and fetched the rope I had seen there. Then I hauled Tyler to a clear space on the floor, and folded his limbs and tied him as the Choctaws tie their prisoners, so that any struggle to escape must strangle him. When I was done, I went and looked out the window again.

Word of Allen's murder had spread. They were throwing stones in earnest now, and not over the walls but directly at the soldiers. Two Justices of the Peace, who had earlier called upon me within the prison, were now standing outside the gate; protected by the line of soldiers, they appeared to be imploring the mob to disperse peacefully.

To the west of St George's Fields, the line of horseguards was now slowly advancing.

I snatched up the musket and ran down the stairs. As I emerged from the storehouse, there came out from the barn a number of men bearing Allen's body upon a door, like a bier, shoulder-high. A great cry broke from the crowd at the sight, and the hail of stones upon the soldiers by the prison became a storm. But the bier and the new-made martyr of the people turned away from the prison and went towards the road going up to the City. I tried now to get myself back through the crowd to the gate.

One of the Justices had found himself a crate to stand on, the better to address the people over the heads of the soldiers. He had the Riot Act in his hand, and as I came near he shouted at the people in desperation, for they were almost breaking through the soldiers' line. 'The Riot Act has been read. For God's sake, good people, go away; if I see any more stones thrown, I will order the guards to fire.'

It was only a goad to them, and now they jeered him and damned him for a helper to the murdering soldiers. He was red in the face with fear, and he declaimed the Riot Act a second time, holding the paper where they might see it.

'Damn the King!' they shouted. 'Damn the Parliament!'

'Good people—' said he, but then a stone struck his chest, and he stumbled down from the crate.

Some fellow had got through the soldiers' line, and now he fixed up a paper below Wilkes's window. The Justice ordered it taken down, which a soldier did, and what defiance or contempt of the King was written there I never saw, for I could make no proper headway through the crowd now, nor get myself clear of them. And I was there in the midst of them when another vicious hail of stones struck the soldiers, and the Justice also, but this time he took the blow upon the face. He bellowed in pain and clutched at his eyes, and with one hand flailing blindly he cried out to the soldiers, 'Fire! Fire!'

The soldiers closed up into three ranks, the front kneeling, and two ranks standing behind, and it was just the practice I had witnessed at the drilling ground by the Treasury. The front of the crowd saw their intent and tried to fall back, but there were thousands behind held them fixed in their places.

'Let me through!' I shouted. 'Let me pass!' I forced my way with the musket, but they were too many for me, and I was not quite to the front when the soldiers fired.

It was like a clap of tropic thunder, and the roar and screaming of the crowd that followed went right through me. I thank God that most of the soldiers fired high (for they were not all monsters, but most of them only men under command, and fearful of their own lives), but the instant they fired the whole crowd seemed to slump as a body away from them.

I held my ground against the people as they screamed and fell back, parrying them with my musket and my elbows, and soon there was nothing between me and the soldiers but only the people who were shot. I dropped the musket then, and ran across to them. Most were lying on the ground and crying out for help, but two were dead. By the triple rank of soldiers the frightened captain was ordering a reloading, and nothing I might do now to stop it.

Then was a rumbling beneath my feet, and a shot from the west side of the field. I turned, and the horseguards were riding down upon the people, and with sabres and pistols drawn. They fired over the crowd and into it, and I saw a woman go down beneath a horse's hoofs, and heavers swinging cudgels at the mounted guardsmen, and trying to break the horses' legs. It was no equal battle, but a scene chaotic and brutal, with women stumbling over the hems of their dresses now, and children abandoned and in terror.

'They are dispersing!' I shouted at the triple rank of soldiers. 'Put up your muskets. Hold your fire!'

But the smell of burned powder was on the air, and the shrill orders of their captain in their ears, and my words were nothing to them. They went forward into St George's Fields in good order, bayonets levelled.

I ran by them into the prison and upstairs, where I found Baxter and Wilkes both standing at the window, and the shutters half-opened.

I hauled Wilkes roughly away from there.

'You will take Mr Wilkes to the warden's rooms,' I told Baxter. 'And keep him there.'

'Unhand me, sir,' cried Wilkes, wrenching free of me.

'You will do as you are advised, sir. It is not a sport there below. You will keep clear of any window. Do you hear me, Mr Baxter?'

'Yes sir.'

I looked out over the field, and the crowd was broken now. Broken, and with some now running north towards the river, and others huddled in small and pathetic bands for safety; and more yet going east to the road up into the City, where Allen's body had gone before them. Two minutes more, and the horseguards and the soldiers ceased their firing, and they moved about the field now unthreatened, victors in a rout that had won them neither spoils nor honour. In different parts of the field the wounded writhed upon the ground, screaming, and in other places people knelt wailing by their dead.

'What will happen now, sir?'

'Now, Mr Baxter? Now we will reap what we have sown here in St George's Fields.'

'It is a massacre,' said Wilkes with some real anger in his voice. 'The ministry has done murder here.'

'The ministry has done that which you have goaded them to,' said I, not facing him, but looking yet from the window. 'You would do better now to pray for those who have died, Mr Wilkes, than to feast upon a hollow indignation.'

'Sir!' said he.

Then over at the storehouse I saw a fellow come out and look about him. It was Carrington's man, Meadows, and he turned and went east towards the City road.

'Keep him in the warden's room,' I told Baxter as I ran out. But though I ran down the stairs and across the yard, and rushed out through the prison gate, by the time I got across to the storehouse Meadows was gone. I spent but a short while searching after him, then came back, hurrying by some poor fellow who clutched a bloodied leg as he hobbled, and then I went into the storehouse, drew my dirk, and mounted the stairs.

On the uppermost floor, I stopped a moment outside the open door. There were but two reasons Meadows might have come here, and only one of which was to give Tyler some assistance. I went in, and straight across to Tyler and cut the rope. His feet dropped to the floor, and I rolled him and loosed the rope from his neck, but I saw at once that it was too late for him. It was not to give assistance that Meadows had come. Tyler had been stabbed in the heart. It was not help that he had got from Meadows, but only the silence eternal.

I called Baxter out from the warden's room where he sat with Wilkes, and explained to him that I must go up to the Lane. 'The trouble is going up to the other side of the river, and I must go with it. There will be soldiers remain here. But if the mob descend upon the prison again, you must send for me.'

'Wilkes wants to be in his own rooms, sir.'

'Mr Wilkes is a prisoner and will do as you bid him. But put that by. Baxter, there is that which I hardly know how to tell you. I will say it plain. Your nephew Tyler has been killed.'

'Sir?'

'He has himself killed Pearce.' Baxter looked stupefied at this, and though I was unsure he had fully taken it in, I must ask him now, 'Had Tyler said anything to you of continuing to search for Pearce?'

'No. But killed – you mean by Pearce or the soldiers?'

'He is with Pearce in the upper floor of the storehouse. You may have the bodies brought over here. It is a pauper's grave for Pearce, and you will know who must look to Tyler.'

'But how killed, sir?'

'It appears that he and Pearce fought with knives. You are sure Tyler said nothing of searching for Pearce?' Baxter looked down to the floor and turned his head. He really could not take it in. I put a hand upon his shoulder now, and very relieved I was that he should take it so. For I saw plainly that he knew nothing of what had happened. 'If you have any need of me, I am at the Lane.'

Upon one of the prison horses I rode up over Westminster Bridge, and found that word of the killings in St George's Fields had gone before me; for there was now a mob outside Parliament, crying like demons against the King and his ministry. Soldiers were now arriving in the square from Whitehall to see them off, and I rode past them and around to the Horseguards Parade. As I crossed the drilling ground, Jenkinson came out from the Treasury with North and some others, and all of them hurrying in the direction of the Army office.

I rode over and made a quick report to them of the soldiers' actions in the Field, and of the movement of the mob north into the town and the City. They asked me a hundred senseless things, to which I only answered at last, 'Wilkes is secure in the prison,' and then I dismounted and Jenkinson stayed by me as North and his fellows continued with a renewed hurry across the empty drilling ground.

'Sir, Pearce is dead down by the prison. It looks that there was some plot against Wilkes's life. If I am not mistaken, Pearce and Carrington were both a part of it.' At this, Jenkinson started. 'I have had no time to make a proper consideration of it, sir. But you must not trust to Carrington.'

'But why should he want Wilkes dead?'

'Why should Sandwich organize the watermen in the City? And why should Weymouth order a Scots regiment down to the prison?

The mob are provoked that they may be destroyed. Wilkes would get the blame of it, and he be destroyed with them.'

There was shouting now in St James's Park, and we saw people armed with sticks and pikes moving toward the King's Palace. There could be no doubt but that Jenkinson was afraid. It was visible in his eyes, and no surprise to me, for the threat of physical violence must be a rare thing to him. I thought he might run to join North and the others, and certainly he hesitated, and nor would I have blamed him had he gone. But at last he braced himself, and turned his face fixedly toward the Palace. He put his hand on his sword hilt and moved forward, and I saw then that he was no coward, and I was glad of it.

But I knew there was no one who might stop the rioting now. It was not love of Wilkes and liberty alone, nor yet hatred of the King, had fanned the mob up to this violent blaze. Privation was the fuel laid down through the long winter, and the murder of Allen and the others in the Field had now thrown a torch into the midst of it. And now it must burn while each man looked to secure himself and his own.

'If the soldiers may be kept to their barracks, sir, as far as that is possible.'

'I shall recommend it,' said he glancing back. 'But the decision is not mine.'

'I must go to the Lane now.'

'God preserve you, Mr Douglas. God save us all.'

CHAPTER FORTY

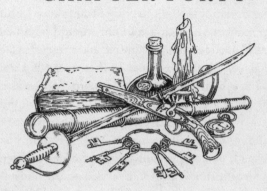

*U*p at Banks's place in New Barrington Street I found the apothecary Collins undisturbed yet by any word of the rioting down in Westminster and St James's. I gave him the news of it quickly, and he at once gave Banks's servants the order to shut up the house and shutter the windows. Then he came at my request to my own house in Holborn. There I unlocked my pistol case and left it with him, giving him charge over the house and Kitty Langridge, to whom I introduced him hastily before buckling on my sword and going down to the Lane.

By the time I got near to St Paul's, the rioting had started in earnest. Bands of men roamed the streets armed with all manner of makeshift clubs and missiles, and my only defence against them was the cry of 'Wilkes and Liberty!' which I used lustily and often, and so kept myself safe till I came to that meeting of streets before the Royal Exchange and the Mansion House. But here was not so much a riot as a pitched battle engaged between the watermen and that part of the mob newly come up from St George's Fields. The mob here was near a thousand strong, and they held the central open ground. But along at the

Royal Exchange steps, and in front of the Mansion House and the Bank, there were brigades of watermen beating back the coal heavers at the van of the mob, and charging out from behind their defences with clubs and muskets in irregular but ferocious sallies, and screaming bloody murder.

I could not get through there without risk of my life, and so I circled wide behind the Mansion House, and came up to the rear of the Post Office. The stable yard was locked, but I banged on the wooden gate with my fist and called for the head groom, and finally the gate opened. I gave him my horse, and then I went up the Abchurch Lane past our door and into Lombard Street. And here I found yet another brigade of watermen, these patrolling with muskets before the Post Office, their line extending to Change Alley, and the mob from either direction pelting them with stones. I retreated quickly, and pounded on the door of the Lane. 'Francis! Gus! It is I, Douglas. Open the door!'

After a minute it opened, and Gus let me in. He closed the door at my back very hurriedly, locked it again, and dropped an oak beam as a bar. When I asked after Francis, Gus directed me into the main Post Office.

'Keep the door barred against everyone who comes now,' I shouted back to him as I went through.

The main Post Office was deserted. There was the sound of glass breaking now, out in the street. I found Francis descending the staircase, and as fast as I had ever seen him move.

'Sandwich is gone,' said he.

'Carrington?'

'I have not seen him since yesterday. What the devil has happened?'

'The soldiers have made a massacre,' I said, and as I spoke there was a great crash of glass where the front window of the Post Office was hit. The shards were still raining down on the stone floor as I grabbed Francis's arm and dragged him after me back to the Lane.

Inside the first chamber, we locked and barred the door joining us to the Post Office. Then we stood quiet a moment and caught our breath, and we heard men running by in the lane outside, and shouting. The sound was muffled, but the banging they made suddenly against our door was quite terrifying; for some reason they quickly ceased their thrashing and passed on.

We went then into the Steaming Room, and locked and barred this door also. I ascertained what food we had, and water, and there was sufficient for a few days if rationed; for Bode and those others that Francis had sent to their homes had left behind them bread and eggs and some few other things. Gus stayed below now while Francis and I went up to our room atop the winding stairs. The moment Francis had locked the door, he turned to me and said, 'Where is the King?'

'St James's.'

'Let us pray he is still there when this is done.'

We spoke no more of the King's fate then, for we could do nothing for him but our work, and neither was there any way for us to know if we were in the midst of only a great riot or a bloody revolution. But the thought was now behind all that we did. We turned out our desks and commenced the urgent business of separating and ordering all the papers, and then I heaped more coals upon the fire and we began the burning of those secret pieces that must be a danger in the light. It was while we did this work that I told Francis what I had witnessed at the prison. He said nothing, but his face was very grave.

'I have told Baxter that it was Pearce who killed Tyler. Baxter will have the better protection the less he knows of the truth.'

'Was it knowledge of the truth caused Tyler's death?'

'I weep no tears for him. I think now that it was Tyler killed Flanagan at the Greenland Dock.' Francis lifted his head sharply from the papers he inspected. 'It must have been when Baxter came to fetch me on the back road,' I said. 'Tyler must have gone into the vat-shed to warn them to flee. But Flanagan – I know not why – resisted it. I could not understand why Pearce would kill Flanagan and not take the bill. But now I think Pearce was gone already. And if Flanagan would not go, Tyler would then have to murder him or risk that Flanagan be captured and talk. And Tyler knew nothing of the bill, and so did not take it. He murdered Flanagan to get silence. And Meadows has paid him in kind.'

'But was Tyler doing Carrington's bidding from the first?'

'Not from the first. But Baxter introduced Tyler to Carrington as a lad who might be taken into the Messengers. Carrington had that gift in his power. I have been the greatest fool.'

'And Carrington would use Pearce to murder Wilkes.'

'It is likely. I have had too little time to consider the whole of it. But it is Carrington at the back of it. And you know who is at the back of him.'

'We must look to the archives,' said he, and went to the rear of the room to fetch more papers for the burning.

We were several hours about this necessary business, and strangely calm it seemed when we settled to it; for all the sound of the rioting outside was muffled by the walls, and through our window we saw only the stable yard, which was kept shut, the head groom and two others there armed with muskets keeping watch on the gate lest any rioter attempt a forced entry.

It was late night before Francis was satisfied with what we had burned and what we had kept, and then we went down to the Steaming Room and took a meal of bread and boiled eggs, and tea. After we had eaten, we fetched out one of the mattresses and Gus carried it upstairs for Francis. Gus then put down a blanket on the floor by the stove in the Steaming Room, and I made myself as comfortable as I might on the translator's narrow bed next door.

The rioting ebbed and flowed through the night, sometimes clamorous and close, and sometimes distant, but never was there absolute quiet. Nor came there any of the familiar cries of the watchmen, or bells sounding from down at the ships; but all was confusion without, and the Lane but a small vessel with hatches battened fast against the great storm.

All the next day we stayed immured within, and made no rash venture into either the Abchurch Lane or the main Post Office, but only listened to the clamour without and awaited, with nerves badly worn now, some abatement of the violence.

Francis, to distract himself, began to work at the Nightingale Code of the French, and a fine distraction it was to him; for the code had withstood every assault of the Bishop through a lifetime, and so must give Francis sufficient trouble to take his mind from the riot beyond our door. He was much vexed, though, to have some necessary books of mathematical tables so close by in the bookcase of his rooms in the Royal Exchange, but unreachable. I sat with him and did very little but only toyed with a pen and paper, and turned through my mind all that had brought us here, from Langridge's murder and up to the death of Tyler. I acted as a foil for Francis to essay his reasoning over the Nightingale Code, but I had no proper concentration.

It was near evening, and I had just remarked the fall in the clamour the past hour, when Meadows came into the Post Office stable yard. Francis saw me step back from the window. Putting aside his futile scribblings, he rose from his desk and came to stand by me. Meadows was now in conference with the head groom who had opened the gate to him. After a few moments, they went in through the rear door of the Post Office and so passed from our sight. I moved towards the stairs.

'You will not challenge him, Alistair.'

'I will not go near him.'

Downstairs, I warned Gus against opening the door to Meadows. 'If there is any attempt to force the door, fetch me at once.'

Upstairs again, I spent some several minutes in useless speculation with Francis upon the meaning of Meadows's return; but in truth, the fellow had any number of reasons to be there, the most likely of which was the securing of the Messengers' secret papers.

'If he has come here, the streets must be passable,' said I.

'You will not go out,' said Francis, and when I offered to fetch for Francis the book of mathematical tables from his room at the Royal Exchange, he repeated it. 'You will not go out. The streets may be passable, but I am sure they are not yet peaceful. You will not put your life in danger, that I may amuse myself in greater comfort.'

'We need not confine ourselves more.'

'We will wait till the morning,' said he, and with such a look that I knew I might venture no appeal, and nor was it worth the trouble I should have by defiance.

But that night seemed to me interminable, for I would be out from the Lane now to discover what had happened in the City and the prison and at St James's Palace. Certainly the clamour outside was much abated, and after midnight it died away almost completely (though there was yet no comforting and familiar cry of any watchman to replace the noise of riot). But I slept at last, and was woken near dawn by Gus's hand upon my shoulder.

'Sir?' said he. 'It is Mr Bode returned, and the translators. Shall I open the door to them?'

I rose and went with him, and spoke through the lane door. And it was indeed Bode and those others, and so I unbarred and unlocked the door to them.

'How have you come here?'

'A hackney to St Paul's, sir,' said Bode coming in. 'He would not bring us further, so then we walked.' And upon my asking if he had been sent, he answered, 'No sir. But I thought Mr Willes must have need of us.'

I rebarred and relocked the door and went with them into the Steaming Room. While I fetched my jacket and sword, Bode told me what he knew of the rioting, which was very little. He had fetched the two translators who lived near to him south of the river, and they had come here, by way of St George's Fields, which place he assured me was very quiet and peaceful. There were no soldiers about there, except close by the prison, and very few other people abroad in the streets, and none of them rioters.

'There are some small fires along the docks, sir. And between here and St Paul's – but are you going out then?' said he in surprise when he saw me putting on my sword.

'I'm going across to the Royal Exchange. You may tell Mr Willes so when he comes down.' I instructed Gus to lock the door behind me, and then I went out into the first chamber, and thence into Abchurch Lane. It was coming on to dawn, and the sun not yet risen, and the light grey and dim. I did not see the broken glass lying by the Lloyd's coffee shop at the corner, but felt it suddenly crunch beneath my boots. Nor was it in this place only, but as I went up

Lombard Street and past the front of the Post Office there was more broken glass, and sticks, and other debris of the riot. The front doors of the Post Office remained intact, but those watermen who had stood sentry there were gone. I was but a short way further on when some fellow moved suddenly at the steps of St Mary Woolnoth, and I drew my sword and gave a shout and went forward.

'For shame!' cried the fellow, turning upon the steps to face me. 'Go to your home!' he ordered, and I saw then that it was the rector of the place.

'I am not here for riot, sir,' said I, sheathing my sword, and then holding up to him my open hand. He had a few more sharp words for me, and I asked him then if he knew anything of the west side of town, and how things stood in Westminster and St James's.

He waved his hand over the City and towards the river. 'Here was the worst of it.'

'Have there been soldiers out?'

'Very few. For which we may thank God, and the King. I think they have been kept to their barracks.'

'Then is it over, sir?'

'We must pray so,' said he, and went up and stepped through the broken door of his church.

At the end of Lombard Street there opened before me a great scene of destruction. By the crossroads the rioters had made a bonfire, which was now a high pile of burnt debris and ash and twisted metal, enough to see that at least one coach had been put to the flames. Half a wheel survived, blackened and useless, and its jutting spokes still smouldering. Every unshuttered window in every building (save only the topmost) was broken, and the pavement strewn with broken furniture from the buildings that had been ransacked and pillaged. There were papers scattered everywhere, over crossroads, on the pavements and in the gutters. And a handful of men lingered also; and these few moving quickly from one broken door to the next, and taking their last chance at scavenging and thievery before the sun should rise fully and the constables and justices come out from their own bolt-holes to drive these wretches off.

At the Royal Exchange steps, I saw a body, which was a young fellow in the livery of a chair-man; his head was stove in by a club, but of the reason for his abandonment there by his fellows, there was no sign.

The great doors of the Exchange had not been breached. But as at the Post Office, there were no longer any watermen standing sentry before them. I went along the side passage and up the private stairs, and in the short gallery above I found that everything was untouched, and no window overlooking the central courtyard broken.

I let myself into Francis's rooms, and went and looked down over the central courtyard and found it empty. Now that I was here, I went into the next room and got the step and climbed up to search the bookcase. It was a few minutes I searched, for his bookcase covered almost a whole wall, and the light was very poor. But at last I discovered the book of mathematical tables, and slid it out, and it was as I turned to get down that I was shot.

I struck against the bookcase and fell, the steps going out from beneath me, and the roar of the shot still in my ears. My left shoulder had taken the ball, and I clutched it as I scrambled to my knees to face the door. It was Meadows. He cursed that he had not taken me with his shot, and then he flung down his pistol and drew his sword. I had no time to draw, and it was but blind instinct fetched out my dirk. And even yet he would have killed me had there not then come a cry of 'Alistair!' from the next room.

Meadows hesitated. And in that moment I drove up at him, and he swung his sword, but I was under his arm and twisting my dirk into his belly and up beneath his ribs. He caught me in the face with his elbow and I staggered back.

He howled then. He dropped his sword and fell to the floor, curling himself into a tight ball, and howling like a beaten child.

Francis rushed in, sword in hand. He looked quickly from me to Meadows, and then he came across, saying, 'Is he shot?'

I held out the bloody dirk. And in that moment Meadows ceased his howling and made a quieter noise, like a terrible struggling for air.

My legs had begun a vigorous trembling, and I sat down. 'He has put a shot into me,' said I, and Francis helped me remove my jacket, and both of us now watching Meadows, and the great quantity of blood pooling out from beneath him. Francis tore open my shirt, and we could both see the wound, which was clean.

'It has passed through,' said he, which was a relief to me; for I had learned to fear the surgeon's knife as much as any poisoning from the lead.

Meadows made one sound more, like a keening, trapped in his throat; and then the sound stopped, all the tightness went out from his body, and he lay still. Francis went and rolled him with his foot. We saw at once that the damned fellow was dead.

'We know now why he came,' said Francis.

'They have missed their chance at me.'

'There will be others. You cannot now stay with any safety here in London.'

CHAPTER FORTY-ONE

*F*rancis would not leave me then. We got Meadows out from Francis's rooms, and discarded the body down at the Exchange steps alongside that dead chair-man. Then we returned briefly to the Lane, where Gus bandaged my shoulder and fetched a fresh shirt for me. After that we made our way to the Post Office stables and the groom saddled two horses for us. As we rode south through the City the sun was rising, and people coming out from the places where they had taken refuge through the great riot. They looked all about them at the destruction, and were stunned and silent, like survivors upon a battle-field. On London Bridge we stopped to look down the river. The red battle flags were all gone from the ships, and though some of the warehouses had collapsed, the fires were out now, and only black plumes and not flames going up into the clear morning sky.

'When Jenkinson sent me to Paris to watch Wilkes, I little thought it should end like this.'

'It had ended very much worse, Alistair, had Wilkes been killed.'

It was the plain truth, but I could take no comfort in it.

We turned our horses and rode on down to the King's Bench

Prison. There we found St George's Fields empty, and but a dozen soldiers outside the prison gate. They were armed with muskets, and standing easy, with a small campfire burning. One soldier knelt by the fire, brewing tea.

Baxter was in the turnkey's room off the lobby, and as we entered the prison he came out to us, and apologized to me that he could not prevent the chief warden returning Wilkes that morning to his old rooms.

'It little matters now, I think, Mr Baxter.'

We crossed the prison yard, and Baxter told me that after those first killings in the Field, and the departure of the mob, it had been very peaceful here. He saw the blood on my jacket but made no remark upon it. 'Is the riot broken in the City, sir?'

'It is,' said I; and I asked then after Tyler, and he said that Tyler's parents had come down and fetched the lad's body away, and that a prison cart had taken Pearce to the burying ground in Vauxhall. Francis offered his own condolences, and Baxter thanked him kindly, and so we came to Wilkes's open door.

Wilkes was at his table, head down and writing, with an inkpot before him, and beside the inkpot a glass of red wine. I signalled for Francis and Baxter to wait for me in the yard, and I went in to Wilkes alone.

'Sir,' said he, glancing up as I entered, but continuing with his scribbling. 'If you have come to turn me out from here, you must speak first to the head warden.'

'I little care what rooms you shall have now, Mr Wilkes. I have come to take my leave of you.' He stopped his scribbling now and looked up. 'I am sure we have each seen enough of the other to last us for some good while.'

'Weymouth and Barrington have written notes of congratulation to the soldiers, that they massacred those innocent people.'

'I cannot answer for that.'

'They shall not keep me from the Parliament, you know. And they shall regret that they wrote such an abominable thing.' He dipped his pen and recommenced his furious scribbling, and I understood then that what he wrote was by way of some answering venom to Weymouth and Barrington's stupidity. Wilkes would send it to the printers, after his usual fashion. It would appear in several newspapers, and the whole town would read it and be enraged either for or against Wilkes, or the ministry, according to their inclinations. It was appalling to me that there should be any congratulation of the soldiers for the massacre. But in this letter that Wilkes now wrote there was a a self-interested intransigence the equal of anything that he answered. He was unchanged by what had happened. He had learned nothing. 'I will not offer you my hand, Mr Douglas.'

'Nor would I take it, sir.'

When he looked up this time, I dipped my head to him, and turned upon my heel and went out from his room.

At Lambeth Palace, I went with Francis directly up to the gallery, and Francis sent the young novice stationed there to find the Bishop. After ten minutes the Bishop came, and said nothing to us at first, but only clasped Francis's arm while his eyes spoke his relief to discover his son unharmed. Then he turned to me, and his face changed when he saw the bloodstain upon my jacket.

'We must speak with you privately, Father,' said Francis.

The novice stayed at his place outside the door while we two went with the Bishop into his private rooms.

I slept that night upon the Bishop's floor, and departed with him the next morning to his palace in Wells.

My removal from London was both so sudden and so complete that I had no opportunity to call upon Mrs Watts, or Banks or any other. Francis took a letter to Collins and Kitty Langridge for me, inviting them to bide in my house awhile, till they should hear from me (and Kitty to be a housekeeper to Collins, for which service I included a payment), and directing them that all enquiries made of me at the house, or any letters that came for me, should be passed at once to Francis at the Lane. And Francis obliged me further by calling upon Mrs Watts and Banks, and some few others, to assure them of my safety, and also, though I discovered this only much later, to give them a false hint of my supposed departure to France.

And I was then no more Mr Douglas for a time, but Mr Maguire, a peripatetic scholar whose desire for a temporary seclusion the Bishop had kindly indulged with a private room in his palace, and the freedom of his library, and with whom the Bishop occasionally dined alone, but never in company.

And so I remained, not for days only, but many weeks, and on into the high summer. What passed in London during those days I learned from the magazines and papers that came into the Bishop's library, and from the Bishop himself, who kept me informed of the progress of Wilkes's affairs which carried on through the King's Bench court. In the middle of June, Wilkes's outlawry was lifted, and the libel trial restarted against him, and he at once opened a case against those who had issued the General Warrant by which his property had been taken. And still he was kept from his seat in the Parliament.

The Bishop gave me to understand that in both the Parliament and in St James's Palace, there were many arguments raging over the cause of the great riot, and whether it was leniency with Wilkes and the mob had caused it, or only the massacre that day in St George's Fields. But he told me that along with these disputes was a general agreement that it should not happen again; for everyone, from the greatest in the kingdom to the least, had been profoundly shaken by the unexampled eruption of violence, and an understanding had now pierced even the dullest wits that no one, not Wilkes, nor the King, nor any mortal man, could pretend to ride or direct such a tempest of despairing passion.

The thing had risen like a great wave through the hard winter, and broken in a blind fury over the City, and all now knew its power, and none would call it back.

With the great crisis passed, and no daily reminder of it to me, I found that I was not sorry to have the compass of my mind turn by slow degrees away from London. I walked often in the parkland and down by the river, and always with one of the Bishop's guards to escort me; but throughout this time there was a natural solitariness hung about me, so that the presence of these fellows made no disturbance to me, either while I walked, or while I sat and sketched the willows and the reeds along the riverbank, and the cattle that came to drink the cool water. All nature was my recreation then, and the blue flash of the kingfisher's wing a delight beyond speaking.

I would attend evensong in the chapel, and then return to my room and read for an hour before taking my supper alone. And a few times Francis, by the Bishop, sent me a piece of correspondence from a foreign court to be deciphered (just as he sent pieces to his brothers), but these were not urgent, nor concerned with Wilkes, and this too I found almost a recreation; for a letter from the Austrian court to the ambassador in London touched me little, and I could decipher such things purely as puzzles to be reconfigured for others to understand.

The rhythm of my days was the rhythm of a monastery, and the quiet both a rare thing and welcome; for it felt that I had been tumbled down a roaring cataract and over the fall, and was now in some gentle side pool while the main river ran on in spate without me.

I did not fear for my life. But always when I was in company with the Bishop he made some allusion to my safety, and to the continuing necessity of keeping me from Carrington's reach. As to those who commanded Carrington, we spoke no word concerning them, nor had we done so since Lambeth Palace, when I had told the Bishop every-thing, both what I knew and what I suspected, and he had listened with that solemnity fitting for a man whose whole life was one spent in service to God and the Crown.

But in spite of everything, Carrington stayed over the King's Messengers. He could not be removed, as the Bishop admitted to me very frankly, early in July; for the man's protectors were too powerful, and the secrets that he knew too many. And though time must slowly diminish the threat that Carrington and those over him now felt from me, yet the Bishop would not permit my return to London till he be satisfied of my safety there.

But at last I began to chafe at my comfortable captivity. Then came a day at the end of July when I received the Bishop's summons to attend him in his private study. And when I arrived there, thinking to have the announcement of my release, I found not only the Bishop awaiting me but also Jenkinson, who rose from his chair to greet me (which civil rising to me was the first time). We had not seen each other since the great riot, and now he took my hand and said some kind words on the service I had done. I averred that his own efforts in keeping the soldiers mostly from the streets had been the greater service, and almost smiled when he did not disagree with me, but instead nodded his acknowledgement very graciously. I asked if I should return with him to London. He looked at the Bishop, and the Bishop to me.

'Mr Jenkinson shares my concern for any premature return by you to London.'

'I cannot remain here for ever, My Lord.'

'No,' he agreed. 'And that is why you must go abroad again, if you are willing – that does not please you.'

'I had thought to have put the Mississippi far behind me, My Lord. That is all.'

The Bishop signed to Jenkinson, and Jenkinson took up from the table a scrolled letter, which was bound in a blue ribbon and sealed with red wax. He passed the scrolled letter into my hand, and only then did I recognize the royal seal. I looked up at them.

'You will not break it open just yet,' said the Bishop.

CHAPTER FORTY-TWO

*T*he sea was flat, and white with sunlight, and dazzling; and though I strained my eyes towards the town I could see no sign of our boat's return. The sailors along from me at the gunwale called down to the native canoes that had come out to us each morning since our arrival in the bay. The blacks held up pineapples, and banana, and several more fruits unrecognizable, and cried up in Portuguese to bargain with the seamen. But the morning heat was coming on now, and when the first of the canoes pushed off from us I took myself back to the small table beneath the shade of the canvas that the bosun had rigged for me near the bow.

Soon the heat would settle in earnest, and then the lassitude of an idle ship would overtake me as it had done almost every day since we had crossed the Line. And so I made no hesitation now, but dipped my pen and drew the paper to me.

My Dear Mrs Watts
    Your letter has found me in Rio, and much obliged I am that you have thought to send me such a chronicle before we disappear into the Pacific, and for who knows how long.

Amelia is truly to marry Jenkinson? I would say that I am astonished by the news (as Amelia no doubt wishes me to say), only that I find that I am neither astonished nor even greatly surprised. Mr Jenkinson has proven himself a more determined gentleman than I had first supposed him, and Amelia must know her own mind. Though you seem to believe I shall think it a poor match between them, I must tell you that you are mistaken.

Though Mr Jenkinson is no bright meteor, putting out a great flash and fire, I think now that he has a light steady enough and will burn the longer for it. Certainly I would trust to him in any affair connected with the Court or Westminster or Whitehall. (And here I see that I have here named almost the whole of government, but as that is no exaggeration of his reach, I will make no amendment to it.) And if he is not so young as he might be, nor as open in his affections, yet Amelia has both the youth and good nature to bring him from himself, and be to him not only an ornament in society, but also the dearest treasure of his heart.

If he is no fool – and I do not think him one – he must love her. And as I trust you, that you have sounded Amelia on whether her respect for him has with it the necessary seed of affection from which her own love for him shall grow, well then, what better match may there be?

You will give my congratulations and felicitations to Amelia. I have written separately to Jenkinson.

I find that I am also little surprised to discover Wilkes still held in the King's Bench Prison, nor even that he makes a small hub there of London society. The man has the weight of a cork, and all the resilience too, and the combined waters of the Thames, the Mississippi and the Ganges could not long hold the fellow under. But I wonder does he ever think of those poor people killed in St George's Fields outside his window? You say there is some general feeling that the sentence he is now under for those earlier libels is very hard. I grant you, it is more than a meeker fellow might have got. But then a meeker fellow had not written the 45, nor been so pleased to be carried here and there by the mob, and so I wonder if

there has not been some rough justice done after all. From your
report, and others I have had, he seems to suffer no loss of any
social pleasure by his continued confinement. He returned to
London a penniless outlaw, was elected while an outlaw, and now
though he is a prisoner, what shall it surprise the ministry or
anyone else if he insist upon his elected seat in Parliament? He
has put the law in a knot upon such questions, and I own myself
glad that I am no lawyer or judge to now attempt the tedious
disentanglement.

But that there has been no rekindling of the mob's fury, and that
Wilkes has made no further incitement of them, is almost the very
best that you might have wrote me, and welcome indeed. Pray God
it stay true this next winter.

I must thank you also that you have been so kind as to look
in upon Collins and the widow Langridge. Though you accuse me
of making a match between them, I do promise you that the
thought never came into my head. It was long after I had hastily
deposited Collins at my house that Francis Willes gave me some
similar intimation; but having it now from you both, I must
presume their connection is no play of Francis's imagination.
And I am pleased that you liked the girl. As to Collins, I will
answer for his good character. For the rest, let nature proceed,
and I could not wish for a better family as tenants of my house.
(I must rely upon you to give them the intimation of it, trusting
to your delicacy above any ill-timed and blundering intervention
from my own pen.)

I shall pass over any account of my summer (for which I think
you will understand the reason, and excuse me), and give you
instead a brief account of our voyage till now.

I lifted my head. There had been a cry from aloft, and on the quarterdeck now an officer had his spyglass trained toward the shore.
Banks was by the officer, and moving restlessly. Now he leaned upon
the rail, and now he pushed away from it. Now he consulted with the
officer, and now shielded his eyes from the sun, looking landward.

It was the ship's boat returning from the town. The ship's dog then sniffing about my inkpot, I waved him off, and dipped my pen.

We departed Plymouth in the late August, and proceeded down by the Spanish coast to Madeira. This part of our journey was but two weeks in duration, but felt to me a year, for I was sick for most of the time (as was Banks and many of his party). I will not say that the seas were unusually rough, but nor were they the calmest I have ever sailed on. The few days that I came upon deck I found Banks struggling manfully against his own affliction, and directing the throwing of a hand-net into the sea, for the capture of the hundreds of small creatures that commonly pass by the hull of every vessel, unregarded. His colleague Dr Solander (whom I think you have met with) has the solid stomach of his seafaring forebears. He hardly notices the rough weather, and moves very cheerfully from the dissection of some indescribable creature brought up from the lower depths, and straight to his supper. I dare say Banks has chosen this fellow very well.

We stayed almost a week in Madeira, Banks and his party collecting and botanizing ashore, while I had the pleasant company of Mr Cheap, our consul there, in Fonchiale, and his wife, to give me amusement. Nor were these my only society, for I stayed a night at the house of a fellow called Heberden (who is himself a physician, and a naturalist of sorts, and a correspondent of Mr Collins) and we two made such a joint assault upon his cellar that I was a short while delayed in my bed the next morning, which caused me to be late for the boat, and our commander Lieutenant Cook must needs have a quiet word with me upon my eventual return to the ship.

After leaving Madeira we continued on light winds, and no great event happening aboard but only the wearying and necessary one of each man accommodating himself to the thought of the many weeks ahead with little prospect of landfall. We passed the Pike at Tenerife in late September, and soon after this I discovered that I might now make sketches without a violent opposition from my head and stomach, and since that discovery the time has gone more quickly for me.

The ship has proven the veriest tub, and Cook the only man aboard who seems pleased with her; though as we approached the Line in late October, and the temperature rose steadily, I own I was grateful for the breadth of her deck as giving each of us the opportunity of unobstructed movement well apart from our fellows.

At the Line was the usual ceremony of Ducking (and I am glad to say without the viciousness masked as humour that you and I have both been witness to), and Banks and Cook paying their forfeits in wine and brandy, the merriment was very general about the ship for some good while.

Southward we were promised an island by our maps, but the island never came; which false promise I think we must grow accustomed to who must soon venture beyond even the poorest charts. The ship falling into Calms at sundry latitudes (I think here is where the packet with your letter must have passed us), I several times went out in the ship's boat with Banks to collect by net and bucket the myriad living things that lie upon the face of the water here.

And so in early November we made landfall at last, a few days north of Rio de Janeiro (which place lies not by a river but upon a great bay). And here off Rio de Janeiro we are anchored as I write you, and the green hills, or mountains I might say, very splendid, and jutting sharp into the sky behind the town. Of the town I can say nothing, as having been refused permission to go ashore by the unaccountable order of its governor. This refusal is a general one, directed against all of us save only our captain and some necessary officers and seamen.

There was a stir upon deck, for our boat was now returned to the ship. I watched Banks come down from the forecastle to question Cook, who was climbing aboard. And hardly had they spoken together than Banks threw up a hand and held it to his head; and very evident it was that the governor of the place had again refused permission for Banks to go ashore. Cook excused himself from Banks now and went below.

Banks is a man in despair, for he must stand upon deck and feast his eyes upon a mighty forest covering the hills, and all about the bay, and yet approach no nearer. Nor will Cook allow any subterfuge to get Banks or his party ashore, for the reprovisioning of our ship must depend upon this obstinate governor, and we dare not give him cause to turn us away.

For myself, I pass the time with sketching, and try to make no fret where I can make no remedy. My consolation is that we are in the hand of God always, and only temporarily beholden to this wretched Portuguese.

And you will see that I have left till the last your own news, which though I confess was a great surprise to me at first, now that I have thought on it seems the most natural thing possible. And whether it is Madras or Calcutta to which you make your return, I cannot think you will want for friends or society in either place, but every door will surely be open to you, and not only for the memory of Mr Watts, but for your own sake.

Though you make no complaint of me, I do assure you I have chided myself a thousand times that I was blind to your unhappiness in London. When I think of it now, I see everywhere such small signs as a wiser and better friend might have recognized, and acted upon, if only it might be to lend an understanding ear and draw you from your melancholy. You make mention of my own troubles this past year, both in the matter of Wilkes and my more private concerns, as if this might be an extenuation for me. Yet there is no excuse for me in it. What is left, but to beg your forgiveness?

London must be a lesser place to me now that you shall not be there. And though I now travel toward the margin of the world, and you across oceans, yet I do not believe that we shall never meet with each other again. The world is wide, as you say, and we but small creatures upon it, and yet I must dare to think that we are something more than the helpless passengers of our several destinies. Though I am under command, and must go where my orders take me, I must be ever the one true pilot of my soul. (Which is to say

*that there are many sailings between Batavia and Bengal, and that
I shall account no diversion extraordinary in this voyage that I am
embarked upon.)*

*As to Madame Cordet, to write her name now is to write the
story entire; she is no more Valerie Beauchamp, and I must not
think of her so. To forget is impossible, but I have all the journey
ahead of me in which to school my heart to sorrow. And you may
depend upon me that I will do it. I am deeply touched by your
concern for me, but I must ask you now to put it by. I shall not
waste my life in pining for what can never be. Instead, I must take
your own self as my example, that the passing of Mr Watts has not
broken you, but you have steadied yourself and gone on, for which
I think I have never said how much I admire you.*

*I shall write no more now, for I must send this by the Portuguese
packet that sails this evening.*

*You will tell Amelia and Sophie (and George), that I keep them
in my prayers, and trust in the day when I shall see them again,
and all in good health and full happiness.*

*And for yourself, I pray this letter find you well and looking
forward to your journey with that same hope and courage that
you have ever urged upon me.*

*Your image has stood at my elbow as I have written; now it
fades, and I must let it go.*

I am as always,

Yours in affection and respect,

Alistair

After dating the letter, I put aside my pen and blotted the last page.
Then I folded all the pages carefully into my pocket, and came out
from the shade and to the rail. The land was very near. And past this
land was an ocean and a world undiscovered, and from which some
of us would not return. I looked up at the high hills. The air was hot,
and the muddy smell of the forest came to me across the calm water.
It was the fifteenth day of November, 1768, and a year now since

Langridge had died. A year of hard lessons to me, in liberty and in life. But where now must I be, but only here; and what now must I do, but only this?

At four bells of the watch, I came away from the rail and went below to break open the royal seal.

The author would like to thank:

Jeremy Trevathan and Catherine Richards, Editorial
Eli Dryden, Editorial Services
Neil Lang, Jacket Design
Iram Allam, Design
Ellen Wood, Marketing

The
EAGLES AT
YORK TOWN
By Grant Sutherland

In August 1781 Alistair Douglas is sent by the British spy network, the
Decipherers, to York Town in the American Colonies.

He is tasked with assisting the Loyalist colonists of Virginia to
organize themselves into a militia and fight the Revolutionaries on
behalf of the King. Douglas goes undercover as a grain merchant aboard
a French military vessel in Chesapeake Bay, where he discovers that
matters have progressed much further than anyone in London had
imagined . . . While Lord Cornwallis turns all his efforts to fortifying
York Town, Douglas intercepts disturbing correspondence suggesting
that they might be protecting themselves in the wrong place.

When a British father and son, Cable and David Morgan, are captured by the French as spies, matters turn critical. Douglas is
determined to do whatever it takes to save them, knowing that if he
can get them back they might just have a chance to reverse British
fortunes before it's too late . . .

An extract of the gripping third novel in The Decipherer's
Chronicles *follows here. The first book in the series,* The
Cobras of Calcutta, *is out now in paperback.*

CHAPTER ONE

I got the fellow in my sights and held him there.

'Militia?' said Campbell; but I could not tell.

The man was coming around behind the rocks on the headland of the cove, his musket held across his chest. He was a hundred yards off from us, advancing cautious and slow. He picked his way about the rocks as though to keep hid from the muddy beach, stopping every few yards to look ahead. But we had made no fire, and the fallen pine behind which we crouched hid us from his view. The fellow came on, looked about, and stopped again. I had a quick suspicion of the reason.

'Alone?' said I, quietly.

Campbell at once turned from me. He moved along behind the fallen pine, gained the cover of the scrub, and then rose and went silently into the wood.

There was shade where the stranger was now, so that he was almost invisible. The barrel of my musket still rested on the pine, trained upon the dark shadow. The last week of our journey had sharpened our distrust of everyone that we met with; for Cornwallis's army had but recently come by, and the whole tidewater country hereabouts was under arms. After my sojourn beyond the mountains I was returned now to the front lines of the war.

After ten minutes Campbell returned.

'Alone,' said he, taking up his musket. While he sighted the stranger I fetched my spyglass and turned it upon the river.

The James River was wide at that place, for we were near where the mouth opened into the Chesapeake Bay; but though I studied the quiet water a full minute there was no sign yet of the boat that must take me off.

'Ride on with me,' said Campbell.

I considered it, certainly. I had considered it all the while that he scouted the wood. Our horses were hobbled by a tidal creek but a short way inland, and we might be gone in a trice if we chose. But two days would then be added to my journey, which I baulked at. We had travelled weeks since leaving the Indian country, and I was impatient now to get myself directly around to Cornwallis in York Town and thence north to New York, where my latest instructions from Jenkinson and the Deciphering Department awaited. But as I turned to answer Campbell, 'No,' he clicked his tongue in warning.

Out from the shadows the stranger was advancing. I put the spyglass on him again. He was no Continental soldier, though he wore the buff breeches and the loose white shirt of a farmer, and had also a farmer's broad-brimmed hat to ward against the sun, yet I much suspected the caution of his advance and the ready state of his musket. In the last farmhouse we had stopped at, though they were Loyalists, they were frightened, and only too willing to see us gone. They had sent a message ahead to arrange my crossing, but I wondered now at the chance of some betrayal. As the stranger came nearer, Campbell sighted carefully, put his finger to the trigger, and only stopped when I whispered, 'Hold. Let him come.'

One minute, and then two, and the fellow came on with the same crablike advance. Upon reaching the small creek that ran from the wood across the beach and down into the river, he stopped. Here he must decide whether to turn back, or to go into the woods, or to cross over the creek; which last choice, if he made it, would bring him within thirty yards of us, directly under our muskets.

Campbell settled upon one knee. The heat was thick in the air, and I envied him now the Cherokee headband that kept the sweat from his eyes. I dipped my own face to my sleeve, and when I looked up again the stranger was stepping into the creek. The water went over his boots, and then to his thighs. But the creek was narrow, and after a few wading paces he rose and then stepped again onto the beach. By his movement, he was a younger man than I had first supposed. His hat was low over his eyes, and his face half-hidden.

Campbell took careful aim. And then the stranger put one muddy boot forward, looked up into the woods, and called, 'We are in the next cove!' and I reached to prevent Campbell firing. 'Mr Douglas!' called the stranger, and straightway turned Campbell's musket aside.

A log-canoe is no canoe but a boat native to the Chesapeake, low-cut and shallow-drafted, used by all the oystermen of the Bay. And it was in Cable Morgan's log-canoe that I now set out upon the James River.

'We must put the girls down at home before we go around. You do not mind, Alistair?'

'Only get me to York Town today,' I answered Cable Morgan, 'and I shall not mind any slight diversion.'

Cable hauled up the sail while his son David (who was that young stranger Campbell had nearly shot) took the tiller. Cable's wife Sally, and their daughter Elizabeth, sat opposite me in the bow. It was only by the merest accident that the whole family was there; for my message had found them upon the Portsmouth side, where Sally Morgan visited a cousin.

'Have you left someone?' asked Cable as we came into the river; for he had seen me look back along the shore. But Campbell had stayed hidden while I went down to the Morgans, and by now he must be mounted and riding up toward the Richmond road. Campbell had troubles enough without my making a general announcement of his presence, and so I told Cable no, that I had left no one behind me.

The sail once hoisted, Cable put out the flatboard over the gunwale and sat there to keep the boat trimmed. It was almost five years since I had last been in company with the Morgans. Five long years of the war. And in that time Lizzy had grown from a babe to a child, and David from a twelve-year-old boy into a young man. Cable looked little changed, his face just as dark from the sun, his smile just as broad and open as I remembered. But though he answered me now some few questions concerning Lord Cornwallis's movements about the Bay, and the disposition of the rebel force near Williamsburg and Richmond, I sensed a reticence in him. His several quick and uncertain glances toward his wife soon gave me the reason. I held off then, for I saw that we might talk more freely once Sally and Lizzy Morgan were set down at the farm.

As we went further downriver I turned my spyglass toward the Bay. Two ships stood out there.

'That to the north is the *Guadeloupe*,' said Cable. 'The other is British too, the *Loyalist*. The *Guadeloupe* shall leave for New York upon the night tide.'

After so many months spent inland, and then the hard journey, they were an unexpectedly cheering sight. At length I closed up my spyglass and put it in my satchel. Then glancing up I found Sally Morgan watching me with an expression quite melancholy. I ventured a smile, but she said only, 'You look tired, Mr Douglas.'

'Aye.'

'Shall you stay a time now on the Chesapeake?'

'I should not think so.'

Her hand rested upon her daughter's shoulder. Though I saw there was more she would say to me, she at last forbore and turned away to look out over the water. A strand of silvered hair had escaped from beneath her white bonnet, the breeze moving it about her face till she pushed it behind her ear. She had passed from thirty years to thirty-five since I had seen her last, and though she spoke of my tiredness it was her own looked the deeper. She remained a slight woman, but with nothing of the lively gaiety I remembered, nor in her eyes the clear-hearted joy.

In less than an hour we arrived at the muddy beach the other side of the James, below the Morgans' farm. While Cable and David made some necessary repair to the tiller, I carried Lizzy onto the beach. Then I fetched the baskets up to the leaning pine where Sally Morgan now stood watching her husband and son at work together down in the boat.

'I shall not take them from you for so very long,' said I.

'I would stop them if I could,' said she, which remark surprised me. For she had ever been a help to her husband, not only when I had first recruited him as a spy for us, but throughout the war, as I had learned from Major Andre and others. She faced me now directly. 'Do not receive this ill, Mr Douglas, but I must ask that you keep from our house while you are here.'

Somewhat taken aback, I said that I should speak to Cable on the matter. She shook her head.

'He shall say only that you must not listen to me. He shall tell you that you are most welcome to call on us.'

'And am I not?' said I. She hugged her arms about her and avoided my gaze. 'Has something happened that I should know of, Mrs Morgan?'

'Your work is very important, I am sure, Mr Douglas. But it is work done in passing. Our whole life is here. It is here that Cable and David must live when you are gone.'

'I understand that.'

'You do not understand. You do not understand what the war has done here.'

'I work as your husband works, that the war shall end.'

'It shall not end here, but only for the soldiers. We must live with our neighbours after.'

'Is Cable suspected?'

'All men are suspected who are not under arms in the militia. And only one man in each family may be excused to earn his family's bread.'

Understanding came to me, and I looked down to the log-canoe.

'David is now of an age to join the militia,' said I, and she nodded. But when I asked had any recruiting sergeant come to demand his service with the Continentals or the militia she again turned her head.

'But they shall,' said she. 'You cannot know what bitterness there is in every quarter, either against the Congress or against the King.'

'And so you fear to have me near your house.'

'I wish to God the war had never been,' said she with a depth of feeling quite remarkable. Raising her eyes boldly to me, she added, 'And though you may despise me for it, Mr Douglas, I tell you truly: I cannot find it in my heart to care any longer who shall win. While you are here now, I beg of you, stay away from my house. And once Cable has set you down in York Town, I would that you ask no further service of him.'

Lizzy came skipping up from the river, calling out to her mother. Sally Morgan took up the two baskets from by my feet, dipped her head to me, and turned quickly onto the path homeward.

'She has read you the Riot Act,' said Cable Morgan, amused as he helped me aboard again; for he had seen his wife talking with me up by the leaning pine, and well knew the meaning of it. 'You must not mind her, Alistair. She likes you well enough. It is the coming here of all the soldiers has frightened her.' He made light of the whole business, though when I told him of her warning that I should keep from their farm, he agreed that it might be as well for our mutual safety. He did not think that he was suspected of spying for the British, but nor did he wish at this moment to invite the closer scrutiny of his neighbours. He spoke all this within earshot of his son, and by some few remarks that then passed between them I surmised that the lad had become a helper in his father's secret business.

Cable raised the sail again, and as we went down toward Old Point Comfort he told me what he knew of Cornwallis's recent campaigning in the south, and of a skirmish nearby between the British forces and Lafayette's rebel soldiers. There was little that I had not heard on my way northward. The one surprise to me was how often he must turn to his son David for confirmation of some number, of either boats or horses or men. The lad was become like a second eyes and ears to the father, and a very close helper indeed.

As we emerged from the mouth of the James River into the Bay, I turned my spyglass once more upon those two ships. The nearest, the *Guadeloupe*, was but two or three leagues off from us.

'What chance you might take me out to her?' I asked Cable.

'It is calm enough,' said he, glancing over the water and then up at the clear sky. 'But you cannot want to leave us so quickly.'

I said that I would write a letter to my superiors in London, and that the *Guadeloupe* might carry it the first part of the journey. Cable made no hesitation then, but reefed the sail and called David to steer for the ship.

The breeze was fresh, and our boat cut clean through the small waves, so that I was reminded of those times I had sailed the Bay with Cable at the start of the war. In those days I had worked with him hauling in his crabpots and dredging with the oyster rakes, and there had been almost an innocence in it; for though I must sketch every landing place and cottage near the shore, and with Cable's help enlist several Loyalist fishermen as the eyes of the British fleet, our day's work would invariably end with a return to Morgan's farm. There young David would meet us upon the muddy beach and help his father rope the sail before we took our catch of crab and fish up to the farmhouse. Sally would cook the evening meal, and with one eye always upon Lizzy in the cot. Then we would do nothing very much, but only talk, and the Morgans with some surprise at my travels, and I thankful to be momentarily becalmed in the bosom of a good family. We little thought in those happy evenings how very long and vicious might be the war.

We were soon to the *Guadeloupe* now, and one of her officers hailing us from the quarterdeck as we came around her anchor-line. But no sooner had I called across to identify myself as Douglas of the Board of Trade and Plantations than the familiar face of Captain Symonds appeared at the rail.

'Douglas is it, by God.'

'You are a long way from Jamaica, sir.'

'Stop your fellows messing about there, and come aboard.'

David Morgan having a great curiosity to inspect a ship-of-the-line, he came aboard with me, while his father stayed in the boat and stood off.

'You shall get your pen and paper soon enough,' Captain Symonds told me as we two repaired to his cabin. David Morgan we had left with a midshipman to make a tour below decks. Symonds called back through the open door for his man to bring in the Madeira, then he offered me a chair.

He was a square-built fellow, rosy-cheeked, and though I had never sailed with him, I had often been in his company whilst ashore in the West Indies; for he was a long-serving captain in Admiral Rodney's fleet. By repute, his captaincy answered much to his appearance: nothing handsome or extraordinary, but dependable and solid. When the Madeira came he gave me a short account of how he had come to be in Chesapeake Bay, and he told me of his current intention to sail north to join Admiral Graves. I asked after Admiral Rodney, and he said Rodney was temporarily returned to London and that Hood commanded in his stead. We had some minutes more talk of this kind, each asking after different ones of our acquaintances now scattered along the coast and across the West Indies. He was disappointed to discover that I had been inland for some while and so had no recent news from London. He confessed himself not unhappy to be leaving the Chesapeake. Cornwallis, he told me, was now entrenching in York Town, and might even winter the army there.

'It shall be a dreary winter for some unfortunate captain upon the York River. Thank God it shall not be me.'

At this moment his First Lieutenant entered to report the sighting of a sail at the mouth of the Bay.

On the poop deck, we found the officers scanning the mouth of the bay. There were two ships coming wide around the cape, standing well out to sea in avoidance of the extensive and dangerous shallows closer in. Seamen now gathered along the *Guadeloupe*'s rail, and some climbed into the rigging; but there were as many more continued their several duties about the deck. Cable Morgan, fifty yards off from us, was standing in his boat with his own spyglass turned likewise upon the mouth of the bay. As I watched him, he dropped the spyglass and went in some hurry to the tiller.

'Sir, there is another sail to the south,' reported the First Lieutenant. And no sooner had this new arrival emerged fully from behind the southern cape than there came another directly in its wake. 'Sir—!'

'Yes, I see the flag,' said Symonds. 'We cannot get past them now, I think.'

'No, sir.'

'Give the order to weigh anchor. Call up all hands.'

The lieutenant hurried to the rail, crying orders to the junior officers.

'They cannot be French,' said I.

'They surely are, Mr Douglas. And more of them yet,' said Symonds; for trailing those first vessels around the southern cape were more ships appearing, and no longer singly but in twos and threes. It was a French fleet, and a large one. And a mystery, and a shock to all of us aboard, how it should come to be in these waters. Symonds, when he was over his first surprise, decided that it must be Admiral de Grasse come across from the West Indies.

'Sir, they are coming around.'

It was the van swinging leeward, while the trailing vessels held their line, continuing wide, to seal up the bay. Crossing to the rail I called out to Morgan. He was already bringing his boat quickly in. Then I ran down to the quarterdeck and almost knocked over a lady and her black maid who had come up to see the reason of the commotion.

'You had better stay in your cabin now, madam,' said I.

'The captain has not told me so.'

'He tells you so now!' roared Symonds from above. 'Get below, madam, and stay below till I call you!'

The woman blanched, but she had the good sense not to argue. She turned the maid about and they went hastily below. After sending a midshipman to seek out David Morgan, I returned to the poop deck.

A few leagues off from us, much nearer to the French, the *Loyalist* appeared to be about the same urgent business as ourselves. But so sudden and unexpected was the French arrival, and so near to her mooring, that it was doubtful the *Loyalist* could now weigh anchor, set sail, and outrun the French van. There were a half-dozen French ships-of-the-line bearing down upon her, and yet more enemy sail appearing around the southern cape. Further north, those first two vessels we had sighted now barred any escape to the open sea.

Symonds called the local Chesapeake pilot to him. Between them they swiftly decided that the *Guadeloupe*'s best chance lay in a run for the York River, thence a dash up to York Town, where we might gain the protection of Lord Cornwallis's guns.

David Morgan appeared on the quarterdeck, seeming in some confusion at emerging from below into the midst of a great scramble of seamen.

'You must go down into your boat now, Mr Douglas,' said Symonds, 'or you shall lose your own chance to get clear.'

But should the Morgans be overtaken and captured, I knew that they would be much safer without me. So I went down and took David across to the rail. His father had the boat already below.

'Is it the French?' Cable Morgan called up to me.

'It is,' I answered. Then I told David to go down to his father; which when he had done, I called down to ask Cable if he thought he could make Old Point Comfort before the enemy.

'Only if you come away now,' cried he.

'I shall keep aboard here and go up to York Town. Cast off now.'

David cast off upon the instant, and they cut away under our bow, making straight for the safety of the shallows near the Point.

'We have a sporting chance,' remarked Symonds when I rejoined him. 'But it looks not so well for the *Loyalist*. It is mere good fortune we did not anchor with her. And look there – still they come.'

The waters about the southern cape were now crowded with sail, and the First Lieutenant called up into the yards for a count of the enemy ships. 'It is certainly de Grasse', remarked Symonds to his offi-cers. 'And it looks to be his whole West Indies fleet with him.' I asked if our own ships in these waters had the guns to dislodge de Grasse should he anchor; for control of the Bay must be vital to our army ashore. 'That is not a present concern to us, Mr Douglas. Let us only preserve ourselves till York Town, it shall be work enough for today.' And so saying he moved away from me to consult again with the pilot who stood by the wheel.

At the capstan the men bent their backs like oxen, and not one of them shirking in the labour. The sight of French ships was a goad much sharper than a mere midshipman's order. Aloft, the seamen moved sprightly along the yards releasing the sails, and the count finally came down from them of twenty enemy ships certain.

I stood well clear of the officers now as the anchor came up to be lashed. The first breath of wind caught our unfurling main sail, and we listed leeward. Far astern of us, three French vessels peeled away from the main fleet to give chase. It was a minute later that a frigate broke from the fleet and appeared to make toward Old Point Comfort. I crossed with some anxiety to the aft rail. But the Morgans had a sharp breeze in their sail, and their log-canoe skimmed over the small waves. They had a good start on the frigate, and they knew the waters and the shallows well. The frigate would quickly close upon them, but I had a fair hope they might outrun her.

After several minutes, and the greater part of the French fleet now spread like a chain across the mouth of the Bay, I asked a lieutenant for another count of the ships. The number returned this time was twenty-four.

'And there must be stragglers yet in a fleet so large,' remarked the young officer who brought me the count. 'There may be thirty by tomorrow.'

'You are not alarmed, Lieutenant?'

'Not alarmed, sir, but struck, you might say. It is a rare sight.' A rare sight indeed, and a very fine and welcome sight it must be for those rebels about the Bay that witnessed its arrival. The breeze ruffled the blue water, and the full white sails of the fleet looked like clouds blown in from the sea. But poisonous clouds they were to us, for that fleet was certainly filled with guns and munitions and French infantry. 'They have got the *Loyalist*,' said the lieutenant unhappily.

Like a fox overrun, she disappeared into the midst of the French pack. Her sails were struck, her flight finished almost before it began. The lieutenant made an oath beneath his breath and then returned to his station near the wheel. The *Guadeloupe*'s three pursuers were under full sail now, but two of them visibly lagging the leader.

'West Indies weed slows them,' said Symonds, joining me at the aft rail. 'They have had no scraping yet. The front ship has perhaps recently joined the fleet. She is the only one may catch us.'

'She does not appear to be closing.'

'She is, but slowly. It shall be a quarter-hour before she brings us within range. You must come for'ard, now, Mr Douglas. These guns may be needed.'

Ahead, the mouth of the York was not easy to discern, the green line of tidewater vegetation being identical both sides of the river. Our Chesapeake pilot kept the wheelman steering straight before the wind.

'One league,' the First Lieutenant reported, peering astern through his spyglass.

Symonds screwed up his eyes against the sun and looked ahead to where the York River and safety must be. 'You are standing us well out,' he remarked to the pilot.

'Sandbar,' replied the pilot, pointing. 'Tack too early, we'll ground.' He must have felt Captain Symonds's hard eye upon him then, for he added, 'Never you fear, sir. I'll not give you to the French from too much caution.'

The wind stayed steady, neither strong nor light, and we carved a clean line through the choppy water. But so too did our nearest French shadow. In a short time it appeared she was gathering speed and closing ever more quickly.

'Half a league, sir.'

All eyes went between the French ship and Symonds, the seamen apprehensive and impatient for the order to tack. But Symonds's gaze stayed fixed upon the pilot. The men at the guns aft began murmuring together, seeming in doubt of the supposed sandbar that kept them from safety. The pilot was unmoved, he continued his quiet orders to the wheelman to hold steady.

At last Symonds broke. 'How long, man?'

'A minute more,' the pilot answered, very calm.

'One minute and no longer.' Symonds then turned to his First Lieutenant. 'As we go about we shall make a pretty target. Prepare the stern and larboard guns.' While the order was passed, Symonds rocked upon the balls of his feet. He clasped his hands behind his back as if to prevent himself from snatching the wheel. But after a minute that seemed an hour the pilot turned to him and nodded.

'Give them a shot from the stern chaser,' Symonds sharply commanded his First Lieutenant. 'Then take us about smart.'

A bellowing of orders cascaded through along the decks and up into the rigging. And it was then that the first French gun fired. A puff of smoke showed at her bow before the clap of thunder reached us. A spume of spray then rose a hundred yards to our stern.

'Fire!' shouted the First Lieutenant, and our two rear guns fired in quick succession. The smoke bloomed about us, the sound of the shots still roaring in my ears as the ship listed sharply and came about. We were becalmed for a moment, but then the wind caught our sail and I clutched the rail to steady myself as we came upright just as easily as we had listed.

Our larboard guns fired next, and the French answered with a broadside. All empty sound and fury. We remained just beyond their range as they beyond ours, and every shot fell useless into the water. As our sails refilled we moved again, and now the French must either risk the shallows and the bar or give up the chase.

'She'll put herself aground,' the pilot muttered, peering astern as if he willed the French to make the rash attempt.

Turning my spyglass toward the Point, I made out the Morgans' log-canoe running close into the shore, and the French frigate standing a quarter-mile off. Should a smaller boat be launched from the frigate, the Morgans might easily outrun them into the James River. And once there Cable Morgan would be certain to elude them, secreting his log-canoe in one of the creeks. With some relief I returned my attention to the nearer danger.

But it was little time the pursuing French captain astern of us now wasted in reaching his decision (indeed, he must have his own Chesapeake pilot aboard who had warned him of the bar). After a minute he swung her away, and she at once set sail to rejoin the main fleet.

In silence our crew watched her go. Captain Symonds removed his tricorn and congratulated our pilot, which though the congratulation was sincere, it was muted; for we had preserved ourselves, but the *Loyalist* was lost, and the French fleet now held the Bay. A quiet and sombre ship we continued against the tide, ten miles upriver to York Town.

extracts reading groups
competitions books new
discounts extracts
competitions extracts
books new discounts events
events books
extracts
new titles reading groups
interviews
events extracts extracts books
discounts
new books events
events new events
discounts extracts discounts

extracts events reading groups
competitions books extracts new